Goodnight Highway

PUBLISHING – WASHINGTON, D.C.

THE SHATTERED BONES

DAVID SANTANA

GOODNIGHT HIGHWAY

For my family.

1

— · —

MARCH 23, 2017, THURSDAY

PASADENA, MARYLAND

Edward slowly opened his eyes. Struggling to focus in a dimly lit room, he only caught a glimpse of an unfamiliar ceiling fan before the pounding pressure in his head forced his eyes shut again. His face grimaced, the throbbing behind his eyes intensified until all he wanted in the world was to press his palms against the sides of his skull, but he felt his arms hindered, anchored at the wrist.

He rolled his head to the side, squinting, and discovered his left wrist zip-tied to a piece of lumber, a carpenter's two-by-four. All at once, he felt the rest of the wood beam pinned between his back and the floor, its edge digging into his shoulder blades. His eyes shot open, and suddenly his headache became an afterthought as he whipped his head to the right, confirming his wrist fastened the same as the left.

Edward yanked at the thin white plastic cuffs, pulling, straining; not enough. His arms flexed to their limit, he pulled harder, spewing profanity, only to find his lips sealed shut with the acrid scent of the tape's adhesive in his nostrils. A rush of adrenaline surged through his veins while frenzied terror flooded into his brain, smothering his thoughts; it felt like suffocating. Desperate, he tried to shout through his muzzle, full-throated, but only a mild hum escaped, and his mind nearly snapped. He frantically scanned the room, thrashing violently to free himself, but finding his ankles tied down like his wrists, he spotted a man seated just beyond and stopped cold.

The air in the room was thick with the smell of fresh paint and carpet shampoo. The only window was covered by a large trash bag, its edges sealed with tape. The only light in the room came from the floor, somewhere above Edward's head. The space was otherwise empty, no furniture, no photographs adorning the walls, no signs of life, except for the man sitting quietly in front of the door, just beyond Edward's feet. He was leaning forward, watching Edward intently. He was perfectly still, his face was emotionless, and he was holding a gun.

In a glimmering memory, Edward recalled the parking lot of his office building at night, fumbling for the car keys in his pocket, a man appearing between the cars with his face shaded by the brim of a Baltimore Orioles baseball cap, a black revolver in his hand. All at once, Edward's memories sprinted through his mind: the inside of the gun's barrel looking like a tunnel to eternity, a voice from beyond saying he was being robbed, not to do anything stupid, and he would go home tonight without a bullet hole, being told to turn around, a flicker of light, the flash of pain in his head, finally, awakening confused in the dim light of this room. The continuity left no mystery. As his panic and terror gave way to horror, he was distantly aware of the wet warmth spreading into the carpet beneath his buttocks, but it was of no concern. There was only the man with the gun now; nothing else in the world mattered.

He stared motionless at the looming figure leering back at him. The man was sitting upon an empty plastic milk crate, elbows on his knees, a stubby revolver hanging loosely from his right hand. A small, electric camping lantern, which had been placed on the floor two feet above Edward's head, illuminated the man's face and cast his shadow high onto the wall behind him like an imposing beast waiting impatiently for its turn to step into the light.

The man was middle-aged and clean-shaven, with close-cropped hair. His neck was thick and defined, and his dark grey hooded sweatshirt did nothing to obscure his muscular shoulders. Edward thought the man was attractive, or would be in any other setting. He had the face of a man who would appear in television commercials for medication or life insurance, certainly not the face of a man who would seriously harm another person. Edward began to scheme how he could negotiate with him, but after a few moments spent in lifeless silence, the two men locked in eye contact, Edward's hope gradually faded. He could sense the heat of the man's gaze upon him, its radiation. It felt pitiless and unrelenting, like a snake in the shadows, watching a field mouse scavenging for food while it slowly wanders closer and closer to its own death. Edward slowly began to understand there would be no negotiating; his fate was already set. Like the imperceptible center of a black hole, surrounded by billions of brilliant stars, all magnificently swirling toward their eventual destruction, Edward was now caught in that same gravity.

After an unbearably long silence, Edward finally inhaled, unaware he had been holding his breath, but now terrified to make a sound, he held his breath again.

"You know," the man finally spoke, and Edward flinched, "I'm gonna be honest with you. I'm feeling a bit conflicted. Not about all this," He casually gestured with the gun in Edward's general direction, "of that, I'm positive, but it's this moment, right here, the conversation, that's where I'm still undecided."

The man stopped to gather his thoughts but found himself momentarily distracted by his captive's miserable appearance. Earlier that evening, Edward had been dressed neatly in a light-blue dress shirt, but now, a few buttons along the front were missing, and his pleated khakis, dirtied from efforts to drag him into the back of an SUV, had become soaked with urine.

The man, Rylan, shook his head, still burdened with indecision, "I keep coming back to 'why'. I don't understand it. I can't fathom what you did, and there are so many questions I want to ask, but at the same time, I'm pretty sure I don't want to know the answers."

A few long seconds were spent in silence with Rylan considering his options before he shrugged, "You know what? The thing is, none of it matters. Nothing you could say would change anything about anything." He huffed, "It would only make me mad anyway, and I need to keep my head on straight for this next part, so I'm just gonna let it go."

He turned his back to Edward, rotating around on the dark blue milk crate he had been sitting on. Edward, sensing his situation becoming increasingly dire, began whimpering and pleading unintelligibly through the duct tape covering his mouth.

Rylan, now facing away from Edward, reached down into the brown leather overnight bag that once belonged to his wife. With the lantern light behind him, he blindly felt around inside, found the pliers first, then pushed them to the side to find the familiar grip of his old framing hammer. He pulled it from the darkness into the light. With its weight now in his palm, he reset his grip, and a silent voice in the back of his mind, fascinated and unconvinced, asked, "You sure?"

He took a deep breath; the air was cool and surprisingly crisp in his nostrils. He closed his eyes. Recognizing his footing now at the precipice, he held the fresh wind in his lungs for an extra second, trying to steady himself for the task. His heartbeat was loud in his ears, nearly drowning out the muffled whimpering behind him. He emptied his lungs hard through his mouth, opened his eyes, and answered himself aloud, "Yes."

Rylan stood up and turned around to look down upon his prey; instantly, the room fell silent. Edward, who had been frantically trying to wriggle free of his bonds while his antagonist's back was turned, abruptly halted. His eyes had found the hammer in Rylan's right hand and were unable to look away.

"Edward, I read somewhere that you liked to have the children call you Eddie Beddy."

Edward's eyes grew wider and he tried to slink into the piss-soaked carpet, letting out a pained groan as he slithered in place. To Rylan, Edward's reaction was an admission of guilt, although unnecessary, and he lowered his head in disgust.

"Yeah, that's what I thought. Well, Edward, the justice system failed you. It failed all of us, really, but we're only talking about Edward Chaffin right now. So here's how you got screwed: instead of getting the privilege of wasting the rest of your days away in prison, three hots and a cot, and whatnot, you got let off on a technicality. Congrats!" he exclaimed sarcastically. "You know, I remember watching the news broadcast from the courthouse. You looked so… so smug, getting the entire case thrown out. The whole fucking thing! You probably felt like you beat the system, like you won something, right? Well, no. No… no, fuck that. I'll tell you this, Edward," Rylan lowered his voice as he knelt beside the subdued man's hip, leaning in close to his face, "there is at least one person in this world willing to do the right thing, regardless of the consequences."

Rylan shifted his weight back to his place beside Edward's left hip as his captive tried to slowly wriggle away.

"Edward, I'm gonna let you in on a little secret, okay? You're my first. Hopefully, won't be my last, but you're definitely the first. So, in full disclosure, I'm basically learning on the fly here, but don't worry, it's fine. It's fine. I'll figure it out as I go along. Anyway, here's the plan, I'm gonna take this hammer and break every large bone in your body, well, ten of them, at least. Then, I'll take this pistol, put a bullet through your brain and we'll be done here. What do you think? Good plan?"

Edward was paralyzed by fear once again. His mind couldn't process what the man said about the hammer. What was he going to, wait, break what?

Rylan nodded, "Okay, I'll take your silence for consent." Realizing his blunder, he winced, "Shouldn't be cracking jokes, huh? Sorry. Look, let's get started."

He clutched Edward's knee, pinning it down to the carpet, then raised the hammer high above his head, aimed for his shin, and swung the hammer down onto the bone.

2

— · —

MAY 3, 2001, THURSDAY

COLUMBIA, SOUTH CAROLINA

A seventeen-year-old Rylan Beam sat on an old stump beside Cranston Pond Road at the start of his mom's driveway. He drew lines in the red clay using the heel of his black Converse sneakers before smoothing them over again with the sides of the shoe. He was waiting for Joey's white Dodge Neon to pick him up for school. Occasionally, he would hear a car and squint down the long stretch of faded asphalt, only to return to the dirt in disappointment. Joey was late again, but Rylan's frustration was tempered by the fact his friend was driving out of his way to pick him up.

Most mornings, Rylan's headphones provided a distraction while waiting, but with dead batteries in the lifeless CD player tucked in his backpack, he was left listening to the South Carolina woodland symphony. The frogs' baritone croak from the drainage ditches lining the sides of the road, a hundred thousand cicadas buzzing like the sizzling of bacon, the wind softly shushing through the cypress and pine, the woodpeckers' hollow drumming echoing through the woods from behind the Hanscome place, even Mr. Dodson's metal wind chimes added a faint percussion from down the road; indeed, it was music if you stopped to listen.

Rylan's family had only moved to South Carolina seven months ago from Las Vegas. His mom, Emily, used her husband's life insurance money to buy a house in her hometown of Columbia. Desperately wanting to escape the part of her life shrouded in the shadow of Rylan's dead father, she moved her two teenage children to a corner of the country they had never seen before.

Rylan became accustomed to moving, periodically, over the years. The cycle of settling down, getting comfortable, then pulling up stakes across southern California and Nevada had become all too familiar, but this was his first time living in the South, and so far, he liked it fine. In his view, the hardest things to get used to were the humidity and the mosquitoes, both being wholeheartedly relentless, but besides that, the people were remarkably polite, and the mustard barbecue sauce was a revelation.

Rylan reflexively smacked his cheek, trading the familiar itch of a fresh mosquito bite for the sharp sting of his fingers. He wiped his cheek with the same hand, hoping to find a mosquito carcass, but found nothing. Dejected, he looked up frowning, but his expression quickly disappeared as a young deer emerged from the woods across the road. Rylan froze, even halting his breathing for fear of spooking the animal.

The deer, a fawn, dipped its head to graze on the weeds growing on the road shoulder. Rylan watched in awestruck silence, fascinated by the beautifulness of the scene, with the sun just high enough in the sky to cast its orange rays on the creature's auburn hide. Some of the hairs in its fur glimmered in the morning light like golden filament. Rylan thought it the most perfect thing he had ever seen. He sat quietly observing the deer chewing the wild grass and envied the fawn's life of simplicity. He mused about how uncomplicated its existence must be; no anxiety about getting to school late, no soul-crushing helplessness when his younger sister bursts into tears over their dead father, and no pressure about figuring out what to do after graduating high school.

Suddenly, the dear's head shot up from the weeds, alerted to something in the distance behind Rylan's new home. A short moment later, the deep bass of a distant explosion reached them.

Fort Jackson was less than five miles away, and occasionally, on less humid days, they could hear the popcorn-popping sound of soldiers shooting rifles on the firing ranges, but they always heard the boom from the larger ammunition. Seconds after the first explosion, there was another impact, and the young deer immediately turned tail and beat a hasty, but graceful retreat back into the thick woods.

Watching the deer bound away into the forest's shadows struck an emotional chord with Rylan, and he felt a familiar heartache start to rise in his throat. The knot blocked his airway and made it difficult to breathe. His eyes began to sting and well up with tears. He swallowed hard, again, and again, trying to swallow his pain, to force it back down into the hollow spots of his soul, where he imprisoned the things he was not yet ready to face.

Rylan immediately jumped up from his stump, searching the area for something to distract his mind from the thoughts attempting to suffocate his sanity, but found no reprieve. The dirt at his feet was nothing but a rusty brown color with patches of weeds, the road was completely empty, and the woods provided only softly swaying branches. He felt panic swelling from his chest into his neck until he spun around towards the house and saw his mother.

Emily was inside the house, gazing through the screen door at her son at the end of the driveway. He had startled her and she flinched as if caught doing something illicit. She smiled sheepishly, smoothing her nurse's scrubs with her free hand while the other held her coffee cup. Having gathered herself, she put an open palm up to the screen door, a warm gesture of greeting to her only son. He looked very much like his handsome father, an unfortunate twist of fate that often tormented Emily, but as a woman well-acquainted with pain, she rolled her shoulders, straightened her spine, and smiled lovingly at her boy.

She was the only person who still called him Rylan. Everyone else called him Rye. When he was born, his father, a semi-functional alcoholic, had convinced her to name their son Rylan, a duplicitous scheme so he could call him Rye, for short, after his favorite type of whiskey. By the time Emily, who had quarreled frequently with her husband about his alcoholism, realized his deception, the birth certificate had already been printed, and she was furious. Since then, she refused to call her son by his nickname, mostly out of shame for her own gullibility.

As Rylan stood looking back at his mother, his anxiety began disappearing. He could tell he had startled her and she was embarrassed, but the blush in her cheeks gave her a youthful look he hadn't remembered seeing before. He felt admiration warming his chest, and right then, all he wanted in the world was to hug her. He stepped forward but heard a vehicle approaching and knew it was Joey even before he turned to see the car. Turning back toward his mom, he flashed an awkward smile and raised a hand to give a subtle wave. She quickly returned his wave but he had already turned away again. He grabbed his backpack from beside the stump, swung it over his shoulder, and waited for the car to stop.

He stole one last glance into the woods, but finding no sign of the deer, he slid into the passenger seat and greeted his friend with a playful taunt.

"Late again, dude?"

Joey didn't respond. He just began driving down the road while Rylan became increasingly uncomfortable. He hesitated to say anything and instead sat in silence, watching the trees speed past and, occasionally, an old house, a trailer park, or a gas station. He wondered if he had somehow irritated his friend, but after a while, he decided the notion was ridiculous.

He floated a soft query, "You good, bro?"

Joey jerked, blinked a couple of times, and glanced at his friend. He seemed mildly surprised to see Rylan sitting there.

"Naw man, I mean yeah, I'm uh..." he trailed off before finding himself again, "I'm just figuring some things out, is all. No need to worry about me."

Rylan was unconvinced. His friend's voice, thick with a Carolina twang, was usually lively and full of humor but had become flat and joyless. He knew Joey well enough to know something was wrong, but their friendship lacked sufficient depth for him to feel comfortable prying. He reined in his curiosity while hoping it wasn't something too serious. They passed the rest of the ride to school in silence, but as Joey pulled to a stop and cut off the engine, Rylan tried again.

"You don't seem okay, bro. What's up?"

Rylan's friend looked distantly through the windshield, passing a few seconds before answering emotionlessly, "Dawn broke up with me last night."

"Oh man," Rylan muttered, remembering how Joey, a high school senior, had planned to propose to his girlfriend right after the graduation ceremony in a month. "Bro, that's..." he paused, trying to find a word, "that's fucked up. She say why?"

Joey grumbled sourly, "Some dude goes to Clemson. He's on the football team or something. I dunno."

The two sat quietly for a little while, lost in thought, until Homer, a mutual friend, ran up and smacked Rylan's window with his hand, making them both jump in surprise.

Homer yelled through the glass at the two friends, "Hey, quit all that huggin' and kissin' in there! Y'all are gonna be late to class"

He grinned, gave them the finger, then jogged off toward school.

"I hate that dude." Rylan said jokingly, "But yeah, we should probably get going."

"Yeah," Joey replied indifferently, making no effort to leave the car.

"Joey, man, you gonna be okay?"

"Honestly, I dunno. She was my life. I was fixin' to marry her. You know?" his voice trembling at the end. He gripped the top of the steering wheel tightly with both hands.

"Yeah, I know," Rylan said quietly, ashamed of his inability to help his friend find solace. While he considered what to do, he looked down at his shoes, now covered with a light coat of rust-colored dust from his driveway.

He tried distraction, "What're you doing after school today? You wanna go to Walmart? I need batteries for my CD player, and

I could use a ride. We can... I don't know; maybe we can talk about it too if you want."

"Yeah. I'll take you." Joey muttered, sounding defeated. He reached over and pulled his backpack from the backseat, staring blankly at the steering wheel for a moment before stepping out of the car. He began trudging towards the main entrance while Rylan hurried to catch up.

The school day passed as usual; gossip, flirting, boredom, and studying, typical high school stuff, but Rylan's thoughts kept returning to his friend. They didn't have any classes together that semester, and their lunch breaks were scheduled in different time blocks, so their paths rarely crossed until after school. As the day progressed, his trepidation only grew. He had never seen Joey so distraught, and he wanted to check on him to see how he was coping, hoping Joey had found some distraction in the day's goings-on.

During lunch, Rylan spotted a friend, Tommy, in the cafeteria lunch line who happened to share a second-period math class with Joey. He rushed to his side, startling his friend.

"Tommy, you see Joey in Calculus today?"

"Damn, Dawg! Don't run up on me like that! I almost swung on you."

"Yeah, okay. You seen Joey in your Calculus class?"

"Well, nice to see ya too, Rye." Tommy shot back sarcastically, "I'm doin' great, thanks for asking."

Someone near the back of the lunch line yelled at Rylan, "Hey, no cuts!"

"Hey, mind your fucking business, guy." Rylan snapped back, "I'm not getting in line. I'm just talking to him."

Tommy grinned mischievously, "He's right, though. No cuts."

Rylan rolled his eyes. "Dude. I just want to know if you saw Joey in class."

"Yeah, I kinda picked up on that the first two times you asked me."

"So?"

"Yes. He was in class, but we didn't talk much. Ms. Pendergrass was teaching some crazy parametric equation bullshit. Dawg, I can't fuckin' wait for this year to be over. Thirty-four more days til school's out." He held out his fist for Rylan to pound.

"Hell yeah, thirty-four." Rylan repeated in agreement, pounding his fist down onto Tommy's, "But, about Joey, you know Dawn broke up with him last night?"

"What? What a bitch!" Tommy exclaimed louder than he intended, then checked over his shoulders to see who had heard him. Lowering his voice to a whisper, he leaned closer to Rylan, "I never liked that bitch. He was gonna propose to her too, right?"

Having reached the front of the lunch line, Tommy grabbed a hard plastic serving tray off the rack. Rylan followed him but didn't grab a tray.

"Yeah, man. Right after graduation."

"Damn. That's all kinds of fucked." His eyes lit up in dawning revelation, "Yo! So, that's why he was so quiet in class today!"

"Now you get it. Just keep it on the low, alright? If anyone else finds out, I don't want it to be because of me, you know?"

"Yeah, I got you," Tommy nodded before turning his attention to the lunch lady waiting on the other side of the counter for him to make his selection.

"Whacha want, baby?" her voice sounded polite, but her facial expression was unmistakably impatient and annoyed.

"Chicken sandwich, please."

Rylan put his hand on Tommy's shoulder and whispered, "I'm gonna take off. I'll hit you up later."

Tommy nodded his understanding and continued ordering his lunch while Rylan wandered off to find a quiet spot to study for the test in Mr. Giovanni's American History class.

A few hours later, after the final bell rang at the end of the school day, Rylan hurried out to Joey's car, but his friend hadn't arrived yet. After ten minutes, the parking lot was nearly deserted, and as Rylan was about to go look for him, Joey finally came walking out the front door. A few seconds later, Dawn stepped out through the same doors, wearing a concerned look on her face. She stood in the arched entryway to the high school, watching her ex-boyfriend walk away from her.

As Joey drew closer, it was obvious something was deeply wrong. He looked deflated; a hollow shell of his old self. Rylan opened his mouth to greet him, but Joey waved him away.

"Don't wanna talk about it. Just get in."

Rylan did as he was told and they drove to the Walmart without a word between them. When they got there, Joey stayed in the car, and Rylan walked in alone. It wasn't long before he returned, sliding back into the passenger seat with an eight-pack of double-A batteries in one hand, and an already-opened bag of Sour Patch Kids candies in the other. He was relieved to find Joey had perked up a little. He even took the bag of candy to pop a few in his mouth before giving it back.

"Rye, man," Joey began, nervously rubbing the steering wheel, "Lemme ask you something. You like this car? It's a good car, man."

"Yeah. It's tight."

"It is *tight*, huh?"

Joey's inflection was meant to tease his friend about his West Coast slang. Rylan thought this was a good sign.

Joey continued, "So, uh, you wanna borrow it for a while?"

Rylan scrunched his face in confusion, "What? Borrow your car? Why? For how long?"

Joey shrugged, "For a while. I don't know. That way you can get to school and such."

The driver turned to look at Rylan for the first time that day and saw the puzzled look on his face. He attempted a smile, but he couldn't hide the quivering at the corner of his lips.

Still confused, Rylan asked, "But don't you need it?"

"Naw, not really," he turned away to gaze out his window and mumbled to himself, "Not anymore anyway."

Rylan suddenly understood what was happening. Horrified and angry, he seized his friend's arm in a crushing grip, "Hey! Fuck no. You're gonna kill yourself?"

Joey snapped his head around to find his friend leaning over the center console, teeth barred. Joey, floundering with his response, turned his face away, but Rylan yanked his arm to bring him back.

"No. You're not doing this shit to me. I can't... not again. Fuck, no. Listen, your family loves you, even your piece-of-shit brother, Darrell; they all love you. You love them too, don't you? Don't you? Of course, you do, but you're not thinking about what happens to them after you're gone, right? So, here, let me tell you: their lives are gonna be fucked! They're gonna spend the rest of their lives in pain, grieving, angry at themselves for not being there for you."

He gripped Joey's arm tighter and continued his tirade. "Asshole! Suicide is the most absolute, totally selfish thing in the world. Look, man, I get it; Dawn broke up with you. It sucks. It hurts, but that pain you're feeling right now; recognize that shit is temporary. You can recover, but if you kill yourself, it's over. It's all over for you, but it doesn't stop there. because, guess what, you've just taken your pain, made it a million times worse, then forced it onto those who love you the most. THAT kind of pain is permanent. It NEVER goes away! Is that what you want for your mom? Your dad?"

Rylan released Joey's arm and threw himself back in his seat, his chest heaving. Joey, wide-eyed and slack-jawed, sat astonished at his friend steaming in the passenger seat.

For a while, there was no sound. Outside the car, shoppers passed back and forth behind the car, but the two friends paid them no attention. After a few minutes, Rylan had calmed down and sat staring blankly through the windshield. When he spoke again, his voice was low and dismal.

"My father killed himself almost three years ago, Joey. I know what I'm talking about. I know you loved Dawn, but she's moved on, and you need to do the same. She ain't worth killing yourself over, man, life is precious."

More silence. It might have been an eternity, but Rylan and Joey wouldn't have noticed. Finally, without a word, Joey turned over the ignition and drove to Rylan's house. He pulled into the driveway and Rylan opened his mouth to speak, but Joey stopped him with a hand on his shoulder.

"Brother, thank you for what you said. I had no idea about your daddy, and I'm sorry. I got some things to think about, but I'll pick you up in the morning, okay?"

The two held eye contact for an extra second before Rylan finally nodded, satisfied. He got out of the car and walked to his front door, then turned to watch Joey backing out of the driveway. He held up his palm to his friend, who returned the gesture before driving away.

Before walking in, Rylan stopped to peer into the woods across the street, hoping to see the deer again, but after a few moments, he turned back toward the house. As he stepped through the doorway, he imagined the fawn had found its way back to its family. The thought made him smile a little.

3

MARCH 24, 2017, FRIDAY

TERRE-HAUTE, INDIANA

Notes: Edward Chaffin in Pasadena, Maryland.
-Get better zip-ties. The skinny ones might break. After I finished with the left leg, he started thrashing again. Looked like he could have snapped the right-side wrist zips. Had to break that arm first before getting back to the legs. Maybe I should just start with the arms?
-NEED SMELLING SALTS!!! Took too long waiting for him to wake up after he kept passing out.
-That first hit, on his left shin, was too hard, big mess, unnecessary. Obviously don't need to swing so hard next time, but luckily Edward is skinny. I think the ~~femer feemer~~ femur (the freakin' thigh bone!) and even worse, the pelvis are going to be more challenging with a fatter person. Not sure how I'm going to work around that.
-GOT TO TAKE OFF THE CLOTHES! Had to hit twice on the right-side shin. Didn't hit cleanly the first time. Need to be able to see the target. "Aim small, miss small."
-Didn't end up shooting him. Didn't want to make a bigger mess after the botched shin job. Choking worked okay. ~~Sufication~~ Suffocation might be the best way going forward. Bring a bag next time.

-The wood frame worked fine but was cumbersome to move and set up. Setting it up the night prior was a good call. Look into PVC pipe for next. A lot lighter. Maybe pre-drill the holes and then lash sections together? That should speed up the process. Make sure the thickness is good enough, though. No cheap shit.

-Location was excellent. Nice and quiet, and no cars drove by. I hate that I stained the carpet. The owners are going to be pissed. Thought about using the garage but was worried about sound control. Maybe use a tarp, next time?

-BIG ONE! On the snatch, I must find a way to get them in the car before knocking them out. Don't think anyone saw, but it's dangerous dragging them in the open. Think of something better.

-Took just over four hours total time. Not bad, could be better, be more efficient.

My anger management counselor from high school, I can't remember her name, dark hair, hugger, smelled great; anyways, she made me write in a journal for about a month. She said it was to force me to make my thoughts and feelings ~~tangeable~~ tangible, so I could see them right in front of me, on the page. It was apparently to help me be more aware of how I react to things when they happen. I don't think it helped much back then, but I know it definitely did after I returned from Iraq. I'm sure a lot of things would have been even worse if I hadn't been journaling then. So, now, I'm sure this path I've chosen will eventually take a toll on me. How could it not? So, as a kind of preventative maintenance, I'm going to pick up journaling again, to try to sort my thoughts and feelings throughout this... journey? Endeavor? Mission? Whatever.

This journal will eventually serve a second purpose. If I'm being honest, I don't expect to survive this. I have a list of names, and I'll see how far down the list I can get. Hopefully pretty far, but we'll see how things go. Regardless, no matter what, ~~I won't be taken alive~~ *I'm not getting arrested. This is a one-way trip for me, and it'll end one day; I imagine some random cop shooting me. You know, the old 'going out in a blaze of glory' thing. I'm cool with it. Well, I've accepted it, at least. But ultimately, that means I won't be around to answer questions, and I'm sure there will be many. Undoubtedly, this journal will be found at some point and analyzed, it being evidence and all that, and it should help give some understanding of my "madness." I'm kidding. Of course, I'm not mad.*

So, let's get right into it: Edward Chaffin. Why'd I do it? Very simple: this piece of shit molested five children, at least five that we know of, then was released just because a cop working in the evidence locker fouled up the chain of custody. That's it. I still remember that shit-eating grin on his face, getting interviewed at the courthouse when they announced the case had been thrown out; it made my blood boil. So, anyways, this guy is now walking free, nose up in the air, talking about suing the state of Maryland, the police force, and everyone else. The fucker is guilty. GUILTY. He knows it. We know it. And now he acts like he's a victim? Nope! I'll pick up that tab. I'll take care of it.

Next, I'm sure the question, "Why did I choose him first?" will be a biggie for investigators. Again, the answer is simple. Just look at him. I mean, practically speaking, the guy just looked weak. From what I see, everything in his body language suggests the submissive type, easy to intimidate, and remember, I'm a rookie at this kidnap-ping-killing stuff. I expect I'll make some mistakes, and I need to be sure I can out-muscle them before shit goes sideways. That's it. That's why he went first. It was a business decision, nothing more, and for the most part, it all went according to plan. Although I will admit I did panic a little when I thought he might break the zip tie on his wrist, but I handled it. I'll fix that in the future. I'll do better.

I understand that not everyone will agree with what I'm doing, especially law enforcement, but in an ethical sense, I really don't feel like I'm wrong here. The way I look at it, I'm doing the American people a service. I'm taking out their trash.

Rylan tossed his pen down onto the pages of the notebook that had just become his journal, then flipped the cover closed, trapping the pen inside. He stared down at his right hand, opening and closing his fist a few times to assess the soreness. When was the last time he had written so much in one sitting? It must have been after returning from Iraq.

As he massaged his hand, his waitress glided past his table carrying a coffee pot, leaving an invisible cloud of heavy perfume laced with the bitter notes of freshly brewed coffee in her wake. He wrinkled his nose at the inharmonious blend of aromas though the smell dissipated as the waitress, the name Sarah embroidered on her shirt, drew further away. He watched as she went, taking note of the way her hips swayed when she walked, and forgave the offending fragrance.

Rylan followed her path as she made her rounds, and although she was physically attractive, it was her demeanor that kept his attention. She hummed along to the country music coming from the kitchen, kept the beat in her steps, and even sang a few lines as she filled coffee cups. When she chatted with the few customers in the dining room, she spoke with a light Midwest accent but called everyone "Darlin" with a drawl as though she was from somewhere deep in the heart of Texas instead of the corn fields of Indiana.

A chromed desk bell rang out sharply, and a sweaty short-order cook called, "Order up," before disappearing into the sizzling, clanging, steamy discord of the kitchen. The sound of the bell snapped Rylan out of his momentary hypnosis. He sighed, popped the last piece of overcooked bacon into his mouth, and gazed out the window.

Beyond the Appleseed Diner's small parking lot and its faded sign, before the endless ridges of empty cornrows disappearing into the horizon, cars and long-haul trucks sped past each other along Route 70. Soon, Rylan's old grey Chevy Trailblazer would once again be traveling amongst them, but for now, there was no rush to get back on the road. He had already driven ten hours straight from Maryland last night before rewarding himself with a hot shower at a cheap motel and an Ambien tablet. Even if Edward's shattered body had somehow been discovered, the police would be searching for a suspect in the Baltimore area, not near the eastern edge of Indiana. Rylan supposed there might be a need for haste in the coming weeks, but certainly not yet.

He glanced at his watch, 11:07 AM, and decided he could afford to linger a little longer. He looked down into his near-empty coffee cup before scanning the room to find his waitress. She was chatting and laughing with a bearded customer wearing a trucker hat. Rylan raised his hand to get her attention, then tapped the air above his coffee cup. She nodded, patted the trucker's shoulder, and sauntered over to Rylan's table.

"Get you anything else?" The waitress, with the name Sarah embroidered on her shirt, asked while topping off his cup, "A slice of Hoosier Pie'd go real nice with this coffee."

He tilted his head, "What's a Hoosier Pie?"

She smiled knowingly, "I'll get you a small slice. Don't like it; it's on the house."

"Alright, then," he smirked, sensing a challenge, "I'm pretty picky, though."

She took a step backward, sassily planted her free hand on her cocked hip, and looked him up and down with a raised eyebrow, "Yeah, you can afford to be picky. But I don't believe it; you look like a sweetheart." She put a hand on his shoulder, leaning in to pick up his breakfast plate, "Let me get you that pie," then walked back behind the counter.

A short time later, Sarah returned with a golden slice of pie, the top slightly sweaty from condensation and lightly browned in some places. She slid the plate in front of Rylan, placed a fresh fork next to the pie, and sat across from him to watch his reaction.

"Now, it's not the best representation of a classic Hoosier Pie, I'll admit, but we buy from a baker a few miles down the road, and he's not half-bad. G'on, see what you think."

Initially taken aback that she had sat down to watch him, he quickly warmed to her company. She was maybe thirty, at most, and her amused expression brought a youthful glow to her face. Her eyes seemed tired, as though she didn't sleep much, but still warm and radiant like the coals of a campfire at dawn. Rylan thought there was something comforting about the way the sunlight came through the window, catching her auburn hair at the perfect angle, vaguely familiar like a faint whisper of something long forgotten. He liked her but didn't know why.

He examined the dessert, shaking his head disapprovingly. "I don't knowww," he teased.

"Stop it." She rolled her eyes, swatting at the air in a dismissive gesture, "Just put it in your mouth. Let it do its thing."

He gawked at her in mock umbrage. She smirked playfully.

"Alright," he smiled before cutting off a bite with his fork and scooping it into his mouth. He closed his eyes to savor the flavor. It was a simple custard pie with notes of nutmeg and vanilla on a buttery crust; not entirely remarkable, but enjoyable nonetheless. Upon opening his eyes, Sarah's face was full of anticipation. He nodded approval, wiping his mouth with a napkin. "That's pretty good."

"I know, right?" she cried in mild triumph, "Now, you can scratch it off your bucket list. And when you get to wherever you're going, you can tell them you had a real-life, honest-to-goodness Hoosier Pie."

"Get to where I'm going?" He asked as he cut another piece of pie, "How do you know I'm not from 'round here?"

"Well, two things. Right off the top, you've never heard of a Hoosier Pie. That's a big one, and two, you're eating here. Nobody from 'round here comes to the Appleseed. It's only travelers that come to sit at these tables." Rylan looked around the dining room, considering what she had said while chewing a second bite of pie.

"You think maybe it's the name of the place why locals don't come here? I get the convenience thing for travelers, stop in, eat, and go, but do you think the name turns other folks off?"

Puzzled by his comment, she thought for a few seconds before responding, "I don't follow."

"Appleseed Diner. Doesn't arsenic come from apple seeds? They're poisonous." He couldn't hide the sly smirk from his face.

Sarah's expression of strained comprehension instantly melted away. "Oh god, you're a damn comedian, aren't you?" She said flatly while Rylan erupted in laughter at her reaction. She shook her head and started to get up from her seat before pausing, "It's not arsenic that's in apple seeds, funny guy; it's cyanide."

Rylan laughed even harder, tears welling up and starting to trickle out of his left eye. He reached for her hand to steady her, signaling he wanted her to stay. She weighed the decision to stay or go, watching him try to control his laughter before she gave in and sat back down.

Still getting himself under control, wiping his eyes, he took a deep breath. "That was funny. I really needed that."

"It wasn't that funny."

"No, no, you're right; the joke wasn't that funny. I was mostly laughing at your face."

"The HELL did you say?" She exclaimed, slapping the table in outrage.

Rylan's eyes flashed wide in surprised shock before he erupted in howling laughter again, shaking his head and waving his hands to indicate he was mistaken. He tried to stop, but the laughter had seized him like an undertow dragging him out to sea.

He laughed uncontrollably for a while as the waitress observed him with growing concern. Eventually, he slowed and then stopped, red-faced with embarrassment. He cleared his throat and began to apologize, but an elderly couple entered the diner, triggering the doorbell chime and drawing Sarah's attention.

Sarah started to stand but paused, and turned back to Rylan.

"Look, darlin', I don't know you, but you look like you might be going through some things" She reached out and put her hand on top of Rylan's. "I hope whenever you get to wherever you're going, you can find some peace. I'll pray for you, okay?" She squeezed his hand, then stood up, "Don't worry about the check. It's on the house. This time." She winked charmingly before hurrying off toward the new customers.

Rylan suddenly felt exposed and vulnerable. His mind raced to replay their conversation. What had he said? Did he accidentally leak something? Paranoia started to tickle the hairs on the back of his neck as the air grew thicker. He reached for his wallet, dropped a twenty and a ten on the table beside the half-eaten pie, then scooped up his journal, pushed his chair back from the table, and stepped toward the exit, sheepishly keeping his eyes on the floor until he reached the door.

He rushed out into the sunshine and sucked in the cool morning air, hardly noticing the stench of fertilizer from the cornfields. After a few deep breaths, he turned to peer through the diner's windows and found Sarah scribbling the elderly couple's order in her notepad. He observed their muted banter as the new customers cheerfully grinned back at her and wondered if he had overreacted. He convinced himself it didn't matter, and that he needed to get back on the road anyway. He peeled himself away from the window, walked back to his Trailblazer, and put the Appleseed Diner in his rearview mirror.

4

— • —

JUNE 15, 2001, FRIDAY

COLUMBIA, SOUTH CAROLINA

Rylan's pulse quickened as he leaned forward, ready to jump up from his seat. He glanced at Tommy and Homer, the two friends seated next to him in the bleachers, and could see they were equally as anxious. Having listened to hundreds of names being called, impatiently waiting for their turn, the announcer finally read the name they had been anticipating: Joseph T. Severn. In unison, the three high schoolers jumped up yelling, "Joey!" They clapped as their friend walked across the stage to receive his diploma. Rylan noticed Joey's mother and father standing and cheering loudly from seats closer to the stage. They were flanked by three unfamiliar people sharing their same enthusiasm, but Rylan paid them no mind.

He was proud of his friend's accomplishment and was genuinely happy for him, but he couldn't help but imagine his own graduation, still a year away; his mother and sister seated in the folding chairs reserved for family members, cheering wildly for him. Then the thought that his father would never see him walk across the graduation stage pierced like an arrow through his joyous daydream, straight into his chest. His father would never be there to give him the firm handshake of acceptance into adulthood, the held eye contact of affirmation, or the nod of acknowledged achievement, none of it. Rylan blinked hard to force the thought from his mind, then refocused on Joey, now nearing the end of the stage, waving his rolled diploma over his head, grinning, and pointing at his parents. The announcer began reading the next name on the list: Janice Severson, and the five friends sat back down as Janice's family and friends took their turn to loudly proclaim their support for their freshly-minted high school graduate.

That evening, Joey's parents were taking him out to a celebratory dinner at his favorite restaurant, Little Pig's Barbecue, and they had invited his friends to come along. Besides Rylan, two other friends, Homer and Tommy, took up the offer. The three of them had arrived in Homer's pickup truck a few minutes before Joey and his family had pulled into the parking lot. They stood patiently waiting in the gravel, the savory aroma of wood-smoked pork thick in the air.

Joey and his parents got out of their minivan along with the three other people Rylan had seen standing at the graduation ceremony. After quickly greeting the boys, Mr. Severn introduced the newcomers, the Jamesons, from his side of the family: his sister, Mary, her husband, Merle, and their teenage daughter, Abigail. They had driven over from a small town near Charleston for the graduation. Everyone smiled and shook hands to a jumbled chorus of hello, howya doin', pleasure to meet ya', and can't complain. Once everyone greeted one another, Mr. Setter invited everyone to go inside.

Standing by the cashier, Mr. Setter ushered everyone past him, counting heads, then stayed behind to square up the fare. The four boys, including Joey, darted here and there along the buffet counter, knowing exactly where to go for each of their favorite foods. The newcomers, unfamiliar with Little Pig's offerings, started squinting and scanning the foods, tempted but unsure of what to select for fear something better might be further on. Rylan had quickly filled his plate and was about to head to the table but detected their hesitation.

"Y'all need some help?" he offered. They turned to look at him with relief. "Don't worry; I got you. They got pretty much everything here, but if you get nothing else, you gotta get the hash. It's the bomb; I'm telling you." Rylan made a slurping sound, licking his lips for dramatic effect. Everyone smiled, Abigail giggled, and Rylan noticed. They followed him as he walked along the buffet. "Next, there's ribs, and these smoked sausages are the best when they're just a little overdone on the ends. Over here, they got three kinds of pulled pork with the vinegar-based sauce, the mustard base, or the tomato base; all three are, of course, delicious." He smiled charmingly at Abigail, and she smiled back, delighted with his rousing review of the buffet. Encouraged, Rylan continued his commentary, "They got fried fish with the skin-on, hush puppies that taste like cornbread, oh, and for dessert, they got banana pudding over here, and this crazy chocolate-peanut-butter-marshmallow madness; they call it Chocolate Delight. It's hella good. I mean, really, anything you're gonna get is gonna be good. It may not be the very best you ever had, but I can guarantee it's all gonna be good food, at the very least."

"Well damn, boy! You work here or somethin'?" Merle cried out with a laugh, clapping a meaty hand behind Rylan's shoulder. Rylan started to reply, but Merle interrupted, "Just messing with ya, Rye. We appreciate you taking the time to give us the grand tour of the place. G'head now and eat. We can figure it out from here."

Rylan stole another glance at Abigail, who looked at him like she wanted him to stay before Merle put a hand on her shoulder to usher her into the buffet line. The young man reluctantly headed over to join his friends, already halfway through their first helping despite nonstop chatter, but throughout the meal, he would discretely peek at Abigail, and at times, caught her doing the same.

Amongst his friends, the conversation eventually turned to the subject of Joey's enlistment in the Army. He was set to ship out to basic training in two weeks; then, after basic, he was to be stationed at a base in Germany. He was thrilled about living in a foreign country, but his excitement was mainly at the thought of doing something different from everyone else. His parents, for their part, had mixed emotions about their son joining the military but were mostly proud and supportive of his decision. They found solace in the fact that there wasn't a war going on, and he was enlisting to be an Army truck driver, not an altogether dangerous job.

"You think the Army's gonna send you to Kosovo?" Tommy queried with a mouthful of mashed potatoes and gravy, "Kelly Crisp said her uncle came back from over there last year and was messed up in the head. Saw a lot of fighting, I guess."

"Naw, Sergeant Thompson, my recruiter, said they're done with all the Kosovo stuff by now. Everybody's come home or already come home by now."

"Yeah, right! They tell you that 'til another war breaks out, and you're sent to get shot up in someone else's country." Homer exclaimed, always talking too loudly. Tommy, seated next to him, backhanded Homer on the shoulder.

"Don't listen to this dumb ass, dawg. You'll be fine. You're only driving trucks anyways, right?" Tommy tried to reassure his friend.

"Hell yeah! Not just them Humvees either, them big ol' semi-trucks too. I got a three-year contract, gonna spend a few years in Germany, and when I get out, I'll have my CDL and can go drive commercial. I'll buy me a brand new Mack or a Peterbilt and practically live on the road." Joey's face lit up with excitement as he spoke.

"You're not coming back to live here?" Rylan asked.

"I'll still have a little place here, but it'd be more of a base of operations for me. I'll come back to visit for a bit, then get back on the highway."

"Base of operations? Look at this guy! Thinks he a soldier already!" Homer mocked, laughing.

Joey, red-faced, tried to suppress a smile, then stood up to throw a brotherly punch over the table at Homer. He connected in the same shoulder in which Tommy had backhanded his loud-mouthed friend earlier. Homer laughed even harder, rubbing the spot of the blow while Rylan and Tommy grinned in amusement.

"Boys!" Mrs. Setter exclaimed from the adjacent table to chastise her son, interrupting her conversation with her sister-in-law, "Joey! Act like you was raised right."

"But he..." Joey began, caught himself, and began to sit down, "Sorry, Mumma." Turning back to Homer, who had stopped laughing but was still grinning, he lowered his voice to a whisper, "I'm gonna fuck you up outside, boy, wait and see."

"Simmer down over there, Joseph, you know I'm just playin'." Homer deflected Joey's half-serious threat.

Tommy attempted to change the subject, "Hey Joey, you get a signing bonus for the Army? I heard Jasper Fischer is getting five hundred, and he ships out next month."

Joey's eyes lit up, "Oh yeah? I didn't know Jasper was joining up too. I'll have to hit him up, but yeah, I got a signing bonus."

"So, how much you get?" Homer questioned.

"None of your damn business, Homer." Joey snapped at his friend across the table, "Stay outta my pockets."

The conversation paused for a few seconds. Joey's friends waited for him to answer the question, but when he scooped a spoonful of banana pudding into his mouth, it became apparent he wasn't going to respond.

"Really?" Tommy interjected incredulously, "Really? You're not gonna say how much you got? What, you think we're gonna rob you? Well, Homer might; can't rule that out, but seriously?"

"Mmmm," Joey hummed with a mouthful, pointing to his lips. He finished eating and wiped his lips with a napkin, taking his time, milking the moment a little longer to frustrate his friends' impatience. "I got seven hundred bucks."

Tommy and Rylan both exclaimed in hushed voices, "Oh shit!"

"That's it? That's all ya got?" Homer feigned disappointment to goad Joey some more.

Joey quickly checked over his shoulder to see if his mom was looking; she was, so he just smiled and waved at her. She squinted her eyes at him, knowing her son was up to something.

Joey turned back towards his antagonist, "You're one lucky fucking duck; I'll tell you what."

Homer grinned and waved over at Mrs. Setter. She shook her head knowingly, unfooled by his grinning facade. Homer had a reputation as a shit-talker and instigator. He enjoyed provoking people to frustration before deflecting their anger at the last minute by saying, "I'm just playin'." It was so frequent it might as well have been his catchphrase.

"So you're living large, then, huh? What're you gonna do with all that cheddar? More importantly, how are we gonna spend it." Tommy joked, rubbing his palms together.

"Y'all stupid." Joey said, rolling his eyes, "I don't get the signing bonus until I've been in the Army for a full year. That way dudes don't enlist and then run off with the cheese."

"Makes sense, I guess." Tommy said, deflated, "But, dawg, you know we gotta do something big before you leave for basic training, though, right?"

Homer scoffed, "Something big? Y'all ain't got no creativity. All y'all ever want to do is come back here to eat. Now, we could probably come up with something new if Rye wasn't so busy checking out your cousin."

Rylan's face flushed bright red. He thought he was being stealthy, but looking around at each of his friends' smirking faces and Homer grinning devilishly like the Cheshire Cat, he knew he'd been caught. He quickly checked on Abigail. She was thankfully engrossed in the older folks' conversation, oblivious to what Homer had said.

"You're a dick, Homer," Rylan said flatly. The three friends burst out in laughter with Rylan unable to restrain a reluctant smile.

The laughter drew Abigail's attention and she noticed Rylan still blushing. Their eyes met and they held each other's gaze for a few seconds, a subtle electricity passing silently between them. She leaned over to say something to her mother, then stood up, made eye contact with Rylan once more, and walked towards the buffet, stopping at the dessert counter.

The boys had almost stopped laughing when Homer said, "You better get after her, Rye. Don't be a pussy. If you don't go, I will."

Rylan shot him a look of contempt, then got up from his seat, knowing Homer was at least partially right. He took one step towards the buffet, then stopped to glance at Joey, awkwardly seeking some sign of permission from his friend.

Joey nodded, "G'head. Good luck."

Rylan nervously ran his hand through his hair, then followed after Abigail.

She was standing at the dessert counter, with her back towards Rylan, wearing a yellow sun dress with a white belt that perfectly complimented her light brown skin. Her wavy hair was pulled back into a ponytail and tied with a wide blue ribbon. As he approached, Rylan noticed a pair of middle-aged men standing at the far end of the buffet, eyeing Abigail. One leaned over and said something to the other, and they both smiled mischievously. Rylan clenched his jaw and tried to refocus his attention on Abigail. He walked up beside her, purposely blocking the old men's view, and casually asked, "You try the Chocolate Delight yet?"

She didn't look up, "No. Not yet, but I hear it's hella good." She quipped, mocking the slang he had used earlier, with a wry smile.

"It is. You're... " Rylan had missed her taunt but trailed off, noticing the way she was grinning. "What?"

"I'm sorry, but who says 'hella good'?" She turned to face him.

Rylan smiled, "Yeah, when I lived in Vegas, I had a friend who moved over from Southern California. He used to say 'hella' all the time. It's like some surfer lingo." Rylan shrugged, "I used to roast him about it when we first met, but I guess it kind of stuck with me. Now everyone gives me shit about it."

"So, you're from Las Vegas?"

"Yeah, kinda. We only lived there for a few years before moving here."

"Were you living in Vegas when they killed Tupac?"

He was surprised by her question. "Yeah, actually I was." he responded, "He got shot the night of the Tyson fight. Next morning, I found out on the news. My friend eventually came to scoop me up, and we drove to the hospital. I swear, there were at least a thousand people out in that parking lot. It was packed! Every car was playing his music real loud so he could hear it up in his hospital room, so he knew we were there for him. It was sad, but it was also kinda beautiful, too, ya know?" His voice trailed off as he looked down at his shoes in mournful thought, "He held on for five more days before they let him go."

They stood together in reverent silence for a few seconds before Abigail asked, "Did you cry?"

Stunned by her question, he jerked his head up, looking at her skeptically. Her face showed a sincerity he hadn't expected. He

slowly lowered his gaze back down to his shoes, humbled, "Yeah."
He reluctantly admitted, "Yeah, I did."

"Me too."

The conversation had taken a dismal turn so Rylan decided
to change the subject. "So... um, you guys are from Charleston,
right?"

"We're actually from Summerville. It's a few miles inland of
Charleston." She answered, then stepped backward, out of the way
of a woman heading toward the desert counter. Rylan followed her
lead, stepping closer toward Abigail.

"I've never been to Charleston, but I hear it's nice." He added.

"It is. It's pretty, and it has this real old-timey southern feel to
it. My mama says it feels romantic when you're walking down the
street, like in Savannah. You been to Savannah? In Georgia."

"Naw. Never been to Georgia either."

"Me neither. Someday though. You wanna take me?" She teased.

Caught off guard and fumbling for a response, Rylan stuttered,
"Uh, um, yeah. Yeah, sure. When do you..."

"Stop." She laughed, "You're gonna hurt yourself. I was only
joking. I don't even know you. You're practically a stranger."

Rylan could feel the heat of embarrassment on his face. "I mean,
your cousin, Joey, he knows me. He can vouch for me."

"Are you serious?" She exclaimed in mild disbelief, "Rye, I was
seriously joking. I'm not going to Savannah with you."

"Why not? Don't I seem like a nice guy?"

"Nice doesn't mean anything. I've seen that movie about Ted
Bundy. He was a nice guy too."

"I'm not Ted Bundy, though."

"I don't know that." She retorted, crossing her arms. "How do I know that you're not some serial killer?"

He stepped closer, doing his best to keep a straight face and appear menacing, "I guess you won't know until I got you tied up in the back of my van."

She searched his eyes for a few seconds, trying to get a read on him. "That's pretty good." She nodded, unsmiling, "Clever come-back, I'll give you that, but that's not how you sweet talk a girl for a date, though."

She stepped around him to walk away, but he loosely grabbed her forearm to slow her down.

"C'mon." He pleaded, "C'mon, I was messin' around. I'm not a serial killer, okay? It's just..."

She spun around, "It's just what?"

Startled by her sudden change of direction, he flinched, straightened himself up, and spoke in a softer tone, "It's just that, I don't know, I like you, okay? And I thought maybe you might... look, can we start over? This got out of control real fast."

"No, I've heard enough." She slowly pulled her arm from his grip, "Rye, just so we're clear, I'm not going to Savannah with someone I just met."

"No, course not, that's not..."

"Please, don't interrupt me."

Rylan stopped talking but was visibly anxious.

Abigail continued, "Let's say we were both joking and leave it at that, okay? It's not a big deal. But..." she paused to choose her words, "Look, you're cute, but I don't know if I actually like you, yet. I'll just say I'm interested, okay? Here, give me your cellphone." She held her hand open and Rylan placed his flip phone in her palm. She talked while she pressed the buttons. "I'm saving my number in your phone. Call me tomorrow night after seven."

"Tomorrow?"

"Yeah. Tomorrow. We only came for you guys' graduation, even though Joey didn't come to mine last week." she added sourly.

"Your... your what? Your graduation?"

"Yeah, my school had our ceremony last Friday."

"Oh," Rylan said flatly.

"What? What's the matter?"

"Nothing, nothing. I'm good."

"No, you looked at me like I just ate the last piece of your birthday cake or something. What's wrong?"

He ran his hands nervously through his hair. "It's just that I haven't graduated yet. I graduate next year."

"Oh," Abigail looked off in the direction of the buffet while she thought, then looked at him before she spoke again, "Okay. Well, look, that's not a deal breaker for me if that's what you're worried about. We can talk about it later, though." She glanced at the table where her parents were seated, then turned back to Rylan. "I should probably be getting back to my parents. You gonna call me tomorrow, though, right?"

"Yeah. Yeah. Of course. Tomorrow after seven." Rylan replied, doing his best to sound optimistic.

"Okay, yeah, it was nice meeting you, Rye." She held out her hand, and he reluctantly shook it, knowing his hand was clammy.

"It was nice meeting me too." He caught his mistake too late, then stumbled to correct it, "I mean, for me. For me, it was nice meeting you too." He snapped his mouth shut, deciding it best to stop talking.

She held his hand for an instant longer, peering into his eyes. The corners of her mouth twitched with the beginnings of a playful smile before she let go, turned, and glided back to her table. Rylan stayed and watched her go.

Abigail's mother, seated beside her husband, had been doing her best to keep a furtive eye on her daughter, but as she approached, she stared past Abigail, directly at Rylan. Her gaze was firm and her message was clear, "I'm watching you."

Rylan decided to go to the restroom before heading back to his table, where his friends were undoubtedly waiting to interrogate him.

Walking through the door, he caught his reflection in the mirror and went straight to the sink. He leaned in to get a closer look at his face.

He thought he had a decent chance with Abigail, but the awkward way their conversation had ended left him unsure. She had given him her phone number, though; an encouraging sign. He nodded to his reflection, resolving to call her tomorrow night and let the chips fall where they may.

5

MARCH 26, 2017, SUNDAY

CARSON CITY, NEVADA

The rain had slowed to a gentle drizzle. Thousands of water droplets clung to the windshield, refracting the green light from the hotel's neon sign like tiny emeralds gleaming against the night sky before the windshield wipers swoosh-swooshed them away. As the grey Trailblazer idled in the parking lot, Rylan peered through the driver-side window into the brightly lit lobby of the Holiday Inn. A man in a faded blue sweatshirt was checking in at the reception desk while his wife stood a few steps away, holding a blanket-wrapped infant to her chest. The mother's face showed concern as she monitored her two adolescent sons chasing each other around the lobby furniture. Rylan observed the two rambunctious youngsters and decided to wait until their dad finished before heading in.

Rylan grabbed a soft taco and a packet of hot sauce from the plastic bag in the passenger seat, then sat listening to the soft hum of the Trailblazer's engine while he ate, squirting a bit of hot sauce onto the folded flour tortilla before each successive bite. Relief started to settle into his shoulders as he realized that his cross-country journey had concluded, at least for a little while. After three days and more than 2,500 miles between Maryland and Nevada, he was exhausted and eager to get some sleep.

While waiting for his turn to check into the hotel, Rylan continued eating and watched the tiny raindrops landing on his windshield dwindle to a stop. He began casually scanning the parking lot out of boredom but halted when he spotted the purple Chrysler PT Cruiser glistening in the rain. His appetite instantly disappeared, but he swallowed his last bite and sat motionless, staring blankly, transfixed by the sight of the vehicle.

Familiar images began to flicker rapidly behind his eyes, suppressed memories of much happier times too painful to remember. He could see Abigail sitting on the living room couch, a glass of wine nearly finished, sarcastically correcting him about the color of her beloved PT Cruiser: "It's not purple, Rye. It's dark plum!" On another day in mid-summer, with sweat stinging the corners of his eyes, he was struggling to install the child safety seat into the car when a still-pregnant Abigail arrived with the grace of an angel to bring him a cold glass of sweet tea and a warm smile. Many years later, on a breezy spring afternoon, as he washed the purple car in the driveway, his daughter gleefully scooped the suds out of the bucket of soapy water only to toss them into the air and declare it was snowing.

A pickup truck suddenly pulled into the hotel's parking lot behind the Trailblazer, and its headlights caught Rylan's rearview mirror at the perfect angle to reflect the light into his eyes. He blinked hard, winced, and swatted at the mirror to redirect the light. Finding himself free from the grip of his recollection, he once again peered into the hotel lobby and saw the family walking to the elevator. He wrapped up the last of his half-eaten taco, tossed it back into the bag, and headed inside.

Five minutes later, with a hotel keycard in his pocket, he had returned to retrieve his backpack from the truck but paused behind the vehicle to check over both shoulders before opening the liftgate. As he stood peering into the shadowy cavern, squinting into the darkness, he thought about the overhead light he had broken two weeks ago while dumping the rear seats at a junkyard and lamented his clumsy blunder. He could barely see anything in the trunk area, but the hotel's exterior lights provided just enough illumination to find the dark blue canvas backpack among the dozens of six-foot-long PVC poles he'd purchased from the Home Depot in Cheyenne. He swiftly slung the bag over his shoulder, closed the lift gate, and grabbed the bag of tacos from the front seat on the way to his hotel room.

Opening the door to room fifty-two, Rylan flicked the light switch as he crossed the threshold and then set his backpack on the floor beside the bed. With a heavy exhale, he slumped down onto the bedspread and ate another taco before digging around in his toiletry bag to find the little bottle of Ambien. He shook the bottle to hear the rattle, trying to estimate the remaining pills by the sound. Disappointed by what he heard, he chose to only take one and slurped it down with water from the sink faucet before undressing to shower. By the time he had finished, he was already drowsy but managed to brush his teeth and hang the "Do Not Disturb" sign outside the door before collapsing, naked, on top of the bedspread.

When he opened his eyes again, the digital alarm clock on the nightstand read 11:17, daylight was peeking around the edges of the undrawn curtains, and he could hear the voices out in the hallway; a family was discussing how much longer it would take to get to gramma's house. He rolled over onto his back, groaning and groggy, with a puddle of drool on the bedspread. He wiped his dampened cheek and stared up at the ceiling, thinking about going back to sleep, but the growling in his stomach argued against it. He glanced at the alarm clock, then groaned again, remembering that the hotel receptionist had said the hotel stopped serving complimentary breakfast at ten.

Annoyed at the prospect of leaving the hotel to find food, he briefly considered last night's leftover tacos but immediately dismissed the idea as repulsive. Reluctantly, he slid out of bed and staggered to the sink to brush his teeth, then dressed himself in a pair of jeans, a black Guns N' Roses t-shirt, and his grey running shoes. As he sat on the edge of the bed, tying the laces, he could almost hear his father's gruff voice, imparting a rare bit of sage advice to an eight-year-old son, "Lace them tight, Rye. A man should always be prepared to run away or chase someone down."

Exiting the building, the sudden brightness of the late-morning sun stung Rylan's eyes, but he kept walking toward his truck as his eyes adjusted. When he spotted the Trailblazer, he noticed the light grey paint appeared pale brown, dusty from the near-transcontinental road trip from Maryland, and just then, the truck's altered color brought to mind the PT Cruiser. The thought immediately seized Rylan's spine, and he stopped mid-stride. He peeked at the spot where the purple car had been parked, but fortunately, it was gone. He leaned his head back to release a bated exhale into the heavens and noticed the impressive hue of the Sierra Nevada sky, cerulean without a trace of a cloud, like a boundless blanket of blue laid overhead. He closed his eyes for a few seconds to enjoy the sun's radiance on his skin before hopping into the driver's seat, feeling unexpectedly optimistic. He started the engine of his dusty SUV and drove south on North Carson Street to forage for food in the way of the modern man.

Thirty minutes later, Rylan was back in his hotel room, eating a cheeseburger on his bed while scrolling through real estate websites on his laptop computer. He was hunting for houses outside of the city. In particular, he was searching for a place with some privacy, preferably a bit of land. When he had searched for houses back in Maryland, most had plenty of trees to provide natural privacy between the surrounding homes, but the area around Carson City was much more sparsely vegetated. As a result, he had to look for houses set away from busy roadways, hoping to reduce the chance that a passerby would notice some suspicious late-night activity in a supposedly vacant house and decide to alert the police.

After almost three hours of search and analysis, he had compiled a list of eight homes he wanted to reconnoiter. He pulled the marble composition notebook out of his backpack and flipped to the back. Taped inside the back cover was a list of twenty-one names with corresponding phone numbers and addresses. At the top of the list, written in all capital letters, were the words: THE GARBAGE ROUTE. He scrolled down to the address corresponding to the name Toni Caisse and added it to the list of locations he planned to visit that afternoon.

The time on his wristwatch read 2:52 PM. He estimated that scouting the nine addresses in the daylight should take him until dinner time, then after that, he would have some time to kill before revisiting the houses at night. He immediately thought about going to the movie theater. The movie, *Logan*, had come out a few weeks prior, and he was excited by the prospect of catching a showtime.

Recognizing he wouldn't return to the hotel until late, Rylan decided to shave his face before heading out. In his reasoning, if he happened to arouse suspicion while out scouting houses, a clean-shaven face would seem more trustworthy than one with a few days' worth of stubble, increasing his chances of talking his way out of trouble.

Standing in front of the sink, he observed each stroke of the razor blade in the mirror with only a passive interest. Though he was careful while shaving, he was far more focused on the debate taking place within his mind.

"What would Edward have said if we had taken the tape off his mouth?"

"He'd beg for his life. Probably offer us all the money in the world to let him go."

"Well, no shit, but would he have answered questions if we asked?"

"Maybe, but he'd just say whatever he thought would keep him alive."

"Yeah, but I really want to understand how his mind works, though."

"What does it matter? That's not what's important here; besides, we wouldn't even be able to trust anything he said."

"What if he thought his honesty would keep him alive?"

"...maybe."

"Right. Maybe."

"Look, we still got a lot of names left on the list. Don't get distracted by that bullshit. Don't make it complicated. Edward was only the first, and we're not stopping."

"But, could we stop, though, right? We wouldn't get caught if we stopped here, walked away, and went on with our life. We're only thirty-eight. We could meet someone new and start over."

"No. We can't start over. There is no starting over after Abigail and Penny."

"But they would've wanted us to try."

"Yes. They would."

Rylan bent over, bringing his face close to the faucet to rinse off the remaining shaving cream. When he stood back up, warm water dripping from his chin, he found his eyes again in the mirror.

"We can stop, ya know? Call it good. Edward could be enough."

"No. It's not enough."

To Rylan, the question of stopping needed no answer. He had already spent nearly a year debating the how, who, where, when, and why of it all. By the time he stood in the hotel room in Carson City, he was already fully committed to the mission and knew his success would only be measured by how far he could go. He had vowed to finish the list or die trying.

Rylan leaned heavily on the edge of the hotel sink, bringing his face closer to the mirror. Studying his countenance, he noticed the fluorescent lights accentuated the fine wrinkles at the corners of his eyes, but besides the bit of shaving cream still clinging to his left earlobe, his face looked the same. Edward Chaffin hadn't changed him. Nothing had changed except one name got scratched off a sheet of paper.

Five months prior, Rylan was still living in Columbia, South Carolina. During the day, he worked as a residential construction worker, surrounded by the banging of hammers and the pop of nail guns, but in the silence of the evenings, Rylan secretly worked on his sinister project. By then, he had assembled a list of twenty-one names and had begun gathering as much information as possible on each subject. He found a website where, for only $19.95 each, he could collect all their last known addresses, social media accounts, and phone numbers. Then, for months, he stalked their social media accounts and gathered information such as employment and relationship status, type of residence, friends' names, religious preferences, hobbies, vehicle model and color, favorite restaurants and coffee shops, and physical fitness habits. Using all the collected information, Rylan spent weeks carefully placing the names in order. He deliberately avoided listing any two consecutive names within the same state, reasoning that the police and, eventually, the feds would be slow to recognize a pattern if he moved across state lines, seemingly at random. After countless nights full of focused research, internal debate, and game-planning, Rylan completed the final version of the list, and he titled it, 'The Garbage Route'.

Finally completing the list, Rylan felt invigorated. Like a pioneer who had forded the first river in an uncertain westward journey, he had crossed a significant milestone that reinforced his resolve. Freshly energized and anxious to begin the work, he purchased a black stub-nose .38 revolver from a gun show, quit his job, and sold nearly all his belongings at a yard sale in front of his apartment. Ms. Radulescu, his elderly neighbor, brought out an old plastic milk crate for him to sit on while he sold his possessions, and he gave her his microwave and a set of steak knives in exchange. In the end, he only kept a few things from his old life: a few sets of clothes, Abigail's old brown leather overnight bag, his framing hammer, a pair of pliers, a folding knife from his Army days, a blue JanSport backpack, and his daughter's stuffed sea otter. That night, he tossed everything into the cleared-out rear of his SUV, turned in the keys to his apartment, and headed north on Interstate 95 toward Maryland.

Two weeks later, after leaving Edward's broken body in an empty house in the Baltimore suburbs, he was already prowling the areas around Carson City for his next venue. Of the eight houses on the list, he had already visited four when he took a detour to visit Toni Caisse's address. The time on his watch read 16:45 when he parked across the street to wait, hoping she was working a nine-to-five schedule and hadn't come home yet. While he waited, he studied the front of her residence, looking to gather any clues that might give him an advantage.

The house was wholly unremarkable; small craftsman-style single-story home, light-blue paint, white trim, and a small front yard framed by a chain-link fence. It was a decent house, nice, but lacked personality. There were none of the personal touches people tend to add to their homes. There were no wind chimes, potted plants, garden gnomes, or house-shaped mailboxes; nothing. Despite her lack of flair, Rylan was relieved to see that Toni's front yard was completely devoid of children's toys, unlike the next-door neighbor's home where colorful Fisher-Price toys littered the grass.

Eventually, an emerald green Hyundai Sonata arrived and parked in the driveway, then a woman with shoulder-length blond hair pulled back into a single braid climbed out. She wore a dark blue skirt with a white blouse and was barefoot. In one hand, she carried a blue clutch purse while her black high heels dangled from her fingers, and in the other, she carried a six-pack of Bud Light beer bottles. Rylan couldn't hear her voice but could tell she was singing as she strolled from her driveway to her front door, swinging the case of beer by the handle like a child with an easter basket. She unlocked the door and disappeared inside, having never looked in his direction.

Rylan stayed to watch Toni's house for a few more minutes, then left to continue scouting the remaining homes on his list. Before long, he was able to winnow the original list from eight down to three, but would still need to revisit them in the subdued light of night before making a final decision. Having completed his daylight recon, Rylan found a brick-oven pizza restaurant adjacent to the movie theater to eat dinner before catching the seven o'clock showing of *Logan*.

He stepped into the darkened theater, packed with eager movie-goers and the oily scent of buttered popcorn. *Logan*, a movie set in the twilight years of the superhero Wolverine's life, was advertised as the character's cinematic swan song, so, going in, Rylan knew his favorite superhero was bound to perish on screen. He was unprepared, though, for how the experience would ultimately affect him.

In his early teenage years, he was enamored with comic books and the hundreds of characters who inhabited their fictional universes. Back then, the only major motion pictures about superheroes were of Superman and Batman, but Rylan could remember laying on the floor of his bedroom, comic books fanned out on the carpet, fantasizing about the kind of movies that could be made about Iron Man, The Punisher, Captain America, and of course, his favorite, Wolverine. Decades later, when so many of those beloved characters were eventually brought to life on the silver screen, Rylan went to see them all and often exited the cinema feeling like he'd finished visiting cherished friends from his past.

When Rylan finally sat down to watch *Logan*, he felt cautiously optimistic that the final chapter in Wolverine's story would be handled with requisite respect, and he was not disappointed. Although undeniably a violent action flick, Rylan was surprised to find the film also full of introspection and compassion. The more subtle moments, especially those exploring the durability of familial bonds, tugged noticeably at his heartstrings, and in the end, he was grateful for the story the director told.

Once the final credits rolled and Rylan shuffled out the doors with the rest of the delighted crowd, he wanted badly to discuss the movie's finer points with someone. He could hear couples and small groups exchanging opinions about the plot, and he wanted to do the same. Gradually, his contentment was replaced by a sour sensation that started in his abdomen, spread throughout his chest, and eventually seeped into his heart. At that moment, he became soberingly aware of how alone he had become. There was nobody in his life with whom he could talk. No friends. No family. No one. He stopped walking and stood in the theater lobby, staring blankly into eternity as cheerful cinema patrons veered around him on their way toward the exits.

His loneliness boldly staring him in the face, his mind inevitably wandered back to the loved ones he once had, who were now all gone from his life. He longed for the times when they had endured hardships and rough patches together, bonding over their ability to overcome adversity, ultimately becoming stronger and wiser after emerging on the other side. Ironically, the more joyful recollections, periods when times were good and life was vibrant, were even harder to think about; those once-blissful memories had somehow become torturous.

Eventually, Rylan trudged sullenly out of the theater into the cool night air. He was mildly aware of the world occurring around him: groups of teenagers hooting and hollering with their friends along the sidewalk, a line of cars snaking through the parking lot as they inched their way toward the outlet, a passing waft of cigarette smoke, and a police siren off in the distance. He stood outside the glass doors feeling deflated and mildly dazed. It occurred to him that he still had work to do, but the mere thought of revisiting the three vacant homes that night was repulsive. He just wanted to return to his room and curl up into the coolness between the hotel's bedsheets.

As he dragged himself to the spot where his SUV was parked, he noticed the gas station on the corner of the street. The lights in the convenience store were on, but the neon-red Budweiser sign in the window caught his eye and flipped a switch in his brain. His mind instinctively carried him back to the subtly smokey scent of Tennessee whiskey and the sweetness of bourbon on his tongue. His heartbeat quickened and his skin warmed, as one's does when a once-passionate lover is nearby. His mouth watered, yet somehow still felt parched and thirsty. Absentmindedly, he licked his lips while unlocking the Trailblazer with the key fob, and as his hand reached out for the door handle, he stopped to reconsider.

At one point in his life, only a few years before, Rylan would have attempted to drown his sorrows in the bottom of a bottle, but he had made a promise he couldn't break. He opened the door, climbed inside, and started the engine.

6

— • —

June 18, 2001, Monday

Columbia, South Carolina

"Hello, I'm Abigail. Is Rylan home?"

"Oh wow! You're gorgeous!" Jean exclaimed through the screen door.

"Oh." Abigail was caught off guard and her face immediately flushed. "What an incredible thing to say to someone." She nervously smoothed her hair with her hand. "You're um, you're Jean, right?"

"Oh, right. I'm so sorry. Yes, I'm Jean." She replied while peeking past the visitor toward the driveway. She gasped in excitement, then pushed open the screen door and stepped onto the stoop beside Abigail. "Is that your car?"

"It is. It was a graduation present from my parents."

"That dark purple is like, so freakin' awesome! I love it."

"Thank you." Abigail beamed.

The younger girl bounded down the steps to get a better look at the brand-new PT Cruiser in the driveway. She circled the vehicle like a bee surveying a flower, then stopped and turned to the new owner.

"Wait, you said you graduated? I don't remember seeing you at school. You went to Thurmond High?" Jean asked.

"Oh no, I live in Summerville. It's near Charleston."

"Ohhhh. Okay." Jean's eyebrows rose in surprise, then lowered in confusion. "Then how do you know my brother?"

"My cousin, Joey, graduated last week..."

"You're Joey's cousin?" Jean blurted out, "He's so hot."

"Um..."

"Uh, I don't know why I said that out loud." Horrified by her own candor, she tried to deflect, "Like, just forget I said that, okay? You were saying..."

"Yeah... anyways, my parents drove up to see Joey's graduation, then we went out to dinner, and that's where I met Rylan."

"*Rylan*?" She exclaimed. "Wow! No one besides my mom calls him 'Rylan.' It even sounds weird coming out of my mouth." Lowering her voice, she asked, "What does he say when you call him that?"

Abigail cocked her head in bewilderment, "He hasn't said anything about it. I know everyone calls him Rye, but on the phone, he mentioned that his real name was Rylan, and I thought it was cute, so I've been calling him that for the past two days."

"I'm surprised he even told you his real name."

"Why is that?"

"Honestly, you should probably talk to him about it. I don't think it's right for me to... "

"Yeah, yeah, of course, yeah." Abigail agreed, "Sorry."

"Nah, you're good," Jean reassured Abigail while her eyes returned to the purple car. "So, you just met Rye last Friday, and then two days later, you drove all the way up here from...."

"Summerville."

"...right, from Summerville, for your first date?" She questioned, in mild disbelief. "How long was the drive?"

"Just under two hours."

"Holy shit!" Her hand reflexively shot up to cover her mouth as if she could still catch the curse word after it had already escaped her lips. She glanced at the front door before continuing, "I'm sorry, but wow, that's a long drive. The boys in Summerville must suck, huh?"

Abigail laughed. "That's not really why, but you're not wrong either. They do suck." The two girls laughed together in the early afternoon heat as a cool breeze blew through the maple tree in the front yard, causing its leaves to cast gently swaying shadows on their faces.

Rylan appeared in the doorway of the house, standing behind the screen door, buttoning up a white short-sleeved shirt.

"Yo! What the hell, Jean? Why didn't you tell me she was here?"

Jean snapped back. "Seriously? She only got here a few minutes ago, Rye. It's not a big deal."

Stifling her laughter, Abigail waved to Rylan, "I just got here. Your sister was admiring my new ride. What do you think?"

"It's great," he curtly replied while glaring at his sister, then turned his attention fully to Abigail. "Can you give me two minutes? I'll be right out."

"Yeah. No, that's cool. I'll be out here with Jean."

While Rylan withdrew into the shadows of the house, Jean turned back to Abigail, dramatically rolling her eyes.

"Brothers are so annoying. You have any brothers or sisters?"

"Nope. Only child."

"Soooo lucky!"

"I don't know, maybe not so much. Growing up, a lot of my friends had brothers and sisters and I'd watch how they were together. What I always admired was that no matter much they'd squabble amongst themselves, when times got tough, they'd always fight for each other."

After a moment considering it, Jean nodded modestly, then gazed towards the front of the house where her brother had been standing.

"Yeah. He's not so bad. He's really been there for Mom and me." Her gaze sagged toward the ground as she thought about her father. "It's been a rough few years."

Abigail put a hand on Jean's right shoulder. "Rylan told me about your dad. I'm really sorry. It had to be hard on you all." She noticed the younger girl's lip quiver, and asked softly, "Can I hug you?"

Jean nodded and was gently embraced by a young woman she had only just met. She threw her arms around the taller girl's waist, rested her head on her chest, and listened to her heartbeat. The two stood motionless together while the wind blew around them.

A few moments later, Rylan emerged from the house and stopped in his tracks. "What the heck is this now, Jean? I turn my back for two minutes, and you're trying to steal my girl?"

Mildly embarrassed, the two girls released each other and avoided each other's eyes. Jean cleared her throat, "Hey, she's my girlfriend now, bro. We're together, so you can go back inside now."

Abigail waved both hands over her head, "Whoa, hey, look, let me stop the both of you. First of all. I'm nobody's 'girl.' I am a woman. Okay?" She declared, while firmly planting one hand on her hip and waving the index finger of the other in the air in front of her, "And secondly, before anyone thinks I'm gonna be someone's 'girlfriend,' I will for-damn-sure have a say in it."

Rylan and Jean snickered while Abigail smirked.

"Yes, Ma'am. My deepest apologies." Rylan replied sarcastically.

"Yeah, sorry." Jean played along, smiling.

"Apology accepted." Abigail turned her attention to her date, still standing in the doorway, holding the screen door open, "So, you finally ready now, princess? Got your makeup all done up? You look beautiful. Let's get going." She turned to walk to her car, winking at Jean along the way. "I'll see you later, okay?"

"Definitely," Jean replied. Stepping towards the house, she made eye contact with her brother as he walked around to the car's passenger-side door and firmly whispered, "I like her. Don't mess this up."

Rylan smiled and nodded in agreement.

The pair filled the short drive to the Pitter-Putter Mini Golf course with idle chatter and playful banter, which continued as they checked in and began a round of eighteen holes. Both were surprised by how easily their conversations had come while on the phone but were worried that it would be different in person; fortunately, those concerns proved invalid. The two discovered an unexpected comfort together, as if they had known each other for years.

While in high school, Abigail hadn't had much time for boys. Her grades had been paramount in her life with everything else a distant second. Her mother had driven home the point that her daughter must be able to stand on her own two feet without expecting a man to prop her up in life because, "more often than not, a man would rather hold you down." While motivated to follow her mother's advice, she did find time to go on a few dates but found the guys tended to be tiresome, beautiful idiots, who were good enough to practice kissing, but not for much more. With Rylan, though, something felt different. She couldn't articulate what it was, which only made him all the more interesting.

She watched him interact with other people at the mini golf reception area, and he seemed to be considerate of others, polite, and even charming; and it didn't seem like an act. He thought he was funny and often was chuckle-worthy, at least, but he was mostly just a smart-ass. She liked it. She thought of Rylan like a good lemonade in the summertime; refreshing and sweet with the right amount of tartness to keep it interesting.

On the fourth hole of the course, Rylan was staring down at the fluorescent-orange golf ball lying between his feet on the bright green artificial grass. As he lined up the putt, he asked, "So, why Penn State? I know you could've gotten in at USC or... I dunno, somewhere else close by, maybe."

He took his shot, and the ball missed tightly to the left of the hole. Grumbling, he walked over to set up the next stroke while his date answered.

"So, my grandpa lived up in Strasburg, Pennsylvania. He'd graduated from Penn State a long time ago and was a huge football fan. Anyways, when I was younger, we would go up to visit him around Thanksgiving and we'd sit together on the couch, watching the game, and he'd teach me about football. He was great. He had this scruffy old grey beard and smelled like pumpkin pie and beer." She recalled with a laugh, "I remember he'd always have a can of beer in his hand, some local brand called Yuengling, and every quarter,

I'd ask if he wanted me to bring him a fresh can of 'Ding-A-Ling' from the fridge and he'd laugh until his face turned red and started coughing." She laughed again, and Rylan watched, smiling, until her laughter faded into melancholy. "Lung cancer took him almost ten years ago." Clearing her throat, she shrugged, "So I wanted to go to Penn State because of him. It's a good school too, though."

"Yeah, it's definitely a good school. It's your turn, by the way." Rylan stepped off the green carpet, and Abigail stepped up to make her putt. "It just sucks that you're going to be that far away, ya know?"

"Aww, you gonna miss me, Rye?" She taunted him with a sad face.

"Shit, not anymore." he countered.

"Nice," she smirked approvingly.

"How do your parents feel about you going that far off for college?"

"They don't really like it but understand. They wanted me to stay closer to home, so when I eventually decided on Penn State, I could tell they were disappointed. I mean, they tried to hide it, but I can tell."

She stopped talking while she putted her purple golf ball. When it dropped into the cup, she retrieved it and started walking towards the fourth hole. Rylan followed her.

"What about you, Rye? I know you hate school, but what are you planning to do after you graduate next year?"

"I dunno. I really can't see myself going to college. I could do it, but I'd be so miserable. I hate school. It's so much wasted time. It's... tedious! That's the word, right? Besides, the husband of one of my mom's coworkers has a construction business, and he told me to go talk to him about a summer job on his crew. If it works out, I think I could do that long term."

Abigail took her tee-off shot but missed wide-left and Rylan stepped forward for his turn.

"You ever do anything like that before?" She asked.

"Construction? Naw, not yet, but it sounds cool... swinging a hammer all day long, huh? I could do that." He beat the air with the end of his putter as if it were the head of a hammer.

"Or you could get a nail gun."

"Hell yeah! Now we're talking." He struck his golf ball too hard and it ricocheted off the frame, nearly rolling back to the start point.

Abigail teased, "Calm down, killer. On second thought, maybe they shouldn't trust you with a nail gun. Stick to the hammer. It's safer."

Rylan shook his head as he stepped off the green. "Yeah, well, we'll see. You know, Joey was trying to talk me into joining the Army. I could do that if the construction thing doesn't pan out."

"Hmm," she replied, lined up her shot, and smoothly tapped the ball. They watched it roll closer and closer to the cup, then stop at the rim. She groaned loudly, then playfully blew a lungful of air at the purple ball. Miraculously, it tipped over the edge and dropped into the cup.

"OHHHHHHH!" The two teenagers cried out in unison. Abigail dropped her putter and threw her arms up into the air. "Did you see that?"

"That was crazy!" Rylan exclaimed and gave her a high-five. "You can't blow on the ball though. That's cheating."

"Cheating? Really? Kiss my ass, Rye. I was like four or five feet away."

"I don't know. It could be the butterfly effect or something."

"You're ridiculous." She rolled her eyes hard. "You're just mad because you're getting smoked by a girl!"

"I don't have a problem losing to a woman as long as she beats me fair and square."

"Shut up, Rye. I was already winning before that shot. You're just not very good."

"How do you know I haven't been hustling you all along?" He replied.

"Hustling me? For what? We aren't even playing for money."

"Alright, how about this? If I sink this next shot, you give me a kiss."

'Wowww. That's pretty bold, baby boy." She squinted her eyes suspiciously while considering his proposal, surprised to find that she was aroused by his audacity. "What if you miss, though?"

Rylan shrugged, "Then I don't get a kiss."

"No way. Then you're not risking anything. Nuh-uh. How about this; if you make the shot, you get a kiss, and if you miss, I get to slap you as hard as I can across the face."

"What? Fuck no!"

"Oh darn. Well, I guess you weren't hustling me then." She taunted him.

"Wait, hold up, let me think."

"By all means. Take your time." She smirked.

Rylan paced a little bit, thinking, his eyes darting back and forth on the faux grass. He stroked his chin while he contemplated the deal. "Alright. Let's do it." He announced and held out his hand to Abigail.

She shook his hand, again surprised by his decision. "Okay then," She grinned, excited by the bet as he started to line up his putt. "You must really want that kiss, huh, Rye? I like the confidence, but I feel like I should tell you," she stepped in close to him and whispered in his ear, "fortune doesn't always favor the bold, baby boy."

"Get out of here!" He gently pushed her away while she laughed gleefully. He tried to suppress the smile forcing its way across his lips but failed. "What's all this 'baby boy' stuff anyways?"

"I don't know. It happened naturally, but I think I like it for you, though. I am older than you, after all, remember?"

"Yeah, okay, whatever." He swatted the air dismissively.

"Aw babe, don't be salty. Here, I'll shut up so you can concentrate on this very, very, veerrry important shot."

Rylan didn't respond. He was busy concentrating on his putt. She watched with mirthful interest as he made incremental adjustments to the angle of the putter face, imagined the ball's path to the cup, and tried to gauge how hard to hit it. It was comical how focused he was on the stroke, but she held her giggles behind a pursed smile.

He slowly drew the putter into his backswing and brought it forward to strike the ball. It began rolling straight, then, Rylan held his breath as it drifted slightly to the left. Abigail, enjoying the fun, leaned on her putter like a cane, stretching her lean frame over the top, then craning her neck to watch the approach. Rylan's ball arrived at the hole along the left edge and rode the rim for a breathless moment before rolling on past.

"No!" Rylan dropped to his knees, playing up the part of the defeated for Abigail's benefit.

"Ohhh shit!" She cried out, laughing as she did a little celebration dance. "I can't believe you missed! Now you got to pay up."

Rylan sighed, "Yeah. I know." He stood up. "Let's get it over with." He put his hands behind his back, leaned forward, and stuck his chin out.

"Man, this is gonna be good. You're gonna tell your grandkids about this!" Abigail taunted while hopping up and down, shaking her arms out to get loose, grinning from ear to ear. "Close your eyes, too. I don't want you flinching and making me miss."

"I won't flinch."

"Eyes closed." She demanded.

"Fine." He conceded. He closed his eyes and waited, his jaw clenched, braced for impact.

"On second thought," Abigail said, "I'm gonna keep this one in my back pocket for now, and I'll cash it in some other time.

Rylan opened his eyes. "What? No, fuck that. Just do it now."

"Nope. You didn't specify a time or place before we shook on it. I won the right to slap you in the face as hard as I can, end of story. So now, it's up to me to decide when to slap the taste out of your mouth." She grinned at him while he stared blankly back at her. "Now, c'mon. Finish this shot so we can move on." She pointed at the family behind them at the third hole, "They've almost caught up to us."

He mumbled, "This is fucked up," as he reluctantly walked over and tapped his ball into the hole. Abigail had already started walking towards the sixth hole, but her eyes were on him while she strolled. She was beaming like a child holding an ice cream cone. She couldn't remember when she had enjoyed being with anyone this much. In the past, when on a date, she felt the need to be cautious with her words. The five boys she had dated had all been fragile things; physically strong, but also insecure and temperamental. With them, she couldn't play too hard. She had to be careful not to say anything too critical, but with Rylan, she sometimes surprised herself with her audacity. Even better, he seemed to be able to handle it and enjoyed the back-and-forth.

They continued playing through the course, laughing and talking, learning about each other. They discussed favorite foods: for Abigail, the refined artistry of hand-rolled sushi, and Rylan, the greasy char of a cheeseburger hot off the grill. When it came to favorite movies, Rylan declared himself an avid movie fan, then exhaustively detailed the nuance of his favorite movie, *Gladiator*, confessing to having watched it three times in the theater the previous summer. Then, when Abigail admitted she wasn't much into movies, Rylan blustered and playfully threatened to end their date entirely. He insisted she was missing out on one of America's greatest art forms and swore he would change her mind.

Feeling defensive, she quizzed him about his favorite book, hoping to gain the upper hand in the discussion, but was stymied when he answered, *The Count of Monte Cristo*. Unconvinced, she questioned him about why he liked the book and was impressed by the depth of his response. After he finished his excellent book report on Alexandre Dumas' classic, she was reluctant to admit her favorite book, *The Princess Bride*, but Rylan immediately began quoting lines from the movie and acting out the swashbuckling scenes using his putter as a sword. She laughed at his antics at first, then unsheathed her own putter and played along.

Later, while walking up to the twelfth hole, Abigail switched gears in their conversation, "Can I ask you something?"

"Oh no, you sound serious." Rylan responded with light sarcasm, "What's up?"

"No, it's nothing like that. Well, I don't know. I'm curious, I guess, and if you don't want to answer, it's totally cool, okay?"

Rylan stopped and turned to her, trepidation beginning to tighten the muscles in his shoulders, "Okayyyy."

"That girl over there, next to the pink windmill, reminded me of your sister, and it got me thinking. Did you guys, I mean your mom and you and Jean; did you guys move from Las Vegas because your dad died?"

He took a step backward and looked off into the distance with his mouth hanging slightly open. "Um."

"Rye, I'm sorry. I shouldn't have asked. I didn't mean to..."

"No." He interrupted, shaking his head, "No, you don't have to apologize. It's fine. I'm just thinking about how to answer. I've never really talked about it to anyone before." He thought about it for a few more seconds, again looking off into the void, squinting as if trying to focus his vision. "Okay, the short answer is 'no,' but the long answer is 'yes.'"

Abigail scowled with strained understanding.

Rylan offered, "You know what? This sun is really cooking today. How 'bout we head back to the concession stand? Get a soda, find one of those benches with some shade, and I'll explain what I mean, okay? We can finish the course after."

"Yeah, that sounds great." They started to walk back to the concession stand, and Abigail put an arm around Rylan's shoulders,

"But, hey, so you don't sound crazy, remember, this is the South, okay, honey, we don't call it 'soda', it's 'coke'."

He shot her a deadpan look, "Thank you so much," he responded sarcastically, "now I won't sound crazy."

She winked. "Good thing I'm here, right?"

"Yes. Lucky me."

After purchasing a couple of fountain drinks, they found a picnic table under an awning, away from the too-loud pop music and the other customers noshing over-priced nachos, french fries, and chicken strips. They sipped their iced beverages under the merciful shade for a short while before Rylan started talking.

"So, I'll be honest," His eye contact signaled his seriousness, "I suggested we get drinks because I needed to stall and think about what I was going to say; and how I was going to say it. Aside from the counselor I was forced to see while we were still in Vegas, I haven't ever talked to anyone about this. Well, Joey knows a little bit, but that's all."

"Rye, if you don't feel comfortable...." Abigail offered but secretly hoped he would continue.

"No, it's fine. It's not any real secret. It's just..." He shrugged and took a deep breath. "It's kind of a long story. You okay with that?"

"Of course." She folded her arms on the table and leaned in closer.

"Alright. So, in total, we lived in Vegas for about three years. We'd moved there from Southern California because my dad imagined he could become a professional gambler." He paused and shook his head in stupefied disappointment, "After we moved, we came to find out he was actually horrible at cards. He lost all our money. He'd come home drunk, and... if you didn't know, at the casinos, if you're actively gambling, the alcohol is free; all you can drink. They want you drunk so you lose; and he did, often. So, as you can imagine, my parents argued all the time. One day, a neighbor at our apartment complex drove my mom to come pick me up early from school, then we picked up Jean, and we drove out to a women's shelter near the edge of the city. She waited until we got there before dropping the bomb on us that she was leaving our dad. She already had bags packed for Jean and me in the trunk of her friend's car. At the time, I was pissed at both of my parents. Later, I found out some other stuff that helped me understand, but right then, literally could not believe what was happening. I was turning thirteen years old, and couldn't even process what she was telling me."

"Woah," Abigail muttered.

"Wait, that's just the start. Like I said, it's a long story."

He grabbed his Cherry Coke and took a few sips from the straw. Condensation beading on the outside of the plastic cup, he touched it to his temples and the back of his neck to cool off.

"Alright," he continued, "we were living in this shelter for abused women, and Jean and I were going to a different school, not allowed to call any of our friends, and couldn't go back to our old apartment to pick up any of the stuff we left behind. We could only go to school and come straight back to the shelter; nowhere else. It sucked, but we did have a lot of time to talk to each other. I found out a lot from my mom, like how my dad had been beating her and choking her. I had no idea."

Rylan paused, and Abigail could see the muscles in his jaw flexing as he clenched down. A vein in his forehead bulged noticeably.

He exhaled hard through his nose and wiped the sweat from his forehead before continuing.

"Sorry. Getting back on track... we probably lived at that shelter for a month-and-a-half, maybe two, then one day, a Saturday morning, I remember because Jean and I were watching cartoons in the living room, my mom called me to the bedroom. I walked in, and she was on the phone. She held the phone out and said my dad wanted to talk to me. At first, I was confused because she had told us that the rules at the shelter restricted us from talking to him, but here she was talking to him... whatever, I took the phone. He sounded sad and said he knew we weren't coming back, but wanted to see us one last time. I told him that he needed to get some help first; then he said he loved me, but I didn't say it back... I still wonder why... but, I just said 'bye, Dad', and handed the phone back to my mom and went back out to watch TV with Jean. Maybe ten minutes later, my mom started screaming. She ran out of the bedroom in a panic, says she thinks he shot himself, then ran back into the bedroom and called the police." Rylan took a drink and a moment to breathe before continuing, "She was right. He'd shot himself in the chest. Dead before the cops even arrived."

Rylan stopped again. The inside of his throat suddenly felt swollen. He tried to take another sip of Coke, but swallowing was difficult.

"You okay, Rye?"

"Yeah. Yeah, I'm okay." He reassured her, though he wasn't really sure. He wiped the sweat from his forehead again and cleared his throat. "You want to know the most fucked up thing?"

Abigail's first thought was to reply, "Worse than that?" but she refrained; instead, she only nodded slowly.

"He was planning to kill all of us." He paused, eyebrows raised, still astonished at the fact, "My mom told me that he had... wait, hold up... I should probably explain first: my dad was a Vietnam veteran, and the way my mom tells it, 'he never really came back.' I'm not exactly sure what that means, but apparently, he'd take a six-pack and go hang out in cemeteries at night, then come home having full conversations with spirits he met there. Ghosts! Mom said one of those times, she was acting asleep, and he was in the room whispering to 'someone' in the corner of the room. He was saying some fucked up shit like, 'No, I'm not going to do that to her. She's asleep. No, the kids are asleep in their room too. Leave them alone.' Some crazy shit like that. I mean, like, WHAT THE FUCK, right?"

"Oh my God," Abigail muttered weakly. She felt dazed though wide-eyed and locked into Rylan's story.

"He had told her once that it would be best if everyone... mom, Jean, me, and him, would all die together so we'd go to heaven together. So... this motherfucker..."

Rylan stopped to get his anger under control, realizing that he had begun to speak louder than usual. He checked his surroundings to see if he had drawn any unwanted attention; he hadn't.

He lowered his voice to a normal volume, "Alright, so, on the day he killed himself, our neighbors saw him take the gun from our apartment and stash it under the driver's seat of the car before walking back inside. Ten minutes later, he ran out to the car and returned with the gun in hand. They called the cops, but not long after, they heard the gunshot. Now, remember how I said he was on the phone with my mom when he killed himself? He'd been trying to convince her to get us all together 'one last time'... now,

I could be wrong, but that sounds like he was planning to take us all with him."

Abigail was speechless. Rylan sat silently for a couple of minutes, absentmindedly rotating the straw in the drink cup lid, stirring the ice cubes beneath. She wanted to say something comforting but couldn't find the words. Her thoughts were like smoke swirling in a jar. All she could do was sit quietly and listen.

Somewhere on the miniature golf course, a teenage boy howled in celebration. Elsewhere, a woman was yelling at a child, evidently named Adam Winthrop Ross, to 'get back here this instant.' The speakers near the concession counter played a Britney Spears song while the popcorn was popping, and the scent wafted on the breeze.

"It's a good thing my mom didn't take us to visit him that day, huh?" He spoke softly then drifted off into his thoughts again.

Abigail sensed the rhetoricalness of the question and didn't answer.

When Rylan spoke again, his voice sounded distant, brooding. "They found him with an empty bottle of tequila and a half bottle of whiskey."

He sat with his mouth ajar, lost somewhere deep in his memories until he eventually flinched and blinked away the vacant look in his eyes. "I'm sorry. I got off track there for a while. What was it that you had asked me again?"

Abigail was stumped, unable to recall her original question, but Rylan remembered.

"Oh yeah, you'd asked why we moved from Vegas, and if it was because of my dad, right?" He shifted in his seat and took another sip of his drink before starting again, "After he died, it was hard on all of us, and I guess we all tried to cope in our own ways. If I'm being honest, I started messing up. Before he died, I was a good kid. I had good grades, played basketball after school, and never got into trouble. After he died, though, all of that changed. I started ditching school, failing classes, stealing, drinking, smoking weed, and getting into fights. My counselor said I was starting to spiral." He shrugged, "She might have been right."

Rylan took another sip of his drink. Abigail managed a nervous smile and took a drink of her own.

"So, somehow, my dad's life insurance paid out and my mom was looking to buy a small house in Vegas, but since I kept getting into trouble, she decided we all needed a fresh start. That's how we ended up here in humid-ass South Carolina where I'm sure we'll all live happily ever after. The end." He put his palms flat on the table, signifying the completion of his tale, before finally adding, "So, to finally answer your question: we mostly moved here because of me, but also because of my dad, too."

Abigail took a long breath. "That was a lot."

"Yeah. Sorry." He looked away in embarrassment. "I didn't mean to dump all that on you."

"No. It's fine. Seems like you needed it."

"I guess so."

She reached across the table and put her hand on top of his. "Thank you for trusting me with all of that."

He nodded, "Thanks for listening."

She slowly pulled her hand back and grabbed her drink. "So, you were a troublemaker, huh?"

He smiled shyly. "Once upon a time, but I'm not a bad guy anymore, though."

"No, I don't think you're a bad guy. It sounds more like you were just too weak to stop yourself."

Rylan recoiled. "What?"

"That sounded harsh. I'm sorry. I don't mean that I think you are a weak person in general. I meant 'weakness' in the sense of a temporary condition. My mom says that from time to time, the world, the universe, and even the people closest to us will hurt us. While we're recovering from that pain, we'll be weak, vulnerable, and likely to do reckless things. While we're in those low spots, it's important to remember, first, that it's normal, and then that it's only temporary. She always says, 'There is no real strength without pain. You must endure it to emerge stronger on the other side.'"

He considered the weight of her words, "That's deep. 'No strength without pain'. I like that."

"Yeah well, it sounds better with her Jamaican accent, but the message is still good."

"I didn't get to talk to her much the other night, but she gave me the stink-eye once or twice at the restaurant."

Abigail sucked her teeth. "She's very protective of me and skeptical of everything. She didn't even want me to come see you today, but don't take it personally; no one will ever be good enough for her daughter."

"Great. It's good to know that she already hates me."

"She doesn't hate you, at least not yet anyway." She smirked, "No need to worry about that right now though since I haven't even decided if you're gonna get a second date."

"What?" Rylan feigned outrage, "Okay, you know what? It's crazy that you say that because I was thinking the same thing. I'm not sure I want a second date with you either."

"Oh really? Well, then I'm glad we're on the same page. I don't want to date a troublemaker anyway." Abigail shot back.

Rylan leaned back a little, nodding in respect. "Good one."

Abigail let her smile spread across her face, pleased with herself but also glad that Rylan could take a joke.

Rylan leaned forward again, "Seriously though, I think I like you. I want a second date."

Abigail could feel a familiar warm tingle on her face and neck as she blushed. "I think... I guess I like you too." She said bashfully, doing her best to hide the reality of her blossoming feelings.

A nervous hush passed between them, both feeling validated and humbled by each other, they searched for something to break the silence, but the moment seemed fragile, and everything else seemed ruinous.

Rylan finally broke the silence, "Abigail, I don't want you to think I'm some bad guy. Yes, I got into trouble before, but when I saw how I was breaking my mom's heart, especially after all she'd been through with my dad... I felt like a piece of shit. I swore to her that I would do better, and I've kept that promise. The old me is gone, okay?"

The sincerity in his eyes was far more substantial than the words he spoke. It made her want to cry, hug him, and push him away all at the same time. They had only spent a few hours together, and even with the phone conversations over the previous two days, of all the fluttering happening in her abdomen, it still felt too early. Or maybe it wasn't too early. She wasn't entirely sure. She was only certain of one thing, that she liked him and wanted to spend more time with him today and tomorrow, and probably more.

"Thank you for telling me that; for all of it. For the record, I don't think you're a troublemaker. Of course, I could be wrong, but I guess I'll let time tell the story. So, yeah, I think I'd like a second date too, but can we continue this one first, or where you... did you want to... like, did you need to go home or...?

"No!" Rylan blurted out, "No. Sorry, no. I don't need to go home. We can get back to the game if you want."

He began to rise from his seat, and Abigail followed his lead. They began walking back out to the course when Abigail pulled the scorecard from the back pocket of her jean shorts.

"So, where were we... ah yes, heading into the twelfth hole with the score at thirty-one strokes for me and a big thirty-seven for Baby Boy Beam. You're getting smoked, kid!"

"What? No way! Gimme that." He snatched the scorecard from her hand and saw she was only teasing him.

Abigail laughed so hard she snorted. At the sound, they both froze, exchanged surprised looks, then erupted in laughter together. Rylan was doubled over laughing until tears streamed down his face. Embarrassed, Abigail laughed even harder until, in a stupor, she stumbled and her heel caught the concrete edge of the walkway. She started to fall sideways, but Rylan instinctively stepped forward to catch her around the waist. He held her in his arms as she regained her footing. As their laughter quickly faded into giggling, they looked deep into each other's eyes, and the glee suddenly vanished.

Abigail swallowed nervously, aware that a pivotal moment had arrived. Transfixed by each other, the world slowed down while their hearts raced. Rylan had only started to lean in when two young boys sprinted past, chasing each other along the walkway.

It was enough to break the spell. Abigail cleared her throat and patted him on the shoulder. "I think I'm good now."

"Yeah." He let her go, feeling slightly embarrassed.

"Thank you." She said sweetly. She watched him, studying his body language for clues to his thoughts.

"Of course." he responded dismissively, "You don't need to thank me. I wouldn't let you fall."

He turned and resumed their stroll toward the back end of the course, but after four steps, he realized that Abigail wasn't with him. She was still standing in the same spot, wearing the sly grin of a scoundrel.

"What?" He asked skeptically.

"C'mere."

"Uh-uh." He shook his head playfully like a child refusing to eat his vegetables.

"C'mon. C'mere." She invited. "Just thought of something."

His curiosity overrode his caution, and he hesitantly walked over to her, "What's up?"

"You probably saved my life." She said sardonically.

"Oh god." He rolled his eyes.

"No, no. I owe you now, and I know exactly how I'll repay you."

"Yeah? How's that?"

"I'm going to slap the shit out of you." She said gleefully.

"What?" He chuckled.

"Yeah. That way, you don't have to worry about when I'm gonna spring it on you."

"I'm seriously not worried about that. I had already forgotten about it."

"Well, lucky for you, I haven't. So let's do it."

He searched her face and saw she was serious. "Whatever. Yeah, let's get it over with." He checked to ensure that no one was coming along, then positioned himself in the middle of the walkway, an arm's length away from her. He put his hands behind his back and leaned forward, chin up. "You only get one shot at this, okay? If you miss, that's it, you missed. So, make it count."

The last thing he saw before closing his eyes was her, struggling to contain her excitement. His eyelids shut tightly as he once again braced for impact. He stood in darkness for five seconds, and as he was about to reopen his eyes, he felt it.

It was meant to be a quick kiss, but Abigail lingered with her lips pressed softly firm against his for a beat longer than she had expected. She could feel his whole body tense, then melt as he leaned gently into her. When she finally pulled back and opened her eyes, she half-expected to see Rylan liquefied into a puddle on the concrete.

When Rylan opened his eyes, his vision was blurred with the swirl of enchantment and confusion in his head, then, gradually, everything became clearer and more vibrant than before. His lips felt warm and tingly, as though electric current flowed just below the surface of the skin. He thought he should say something to her, but as he licked his lips to speak, he discovered the lingering taste of her lips on his, and he only managed to utter, "Whoa."

"Alright, Baby Boy, don't go fainting on me. Let's go finish this game." She strode away, while Rylan, still stunned, followed.

7

—·—

MARCH 29, 2017, WEDNESDAY

CARSON CITY, NEVADA

Rylan walked along the darkened sidewalk on his way to Toni Caisse's house, periodically tugging on the brim of his brand-new baseball cap. Having just purchased it that morning, he hadn't had a chance to break it in, and the cap was stiff. The inside, behind the orange embroidered SF logo, was especially rough and pressed uncomfortably against his forehead.

As a matter of principle, Rylan refused to wear hats from any other sport besides baseball, clinging passionately to an irrational belief that ball caps should only be for baseball teams. Although keenly aware of how absurd his stubborn stance on headwear was, especially since he would be burning his entire outfit once the job was finished, in his mind, his principles were nearly shatterproof.

He wasn't a fan of the San Francisco Giants but figured that wearing a cap representing a local team would help him to blend in. Unfortunately, the State of Nevada didn't have a major league baseball team, and the closest teams were the Giants and the Oakland A's, both from California's Bay Area. So, that morning, while shopping for his "work clothes" at Walmart, he opted for the more subdued black and orange Giants cap over the bright yellow and green of the A's.

He'd had the taxi driver drop him at a fake address a mile from his next victim's house, and while he began to cover the remaining distance on foot, he was satisfied with how the dark grey hoodie and blue jeans blended into the shadows. While he hiked, two things were stuck in his mind: the new Taylor Swift song that had been playing on the taxi's radio when he stepped out, and the word "savagery".

Two days ago, while scouring through clips of news broadcasts from the Baltimore area, he finally came across the story he had anticipated. The video clip was posted online with a bold red 'Breaking News' banner on the bottom of the screen.

"Pasadena police, this afternoon, have confirmed that a man has been found mutilated and brutally murdered in the vacant home you see behind me, nestled in a once-quiet neighborhood near the corner of Chestnut and Leigh Road. For the past two months, this modern-colonial three-bedroom house had been listed for sale, but as of 10:30 this morning, it is off the market and has now become an active crime scene. The police haven't yet identified the victim or indicated the cause of death, but what we can confirm is that a real estate agent entered the residence at 7:30 this morning to prepare a showing for potential buyers and horrifically stumbled upon the grisly discovery. No other details have been made available at this time, but one senior officer that I spoke with said he had 'never seen this level of savagery' before in his career. We will, of course, be closely following this shocking story as it unfolds and keep you up to date. This is Tad Smiley, on the ground in Pasadena, for FOX45."

While Rylan listened to the reporter's words the air around him seemed to constrict a little. He knew the police would start coming for him now and he felt pressure in his abdomen and a tightness behind his ears. He began second-guessing his actions in Maryland and for a moment, became convinced of his own recklessness. He eventually dismissed the concern and told himself, "What's done is done. Just do better next time." He tried to refocus his energy on the upcoming encounter with Toni Caisse, but something from the news clips had lingered in his thoughts.

The word 'savagery', from the FOX45 reporter's piece, had stood out to Rylan and he couldn't shake it from his mind. He ruminated on it, at times, for the next two days while he made his final preparations, and finally, as he crept through the night towards Toni's house, the question resurfaced again.

"I mean, when you look at it on the surface, yeah, we broke his body with a hammer and then strangled him. That's got to count as savagery, right?"

I don't know. Brutal? Yes, for sure. But savage? When I think of the word savage, I'm thinking of a wild animal. Gnashing teeth, snarling, shredding flesh, something like that. What we're doing is more... I don't know, humane, maybe?"

"Humane? Seriously? With a hammer? Breaking a person, a human being's bones. Torturing them. Nowhere, not in any universe, is that humane."

"Okay. Okay, yeah, that's fair. But I just, I don't feel like savage fits what we're doing. I feel like we always maintain control, we have a plan, we're not excessive... okay, that one is probably debatable, but I mean, it's not like I'm some animal out here, ya know?"

"Alright, how bout this; staying with the same logic, a lion, or more likely, a lioness, tears the throat out of an antelope; that would be savage, right?"

"Yeah, sure."

"But that lioness is always in complete control of herself. She's not some frenzied animal, all rabid and foaming at the mouth. She is methodical, focused, violent, and efficient. It's more that the act itself is savage than the attacker."

"Hmm. I still don't like it, but I can see the point. Savagery it is, then."

Rylan tucked his hands into the warm front pocket of his hoodie as he continued the short hike. The drab yellow glow from the streetlights illuminated the sidewalk at regular intervals but left generous stretches of undisturbed night in between. Rylan was careful to pause in these shadowy gaps and feign tying his shoe whenever a passerby approached, or a car passed.

Two blocks away from Toni's house, Rylan checked the time; 9:57 PM. He had hoped to arrive at her door around 10:00 PM and was pleased with his progress.

As he crossed the last intersection, her house came into view. Her car was in the driveway and the lights in the house appeared to be off. Rylan scowled knowing the darkened interior signaled a potential issue if she had already tucked herself into bed.

He passed the last streetlamp before her house, and with the light behind him, swiftly adjusted the revolver in his waistband to ensure an easy draw when needed.

As he walked in front of her house, he made one last scan of the homes on the street and saw nothing that would give him pause. He briskly walked up her driveway, peering into her car as he passed by. The inside was littered with trash, mostly fast-food containers, some clothes, and loose papers. He continued up to the house, glad to see the blinds were drawn.

He stepped up onto the stoop with the porch lamp shining brightly in his face, and quietly checked to see if the screen door had been locked; it hadn't. Pleased with the conditions, he repositioned the ball cap further up on his head so his face could be easily seen, then took one last deep breath, rang the doorbell, and took a few steps back from the screen door.

Almost fifteen seconds passed before Rylan could hear someone's slippers shuffle behind the door. It didn't open, so Rylan assumed they were using the peephole to assess their late-night visitor. A woman's voice sounded annoyed and suspicious through the door. "Who are you?"

Rylan played sheepish and apologetic, snatching the hat off his head in an exaggerated gesture of respect, "I am so, so sorry to be bothering you this late, ma'am. Are you..." He pulled out a hand-addressed envelope from his back pocket and pretended to struggle to read the name he had written on the front, "is it Toni Chasse?"

"You mean Toni Caisse?"

He re-read the envelope, "Oh crap, yeah, sorry about that. It's been a long day." He chuckled at his blunder, making sure to flash his smile towards the peephole, "I'm just barely getting home from work, but I figured I'd try to drop this off on the way. The mailman must have put it in my box yesterday by accident. I'm Benny, by the way; I live four houses down from here."

For a few tense moments, there was only silence. He forced himself to stand still, smiling, and then he heard the snap of the deadbolt as she unlocked the door. In a blink, he threw the ball cap back on his head, snatched the screen door open, and pulled the pistol from his waistband.

Just as Toni twisted the doorknob from the inside, Rylan rammed the door with his shoulder from the outside. The door burst open, smashing hard into her chest and knocking her onto the living room floor. As she flopped onto the carpet, Rylan stepped into her entryway and closed the door behind him.

"Don't scream, or you will be dead before the cops even get here." His voice came out like crushed gravel.

She lay on the floor, propped up on one elbow with her other hand held up in a defensive pose. He stood imposingly at her feet with the gun pointed at her face, then held still for a moment to let everything settle. He watched as her facial expression rapidly evolved from initial confusion and surprise into revelation and terror. Once he was satisfied that she had grasped the severity of the situation, he spoke again.

"This is a robbery," he declared. "First things first: Do not scream. Don't yell, and don't try to run. I promise you cannot outrun these bullets."

He cocked the hammer for emphasis. She gasped.

"Now, is there anyone else in the house?"

She hesitated.

"Yes or no?" He growled.

She flinched and shook her head.

"Good. Don't move."

He stood at the edge of her living room scanning the surroundings. All the lights in the house were off except for a light coming from her bedroom, near the back of the house.

The house smelled of McDonald's french fries and cat piss. Papers were scattered on the dining room table, and empty beer bottles sat on the coffee table beside a brown take-out bag with the familiar Golden Arches printed on the side.

Rylan brought his attention back down to Toni, who looked like a mannequin posed suggestively on the carpet. Her blonde hair looked damp, and she was wearing a light-pink bathrobe. The waist tie still held, but the robe was split open below the waist, exposing her thighs and the blue panties she had on.

He thought she looked alluring, even seductive, despite the terrified look on her face. He tried to remember how long it had been since the last time he was with a woman. He could recall the woman's face, a one-time chance encounter with a woman he'd met at a grocery store, but how long ago was fuzzy, maybe six months. He shook away the thought and refocused himself.

He stepped backward toward the front window and peeked through the blinds, quickly surveying the street and neighbors' houses, then snapped back around to make sure Toni hadn't moved from her spot; she hadn't. With the gun still pointed at her, he squatted at her feet, then slowly reached down and pulled up one of the sides of the robe to cover her legs.

He spoke softly, knowing he needed her to calmly go along with the next phase of his plan. "Where is your purse? Out here?"

She shook her head.

"In the bedroom?"

She nodded.

"Okay, look, this is how this is going to go. You're going to get up and go to your bedroom. I will follow you. You will get your purse and get dressed. You have a pair of leggings, like yoga pants?"

She nodded.

"Good. Put those on and a T-shirt too. Now listen," he paused to let her process what he had told her, "Listen. You and I are going to take a little ride to an ATM; then, once I get the cash, I'll bring you back. Understand?"

Rylan watched her hazel eyes dart back and forth between his left and right eyes, searching for some sign of his trustworthiness. He could tell she desperately wanted to believe in the promise of her safety, but the ominous presence of a gunman who had bulldozed his way into her living room was too much to bear. Her eyes welled with tears then started to weep as her face rendered like butter in the sunshine. Rylan couldn't help but feel sympathy for her. A hard-wired result of societal evolution over many millennia, it was difficult for him to see a woman in distress and not feel compelled to provide aid, but he fought away the urge by remembering the reason her name was on his list.

"C'mon. Let's go get dressed."

He grabbed her by the elbow and helped her up. She sobbed and slowly trudged to the bedroom, nervously peeking at the man behind her every few steps along the way.

Her bedroom was messy. More empty beer bottles sat atop a cluttered desk with an overflowing waste bin underneath, a wet towel was casually discarded on the carpet, dirty clothes were tossed loosely into one corner of the room, and a pile of clean clothes sat on the bed alongside an open bag of Doritos and a paperback novel by Stephen King. A tabby housecat, laying on one of the bed pillows, slowly raised its head as its owner re-entered the room with a strange man in tow, then lowered its head back down and closed its eyes.

Rylan followed Toni to the dresser and sat on the edge of the bed while she pulled out clothes. She turned away from him to dress and as she let the robe fall to the floor, her bare back revealed a spectacularly chiseled physique, its topography changing with each new movement. Rylan immediately felt a tingle in the front of his pants. The way her panties accentuated the shape of her buttocks, and the discovery that she hadn't been wearing a bra, did nothing to quell his surging urges. He tried to distract himself by browsing the room while he waited, but in the corner, beside the nightstand, he noticed a bassinet with a baby doll swaddled in a yellow blanket inside. He shivered and turned away.

He gazed at Toni's silhouette, marveling at how impressively fit she was, then wondered how she could have a home so littered with fast food containers and beer bottles, yet possess the discipline to maintain such a splendid figure. He watched the muscles in her back flex and relax while she put on a blue sports bra that matched her panties, then pulled on a loose-fitting black T-shirt.

When she finished dressing, she placed both hands flat on the dresser. The wood creaked as she rested her weight. Rylan could tell she was trying to get a grip on herself. He gave her some time, imagining she was talking herself into an optimistic point of view: "Just do what he says, then when he lets me go, call the police." He pitied her. She had no idea how the night would end.

He stood back up from the bed with his pistol pointed at her. "Alright, time to go. Grab your purse and your car keys."

She wiped away her tears, and as she slowly turned to face him, he recoiled in astonishment. Her t-shirt was identical to the Guns N' Roses shirt he had worn on his first day in Carson City. As incredible as the coincidence was, he brushed it away immediately. Toni's sudden change in demeanor was more concerning.

She wasn't a tall woman, maybe five foot and four inches, but at that moment, she seemed taller. Her upright body posture, starkly different from the lumbered and defeated way she had walked into the room, projected confidence and resolve, but Rylan could tell she was bracing herself with the dresser to hide the unsteadiness of her legs. Her pursed lips, bent into a slight frown, were meant to signal defiance but instead trembled subtly. Rylan respected her courage to even attempt such a valiant show of strength, but ultimately, the frightened and desperate look in her eyes betrayed her true demeanor.

He tried to hide his amused smile, like a parent who had caught their child accidentally using a curse word, then chose to not acknowledge the offense.

"Good. Now make sure you grab a sweatshirt or a light coat. It's a little chilly out tonight."

Her body seemed to deflate and she looked to be near tears again as she grabbed her purse off the dresser and trudged out of the bedroom. They walked through the dimly lit house and stopped at the front door. Toni grabbed a dark green jacket from the coat closet while Rylan peeked through the blinds one last time.

"Alright, listen, you walk in front of me. Nice and casual. Don't try anything stupid. Remember, I have the gun. Get in the driver seat, and I'll get in the back seat directly behind you. You drive, and I'll tell you when and where to turn. Got it?"

"Yes." She spoke for the first time since he had shoulder-checked his way into her life. "Can I ask a question first?"

"Sure. What is it?"

"If I do what you say, do you promise you won't hurt me?"

"No, but if you don't do what I say, I can assure you, you will be hurt. Now let's go." He side-stepped away from the door to let her lead the way.

The two marched to the car and got in, with Rylan pushing aside a few crumpled clothes and empty shopping bags to take a seat behind hers. Toni started the vehicle, and as Rylan directed her to turn left out of the driveway, she took one last glance back at her home and then drove off into the night.

After a ten-minute drive spent in silence, except for occasional route directions from the rear seat, they arrived at a bank. The branch was closed, but Rylan guided her to a drive-up ATM at the rear. As they approached, Rylan, wary of the security cameras, pulled his hat down lower on his brow and raised his hoodie to obscure as much of his face as possible. Toni pulled in close to the ATM, put the car in park, and rolled down her window.

Rylan asked, "Okay, how much do you have in savings?"

"Around fifteen hundred." She reluctantly admitted.

"That's pretty good. Let's just do five hundred since most of these banks have some sort of daily withdrawal limit."

Toni inserted her debit card and navigated the on-screen menus to process the withdrawal. Once she had the cash in hand, she handed the money to Rylan.

"Alright, Toni. You've done a great job. Now for the last piece: I'm not taking you back to your house. Instead, I will give you directions to where I want you to drop me off. Got it?"

"What?" She groaned incredulously.

"Look, it's almost over, okay? Let's get moving. Take a right on that street there, then go straight for a while."

"What the fuck?" She complained under her breath, then drove on into the unknown.

***

Once they had journeyed beyond the city limits and were traveling along the back roads, there was nothing but the hum of the tires on the roadway and the endless hypnotic procession of ragged white lines painted along the median.

As they drew further away from town, the open spaces became wider until it seemed miles stretched between homes, and with the crescent moon only showing a paltry sliver of the sun's reflected light, the darkness outside the car's windows was almost absolute.

In the silence, Toni began to feel claustrophobic. She could sense something was deeply wrong with the world around her, not just that she had been robbed, but that something more sinister was afoot. She felt like they had stopped moving entirely and the faded grey asphalt passing beneath the vehicle was just an illusion playing repeatedly. It felt as though the Night had reached out and seized the car from behind; its cold fingers wrapping them in the void, keeping them trapped in a singular moment in time. She sensed the Night, a creature unfathomably enormous, ravenous, had gradually crept into the car, surrounding her, trying to swallow her whole, with only the lights of the dashboard keeping the suffocating blackness at bay.

"Up here." Rylan suddenly spoke.

She jumped at the sound of his voice, swerving the car out of her lane.

"Slow down." He added, "The driveway is coming up."

Toni slowed the car to twenty, fifteen, then ten miles per hour, squinting to see anything through the darkness.

"Take this next right." He directed.

As she slowed further, she could barely make out the mailbox along the right side of the road, then the gravel driveway just beyond. She steered the car down the driveway, and the headlights revealed a small two-story house a short distance away from the road with a For Sale sign in the front yard. She parked in front of the garage beside a dusty grey SUV but kept the engine running, hoping for a quick turnaround.

"Well, this is it," Rylan stated nonchalantly. "Thanks for the ride."

While waiting anxiously for him to get out, she could hear him crumple up a piece of paper behind her, then a white ball suddenly flew into her peripheral view and landed on the floor in front of the passenger seat.

"I guess I don't need that envelope anymore, huh? Hey, listen, Toni, I want you to know I really appreciate your cooperation." He patted her shoulder, startling her again.

He opened the rear door and the car's interior overhead light automatically clicked on. His shoe crunched the gravel underfoot as he stepped one foot out onto the driveway, and she reached for the gear shifter, wanting to speed away as soon as possible, but she paused. There were no other footfalls on the gravel, and the rear door hadn't closed yet. Toni looked in the rearview mirror to see him still seated.

"You know what," Rylan spoke in an apologetic tone, "On second thought, I should probably keep that envelope. Can you grab that for me?"

Toni squeezed the steering wheel and grunted her frustration. She snapped her head towards the floor on the passenger side to locate the crumpled envelope and found it sitting delicately on a merlot-colored sweatshirt she had worn last winter. She unbuckled her seatbelt and stretched out over the center console to retrieve it. Just as her fingers grazed the ball of wadded-up paper, it felt like a lightning bolt struck the back of her head, and then everything went black. The Night had finally taken her.

8

—·—

MARCH 29, 2017, WEDNESDAY

CARSON CITY, NEVADA

The first thing Toni became aware of was how cold she was, before the aching pain at the base of her skull claimed her full attention. Opening her eyes, dizzy, nauseous, her mind was bombarded with new information; she was on her back, spread-eagle, wrists and ankles bound, tape covering her mouth, and her shirt was missing. Her eyes darted back and forth, processing, overwhelmed, her thoughts stuttering, she reflexively twisted and fought to free herself from the white PVC poles holding her captive. Scanning the room for aid, she found only an empty milk crate at her feet and a camping lantern on the floor above her head, both objects well out of reach. A blue tarp had been laid underneath her, and another had been hastily taped to a wall, likely covering a window. She seized upon the window as her only chance for salvation.

She screamed, trying to muster up enough force to overpower the tape, but only produced a moderate hum. She tried again, harder still, with the same result until her vain efforts finally faded into sobbing. As she wept, her mind stitched together the events in her car, the remote location of the house where they had stopped, and the dire situation in which she had awoken. The possibility that she had been abandoned in that desolate room crossed her mind and she slipped further into despair.

Suddenly, the door swung open and her captor rushed into the room, the look of concern quickly dissipating once he confirmed his victim was still secured.

"Damn, you woke up faster than I expected." His nervous smile showed relief.

He carried a brown leather bag, and dropped it beside the milk crate, pulled the stub-nose pistol from his waistband, and then sat down.

"I had to take a piss." He chuckled, "You almost literally caught me with my pants down." He grimaced at his joke. "I apologize. I don't mean to make light of the situation. I have this terrible habit of making dumb jokes in tense situations. I've got to do better there. It's just not professional."

Toni, frozen in fear when he walked in, now started sobbing again, slowly squirming, and pulling at the zip-ties while the tarp crinkled beneath her. Her body was stretched out in the shape of an "X", framed within a white square made of PVC pipe. She was wearing only a light blue sports bra and matching panties that peeked alluringly out of the top of her low-waisted black yoga pants. Her athletic arms and legs flexed and released in a sensuous rhythm while testing the strength of the restraints, her abdomen constricting like a serpent as she twisted and writhed. She looked incredible, and Rylan felt ashamed of how tantalizing he found her.

"Stop. Stop moving, please." he pleaded, "Just stop."

She did, but the desperate appeal in her eyes was unmistakable,

"Thank you." He tried to shift his focus, checking his watch; 11:12 PM. "Listen, I wanna try something if you don't mind. But first, you remember the drive out here, right?"

Toni was motionless.

"Right?"

She nodded twice.

"Okay, so you remember how far out we are. There isn't another house around for almost a mile. I chose this place very carefully."

Her eyes widened and tears leaked from the corners.

"Nobody is coming to help you." He spoke each word separately to add gravity, then let the sentence sink in.

Toni gagged, and her eyes rolled listlessly while her body went limp. Rylan thought she was passing out, but she slowly recovered control so he gave her a minute to get ahold of herself. As she stared up at the ceiling, moaning, he spoke softly, almost sweetly.

"Toni, I want to take the tape off your mouth and talk to you for a little bit."

Her head lifted, and she looked at him with confused disbelief.

"Yeah, I know. It's a crazy idea, but even if you scream, no one will hear it. Here, I'll show you," He sucked in a huge breath, pointed his face toward the tarp on the wall, then let out a deep roar from the gut, "HEEELLLPPP MEEEEE!"

Toni flinched at the outburst, then watched helplessly as he bellowed, his face reddening and the vein in his forehead bulging. Her fear was paralyzing, and all she could do was breathe in ragged gasps through her runny nose.

He stopped yelling and quietly watched her reaction. She was wide-eyed and unmoving.

"Okay, I'm going to cut the tape off now. Don't move. I don't want to cut you unintentionally."

He stood up and pulled a folding knife from his front pocket, flicking his wrist to snap it open. She drew back into the carpet, crunching the blue tarp. He stepped inside the white plastic frame to which Toni was captive, then knelt beside her.

He held the knife a few inches in front of her face and reiterated, "Don't. Move."

The blade was ice cold as it touched her jawline, and Toni resisted the urge to pull away. Rylan carefully picked at an edge of the tape wrapped around her head and cut it, then used his fingertips to get a grip.

"Alright, ready? This is gonna hurt." He cautioned.

She shut her eyes tightly then he tore away the portion covering her mouth. Her eyes shot open, and she shrieked in pain while Rylan quickly sliced off the loose strip of tape, folded the knife, and returned to his seat on the crate.

Toni exercised her newly freed mouth, stretching and clenching despite the burning sensation on her skin. The acrid aroma of the tape's adhesive wasn't enough to deter her from licking at her inflamed lips and discovering the noxious taste exceeded the strength of the smell.

She glared at her captor and softly demanded, "What do you want from me?"

"I just want to talk."

Toni carefully considered what she wanted to say next, "But... why? If you just wanted to talk, we could have stayed at my place. I could have put the coffee on. We didn't have to come here."

Rylan nodded, respectful of her reasoning, "You are quite an impressive woman, Toni Caisse."

"And what was your name, again? Bradley, was it?" Her voice had changed; it was now soft and smooth, like fleece.

"Benny." He replied.

"Oh yeah! Benny." She smiled, "I like that better. Benny, it's really cold in here. Do you have a blanket, or could I have my shirt back? Please?"

"Yeah, it is a bit chilly in here, huh?" He stood up, "Hold on, I'll get your shirt." He walked over to the brown leather bag, pulled out her black t-shirt, then returned to her side. "I have to apologize, though; I cut up the side of your shirt here. It was easier to get it off this way, but the bright side is that it now opens up kinda like a blanket."

He spread the cotton fabric over her nearly bare torso, with the Guns N' Roses logo facing up. He noticed the look in her eyes was different now; through tear-swollen eyelids, there was a tenderness that wasn't there a minute ago. She smiled at him shyly, and he smiled back.

"Thank you, Benny. That's mighty nice of you." Her voice had become even softer still, like silk on skin.

"No problem." He said as he walked back to the crate.

"Hey, Benny," She started, in her silk soft voice, "Why don't we just go back to my place? We could have some coffee and talk. I have some pie in my fridge too. You like pie?" She shifted her hips slightly but noticeably. "We could get a little more comfortable and... talk. We can talk as long as you want."

Rylan sucked his teeth. "That sounds amazing."

Sensing an opportunity, Toni went for it, "You don't need to do, whatever this is, Benny. I mean, you find me attractive, don't you?"

"Of course, I do."

"Well, I must admit, I find you attractive too, Benny. We don't need any of this other stuff. We can forget that this ever happened. Okay?"

Rylan studied her face, all seduction and allure, except for the shadow of desperation behind her eyes.

Rylan scoffed, "You know... I have a question, that shirt you picked out tonight, Guns N' Roses, why did you pick that one?"

A flicker of angered frustration crossed Toni's face, but it was gone in an instant and her flirtatiousness had returned. "Why? You like GnR? This is actually my lucky shirt, or at least it was..." she pouted, exaggeratingly.

"Well damn, I am sorry about that."

"It's okay. Maybe you could make it up to me someday." She subtly batted her eyes.

Rylan was astounded. He couldn't help but admire her guile. "Toni...."

"Yes, Benny." She answered sexily, dripping with eagerness.

"I don't think it's fair to lead you on. I'll admit, any guy would be stupid to turn you down, but..." he leaned toward her, "It's not gonna happen, so let's drop the Catwoman act."

Her facial expression immediately switched into one of rage. "What the FUCK do you mean fair?"

Her body jerked upward into a near-seated position with only her wrist restraints holding her back. Rylan recoiled and nearly fell backward off the crate.

"What the fuck is THIS, motherfucker?" She snarled, "How the fuck is this shit fair? This is BULLSHIT! I don't even fucking know you! I've never done shit to you. Why me? Why the fuck are you doing this to ME? Why?"

He kept his voice steady, "I'm here because of Megan."

Understanding washed across her face, her breath hitched in her throat, and she crumbled back down onto the tarp. The remains of the T-shirt slid off her abdomen and came to rest beside her. Rylan let her lay there, staring up at the ceiling fan. She began to sob again, then, after a while, her sobbing quieted.

"So, so what then? You're here to, what, kill me?"

He hesitated, then admitted, "Something like that."

"Can you at least tell me who's paying you to do this?"

"No one is paying me."

"What does... wait, then... what does that even mean?" Her head came back up, and she looked at Rylan in bewilderment. "If no one is paying you, then you're what... just doing this on your own?"

"You could say that. You murdered your daughter, Toni. It's not right that you're still breathing when she isn't."

"Who, who are you?" Her anger began to boil.

"You can just keep calling me Benny."

"Yeah? FUCK YOU, Benny! Who the hell do you think you are? You think you're some hero? A fucking vigilante or something?"

"A vigilante?" He scoffed, then stopped. The word echoed somewhere in his memories. "You know what? When I was... I don't know, maybe four or five, I wanted to grow up to become Superman. Back before I learned it's not really possible, you know, physics and all," He chuckled. "But then, I looked to Batman and thought, maybe I could become him instead. He doesn't have superpowers so he relies on his brain, brawn, and a big bank account to fight crime. He can't string up bad guys in a spiderweb, can't fly them off to jail, can't teleport, can't read minds, nothing like that. Most of the time, he has to literally beat the shit out of the bad guys to capture them."

"Are you fucking kidding me?" Toni spat out in disgust, "I got kidnapped by some asshole who thinks he's Batman?"

Rylan laughed, "No, but let me finish, though. Eventually, it dawned on me that Batman has this fatal flaw: he's not willing to go far enough. He has a limit. He still operates by a set of rules, laws, a moral code, when the bad guys don't. That's why the Joker and the other villains keep coming back time after time. The consequences aren't severe enough. Think about this; the Joker's probably been captured and locked up hundreds of times, right? But he always escapes, kills even more people, then gets captured, put back in prison, and does it all over again. THAT is fucking insane! What if one time, Batman caught the Joker and hung him from a fucking light pole with his guts spilled open? Imagine how many murders and rapes he'd prevent if the criminals in Gotham knew Batman would straight-up eviscerate them?"

He guffawed at the idea while Toni observed him with a mixture of horror and disbelief. His grinning laughter, illuminated by the electric lantern in that desolate bedroom, was the single most terrifying thing she had ever seen. At that moment, she understood Rylan more deeply than anyone else in his entire life.

Eventually, he stopped laughing. "That's why I'm more of a Wolverine-guy. That dude don't give a fuck." He checked his watch: 11:38 PM. "Alright, let's get back on track. I want to know why you killed your daughter."

Without a word, Toni laid her head back down to stare at the ceiling again. Rylan waited a few minutes in the cold silence, allowing her time to compose a response, but none came.

"Alright," He stood up, "I guess we're done talking then."

He reached down into the leather bag and began rummaging in its contents. His movement drew Toni's attention, and she lifted her head to watch him. When he stood back up, he had switched the pistol into his left hand and now held a hammer in his right. Perplexed by the need for the tool, she watched him walk around her left side. The tarp crinkled as he stepped inside the PVC pipe frame, into the empty space below her arm, then knelt beside her.

She watched him place the pistol on the floor, just outside her reach, and an ember of hope sprung to life inside her. She was sure she could find a way to reach it. Maybe, while he was busy with whatever he was using the hammer for, she could quickly shift the whole PVC frame towards the gun and snatch it. She would have to move fast though, and would probably only get one shot at it, but it was worth the risk.

She was completely focused on the gun, shifting her body weight to her lower half, preparing to push off and pounce. She made her final mental calculations when abruptly, Rylan grabbed her arm at the elbow, pinning it down to the floor under his weight. She didn't even have enough time to be confused. She barely glanced up in time to see the hammer raised in the air above Rylan's head before it suddenly became a blur, and her whole world exploded in pain.

The sound of the hammer's head smashing through the bones in her forearm, then thudding against the wood flooring beneath the carpet, sounded surprisingly benign, like the sound of a baseball pitched against the side of a house. A few warm blood droplets splattered up into Rylan's face. He knew immediately that, as with Edward, he had swung too hard with the hammer. Her skin had burst open like a smashed banana.

Rylan glanced over to ensure Toni hadn't passed out yet. Her eyes looked as though they would shoot right out of their sockets. Gawking at her mangled arm, she screamed as hard as she possibly could, but no sound came out. She ran out of air screaming in silence, then gasped for breath greedily as Rylan scooted closer to her torso.

In a blink, he pinned down her upper arm near the shoulder and drew back the hammer for another hack. In shock, Toni's reflexes were fast enough to just begin yanking her arm away, but it wasn't enough. She watched in horror as Rylan's bloodied hammer crushed the largest bone in her arm. The impact sounded like a champagne bottle popping its cork.

Rylan winced as Toni found her voice, screaming in full force directly at the side of his face. The shrieking resonance in his ear caused him to jerk away, and he slumped onto the floor a few feet away. Toni carried the high octave of her scream until her voice finally dimmed and was dragged down with her into unconsciousness.

Rylan sat on the carpet, rubbing his left ear. The pain had subsided, but the ringing was still reverberating deep inside. Toni had passed out, and her body went limp. A clear puddle began spreading out on the tarp from beneath her thighs, and another puddle, appearing crimson on her skin but purple on the blue tarp, was oozing out from her once-perfect forearm. He stood up, grunting in frustration at his own sloppiness, retrieved the pistol from the tarp, then tread over to the leather bag to collect the roll of duct tape and the smelling salts.

When he turned around, he stood gazing at the unconscious woman on the floor. He had meant to revive her and get back to work, but his curiosity started tempting him again. He decided to try talking to her one more time, so he sat down on the crate and waited for Toni to wake up.

He compared his experiences with Edward and Toni, noting how much easier it had been with duct tape covering Edward's mouth the entire time. Rylan's verbal interaction with Edward had been minimal, and it was easier to dismiss him as less than human, but with Toni, he had come to view her, and to a degree, respect her as a person, despite the horrific actions of her past. Her unrestrained cries of agony had tugged at the tender parts deep inside his chest as if they had been snagged by a fishing hook, and it took every ounce of his willpower to ignore his impulse to be merciful.

After a short while, she woke, first with a labored groan as she began to stir, which grew into a pained howl as she moved her left arm, and her eyes instantly popped open. She glared at her smashed arm and screamed, spraying spit droplets clear past her lifeless hand. In a panic, momentarily disoriented, she whipped her head around to check her other arm and then began scanning the room, stopping abruptly at the man seated just beyond her feet. The sight of Rylan brought her back into her tortured reality. Her head flopped back onto the tarp as her scream became a wail.

He let her carry on for another minute, then tried to get her attention. He called out her name, but her wailing just got louder, as if she was trying to shout over him. Frustrated, he tried again, only to receive the same result; then, he violently seized hold of her right ankle. She stopped immediately, and her head shot up, eyes wide, to see what he was doing to her leg, but he was only looking back at her.

"Hi." He said through barred teeth, a sour grin pulled tightly across his face. He released her ankle and sat back on the crate. "I'd like to revisit our conversation if you don't mind. I'd like you to tell me why you killed your three-year-old daughter."

She didn't respond. She was completely petrified.

His patience running thin, he felt his blood start to surge. He closed his eyes and took a deep breath before speaking again.

"Toni, you have eight more bones that I am going to break."

She gasped.

"We can talk for a while longer, or we can skip ahead to the bad part. The choice is yours."

Toni closed her eyes and started crying.

Rylan was sympathetic but unwavering, "I know it's hard, but you're going to need to come clean. And hey," he reached out and tapped her left foot, "look at me."

She opened her reddened eyes.

"I think it's important that I say this out loud, so we're both on the same page: I know you're a liar. Truth be told, you're a world-renowned liar, Toni, and you don't get a legendary reputation like that for being particularly good at it. So with that in mind, if anything you tell me sounds outlandish or even deviates a little bit from the facts laid out in your trial, I'm picking up the hammer again. I'm not going to play games with you. This is already your second chance, and I promise you there will not be another. So... tell me, why did you kill Megan?"

After a few seconds, with tears still streaming down her cheeks, she lowered her head back to the floor and sighed deeply. There was a long silence, enough that Rylan was ready to reach for the hammer, but Toni finally spoke.

Her voice was ragged and hoarse from screaming, "She wouldn't wake up. I tried and...I...I tried, but she wouldn't." Toni broke down, bawling and trying to talk at the same time, "I loved her. I loved her so much."

She cried out, wailing, years of repressed agony released from the depths of her soul. Rylan couldn't help but cry, too; he knew well the self-loathing torment of a parent who outlived their child.

"I saw her; she was in bed when I came home. It was late, and she just looked asleep..." Toni sobbed loudly, "And, and then, I kissed her on her head, and she felt cold, so I covered her with her butterfly blanket then I went to bed. In the morning, I tried to wake her, but she... she... she was so cold. I shook her... and I slapped her... but she just wouldn't, she wouldn't wake up."

"How did she die, Toni?"

She shook her head slowly, "I don't know; probably the pills. I swear to you, I would usually only give her half a Zanax before I went out, but a couple of times, she was still awake when I came home. So, one night, the party was gonna be a little further away, so I gave her a whole pill, but when I came home, like around 3:00 AM, she was awake, crying, and had thrown up all over her bed and the carpet. I mean, I felt bad for her, but can you imagine cleaning dried vomit off the carpet in the middle of the night while you're already drunk?"

Rylan appeared motionless and silent, but in his palm, he squeezed the revolver hard in growing anger. His hand made a dull creaking sound as it constricted tightly around the lacquered wood of the pistol grip.

Toni continued her confession, her mouth getting dry and sticky, "The last time, I remember crushing the pills up and putting it in her chocolate pudding. I thought it would be a little easier on her tummy."

"How many pills did you give her?"

"I don't really remember. I do remember that Jonah had come over earlier that afternoon. We had smoked some foils together, so... I was really high. I'm not sure, but I couldn't have given her more than two, though... maybe."

Rylan shivered as fresh fury rushed through his body like venom in his veins. He immediately hugged himself, flexing his muscles hard to vent the negative energy, a trick he had learned in an old anger management class. Slowly, as he focused on his pulse and deep deliberate breathing, he relaxed his muscles.

While Rylan fought with his temper, Toni stole a peek at her broken limb. The swollen left arm, numb in some places and throbbing everywhere else, was already deeply discolored. The skin looked like a sausage casing containing a nebulous mixture of mincemeat, merlot, and mustard, with splotches of grape and blackberry jams, and an inch-long rip near the bottom of her forearm was slowly oozing bright red blood. The sight made her gag and retch; she quickly turned away.

Rylan, having regained control of himself, straightened his spine, and then exhaled. "Okay, let me sum this up and make sure I understand what you're telling me: you drugged your three-year-old daughter so you could go out partying with your friends. She overdosed, you hid the body, and claimed that she was taken by a babysitter that never existed... but wait... are you saying that..."

He paused, mentally putting more pieces of the puzzle together until his mind exploded with realization.

"Oh, you're pretty fucking clever aren't you?" He sneered. "You're saying the pills were her babysitter? So in that way, her babysitter actually did take her?"

Toni didn't reply.

Rylan shook his head in disbelief. "Alright, that's about all I can handle." He reached down, grabbed the roll of tape and the hammer, then stood up. Toni started to groan and tried to push off with her feet to get away from Rylan, but the zip ties were enough to prevent her efforts. "Thank you for the conversation and, more importantly, for your honesty, Toni." He started walking around her outstretched body, towards her head.

"Waitwaitwait, wait a minute, just stop for a minute," Toni sputtered with the urgency of an auctioneer while trying to squirm away. "Ben, Benny, please, listen, we can, we can keep talking. Let's change the subject, okay? What do you wanna talk about, Benny? Anything. Anything. Just talk to me, Benny, please!"

As she frantically pleaded, Rylan came to a stop directly above her head. He paused, having thought of something, "Have you seen that movie, *Logan*?"

"What?" Toni stopped squirming, stopped pleading, stopped blubbering. She was genuinely baffled by his question.

"*Logan*. It's a new movie about Wolverine. Just came out a few weeks ago. Have you seen it?"

She hadn't, though she was scared to admit it, afraid of giving the wrong answer. For the first time since she was a child standing in her mother's kitchen, being questioned about stealing cookies from the pantry, she thought that maybe honesty might be the best policy. She told Rylan, "No," but her response sounded more like a question.

"Damn. That's a shame." He reached down and placed the pistol and hammer onto the tarp beside Toni's right elbow, then stood back up and started scratching at the edge of the tape with his index finger. "The whole thing was beautiful and closed out his story really well. It was the kind of send-off that he deserved. I have to admit, I even cried a couple of times."

Once he had peeled up enough of the tape's edge to grip, he returned his full attention to the woman on the floor at his feet. She was trembling, and despite the chill in the air, she was sweating.

"That sucks that you didn't get to see it."

He suddenly dropped down to both knees, with one on either side of Toni's head, squeezing to brace her in place. She panicked, thrashing like a rabbit caught in a snare, screaming "no" repeatedly. Rylan tore a long strip of tape from the roll and used his teeth to rip it off while she screeched for him to stop. Grabbing hold of her lower jaw, he pulled her mouth shut, then slapped the tape strip down across her lips; then, as if performing CPR, he pushed down to hold it into place. He could feel the vibrations from her muffled screams through his palms.

After a moment, he released the pressure on her mouth and saw that, despite Toni's best efforts, the tape's seal was still holding.

"Hey. Hey, listen. Calm down for a second. Listen," Rylan spoke in a calming tone, and Toni's muted screams settled into sobbing.

"I know it probably doesn't mean anything to you, but I guess, for my conscience, I want you to know that I take no pleasure in any of this. You'd probably ask: 'Then why do it at all,' right? The bottom line is, it's not right that you get to keep on drawing breaths when you snatched away your daughter's."

Toni squeezed her eyes shut, knowing he was right.

Rylan added softly, "The fact of the matter is, through their own choices, some people have forfeited their right to live."

He released his knees' pincher grip on the sides of her head, and she opened her eyes. Loose strands of her hair had stuck to her tear-soaked cheeks while others were trapped under the duct tape. She sobbed while Rylan reached for the hammer. He held it up to his eye level, examining it pensively; the tiny drops of splattered blood, some smeared, had begun to turn a dark rusty brown near the edges.

"You're probably wondering: why the hammer? Why not just shoot you and be done with it? Well... it's not only about you. People need to fear consequences. I mean, consequences are what underpins our society, right? If there were no consequences, people could do whatever they wanted. There would be no limit to crime, corruption, or human depravity. Look, we already have laws in place to discourage bad behavior, right, but it's obvious that the punishments for certain crimes are not severe enough to deter people like you from making the wrong decisions. Ultimately, where our society falls short is that we refuse to consider any punishment beyond the death penalty. We've placed death at the very end of the spectrum in terms of consequence, but I think death should be somewhere closer to the middle of the spectrum. There are far worse things than dying. Hell, some people would beg for death to end their suffering!" Rylan sneered at the absurdity. "Well, after people see what I'm doing, they might make better choices." He shrugged, "Then again, maybe not... but it's worth a try."

Toni, still sobbing, had listened attentively to her captor's rant, hoping to find something within his words, anything she could leverage for more time, some way to survive; but found nothing.

Rylan looked down into her hazel eyes, and for the first time, he saw true hopelessness, and it broke his heart. Reaching down, he gently swept away the strands of honeycomb-colored hair still clinging to her cheek and tried to ignore his heartache, knowing he had to finish the job.

"Look, I understand that you may not have intended to kill Megan, but the fact remains you stole an entire lifetime from your little girl. Simply killing you, after you've been able to spend thirty years enjoying the tragic magnificence of life, is not even remotely equivalent. So... here we are..."

He reluctantly scooted to the right. As he clenched her upper arm, surprised by the coldness of her skin, he was confounded by her lack of resistance. He glanced at her face, but she turned away from him, eyes squeezed shut and jaw clenched. She had accepted her fate and Rylan simultaneously detested her capitulation and admired her strength.

He brought his attention back to her arm and was faced with an unexpectedly unnerving sight. Goose pimples had popped up on the surface of her chilled skin. Immediately, his mind recalled the last time he had seen gooseflesh on a woman's arm. The thought made the tiny hairs on the back of his neck stand up. He slammed his eyes shut against the memory of his wife lying in bed, years before her death, wearing nothing more than a seductive smirk.

Sensing his emotions unraveling, he quickly drew the hammer overhead and fought to find his aim through a fog of emotion.

9

AUGUST 3, 2001, FRIDAY

COLUMBIA, SOUTH CAROLINA

"Babe, seriously, I don't want to argue about it; just get whatever you want," the annoyance in Abigail's voice was apparent.

Even though she was facing away from him, looking out through the passenger-side window, Rylan could sense the rolling of her eyes. Instantly irritated, he stopped scanning the drive-thru menu and turned to her.

"What? What's to argue about? I'm not trying to argue with you. Just pick something off the menu. You want some nuggets? A cheeseburger?"

"I don't want anything." She snapped back, "YOU said you were hungry. All I said was there's a McDonald's a few blocks down. That's it. That doesn't mean I'm hungry too."

Irritation becoming anger, his face turned red. "Well fuck it then!"

He jerked the steering wheel and stepped on the gas, tightly swerving around the red car ahead of them in the drive-thru. He sped off towards the street, barely stopping to check for oncoming traffic before accelerating again, tires screeching on the asphalt.

Wide-eyed and terrified, Abigail had braced her hands on the dashboard in front of her while Rylan whipped the purple PT Cruiser out of the McDonald's parking lot. Now settled on the roadway but still speeding, she punched Rylan's right shoulder.

"The FUCK, Rye?" She screeched at him, then hit him again in the same spot. "The fuck is wrong with you? You know, I don't need this shit right now. Pull over."

He ignored her.

"Rye, Pull over. I'm not playing. You can fucking walk home from here. You're not going to wreck my car because you can't control yourself."

He continued to ignore her.

She leaned over to him, three inches from his ear, and yelled, "Pull the fuck OVER!" Screaming the last word.

He flinched and snapped his head around to glare at her, growling through barred teeth. She had seen him angry before, but never rage. He looked as though he might bite her face. She jerked away, recoiling back to the far side of her seat.

Seeing her startled reaction, his facial expression immediately switched from rabid to regretful. He drove on silently for a few more seconds before pulling into the parking lot of Gentle Dental Dentistry. He shifted the car into park and continued to sit in silence, squinting through the windshield as the mid-afternoon sun shone in his face. Abigail hadn't moved.

The two teenagers had been dating for almost two months, and the whirlwind summer was coming to an increasingly somber close. Abigail was set to begin her freshman year at Penn State in two weeks, and Rylan would start his senior year in high school the following week. They had avoided the onerous discussion about the future of their still blossoming relationship as long as they could, but both were dreadfully aware that the reckoning was rapidly rising on the horizon. The tension between them had been slowly ratcheting up and had now become too strong to ignore.

"I'm sorry," he spoke softly, turning to look at her, "For real, Abby, I'm sorry. I don't know what's wrong with me. These past couple weeks, I've just... I've just been on edge; I don't know." Slowly shaking his head, "I don't know."

Abigail relaxed, shifted into a more natural posture in her seat, and repositioned the seatbelt back onto her shoulder. She took a deep breath, folded her hands between her thighs, and blurted out a thought she hadn't yet decided how to say.

"I think we need to break up Rye."

"What? Wait, over this? I just..."

"No. Not just this." Shifting nervously, she folded her arms across her chest, "I'll be in Pennsylvania for college in a few weeks, and you're still gonna be here." She paused and braced for Rylan's response, but he said nothing. His reticence only made the conversation more agonizing for Abigail, and she continued talking just to fill the air, "I like you a lot, Rye, I really do, but I don't think long-distance relationships work out. Do you?"

While she was talking, a blue sedan parked in the space next to Rylan's door. A woman got out and began to pull her toddler son from his car seat. She told him that if he didn't fuss while the dentist checked his teeth, they would stop at McDonald's for ice cream cones on the way home. Rylan waited until they had walked away before responding.

"I don't know, honestly," he sighed. "We could try to do the long-distance thing, but you're going to meet new people, new dudes up there on campus, you know?"

"What if I don't want anyone new?" Her voice cracked.

Rylan found her eyes. He could see she was fraught with conflicting emotions and was looking to Rylan to do something, or say something, but he had no words. Struggling with his own conflict, he knew he couldn't ask her to stay, though it was all he wanted. Helplessly, he reached out and softly held her hand.

He whispered, "I don't want to lose you either."

She started to cry and leaned sideways into his chest. Rylan held her while she sobbed, rubbing her back, and after a while, he cried too.

10

— · —

MARCH 30, 2017, THURSDAY

LAKE TAHOE, NEVADA

Rylan jumped out of bed, fists up, ready to fight. Briefly disoriented in the darkened hotel room, he quickly regained his bearings, then slammed his hand down onto the alarm clock blaring obnoxiously on the nightstand before flopping back onto the bed.

He lay on the bed sheets feeling jittery and unsettled, wondering if it was because he had awakened so roughly, or as a result of last night's dreams, which had clearly been upsetting, evidenced by the bed covers kicked off into a pile on the floor.

As he stared at the ceiling, his mind continued to project the image of Toni, his last victim, finally turning away from him, her spirit crushed. That singular memory, for some reason, had left an indelible mark on him. The night prior, it had played repeatedly in his mind while he sat alone in his Trailblazer, trapped on the highway for hours, waiting for the unseen wreckage of a jack-knifed tractor-trailer to be cleared. Eventually, he gave in and rented a room at a Lake Tahoe motel for the night.

Now awake, his apathy felt thick and heavy, like crawling through mud, but he eventually mustered enough energy to roll out of bed again, but just stood in place, slumped and loose, his gaze down as if surveying the rug. He knew he should get back on the road toward Santa Monica, but he felt leaden and lethargic. It became a monumental test of willpower to resist the urge to crawl back into bed, but he managed to drag himself over to the window and draw the curtains. A blast of sunlight burst through the window and he was left squinting at the blinding brightness while his eyes adjusted.

It had been many years since Rylan had seen snow in the daylight. Of course, he had seen the snow last night, but the breadth and depth of the landscape had been obscured in darkness and as he stood at his hotel window, he was completely enchanted. Two inches of snow topped almost everything in sight, glistening in the afternoon sun like powdered diamonds and instantly, he wanted nothing more than to be outside.

Infused with fresh energy, he quickly brushed his teeth, dressed, and slung his backpack, then opening the door, he felt like Dorothy stepping out into the land of Oz for the first time. The air was clear, brisk, and vibrant, with a fragrant note of pine. Despite the snow on the ground, the early spring temperature was surprisingly pleasant, and Rylan was comfortable with just a sweatshirt as he wandered out to the sidewalk to better take in the scenery.

The motel was located along Lake Tahoe Boulevard, the town's main street, which had been recently plowed, leaving a nearly foot-high embankment along the road shoulder. He watched the cars and trucks drive by with dirty slush and road salt clinging to their sides; their tires on the wet asphalt sounded like Velcro strips being pulled apart. In both directions along the street, he could see giant spruce and pine trees standing at random intervals, like gently swaying sentinels keeping watch over the town. He marveled at the white-capped mountains beyond the rooftops that seemed close enough to touch.

Spotting a sign for Heidi's Pancake House less than a block away, he decided that midday breakfast sounded good and started hiking in that direction. As he neared the restaurant, a glimpse of the cobalt-blue waters of the lake became visible between the hotel buildings to his right, and all of a sudden his hunger became an afterthought. He could feel a pull, like magnetism, towards the shoreline and was powerless to resist.

The beachfront hotels had been obscuring much of the view, but once Rylan passed them, the entire breathtaking panorama was revealed, and he stopped to take it in.

The beach was completely covered in white, smooth in some places, while in others, human and animal tracks had disturbed the surface of the snow. The water at the edge was impossibly clear; enough to see every one of the rocks and tiny pebbles lying beneath the gentle waves as they lapped at the shore. Further out from the beach, the intimidating depth of the lake created the most intense dark blue Rylan had ever seen. He gazed up at the surrounding mountains cradling the lake like the hands of God, trying to keep the crystalline waters from slipping through his fingers. There was a sublime quiet in the air that felt as deep as the lake itself. The only sounds Rylan could hear were the ducks and the geese, whose calls seemed to echo for miles.

After some time, Rylan followed a shoveled walkway leading up to a long pier; there, he found a bench on which to sit and absorb the energy of his surroundings. He gazed up at the steep slopes, covered with millions of evergreen trees that looked like they had been generously dusted with sugar. He sat and watched a hawk high above the treetops, beating its wings only briefly to climb, then glide like a dignified ruler riding the breeze to gracefully survey its domain.

He recalled a time, many years prior, when he was in the Army, and his unit had spent a week in Camp Beuhring, Kuwait, finalizing preparations for their move into Iraq. They had arrived during the middle of the night, and waking on his first day in a foreign country, he stepped out of the tent into 105-degree heat at 10:00 in the morning and was awestruck by the view. There was absolutely nothing. The land was completely flat and featureless, just an endless expanse of pale sand in every direction, as far as the eye could see. Right then, he decided that if Hell was a real place, it would look exactly the same as that desolate desert. Years later, seated on a quiet pier nestled in the Sierra Nevada mountains, Rylan decided that Lake Tahoe was the spiritual opposite of the deserts of Kuwait; it must be what heaven looked like.

The laughter of children broke him from his thoughts, and he turned around to see a group of three kindergartners on the beach, colorfully dressed in puffy snowsuits, boots, and mittens, throwing handfuls of shapeless snowballs into the lake. They were teasing and challenging each other to throw further than the last. Their glee was infectious, and Rylan found himself laughing along with them. After a while, a woman's voice called after the kids, apparently siblings, and they dutifully clomped through the snow back to their ground-floor hotel room.

Rylan remained on the pier for a while, breathing in the magnificence of the lake. He felt calm and unburdened for the first time in a long time and was reluctant to relinquish the feeling. He decided to linger and watch the ducks floating on the lake with their ducklings in tow.

Eventually, his thoughts wandered back to Toni. He tried to ignore it, but it kept floating to the top of his mind. As his efforts proved to be in vain, he decided to pull his journal from the backpack and begin writing again.

Notes: Toni Caisse in Carson City, Nevada.

-PVC pipe worked well. After I had pre-drilled the holes for the zip-ties, it was easy to set up. They're lightweight but might be too light. Toni was able to shimmy and shift the whole frame a few times. Could become a problem.

-First swing was too hard again. Broke the skin again. Not a big mess this time because of the tarp, but I've still got to do better.

-The tarp was a great call, by the way. Kept blood and urine off the carpet. Hopefully, the homeowners appreciate the consideration.

-Venue selection was great. Very secluded. No neighbors for at least a mile. I wish they could all be like that.

-"Benny" at the front door worked perfectly. Will definitely use that one again, but honestly, it's pretty disturbing how easy that was... (more on this later)

-The whole robbery thing was a good idea to get her to go along with everything, but I can't keep her money. Doesn't feel right. I need to find a children's charity and donate the cash. Maybe donate it in Toni's name. I like that.

-Make a legit list of questions to ask next time. Improvising was okay, but it needs to be more thought out.

-*The smelling salts worked well too. I only had to use them three times with Toni, but it helped speed things along.*

-*Overall, I think everything was pretty efficient. Time-wise, it took 3 hours and 15 minutes (almost 45 minutes less than Edward), and most of that was us talking. I don't think I can continue looking at total time as a measuring stick for efficiency if I'm going to keep having conversations with them.*

She really pissed me off when I asked how her daughter died, and all she talked about was how ~~inconveen~~ inconvenienced she was with having a child. She took no responsibility for anything. I wanted to smash her face in with the hammer. But then again, what the fuck did I expect her to say? That she didn't do it? Maybe deep down, I was hoping she would tell me it was all just a horrible accident. ~~But what if she did say something like that? What if, for example, she said she didn't do it, and somehow I believed her? What am I supposed to do then, let her go? Just be like, "Hey, I'm real sorry about all this. I see now that it's not your fault. You can go home now." Obviously, I can't do that, right?~~

Now that I have something to compare it to, when I was in the room with Edward, he seemed more like a ~~task~~ chore than a human to me. That may not make much sense, but I really don't know how to explain it with words. With Toni, on the other hand, it was different. Even though I hated her for what she did, I still found myself fighting against my own sympathy for her.

There were at least three times when I wanted to call it off: at the very beginning, when I came through her door and saw how scared she was, and then two more times after I went to work with the hammer. Each time, It was the sound of her crying that was tearing me up inside.

Was it because she's a woman?

Maybe. Probably.

After my dad died, all the most important people in my life were women, and now they're all gone. Maybe that has something to do with it.

Regardless, I don't know what to do about it going forward. Before getting detoured to this incredible oasis in the mountains, I was on the way to Tiffany Albrecht's house in California, but I'm having some ~~real reservasions concerns~~ reservations about going there now. The thought of it makes me nauseous. ~~I feel like I'm dying inside~~ I'm seriously dreading it. I think it's best, for my sanity at least, if I try to head up north and visit John Burbules in Idaho first. I'm not ready to do another woman yet.

I think I'll stay here an extra day too. Tomorrow is actually my birthday, and while I haven't celebrated it in years, I can't think of a better place to spend what may be my last birthday. Besides, I could use the break.

Before I close up my notebook, I want to revisit one of the bullet points above: how easy it was to break into Toni's house. I simply stood on her doorstep, told her I was a friendly neighbor returning some misdelivered mail, and she opened the door right up for me. Now, she didn't strike me as a gullible or stupid woman, so if she could fall for it, anyone else could, and it's blowing my mind right now. I mean, there are some truly horrible people out there!

YES! I am aware of the irony of what I'm staying.

Think about it, though. On the news, from time to time, we all hear about criminals breaking into people's houses and doing un-

speakable things to innocent people, but that's only the assholes that got caught. There are others, still out there, hiding in plain sight, preying on innocent people right now. It makes my fucking blood boil. I wish I could smash their skulls open. I know there's nothing I can do about it, but FUCK! It just makes me so goddam angry.

Alright, I'm done venting for now. I'm going to try to calm down; maybe get something to eat at that pancake place I passed on the way over.

By the way, and just for the record: I really do hate lying to them, but I haven't come up with a better way to get them in the car.

11

— ◆ —

April 1, 2017, Saturday

Sterling, Virginia

The fresh-faced FBI agent, Helio Sangria, pushed open the wooden gate leading to the backyard. He closed it quietly behind him and straightened his dark blue three-piece suit before continuing across the freshly cut grass. Scanning the people socializing in the yard, he quickly found the man he sought and began to close the distance. As he approached, the aroma of charcoal smoke and the sound of meat sizzling became stronger. The well-heeled man carefully studied the man tending the grill as he drew nearer. The cook held a beer bottle in one hand and a long spatula in the other, and he slowly swayed to the music while deftly side-stepping the smoke rising from the coals. Helio stopped beside the grill and stood silently for a few moments, surveying the meat on the grate. Neither person acknowledged the other's presence until the visitor spoke.

"Why didn't you just cater this thing, Frank?"

"Because I like grilling, Leo. It's the greatest of American pastimes." Slightly annoyed, Frank used the shortening of his former partner's first name, which he knew he despised.

Helio huffed. "It's a waste of time, is what it is. You've earned enough to pay someone to do the work, or maybe some of these freeloaders could have chipped in to pay for the catering." He gestured to the dozens of mingling guests scattered around the large backyard.

"They're not freeloaders. They're friends."

Helio scoffed, "Colleagues, at best."

"Look, I'm not going to do this with you today. I invited them. They're my guests. That's it. There are people here that I genuinely don't like," Frank made sure to make eye contact with the younger man, "but that doesn't matter. They took time out of their day to come to my retirement party, so at least for this afternoon, they're my friends."

Helio scanned the crowd, "I disagree, but I'll respect it."

"Oh, well, that's very gracious of you," Frank responded sarcastically.

"Frank, I didn't come here to argue. This is your day, and I came to show my support for you and your distinguished career at the Bureau."

Frank nodded slowly, "I know that's nearest an apology I'm going to get from you, so I'll take it."

Helio stuck out his hand, and Frank put his spatula down to shake it.

"Now, you're aware this isn't a formal barbecue, right?" Frank quipped.

Helio squinted, puzzled.

"The suit, buddy." Frank returned to his grill, "You're very overdressed."

"Perhaps, but you know...."

"Yep. I know, I know." Frank interrupted, "Image is everything, right? Especially for the great magician, Helio Sangria! Got to maintain the illusion and all that crap, huh?"

"Magician?"

Frank gulped down the last of his beer. "I've seen you pull some rabbits out of thin air, buddy. Don't know how you do it, but...."

"Francis!" A woman's voice called out from inside the house.

"Yeah, hon'?"

"The rest of those burgers done yet?"

"Almost. Two minutes, tops."

"Hey, *Francis*!" a jeering voice yelled from amongst the guests in the yard, "Don't burn those patties."

"Dillon!" Frank exclaimed, over the sound of the music, after spotting his heckler near the fence. "Hey, buddy! I'm so glad you came today! Come over here and kiss my ass!"

The gathered guests laughed, along with Dillon, who raised his beer bottle as a salute. Frank flashed a sly grin in his direction, then turned his attention back to Helio. He studied the young man, as he had done many times over the past year, with a curious mix of admiration and pity.

"How's the shoulder doing?" Frank asked.

"It'll heal."

"Well, no shit! How's it feeling?"

"Sore. Burns sometimes, but it's manageable."

Frank reached down into the small blue cooler beside the grill, pulled a bottle of beer from the ice cubes, and offered it to Helio, who shook his head, then Frank kept it for himself.

"Helio, can I offer you a little piece of advice?"

"I'm listening."

"When you were in the hospital, do you remember how many of these other agents came to visit you?"

Helio shook his head, "Just you and the Assistant Director."

"That's right. Just me and Coffey, and she only came because it was her job to be there." He paused to let Helio digest the statement, then continued, "How do you read that?"

"You want me to thank you for visiting?"

"What? No!" Frank was stupefied, "Goddam, for someone so brilliant, you're stunningly dense sometimes."

"What's the point here, Frank?" Helio responded impatiently.

"An agent gets shot by a perp, and none of the other agents in his section visit him? That NEVER happens. Never. You may not realize it, but you've only been here for a year and have already set fire to every bridge in the vicinity."

Frank paused again, expecting a response, but his partner remained emotionless.

"Helio, hear me, you're a brilliant young agent, but you're also an arrogant prick that no one wants to work with. Right now, you probably don't give a shit about that, but you soon will. So far, you've had me and my thirty years' worth of connections to use, but now that's all gone. You'll have to forge a whole new network on your own. How long before you come back from convalescent leave?"

"Ten days."

"Okay, a week-and-a-half. Helio, for the love of God, don't go back to the Bureau acting like the same old asshole. Somehow, somewhere, find some humility and grace."

Frank began to pull the burgers off the grill. Once finished, he lowered the grill lid and lifted the platter, ready to carry it to the picnic table, where the side dishes and condiments had been arranged. He paused to look at Helio.

"You have anything to say?"

Helio locked eyes with the older man and replied dryly, "Noted."

"Jesus!" Frank rolled his eyes and walked off, frustrated but also relieved that Helio was no longer his problem to deal with. He yelled to the guests, "Let's eat!"

Helio watched as his coworkers and their families happily coalesced around the picnic table. He spotted Assistant Director Coffey walking out of the house with a few people, then watched as his boss stopped and stood just outside the sliding glass door, waiting for everyone else to get their food. Eventually, she noticed Helio standing to the side, and the two acknowledged each other with a single nod. Neither interested in conversing with the other, they turned their attention back to the throng of hungry people.

He lingered a little longer, leering. To him, they all looked like newborn pups pushing each other aside to get their greedy mouths around their mother's teat. They disgusted him, but their hunger that afternoon was merely a minor provocation to him; the true source of his revulsion was much deeper.

Helio counted eleven FBI agents from the violent crimes division present with their families. He detested each of them and was sure the feeling was mutual. Many were seasoned veterans of the Bureau who had sacrificed large portions of their lives to capture violent criminals from circulating within society, but in Helio's distorted view, their years of dedicated service were irrelevant. They had allowed themselves to grow slow and inept, and their lethargy was slowing the entire branch's forward motion. He argued that they should be relegated to supporting roles, allowing the younger, hungrier dogs to run faster. His views were only compounded by the fact that most of the agents came from wealthy families and had graduated from Ivy League universities, which he read as a sign they had been gifted their status instead of earning it.

Over his first year at the Washington D.C. office, he had found many other reasons to dislike his colleagues, but in truth, the main wellspring of his bitterness was borne of his own racism, influenced heavily by his parents' experiences after immigrating to America.

Many years before Helio was born, Luis and Magdalena Sangria decided to move to the United States to avoid a deteriorating situation in Mexico City. Despite their dreams of a better life north of the border, heavy restrictions against Mexican immigrants to America meant the process would take up to ten years. Fortunately, with their advanced degrees in mechanical engineering and nursing, a family friend who worked at the American embassy was able to pull some strings to shorten their process to five years.

Accepting the five-year wait, the young couple was determined to save as much money as possible and learn English, but in the third year, tragedy derailed their plans.

One day, while walking home from school, Luis's younger brother was approached by three cartel members who surrounded the teenager and demanded he start transporting packages of cocaine for them. When he tearfully reused, they pinned him down on the sidewalk and chopped off his right hand with a machete; a gruesome practice meant to make an example of those who opposed their demands.

Weeks later, while driving home, Luis spotted the trio of gang-sters hanging out on a street corner. The sight of them huddled together, joking and laughing, was too much to bear, and in a fit of rage, he stomped the accelerator and ran them down with his truck. As he sped away, sobering from the surge of adrenaline, he rushed home with the fear that the cartel's retribution was swift at his heels. He collected his wife, scratched together as much money as they could, then fled to Juarez and paid a sizable price for illegal passage into America.

Eventually, they settled in northern Arizona, where, despite their college degrees, they worked as farm laborers alongside hun-dreds of other illegal immigrants. It was an arduous livelihood they accepted as temporary, expecting that they would gradually earn their way up from poverty. As they made their way, Luis and Magdalena's experience was unique compared to most of their fel-low undocumented coworkers, because they had learned English before they crossed over the border. It was an ability they kept hidden to avoid attracting attention from the other immigrants with ties to the gangs in Mexico, but their language proficiency presented the couple with a unique situation; they understood English while those around them assumed their ignorance.

Throughout their early years in Arizona, they witnessed their bosses, often white, ridicule and denigrate the Latino immigrants for their own entertainment, often while wearing a smile to mask their true intent. Over time, as Luis and Magdalena witnessed more and more derision and ill-temper directed towards their fel-low Latinos, their resentment turned to animosity toward white people when they realized the ability to speak English was still not enough to gain respect. The young couple observed how Hispanics who spoke the language fluently, though with a Spanish accent, were still spoken to condescendingly, as if simply having a Spanish accent indicated a low intelligence.

As the years went on, their lives gradually improved. They found better jobs, Luis in construction and Magdalena as a midwife, and they were doing well enough to settle into their new lives, but still, their aversion towards white people never subsided.

Eventually, Magdalena became pregnant and gave birth to Helio, and from the moment he learned to talk, his parents were diligent in correcting any sign of a learned Spanish accent in the young boy's voice. They taught young Helio that white people would never accept him as an equal because of his brown skin, and that he would need to work twice as hard just to have a fraction of the opportunities white people were given by virtue of simply being born with pale skin. As a result, young Helio grew up untrusting and skeptical of everyone's motives.

He never had a steady girlfriend and only a few friends and, even then, kept them at arms reach. As a naturally athletic child, he wanted to play organized sports in school and tried soccer and baseball, but frequently quarreled with teammates, so he gravitated to sports focused more on individual achievement; track, wrestling, and chess. As a student, he was an over-achiever, frequently taking advanced placement classes and receiving top marks, which eventually earned him an academic scholarship from Arizona State University, where he enrolled to study law. The original plan was to become a lawyer, but his dormitory roommate's father, who worked for the FBI, convinced him that his talents could be better used as an investigator.

Six years later, he stood in his now-retired partner's backyard, questioning his career choice. As he scanned the yard, all the smiling and laughing should have elicited a buoyancy in his attitude, but instead had the opposite effect. Of the fourteen agents who attended Frank's retirement party, all were white men, except for three: a Ukrainian woman, and two black men, one of whom acted white to fit in with the crowd. Helio was self-aware enough to recognize that his cold contempt for his colleagues, simply because of the color of their skin, made him, by definition, a racist, but he felt entitled to his rancor.

Just as Helio was about to leave, Frank's wife, Bao, a petite woman of Vietnamese descent, noticed him standing alone by the grill and began walking in his direction. During the few times they had spoken to each other, she had always been pleasant to Helio, in the cordial way of a practiced hostess, but they had never exchanged more than passing pleasantries. Helio wanted to turn and walk away before she arrived but felt it would be in poor taste.

"Helio! When did you get here?"

He checked his watch, "Eight minutes ago."

"Oh, great timing. Come get some food."

"I appreciate it, Bao, but I was just leaving."

She was moderately surprised but also not. "You just arrived! Stay for a while."

"No. I think I'm going to leave. Thank you again, though." He began to turn away.

"How is your shoulder?"

Helio turned back to her, "It's getting better. Burns sometimes but manageable."

"That's great. How's your son doing? I haven't seen him in a while?"

"My ex moved to Richmond two months ago. Jack lives with her."

"Oh, I'm so sorry to hear that."

"It makes the most sense. I spend a lot of time at the office."

"Well, at least it's only a few hours away. A son will need his father as he grows older."

"Perhaps."

"Hmmm." She groaned with a disapproving look on her face.

"Why are you looking at me like that?" He asked defensively.

"It's nothing." She shook her head. "Helio, do you think you will come visit us again now that Francis is retired?"

Helio thought about it, "I suppose not."

"Well, I would like to tell you something, if you don't mind."

"Go ahead, Bao." He was becoming annoyed and shoved his hands into his pockets.

"As you can probably imagine, Francis and I talk a lot about his work. It's a heavy burden sometimes, and I try to help him shoulder the weight when he lets me."

"Are you saying that he disclosed details of ongoing investigations to you?"

Bao frowned at him with such deep pity that Helio felt uncomfortable.

"Honey, you're missing the point."

"Then please, by all means, show it to me." He replied patronizingly as he glanced at his watch.

"You can't do it all by yourself, Helio. Sustained success is always dependent on the quality and depth of your support systems."

Helio was taken aback by her words, surprised more by the source than the wisdom itself. "Where did you hear that, Bao?"

Despite the clear chauvinism in his response, she smiled kindly, "I wrote it."

"Wrote it where?" He asked in confusion.

She laughed softly as if he was making a joke, knowing he was not, "I wrote a book a few years ago about the strategic positioning of air-combat assets, logistical support, and the effective employment of high-altitude and space-based surveillance in the days before a military invasion of a foreign nation."

Helio straddled the line between disbelief and amazement, "Are you serious?"

"Of course, I am."

"YOU?"

She softly rubbed his upper arm. "Honey, I'm going to act as though I'm not offended, okay?"

"But, how? How did you write a book like that?"

"I wasn't always a housewife, Helio. I commanded an intelligence squadron in the Air Force before retiring as a Lieutenant Colonel."

Helio could not hide his astonishment.

"Yup, little old me." She shrugged in modesty. "I know I don't look like it, but maybe there's a lesson to be learned there, too, Helio."

He formed his lips to talk, but Bao cut him off.

"But that's not what I wanted to talk to you about," She waved her hand in front of her face, "I wanted to tell you that Francis spoke a lot about you, and he used to say how much he wished he had your ability starting out at the Bureau, but he also said you act like the whole world is against you and you're fighting alone. Helio, I'm not sure what gave you that worldview, but I just want you to know that some people sincerely want to see you succeed in life. If you truly feel the world is full of enemies and you're at war, the first thing you must recognize is that you're tremendously outnumbered. You must build a deep support network of allies, or you will lose simply by attrition."

Helio held eye contact with Bao while he contemplated her sagacity. She held his gaze, sensing that he was testing her conviction. Helio eventually broke eye contact and looked over at Frank, who was chatting with a small group by the picnic table. Before long, he caught Frank glancing in the direction of his wife. Helio could understand Frank's husbandly concern for his wife and tried to reassure him with a nod. Frank nodded back, then returned to his conversation while Helio returned his attention to Bao. He searched her face as if analyzing a crime scene and found only hopefulness and legitimate compassion.

"I hear you, Bao. I hear you." He swallowed hard. "To be perfectly honest, that's going to be difficult for me, but... I hear you. I'll work on it."

"That's all I ask, honey."

"Thank you."

"You're very welcome, Helio, and if someday you decide to come visit Francis and me, the door is open, okay?"

"I may do that," Helio responded sincerely.

"I hope so. Good luck out there, and stay safe, okay?" She hugged him.

He stiffened at first, then wrapped his arms around her too.

"I'll do my best."

"I know you will.

He walked around to the front of the house and then to the white BMW parked along the curb, feeling simultaneously emboldened and unsure. He knew that Bao had given him what could prove to be very good advice, but he found himself ruminating on Frank's words about needing to build new bridges. Engineering had never been his forté, and the bitter pill of learning to mask twenty-six years of festering hatred seemed like an insurmountable obstacle; nevertheless, he knew he had to find a way. Sensing a new challenge appearing on the horizon, his pulse quickened with anticipation. He started the car's engine, reversed enough to maneuver between the other parked cars, then, shifting gears again, he thought to himself, "I can't wait to get back to work," before driving away.

12

SEPTEMBER 11, 2001, TUESDAY

COLUMBIA, SOUTH CAROLINA

Rylan slung his backpack over his shoulder and joined the mob of high schoolers streaming out of Mrs. Willard's homeroom. As he neared the door, Ms. Hicks, the English teacher from the adjacent classroom, was trying to push against the swell of students to get into Mrs. Willard's classroom. She looked distraught and anxious. Rylan stepped to the side so she could pass, then walked out into the hallway thoroughfare, but before he was out of earshot, he could hear Ms. Hicks call out to Mrs. Willard by her first name, Janet, and asked if she had heard. Disinterested in the personal lives of his teachers, Rylan paid their conversation no mind and joined the traffic in the hallway.

As he neared his locker to retrieve the Spanish textbook for his second-period class, he could see Tommy heading toward him. They exchanged head nods, and Tommy arrived just as Rylan opened his locker door.

"Dawg," Tommy exclaimed excitedly, "I got something to tell you."

"Wassup?"

"Monica just told me that Veronica likes you."

"Veronica? What Veronica?"

"Little Veronica, dawg. You know."

"Oh yeah," Rylan replied, his memory catching up, "Yeah?"

"Yeah, dawg." Tommy nodded with a sly look on his face.

"Huh," Rylan considered the possibility.

"Don't give me none of that bullshit about your ex-girlfriend in college either. Y'all been broken up for almost two months now. Time to get yourself a new chick."

"Shut up, dude." He pushed Tommy back a few steps, closed his locker, and started walking toward Mrs. Grice's class. Tommy, who was also in the same second-period Spanish class, walked with and continued to hound his friend.

"You know I'm right. Veronica is 'burn-your-fingertips' kind of hot. I dunno what she sees in you, but you got to jump on that before it's too late."

"Too late for what? Is someone gonna slide in and steal her first? Who, you?"

Tommy reset his glasses higher on the bridge of his nose, "Maybe."

"Yeah, okay!" Rylan mocked sarcastically, "Lucy would beat your ass, bro."

"No way, dawg. She'd totally understand. Veronica is way hotter than Luce is, anyways."

Rylan raised his hand in the air and yelled into the mass of students scurrying in the hall, "Hey, Lucy!"

A few students turned their heads in their direction. A small group of teachers, huddled together in the hallway, also momentarily turned toward the outburst before returning to their earnest discussion.

Tommy quickly pulled Rylan's arm down and nervously scanned the crowd for any sign of his girlfriend until Rylan's laughter gave away the prank.

Tommy looked at his friend with faux disdain, "Why you gotta be a dick, Rye?"

"Hey, bro, I just thought Lucy would've liked to hear your thoughts on Veronica. You don't think so?"

As they passed the huddle of teachers, Rylan noticed that Mr. Westbrook, the guidance counselor, was also amongst the group, along with Mrs. Grice, who all looked troubled. Rylan became curious as to why they would be standing in the middle of the hall and what they were so concerned about, but Tommy distracted him.

"Hey man, let's get back to the main point here: you gonna ask her out or what?"

The group of teachers abruptly marched off together toward the administrative office, and Rylan stopped in the doorway to watch them stride away.

"Where're they going?"

"Who cares." Tommy groaned, "Stop ducking the ques... huh, yeah... that is kinda weird. Man, if Mrs. Grice is late to class, I'm gonna call her out on it next time I'm late." He stepped through the door wearing a devious grin. Rylan followed.

The classroom smelled strongly of potpourri, which their teacher kept in abundance around the room to mask her students' inadequate personal hygiene habits, and a warm breeze through the open windows brought in the scent of fresh grass clippings.

Rylan and Tommy continued their banter as they arrived at their adjacent desks and pulled out the textbooks from their backpacks. Other students were doing the same, chatting and preparing for the day's lesson, but Rylan started daydreaming.

He knew Tommy was right, that he needed to move on from Abigail, and that only a fool would pass up an opportunity to date Veronica. She was easily one of the hottest girls in school, and she liked wearing those knee-high socks with short skirts that drove Rylan crazy. He began to envision how he should ask her out, but the school bell rang and snapped him out of his imagination.

He scanned to room and noticed that Mrs. Grice hadn't yet returned and some students started exchanging confused glances. The class had never started without their instructor perched like a hawk on the stool at the front of the room, greeting them with a cheery, "Hola, clasé!"

"Fuck yeah!" Tommy leaned over to Rylan and softly exclaimed, "That's a get-out-of-jail-free card. I'ma keep it in my pocket for a rainy day."

After about twenty seconds of gradually building unease, Frank Maxwell, the resident class clown, walked to the front of the room and sat on Mrs. Grice's stool.

"Hola, Class. Mi nombre es Frank, but y'all can call me Señor Maxwell. I'll be y'all's Spanish teacher, or your Maestra, for today." His classmates giggled at his boldness and his butchered Spanish conjugation. "Okay, now g'head and turn in y'all's homework assignments to the front and open up them textbooks to chapter... what chapter were we on, again?"

Mrs. Grice suddenly strode through the doorway, pushing a television cart ahead of her. Señor Maxwell jumped up from the stool and quietly slipped back behind his desk, wearing a wily smirk on his face. She ignored him while she parked the cart beside the stool and plugged the cord into the wall outlet.

Through the door, other teachers were hurriedly wheeling TV carts through the hallway toward their rooms. Rylan wondered how many sets of TV carts the school had stored and where. Mrs. Grice returned to the front of the room and turned to face her students. She was visibly flustered and tightly clutched the remote control with both hands in front of her bosom as she began to speak, her voice uncharacteristically unsteady.

"Um, I am about to turn on the news and, uh, there is something that... something has happened in New York City, and we're not sure if it was done on purpose or what it means, but um, Principal Davidson said we need to make sure you're aware of what's going on."

She clicked the TV remote, and Elmo, the puppet, appeared onscreen, talking to Oscar the Grouch about the importance of patience. Mrs. Grice pushed another button on the remote, and the picture changed. A news broadcast showed two nearly identical skyscrapers standing tall above a metropolitan skyline, but one of the towers appeared to be lit like a cigarette with a massive plume of black and grey smoke billowing from the top. The video switched to a different angle, and it showed the smoke pouring out of a long-jagged gash in the side of the building. The entire sight was confusing for so many reasons.

One student asked, "Is that in New York?"

Before anyone could answer the first, a second student asked, "Is this happening right now?"

Mrs. Grice, wide-eyed and transfixed by the images, answered without looking away from the television. "Yes. It's the World Trade Center in New York City"

"How could that happen?" Tommy asked.

After a moment, Mrs. Grice responded in a distant voice, "They don't know yet. Maybe it was flying too low...."

In an instant, a large passenger airplane briefly appeared in the frame, then disappeared into the side of the second building. Flames exploded from the site of the crash. Everyone gasped and held their breath, and everyone everywhere fell silent.

A clearly shaken female news anchor was the first to break the silence, "An, uh, a second airplane has... has, uh, crashed into the World Trade Center. The South Tower... Gary, these can't be accidents, right?"

"Cathy, I... I don't...." The male news anchor choked up, and could not finish his sentence.

There was another speechless moment before the news crew finally found their footing and restarted their commentary, but the conversation had now shifted. Talk of a tragic accident and what might have caused it, turned to discussions about hijacking and acts of terrorism, speculation about who could be behind it, and if there could be additional attacks.

In Mrs. Grice's classroom, there was complete bewilderment. Students and teachers alike were hypnotically drawn to the video feed, struggling to process why anyone would want to crash an airplane into a building on purpose, let alone two. Their strained comprehension was exacerbated by the news anchors' conjecture about terrorism, foreign enemies with even more foreign-sounding names, political responsibilities, and a possible military response. It felt like the world had stopped, then, suddenly began moving faster than before.

Eventually, Rylan's classmates began to ask more questions from their teacher, who unfortunately didn't have many answers to offer.

They sat with their eyes glued to the television, spellbound by the newscast while experts described the scene as rescue efforts commenced. A news correspondent reported that since the elevators in the towers were destroyed in the crashes, full-scale evacuations were proceeding through the stairwells, but the fire rescue teams, needing to use the same stairs to go up, had yet to make it to the crash sites because they were climbing against the swell of panicked people trying to get out.

An ash-covered fire chief, appeared in an interview explaining that the rescue teams had to climb 110 flights of stairs while wearing full fire-resistant gear, carrying air tanks, and other rescue equipment, on the way to reaching the trapped survivors. As the students waited in suspense for updates on the rescue efforts, they watched in horror as, what was originally mistaken for falling debris was discovered to be people who had been trapped on the floors above the crash site, jumping to their deaths rather than wait for the flames to overtake them.

Mrs. Grice turned away and held her head in her hands. Frank Maxwell muttered, "Oh fuck". Rylan wanted to cry. Others did. No one could imagine the intense fear that would drive someone to jump out of a building from more than one hundred stories up.

Mrs. Grice resolved that she had seen enough and decided to turn off the television, but as she pointed the remote at the console, the news crew said they were getting new information about another airplane crashing into the Pentagon in Washington, DC, and the teacher slowly lowered the remote.

The newscasters, lacking access to video cameras trained on the Pentagon, had an eyewitness on the phone, who confirmed that a commercial airliner came in low and smashed into one of the sides of the military headquarters. The female news anchor declared that there was no question that America was under attack.

"WHAT THE FUCK IS HAPPENING?!" A young woman's voice, erupting in hysteria, cried out from a neighboring class-room.

The raw emotion in her voice was enough to push some students over the edge. In Rylan's class, a few started to sob, a few more folded their arms on their desks and hid their faces, and others began praying. Rylan tried to fight back his tears, but failed, then hid his face in his folded arms. He prayed for the people still trapped on the highest floors of the Twin Towers and hoped they would find the courage and patience to wait for the rescue teams.

At 8:45 AM, the entire school collectively jumped at the sound of the school bell, signaling the end of the second period. Rylan's classmates sluggishly stood up and began their arduous journey to their next class. On his way out, Rylan glanced over at Mrs. Grice, who had retreated to the back of the room to sit with her back against the wall. She looked like she had suffered a concussion, a condition Rylan saw mirrored in many others as he drifted through the rest of that morning.

Out in the hallway, which would usually be bustling with the sounds of teenage gossip, laughter, and flirtation, the mood had instead turned eerily somber, and most of the people wore the dazed look of lumbering zombies. Tommy had rushed off to find his girlfriend, Lucy, as did other couples seeking refuge in each other's embrace. Close female friends also hugged each other in commiseration, while male friends stood around each other scowling with folded arms or hands stuffed into their pockets. The sense of trepidation was heavy in the air already thick with fear, sadness, and anger. No one was sure how many more attacks were coming or if they would even survive the day. The despondency in everyone else's faces augmented Rylan's gloom, and he couldn't wait to seek refuge in his next class, which was, thankfully, only three doors down from Mrs. Grice's room.

Mr. McNabb's Biology class was set up like a science laboratory with tables and stools instead of the more common desks and chairs. As Rylan walked in, he noticed that Mr. McNabb had dragged one of the students' lab stools over so he could sit about four feet away from the television cart at the front of the room. The teacher was leaning forward with the eagerness of a child watching cartoons, though his bushy eyebrows were deeply furrowed, and the corners of his mouth had been pulled down into a stiff frown. More teenagers gradually lumbered into his classroom, but he never even looked up or acknowledged their presence.

Rylan dropped his backpack on the floor beside his assigned lab table, sat down, and held his head in his shaking hands. He felt nauseous and disoriented, like the floor beneath him was slowly crumbling, but he was unable to move. The last hour had seemed like a horrible dream, and he just wanted it to stop. He prayed again, but instead of praying for the people still in the towers, this time, he prayed for himself. He begged God for calm, for relief from his anxiety. He was trying hard to restrain himself but wanted to smash something. His skin buzzed with electricity, as if the muscles just beneath the surface were firing like the pistons of an idling car, just waiting for someone to press the accelerator. He pushed his palms into his face, digging his fingers into his forehead, as he appealed for help controlling himself.

Multiple gasps and exclamations came from his classmates, abruptly jarring Rylan from his prayer. The already frazzled teenager popped open his eyes, turned toward the television, and watched helplessly with the rest of America as the Twin Towers crumbled to the ground, as if in slow motion.

"Did everyone get out?" Cinthia Jacobs, standing with a group of students near the TV, clutching her biology book tight to her chest, demanded in a shaky voice full of urgency.

No one answered.

On-screen, an enormous dust cloud was rolling out, in every direction, on the street, like an inverted mushroom cloud from a nuclear explosion. It engulfed everything and everyone.

Cinthia pleaded again in vain, "Did everyone get out?"

A few moments later, the newscaster said, "Our hearts are with the families of those lost in this devastating collapse…"

The finality in his words became an unexpected catalyst as Rylan's anger flared into rage. He upended the table in front of him. It crashed loudly onto the floor, and everyone flinched; many ducked as if they were under attack. Rylan's classmates swung around in time to see him snatch the stool he had been sitting on and fling it against the white-painted cinder block wall behind him.

"FUCK THIS SHIT!" he roared at the broken stool, his voice cracking at the end.

He turned around and saw his teacher and fellow students gawking at him, some peering from beneath their tables. No one said a word, but two more teachers promptly appeared in the doorway, panting, searching to discover the source of the commotion. Rylan, still seething, broke into a sprint, pushing past everyone on his way through the door, through the halls, and out into the sunshine.

He bolted across the school's front lawn and then ran through the parking lot until he reached the street. He stopped on the sidewalk, gasping for air with tears streaming down his face, looking back at the two-story brick institution he had just escaped. He knew he should go back, but the embarrassment was overwhelming. He decided to walk the four miles home instead.

Rylan had been curled up, asleep for hours beneath the blanket on his bed when someone gently nudged him awake. He peeled back the covers to see his mother and sister standing in his room. For a fleeting moment, the events of that morning were like a forgotten dream, but then it all came back to him.

"You okay, Rylan?" Emily softly queried.

Rylan's first instinct was to say he was fine, but he didn't want to lie to his mother, so he just shook his head.

"I know," she nodded somberly, "me too." She sat beside her son, on the edge of the bed, and started rubbing his shoulder while Jean stood quietly near the bedroom door, trying hard to keep herself together. Emily continued, "Principal Davidson called me at work and told me what happened. You're not in trouble. Apparently, there were a lot of other incidents in school today. Jean said there were a bunch of fights, the cops were called a couple of times, and I guess a lot of parents are picking up their kids early."

"Dee got arrested," Jean stated.

"What? Deanna?" Rylan replied, though not entirely surprised.

"Yeah, she pushed some freshman boy down the stairs. Broke his arm."

Emily gasped, horrified, "What? Why would she do that?"

Jean shrugged, "Don't know. My friend Janey was there and said that Dee never even said a word to the kid. He was just in front of her, going down the stairs, and Dee pushed him from behind."

"That bitch has always been crazy." Rylan blurted, then shot a sideways glance at Emily, "Sorry, Mom."

"No, she must be." Emily agreed, "That's so horrible. Oh my God. I'm at least glad they arrested her."

"I must have missed a lot," Rylan muttered.

"There's going to be a school assembly tomorrow morning at eight," Jean informed her brother, "probably for the principal to talk about the attacks in New York. Group counseling sessions are available to students and teachers, starting tomorrow at lunch too."

"That's a good idea." Emily acknowledged, "It's been a scary day for everyone, for teenagers, especially, I imagine there's a lot of confused emotions right now."

"Everyone looked like Night of the Living Dead, Mom," Jean remarked.

"That's what I thought too; a whole school full of zombies," Rylan added.

"Except for the fights and the cops, just creepy quiet all day." Jean trailed off but then remembered, "During fourth period, the choir from Mr. Sprink's class walked through the halls singing the National Anthem. The teachers and some of the students came out into the hall to listen, and all the teachers started crying. It was really sad, but the singing was also kinda; I dunno...."

"Uplifting?" Emily offered.

"Yeah."

Emily sighed heavily. "I know it's been an unbelievably awful day for everyone, and I know it's probably selfish to say, but at least the two of you... us, the three of us, we're safe. Thank God."

Rylan had been reluctant to ask but knew he had to, "Were there any more attacks?"

Emily replied, "Besides the Towers, the Pentagon, and the flight that went down in Pennsylvania? No. That's all we know of, for now, and I can only pray that it's the end of it."

"What flight in Pennsylvania?" Rylan was confused.

"Did you leave school before they..." Emily saw the confusion on her son's face and knew the answer to her question, "Oh, Rylan, yes, another flight was hijacked. Somehow the passengers heard about the other planes hitting the towers and fought back against the terrorists on their plane, but unfortunately, they crashed into a field somewhere in Pennsylvania. The news said that the FBI, police, or whoever, thinks the hijackers intended to crash it into the White House."

"Those passengers were heroes. I can't even imagine how...." Jean began but was interrupted.

"It crashed in Pennsylvania? Where? Was anyone on the ground hurt?" Rylan demanded, with a surprising urgency in his voice. He quickly swung his legs over the edge of the bed to sit upright next to his mother.

Emily shook her head, "No. I had thought about Abigail too when I heard the news, but no, it wasn't anywhere near her school." She reassured him and started softly rubbing his back. "The flight crashed into a field somewhere further to the south."

Rylan exhaled, then took another deep breath before turning to his mother, "I'm sorry, Mom, I tried so hard to control myself this time, but when the buildings collapsed, I just got so angry. I couldn't hold it in."

Emily hugged her son tightly. "I know, Rylan. I know. I know it's hard." She tightened her embrace as she tried to stifle her tears. "We might need to find you another counselor out here."

Rylan didn't answer, but he knew she was right.

Jean interjected, "A lot of the boys at school are talking about joining the Army to go after the Afghans."

Rylan pulled away from his mother, "Afghans? Is that what the hijackers are called?"

"They're not Afghans, Jean, that's a type of rug. Apparently, they are from Afghanistan, but they're from some terrorist group called... 'All-Cada', or something like that."

"What the heck is an All-Cada?" Rylan asked.

"Tom Brokaw on the news says that they want some kind of holy war against America. I don't understand what that's supposed to mean, though." Jean offered.

"They want a war with us? With America? Are they crazy? We'll slaughter those motherfuckers." Rylan exclaimed.

"Watch your mouth, Rylan." Emily chided.

"But Mom, they came to our Country and crashed airplanes into our buildings! We didn't even do anything to them! Just 'cause they don't like Americans? Hell no, mom. We have to hit back."

"Rye is right, Mom, we gotta." Jean agreed.

"I'm not disagreeing with either of you, but right now, in this room, we need to calm down. WE don't make those kinds of decisions. I'm sure President Bush and the rest of them in DC will figure out how to handle it with the All-Cada. WE need to worry about how to handle our own selves."

"Well, I know how I'm handling it. I'm joining the Army, or the Marines, or one of them."

"No, you're not." The finality in Emily's voice shocked Rylan, who immediately felt defiance warming his skin.

"What do you mean: I'm not?" His words were sharpened by outrage. "I turn eighteen in six months, and like Jean said, a lot of the guys in school are going to enlist too. Plus, you know Joey is already stationed in Germany, so they're probably sending him to Afghanistan right now."

Emily, sensing the conversation had turned in a combative direction, stood up from the bed, and faced Rylan to assert her authority on the matter.

"Rylan, you would need my signature to enlist before your eighteenth birthday, and I'm not giving it. That's non-negotiable. I know you don't like it, and I'm not asking you to, but please respect my decision as a parent. If you still want to enlist after your birthday in March, that's entirely your choice, and I will respect it and support your decision, but as for right now, the answer is a hard no."

Rylan seethed. It sounded right that, given his age, he would need her permission to enlist, but it didn't make it any easier to accept. He could see that this was an argument he couldn't win, so he held his tongue but glared into his mother's eyes to demonstrate his resolve. Unflinchingly, she returned his glare, firmly communicating her entrenched position. After a short but uncomfortable few moments, Jean tried to break the tension between a mother and son, trying to stare each other down like professional wrestlers in the middle of the ring.

"Um, Mom, you had said you wanted to go to church, did you want to go now or after dinner?"

Emily inclined her head slightly towards her daughter but continued to hold eye contact with Rylan for a few beats longer.

"We can go now, baby; then we can pick up some dinner on the way home." She turned back to her son, "We're going to head over to the church. Pastor Watters is holding a vigil for the victims and families of the attacks in New York. You want to come?"

"No, thanks." He responded through barred teeth.

Emily almost rolled her eyes at Rylan's petulant behavior but caught herself before sinking into immaturity.

"Fine." She said curtly, "We'll be back in a couple of hours."

Rylan laid back in bed, covering himself with the blanket as his mother and sister left the room. From under the covers, he could hear their footsteps on the hardwood as they walked down the hall, and then the sound of the front door opening, then closing behind them. As he imagined his loved ones driving off, leaving him alone in the house, his desire to be with his family finally overcame his sulk, and he threw off the blanket, slipped on his shoes, and ran after them.

13

—·—

April 3, 2017, Monday

Caldwell, Idaho

Rylan pulled his Trailblazer onto the shoulder of Chicken Dinner Road and sat carefully surveying the house in the distance. Because of the wide-open countryside in that part of Idaho, with large patches of farmland separating homes, Rylan had parked a quarter mile away to avoid being noticed but still had an unobstructed view of the light grey ranch-style home belonging to the next person on the Garbage Route; John Burbules.

The house's long front lawn was remarkably well-maintained, with mowed grass that resembled an emerald carpet more than anything organic. A fifteen-foot flagpole was planted in the middle of the yard with the POW/MIA flag flying a few inches below Old Glory. The American flag's vibrant colors presented a stark contrast against the overcast sky in the background, the thick clouds greyed by the coming rain.

The remote location of John's house would otherwise have been a boon for Rylan, but after idling on the side of the road for nearly five minutes, he noticed that not a single car had passed by in either direction since he had stopped. With such little traffic, an unfamiliar vehicle stopped by the wayside would likely draw attention.

Ironically, a white pickup truck soon appeared in his rearview mirror, slowed, and then unexpectedly stopped alongside his Trailblazer. The white truck's passenger side window rolled down, and an old man called out from the driver seat.

"Good gracious, son, you must be lost."

Rylan's blood ran cold. He felt like he was seeing a ghost. The old man's face was the same face he had seen in copies of old newspaper stories posted on the internet. It was the same face he had studied while researching for his excursion into Idaho. It was John Burbules.

Rylan attempted to suppress his shock, fearing his facial expressions would arouse the old man's suspicions. "Um, uh, sorry?"

"South Carolina plates." The old man pointed towards the rear of the Trailblazer, "Don't see those up here much." He smiled warmly.

Rylan forced an awkward smile across his face. "No, I guess not."

"You alright?" John asked politely. His southern accent had faded over the years but was still noticeable.

"I'm sorry?" shaking his head in confusion.

"You alright? Having car trouble?"

"Oh! No. No, sorry, I, I mean, I was going to, trying to find the winery, um, the Chappelle Winery. Sorry. I'm getting a little flustered." He closed his eyes and shook his head, "Let me start over. I was going to the Chappelle Winery, and I think I made a wrong turn."

"No, not a wrong turn. You missed the turn back there, should've cut right onto Lowell Road."

"Ah! That makes sense."

"You sure picked a day to visit, though; it's about to rain soon."

"Yeah, sorry. I should have checked the weather before heading out this morning."

John cocked his head to the side, "You sure do apologize a lot, son."

"Yeah, I guess I do," Rylan conceded with a small chuckle. "Sorry about that."

Catching his blunder, Rylan shot an embarrassed glance over at John, who was shaking his head disparagingly.

"Well, enjoy the vineyard." John raised his hand, cordially ending the conversation, and was ready to drive away.

Rylan sensed an opportunity slipping away.

"Hold up!" He blurted out before he even knew what he was doing. The white truck lurched forward, then stopped in a jerk.

John leaned over the passenger side, "You say something?"

Rylan was silent, gripped with indecision, fearing he had made a mistake. His mind raced to decide if he should go with it or apologize again to the old man and let him continue on his way.

"Yeah, I uh, I really hate to do this, but um, do you live near here?"

"Yes, I do," John replied skeptically.

"Could I possibly use your restroom? I promise I'll be quick."

John's facial expression belied the awkwardness of the request.

Rylan tried to put on a charmingly pitiful smile. "Please? I wouldn't ask if it wasn't an emergency."

"Sure." He reluctantly consented, "That's my place, two houses up on the left. You can follow me."

"Thank you! Thank you so much." Sensing John's apprehension, Rylan attempted to win him over with excessive gratitude, but the man in the pickup truck seemed disinterested as he drove off toward his home.

During the short drive, raindrops began to patter upon the windshield as Rylan considered the enormous risk he was taking. He was hoping to get a good look at the interior of the house without drawing suspicion but also knew he needed to be prepared for anything. He quickly felt around inside his backpack for the pistol and was able to wedge it into the waistband of his jeans before finally parking in the driveway.

John had already parked his truck in the garage and was standing near the rear bumper, motioning for Rylan to enter the house that way.

Through the garage, John opened a door, and the two men entered a large room being used as a combination laundry room, pantry, and wine storage. Rylan noted the meticulously organized and labeled containers of foods and toiletries uniformly stocked on the pantry shelves and thought it looked like the work of a doomsday prepper.

"Shoes off, if you don't mind." John directed as he pulled off his shoes and placed them neatly on the linoleum near the door. Rylan mimicked his host's behavior.

Without even a second glance at Rylan, the old man approached the old washer and dryer in the corner of the room while pointing to the hallway on the far side of the room.

"Restroom is the second door on the right."

He started pulling clothes from the dryer and loading them into the empty basket on the floor. Rylan thanked him, then walked towards the hallway, appreciating the scent of freshly cleaned fabrics from the dryer as he passed.

Walking slowly through the hall, he browsed the framed pictures hanging on the wall. He was surprised to find, in most of the photos, a much younger version of John posing with a woman whose skin was the color of milk chocolate; a sharp contrast to the doughy skin of the man Rylan had just met. In many of the pictures, the couple held each other closely, and in others, they kissed sweetly. The photos had been taken in different places the two had visited together: a hiking trail along a mountain range, a cruise ship at sea, a street-food vendor somewhere in Japan, and a Christmas market near an enormous gothic church in Germany. Rylan thought the pair looked happy, and judging by the images, had enjoyed a pretty good life together for several years.

Rylan continued to the end of the hallway, then quickly scanned the living room, trying to memorize the layout, before backtracking to the restroom and closing the door behind him.

Not really needing to use the restroom, Rylan simply stood at the sink, waiting, and wasting time. He could see, through the window, that the rain outside had intensified, and he dreaded his impending scamper back to the SUV.

He gazed at his reflection in the mirror and questioned the benefit of such a needless incursion into John's home. Besides leaving with some intriguing questions regarding the photographs in the hall, he couldn't find a way to justify his impulsive decision.

After a few seconds, Rylan heard John stroll through the hallway into the living room. He stood at the sink for a little while longer, and once he felt like sufficient time had passed, he reached out for the doorknob, then stopped, and realized that he should first flush the toilet and wash his hands, in case John was paying attention. As he dried his hands, he checked himself in the mirror one last time, making sure the butt of the pistol was well-concealed under his shirt, then practiced a charming smile and stepped out into the hallway.

He spotted John seated on a recliner in the living room, folding laundry. He walked in that direction and stopped at the end of the hall to thank his host.

"Sir, I cannot thank you enough."

"No problem at all. Christian thing to do." John said dryly as he rose from the chair and walked toward Rylan.

The older man was sixty-five years old but looked slightly older. He stood a few inches taller than Rylan but thin and wiry compared to the thick musculature of his younger guest. As he approached, Rylan noticed John's facial expression was flat and emotionless. It was clear he was unwanted in the man's home.

"Yes, sir, it is." Rylan flashed the charming smile he had rehearsed. "By the way, I didn't catch your name...."

"I'm John."

"Well, John, I'm Paul." The younger man held out his hand to shake, "I guess our parents were really into the Apostles, huh? Or was it The Beatles?"

John initially furrowed his brow in puzzlement, then finally cracked a warm smile and shook Rylan's hand.

"The Beatles? If you'd have known my old man, you'd know better. His taste in music was real simple: Bluegrass or nothin'." He jovially responded to Rylan's quip. "Besides, I was already in grade school when the Beatles started."

"Oh. Well, Apostles it is then!" Rylan turned up the wattage on his smile.

"Praise be! So, what're you doin' way up here from South Carolina anyway? Can't be just for the winery. I mean, the wine is good but not worthy of that kind of a journey."

"Yeah, well, that's kind of a long story," Rylan deftly tried to avoid the question, knowing he didn't have a good answer, "besides, I should probably get going."

"Golly, son, you in a hurry? It's really comin' down out there."

Both men turned to peer through the large picture window facing the backyard. They could see for almost a mile as the rain battered the landscape. From within the safety of the house, the turbulent scene outside was beautiful to watch and strangely serene.

John turned back to his younger guest, "You're welcome to stick around for a little while if you'd like. I'm just folding laundry, but I wouldn't mind hearing your tale. It's been many years since I've been down south."

Surprised by the offer, Rylan knew the correct answer was to thank him for his generosity and leave immediately, but at the same time, he felt compelled to stay and see where the conversation would lead.

"You know what, John, I think I'll take you up on that. As long as I'm not intruding...."

"Baaah!" The old man waved his hand in a dismissive way, "course not. C'mon over here and have a seat." He turned and walked toward the sofa.

Rylan followed, but as he sat, John continued walking to the far wall and stopped in front of a liquor cart, behind which, a large, ornately carved wooden crucifix hung on the wall. Arranged around the wooden cross were old, framed photographs, many yellowed and weathered, of US soldiers in Vietnam.

John spoke with his back turned to Rylan, "Can I fix you a drink, Paul?"

"Oh, no, thank you. I don't drink."

Rylan saw John's back stiffen, as though alerted to something, then he realized his mistake.

"You don't drink?" John turned around to examine his visitor, "Then why in God's name are you going to a vineyard?"

"Ah! Yeah. That does sound odd, doesn't it?" He nervously flashed his charming smile again. "My um, my wife; ex-wife, actually, this winery was on her bucket list."

"I don't follow, son. You say that winery was on your ex-wife's bucket list, but... aren't you here by y'self?"

"Yes. Right. She died three years ago, and a few months ago, while I was finally going through some of her old stuff, I found this little notebook. Inside, on one of the pages, she had written out a list of places she had wanted to visit, and I guess... I don't know; I guess I just wanted to do it for her. That sounds stupid when I say it out loud."

"Not at all. I understand." John looked pensively down into his whiskey glass, then absentmindedly swirled the two ice cubes around before turning to finish up at the liquor cart.

With John's back now turned, Rylan felt relieved and silently proud of his quick thinking but also dismayed that John had nearly unraveled his ruse. He second-guessed the decision to stay instead of leaving but felt a hasty retreat now would arouse suspicion. He realized he was stuck and would have to weather the storm. He looked around the room to focus his attention.

The interior of the old man's house was roughly what Rylan had expected but with some interesting twists. Everything was neatly organized and clean with lots of polished wood surfaces, including the floors, and the kitchen was all stainless steel appliances and granite. The house smelled like worn leather, furniture polish, and stale cigar smoke, but also like banana bread. The heads of three large elk were mounted high on a wall, all posed as if gazing longingly toward the window at the back of the room. Beside the front door was a full-sized whiskey barrel with an expertly carved and painted wooden statue of a rodeo clown inside, with its head whimsically peeking above the rim. On one wall hung a painting of Teddy Roosevelt, confidently seated atop his horse, and then nearby, a one-foot-tall bronze statue of a battle-worn Confederate soldier carrying the rebel flag was displayed as a centerpiece in the middle of the dinner table.

"I think it's a noble thing you're doing," John stated.

Rylan, who had pivoted in his seat to peruse the room, quickly spun around, startled by the older man's voice. "Wha.. what's that?"

"Your odyssey," John remarked as he took a seat on the recliner beside the half-empty basket of clothes, the other half already neatly folded in stacks atop the coffee table, "You're honoring your wife by keeping her memory alive. It's a noble thing."

Rylan was momentarily stunned by the old man's words but quickly recovered, "Right. Yes. Exactly." He responded, then after a moment, he softly added, "Thank you."

John just nodded, and the two men sat, silently pondering their paths in life. Soon, the silence became uncomfortable, and Rylan decided to say something.

"Those photos over there," He nodded towards the wall behind the liquor cart, "is that Vietnam?"

"Yeah." John turned to look briefly at the wall, then turned back to Rylan, "Yeah. Some good men in some bad bush over there."

"My dad was there too."

"Yeah? What unit?"

"Don't know. We never got a chance to talk about it."

"Mmmm." John knowingly nodded, "Cancer, the bullet, or the bottle?"

"Sorry?"

"Your old man. He died, right? What got him? Cancer, the bullet, or the bottle?"

Rylan considered John's words for a few seconds before he understood the question, "The last two."

"Mmmm," John grunted. "A lot of us that came back, went out that same way. Did you serve?"

"Serve? Oh! Yes. Army. Three years. Two tours in Iraq."

"Well, then, thank you for your service." He tipped his glass of whiskey as a salute before taking a sip.

"No, sir, thank you. You guys got one hell of a raw deal."

"How's that?" John probed, curious about his guest's views.

"Well, for one... getting drafted! How crazy to think that someday, out of the blue, you get a letter that says you're being forced to enlist and headed off to some foreign jungle to fight a war. That's so incredible to me."

John's gaze wandered up into the ceiling rafters. "I remember that day like yesterday. I'd just been hired as an engine mechanic. I was so excited to come home and tell my folks the good news, but when I walked in, mama was in the kitchen cryin', readin' my draft letter. It'd just been delivered to the house."

"Damn... what's, even more fu... more screwed up is that, at the same time the government was forcing men and boys into the service against their will, they were also testing drugs on the soldiers to try to boost aggression, right? I remember reading an article about entire companies of soldiers being given hallucinogenics just to see what would happen, and apparently, one of those companies was out at night, patrolling their piece of the jungle, and stumbled upon the enemy, started shooting, and killed everyone. Then, when they started searching the bodies for intel, they discovered that 'the enemy' was really another company of American troops out patrolling in the dark. I mean, I can't even imagine experiencing something like that, and then having to carry it with you after..."

While Rylan paused, he saw John, again, staring wistfully into his glass of whiskey and ice. The blank stare on his face implied that he had retreated into a distant place in his memory; though not completely detached from the present, he managed a grunt.

"To me, though," Rylan continued, "the most mind-blowing thing is what happened when you guys came home. Look, I can only speak from my experience, and being deployed, away from my family for twelve months, was devastating. I remember being out there on patrol, or guard duty, or whatever, and every single day you're dreaming... dreaming with your eyes wide open about home; the smell of your mom's cooking, the sound of your friends laughing, the texture of your dog's fur, a cold beer in your mouth, the bitter taste of your girlfriend's perfume when you kiss her neck. All of it. It's painful to think about, but you can't help it because it also gives us hope; makes us believe that someday we could get back to our loved ones, and..."

Rylan leaned closer to John, who looked up from his whiskey to see the intensity in the young man's stare.

"I'm sure you guys felt the same thing out there in the jungle as we did in the desert, right? Just praying every day for it all to be over, so you could finally get back home to the safety of America, right? Well, the difference is, when my generation came home, complete strangers greeted us with handshakes and hugs. They called us heroes, and every once in a while, if I went to a restaurant in uniform, a random person would pay for my meal. But for you guys... you guys came home after an absolutely incomprehensible, horrific war, and then were literally spat upon by America. Vilified and rejected by the public, then blackballed by businesses that blocked returning veterans from getting jobs, which led to such high rates of poverty, homelessness, alcoholism, drug use, suicide... you guys were basically punished, by the citizens of your own country, for being forced into a war by the government. Has something like that ever happened, on such a massive scale, in the history of civilization? I can't even fathom what that was like, so, sir..." Rylan extended his hand to John, "from one vet to another, sincerely, thank you."

John shook Rylan's outstretched hand. "Looks like you spent a good bit of time thinking on this subject."

Rylan smiled bashfully, "Let's just say I had an interest in understanding the plight of the Vietnam veteran."

John grunted, signaling his understanding. "Tell me, what did you do in the Army, Paul?"

"I was an Infantryman."

"Ah! So, you're a killer, then?"

Rylan's eyes narrowed, "You could say that."

"You do a lot of hunting?"

"Depends."

"On what?"

"On the 'what' I'm hunting." Rylan smiled.

John took a moment to consider his guest's response, "That's fair. After all, 'there is no hunting like the hunting of men', right?"

Rylan recited the rest of the quote. "And those that have hunted armed men long enough and liked it, never care for anything else thereafter."

"Impressive. You read Hemingway?"

"No. Not really. I picked up the quote from an article in a magazine while I was in Iraq. Stuck with me."

John sat back in his chair, appraising Rylan, "You're an interesting fellow, Paul."

"What do you mean?"

"There's something about you; I can't put my finger on it, but... for example, there's not many men who'd ask someone they just met, let alone someone they met in passing, to use a restroom in their house. And then, there're very few people with the same depth of consideration and concern for others you've shown in your little speech about 'Nam."

"Yeah, sorry about that; I've been rambling a lot lately. I talk too much when I'm nervous or uncomfortable."

"Am I making you nervous, Paul?"

"No. Of course not."

"Hmmm." John took a sip of his drink but kept his eyes on Rylan, "You also seemed evasive when I asked if you hunt."

"Evasive?"

"It's usually just a yes or no question, but that's not the kind of answer you gave me."

Rylan didn't respond. The two men sat in uncomfortable silence, assessing each other.

"What does that mean to you, then, John?" Rylan's tone had shifted slightly, becoming more firmly underpinned.

"I don't know yet," John answered. Rylan saw the skepticism on his face, and then all of a sudden, John's doubtful expression disappeared, replaced by a too-wide smile, "Nothing! Nothing. It doesn't mean anything. I'm just messin' with ya, son."

He laughed, and Rylan smiled, but both men could sense a slight tension in the air.

John turned to look thoughtfully through the large rear-facing window. Rylan followed his host's gaze, and they both sat quietly appreciating the vista, the unrelenting onslaught of droplets bombarding the terrain, with lightning occasionally crackling across the sky. A few voiceless minutes passed as the two men sat admiring the beauty of the weather, and before long, Rylan's mind began to wander.

He thought about Lake Tahoe. It amazed him that an unplanned stop along his route, which should have only lasted enough time for a good nap and a shower, had turned into a three-day vacation, one he didn't know he needed. He thought about the spectacular view of the mountains from the ski lodge where he had finally learned to snowboard. He thought about the casino where he won seven hundred dollars one night, only to lose it the next. He thought about the little rowboat he had rented one warm day to float on the lake and let the waves rock him to sleep.

"How long you say you've been in Idaho?" John's voice brought Rylan back from his memories.

Rylan cleared his throat. "I got in yesterday morning."

"Where you staying?"

"The Nampa Holiday Inn."

"Oh yeah, down there by the Idaho Center. That's a nice place. You know, there's a great little Mexican restaurant right near there called El Rinconcito."

"Yeah! I had dinner there last night. The hotel clerk recommended it."

"That's some of the best Mexican I've ever had, as God is my witness."

"You're not kidding. It was a surprising find, especially in Idaho."

"Yeah, well, we have a lot of Mexican folks up here on account of all the migrant work. They come up from Mexico and whatnot, work the fields and farms, have babies, and set down roots. Good folks, mostly. Of course, you'll get a bit of the criminal element in with the good sometimes, but I imagine that's the same everywhere."

Rylan didn't respond. He was mulling over John's words and wondered why he felt it necessary to include the last part.

"You drink coffee, Paul?" John asked.

"Huh? Oh. Yes, sir."

"I might brew a pot," he stood up and began moving towards the kitchen, "you like a cup?"

"That sounds great, John. Thank you."

"I just made some banana bread this morning too. It's got chocolate chips in it. How 'bout a slice?"

"I'll say this: if it's half as good as it smells, I'll pay you for it."

"Baaah!" John waved away the thought with a prideful smirk.

Rylan watched John move around the kitchen for a while, and it occurred to him that he had been enjoying Mr. Burbules' company a little too much, and he reminded himself to stay on his toes. He discretely adjusted the pistol in his waistband, providing a brief relief from the hunk of metal that had been burrowing into his abdomen since he had sat down.

"John, can I ask you a question?" Rylan raised his voice to be heard by the man in the kitchen.

"Shoot," John called back.

"I noticed that statue you have on your dinner table. It's beautiful. Where'd you get that?"

"You like that? It was my grandpappy's. His old man served under Stonewall Jackson at Chancellorsville."

"Oh wow. That's incredible. I can't imagine you see too many Dixie flags up here in Idaho."

"You'd be surprised."

"Yeah?"

"Yeah. Hold on a sec, though. I'm fixin' to be done here. You want any cream or sugar?"

"No, thank you. Black is fine."

Rylan could hear metal utensils clinking against ceramic; then, after a few moments, John returned carrying a mug of coffee in each hand, with saucers balanced on top, each holding a thick slice of homemade banana bread. Rylan stood to grab his share, then sat back down as John continued his thought.

"These youngsters in your generation think the flag makes them look tough. Doesn't matter where you look, just find some farmland anywhere across the country, and you'll probably find some teenager with an Old Dixie flag sticker in the back window of their pickup truck. They're also the same ones who'll fly Old Glory from their porch, while swearin' up and down that they're patriotic, never minding the obvious contradiction. I think it's just a bunch of ignorance. Most think it stands for redneck pride, white power, rebelliousness, or some other paranoid general distrust of the government."

"Huh. Then, what does it mean to you?"

"To me? I'd say it represents a failed attempt to steal land away from the country."

"Oh?" Rylan was astonished by John's statement.

"Lotta folks in the South wanna portray the war as some righteous fight against government overreach, but that's a big load of cow manure. That war was purely about money. They always are. Ya gotta remember, back then, the South was mostly farmland and plantations. The white folk were makin' all their money off tobacco and cotton crops without havin' to pay a dime to their captive workforce, but above the Mason Dixon, the story was different. The North, with all the factories and industrial infrastructure, had a massive workforce from the huge populations living in them big cities, to which they routinely paid wages. So, for the South, freeing the slaves would've meant they'd have to start paying wages to their new 'employees', and they didn't want to do that. So, while the issue was being debated, the Southern leaders decided to break away from the nation and take their farmland with them, and well... we already know how that worked out."

"John, not to change the subject, but this banana bread is spectacular."

"Well, thanks. I'm glad you like it."

"Is that bourbon and vanilla?"

"Sure is."

"It's outstanding! Thank you for this, John." Rylan said as he finished another mouthful. "Getting back to what you were saying though... the accent in your voice; you grew up in the South, right?

"Right outside Raleigh, North Carolina."

"I can't imagine your views about the Civil War went over well in Raleigh."

"Lord, no! They'd have deep-fried me in oil! Right there along-side a fresh batch of buttermilk-battered chickens!" Both men laughed. "I didn't come up on this perspective until many years after I'd moved away."

"Why'd you move away?" Rylan probed.

John paused to think about how he wanted to answer, "Let's just say I got myself into a bit of trouble when I was a youngster. My family figured it'd be best to start over somewhere else." John shifted uncomfortably in his seat before trying to change the subject, "But, you know, that statue over there sure has been one of them 'conversation starters'. Everyone that comes into my house seems to have somethin' to say about it."

"I'll bet! But purely from a craftsmanship standpoint, it's beautiful." Rylan noted. "You mind if I ask you another question, John?"

"Son, you don't need to ask permission to ask a question. Just ask. If I don't like the question, or just plum don't want to answer, I'll surely let you know."

"Fair enough." Rylan smiled, "In the hallway, on the way to your restroom, I noticed a bunch of pictures on the wall; looks like vacation photos."

John had been taking a sip from his mug, "Yeah?"

"There was a woman in the photos. Your wife?"

John looked uncomfortably into his coffee, the steam rising like ghosts disappearing into the ether, "Charlene... She was my wife."

"Oh."

"Why you ask?"

"Well, the um, the confederate statue, and well, you know, she's black...."

"Yup. That doggone statue caused a lot of bitterness between Charlene and me for many years. I understand the confederacy carries a heavy symbolism tied to slavery, and it's hurtful to black Americans, and rightfully so, but at the same time, she understood it being a family heirloom and its importance to me in that way. God bless her; as much as she hated it, she still let me keep it in the house, not as prominently displayed as it is now, of course, but she allowed it."

"She seems like an interesting person. I'd like to meet her."

"Yeah, well, we divorced almost five years ago. She lives in Oklahoma now."

"Oh. Sorry to hear that. So you live alone, then?" Rylan probed, but immediately regretted the way he said it.

John cocked his head at the peculiar question.

Rylan hastily tried to cover his tracks, "It sucks, living alone after being married, huh? You keep wanting to call out to them for random things; bring you a towel when you get out of the shower, or to ask if they want anything from the fridge while you're up from the sofa. It's crazy."

"I suppose," John replied flatly.

"You know, my wife almost divorced me right before she died. Because of my drinking, mostly."

"Hmmm."

"How about you two?" Rylan asked.

"Hmmm?"

"Why did you two divorce?"

John shifted in his seat, sipped his coffee, then stroked his beard.

"That bit of trouble I had gotten into when I was a teenager, I never told her about it, and she eventually found out about it on the internet, and that was enough for her to leave."

"What?" Rylan feigned surprise, though, in full knowledge of the exact incident John was tiptoeing around, "What did you do?"

"It's not something I ever talk about. It's of the sort of thing you'd wish never happened."

"I see. I apologize, John, that was rude of me. I'm a curious-type person by nature. I didn't mean to pry."

Lightning flashed, then three seconds later, thunder loudly followed, and the two men flinched. They exchanged embarrassed looks, and John decided to use the moment to switch gears in the conversation.

"So, we had spent a little bit of time talking about war earlier, and you said you did two tours in Iraq, right?"

"Yes, Sir."

"Tell me, what did you learn?"

"About?"

"About yourself? About life? Did you learn anything?"

Rylan's eyebrows shot up; sensing the enormity of the question, he was unsure where to begin. "So much." He muttered before clearing his throat, "About myself... I suppose I learned that I'm capable of a lot more than I would have even imagined; I can endure a lot of pain, in all its forms. That I can keep grinding my way through adversity. About life? I guess... I learned that life is spectacularly, impossibly fragile."

"Hmmm." John looked up at the ceiling while he pondered Rylan's words, "Impossibly fragile... what do you mean by that?"

"I mean that it's mind-numbing how easy it is to kill someone."

"Whoa now! What's that you say?"

Rylan chuckled at John's reaction. "No, what I mean is that it's not difficult, in a purely practical sense, to kill someone."

"Lord!" John exclaimed, relieved, "You had me fixin' to go grab the shotgun."

Rylan chuckled again, then continued, "But, I'd also say that, emotionally speaking, for most people, killing another person is a very hard thing to do. Most people who've killed another person suffer mentally and emotionally from re-living the memory of it. Recurring nightmares, hallucinations, anxiety, and panic attacks; nowadays, we call it PTSD, but I think your generation called it shell shock. The doctors say it stems from feelings of guilt after taking another person's life but see... I don't think that's quite right. Don't get me wrong, I agree there are elements of guilt contributing to that kind of PTSD, but at the root, I think it's more about the revelation of how truly easy it is for a person to die, and the discovery that you, too, could die just as easily."

Rylan could see John ruminating over the younger man's words. Another lightning bolt flashed outside the house, then the thunder boomed shortly after. Rylan leaned forward, ensuring he had caught John's full attention before attempting to bring his point further into the light.

"When you take someone's life, up close, seeing your reflection in their eyes when the light goes out; it changes you. For a person, the insecure creatures that we are, to all of a sudden, be faced with that truth, the immutable brittleness, the fragility of life... in a blink, becoming aware that we've been walking through our lives with only these weak bones and soft flesh for protection, that our entire existence is so delicate, so vulnerable; that's terrifying, John."

"Hmmm." John could feel Rylan's words ring with faint familiarity, "There may be a great deal of truth to what you're saying here, Paul, and I'll admit I'm much less philosophical about it all, but I don't believe everyone's experience is the same. Regardless, I'll say this; listening to you talk about it, it seems you've had a very intimate ordeal."

"You could say that." Rylan sat back into the sofa and sipped his coffee. "Death has never been a stranger to me. What about you, though? Vietnam was a long time ago, but does it still mess with you?"

"Of course it does. It's not something that ever really stops. There are stretches of time when it's not as bad, but something always comes along and triggers the memories again."

"That's horrible," Rylan grumbled, unnerved by the thought of his memories continuing to torment him for the rest of his life.

"And even if, over time, the memories do start to fade, or wear thin in spots, your imagination just fills in the gaps. What I see when I close my eyes now is probably not the same as how it happened almost sixty years ago, but you know, when you dream, there ain't no boundaries, no distances that can't be crossed, no details that can't be fabricated. Your mind will just take whatever information you have left, then just make up the rest."

"That's crazy." Rylan tried to digest the concept, "We sure do pay a heavy price, don't we?"

"Hmmm." John nodded in agreement. "So... this thing you say, 'the fragility of life', do you remember when that hit home for you?"

"Yes. Yes, I do. Burned into my memory."

"Care to share?" he asked before sipping his coffee.

Rylan rolled his shoulders and cracked his neck. "First deployment to Iraq. One afternoon, my platoon was on QRF, and we got called up. We began movement to the location and got briefed on the situation enroute. Apparently, the Marines had gotten one of their Humvees blown up on a road cutting through a known minefield. They shouldn't have been in there in the first place. I remember we were on the way, and everyone in the Humvee was complaining about Marines and how they were always doing stupid jarhead shhh... stuff. So, we're nearing the grid coordinates, and it's out in the middle of a half-mile-long stretch of open field; nothing out there but rocky desert, scrub brush, and years and years of accumulated trash scattered everywhere. We stop the trucks about two hundred meters short, then dismount. I go along with my platoon leader and squad leader, and we move, on foot, to link up with the Marine Sergeant on the ground. I can still see him clear as day; he was standing by himself in the middle of the field, with a couple of huge trash bags on the ground beside him, and his troops were off in the distance, walking around the field, scanning through the trash. We finally get there, and my platoon leader starts getting a status report on the Marines' situation. So, I'm standing beside my squad leader, listening to the briefing, but I'm confused, so I ask the Marine, 'Where exactly is the wreckage, Sergeant?' He glanced at me for only a second, but I could tell he was barely hanging on, just completely stretched to the breaking point, you know? Then he points to an empty space, about another two hundred meters away, where the road bends to the right, and I'm starting to feel embarrassed because I'm still not understanding. He says, 'There is a crater over there. It's about thirty meters in diameter and about ten meters deep, but there's nothing in it. It's all out here. The biggest piece we've found so far is half an axle.' My jaw dropped. Right there. That was the moment everything changed. It was like someone slipped a filter in front of my eyes, and I could finally see the field I was standing in. There was trash everywhere, but it wasn't just Iraqi trash; I could now see the shredded chunks and bits of Humvee out there. I mean, we were two hundred meters away, and there were pieces still further away than that! The Marine then says, 'My men are trying to find as much of the bodies as we can.' Again, I heard the words clearly, but I was stupefied by what he was saying... 'trying to find as much of their bodies?' Then it dawned on me that what I had mistaken for mostly empty trash bags at his feet were not trash bags at all; they were body bags. The whole time I was standing there, it hadn't even occurred to me because they didn't look like body bags. They weren't shaped right; you know what I mean? There were only a few pieces inside each." Rylan choked up, and his eyes filled with tears, "I mean, seeing them out there... the, the Marines, out searching through the rubble, and the sand, and the trash, trying to find what was left of their brothers; that changed me."

"God bless," John mumbled, his words heavy with sympathy for the Marines' ordeal.

"How about you?" Rylan's voice was trembly from fighting back tears.

John furrowed his brow, unsure of the question Rylan was asking. "What about me?"

"Do you remember when it dawned on you; just how easy it is to die?"

"My Lord! That was a long time ago," John stretched his back before beginning, "My first day in 'Nam, a Huey dropped me off at a support base a few clicks southwest of Da Nang. I met up with my platoon and the next morning, we started out on patrol. The sweltering jungle was so thick you couldn't see more than ten feet in front of you, so humid even the trees seemed to be sweatin', then from somewhere up front, the signal comes back to halt and get down. So, we're fixin' to get down, and just like that, pow, the VCs started lightin' us up. I heard all the shootin' and the yellin' up front, but I couldn't see a dang thing but a bunch of muzzle flashes through the leaves. They had me in the back of the column carrying the extra ammo for the Sixty, so me and Wilson, the Sixty-gunner, had to high-tail it all the way up to the front with bullets buzzin' and crackin' through the air all around me. Son, I have no shame in sayin' I pissed myself as I ran. There ain't no fear like the fear of certain death, and make no mistake, I was sure I was gonna die right there. I was cryin' and runnin' and calling out to the Lord to save me, and thankfully he heard my voice. We finally made it up to the front, got that Sixty singin' that sweet song of suppressive fire, then Sarge called in the mortars and blew them heathens up. So then, afterward, the firefight is over, and we sweep through the objective. There's bodies everywhere, and we start searchin' through 'em, collecting intel, callin' in reports, and everything like we're supposed to do, and by then, I was feelin' pretty good about myself. I had survived my first firefight, and handled myself pretty well, all things considered. So anyway, once we finished searching everythin', we were fixin' to move out, and somebody yelled out, 'ON THE SIX!' We turned around, and there were at least fifty Vietcong coming up outta the ground behind us. It looked like a dang zombie movie, but those zombies had AK-47s, and they lit us up. We tried to return fire as best we could, but they had us dead to rights. All we could do was break contact, and they mowed us down as we ran away. I saw Wilson turn his head... clear as if it happened yesterday, he'd turned to look back over his shoulder while we were runnin', and two bullets tore his face right off. Two big strips just ripped right across his face, like that, and he went down; then you know what I did when I saw that? I ran harder."

"Well, what else could you do? If you'd have stopped to help him, you'd have been killed too."

"Exactly. We lost twenty-six good men that day, and it's only by the grace of God that it wasn't more."

"You said they were coming out of the ground behind you... they had been hiding in tunnels?"

"Bingo. Those damned rat holes."

"Geez." Rylan ran both hands through his hair. "I can't... I can't even imagine what that's like."

"Oh, I'm sure you can imagine it, but I swear to you, it ain't nothin' like the real thing."

"I believe it. You know, think about my generation's wars; it's seventeen years now that we've been engaged in the wars in the Middle East, both Iraq and Afghanistan, and they've been so devastating for everyone involved, but it blows my mind to think about all the extra stuff y'all went through before, during, and after. I don't think my experience of war can compare to yours."

"I'd say, don't try to compare them. It's not a competition as to 'who had it worse'. War is always changing. Think, way back in the ancient times; we had cavemen goin' at each other with sticks and rocks, then it became swords and axes, then arrows, then guns and cannons, then airplanes droppin' bombs, then long-range missiles, and now, what's this stuff they're working on, drones? The fighters keep getting further and further away from each other while we keep inventing more efficient ways to kill each other in large numbers. Pretty soon, we're gonna have young kids, straight outta high school, flying those drones from their living room, just like they're playin' a video game, except it's gonna be real, and the drone is gonna be in some third-world country on the other side of the world."

"You're not wrong, John."

"I know it. It's just the way of the world." He swallowed the last of his coffee, placed the mug on the table, and then sat back in his chair, assessing the young man sitting across from him. "Paul, I'm gonna ask you something, and I would deeply appreciate it if you would be honest with me."

"Of course."

"Why are you here?"

"I'm sorry?" Rylan replied, genuinely confused by the question. "What're you doing here?"

Rylan was silent, thinking about what to say, but then John continued.

"Lookahere, son, I don't fashion myself a particularly smart man, but I surely ain't a dummy neither. Now I've been sittin' here, enjoyin' our conversation, but also tryin' to figure out what your business is here in my house. I recognize I invited you in and even invited you to stay and wait out the storm a bit, but somethin' feels off. Don't get me wrong, you seem like a nice enough fella, but I've known many 'nice men' who were not nice men at all, and I just wanna know what your intentions are."

Rylan looked out the window. The storm wasn't showing any signs of clearing. He turned back to John, a man he had come to like and even admire in some ways. He weighed the potential risk of revealing a portion of the truth and decided to give it a shot.

"Okay, John. I'll be honest with you. I came here to ask you about Redemption Baptist Church."

The old man slumped back in his chair, and all emotion drained from his face. "I knew it. I had a feelin'."

"Look, I'm sorry I lied to you, but there's probably no chance you'd have talked to me if I'd been upfront about it."

"No, you're right. I'd have left you on the road out there."

"I just, I just have some questions about what happened..."

"I'm sure you do, but would ya' just hold up for a second, though?" He checked his watch, "It's about time for my pill, and this'll likely be a long conversation. Gimme a sec, huh?" He stood up and walked towards his bedroom.

"Of course! Of course!" Rylan replied, relieved John had taken the news so well.

Having expected much more friction, he now relaxed and sipped the last of his coffee while the old man retrieved his medication. Soon, he heard John's footsteps on the old hardwood, returning from within the bedroom. Rylan leaned forward to place the empty mug onto the coffee table and realized the footfalls had ceased, then he heard the unmistakable shuck-shuck sound of a pump-action shotgun chambering a shell.

"Don't you move." John's voice was cold as ice.

Rylan froze in place, his arm still outstretched, fingers touching the rim of the mug resting on the table. Keeping his body still, his eyes darted to the left to see John standing in the doorway to the bedroom with a black shotgun leveled right at him. His heartbeat spiked, but outwardly, he appeared composed. "John, John, slow down...."

"Stop talking. You don't speak unless I ask you a question. You hear me?" His words were emotionless and calm.

"Yes. Yes, I do."

"What are you? Some reporter?"

"No sir, I'm not a reporter."

"Then what? Someone's family send you?"

"No one sent me."

"Then why, in God's name, did you come here?"

"I just want to have a conversation with you."

"A conversation?" John spat out the words, disgusted at the thought. "Boy, your mama should've taught you not to stick your nose in business ain't yours. I have half-a-mind to shoot you dead in my living room and say it was self-defense, but I know the Lord would have something to say about that come judgment day, so I think it's best you leave before I change my mind."

"Alright, John." He slowly raised his hands, "No problem. I'm getting up now." He looked down as he stood, trying to seem submissive, but also checking to make sure the butt of his pistol wasn't bulging through his shirt.

"Right. Let's walk it nice and slow. Nothin' sudden. You're goin' back out the same way you came in." John directed.

Rylan began walking through the hallway, past the restroom, past the pictures of Charlene and John's vacations, then into the fluorescent light of the utility room. As they walked, John stayed two steps behind with the shotgun pointed at Rylan's back. Halting at the door to the garage, the younger man stooped and began putting on his shoes.

"And don't even think about comin' back around here again. As soon as you're gone, I'm callin' the Sheriff's department to report you for trespassin', and if you come back here, I'ma be completely justified in puttin' you in the ground."

Rylan's shoulders slumped as he pulled his other shoe on. It hadn't occurred to him that John would report him to the police, which would undoubtedly result in a description of him and his vehicle on record. He was grateful that John had pointed out this oversight, but simultaneously, he also wished John hadn't mentioned it because now Rylan was forced to act. Aware he had not prepared himself or his equipment to be ready to kill John that afternoon, simply thinking of all that must be done next was exhausting. He stood up and looked at John with genuine disappointment on his face.

"Sir, I owe you an apology. I can see now that I've made a series of bad decisions here, and I can promise you that, once I leave, I'll never be returning to your home."

"Oh, I know it. Just you don't forget it."

"I won't."

Rylan made mental notes of how John was holding the shotgun, how he was standing, and how far away, and then he turned around to face the door to the garage. He made a show of reaching out for the door handle, then stopped. He took a half-step backward and exaggerated patting each of the pockets of his jeans.

"Phone. Wallet. Keys? Crap!" He exclaimed, then exhaled and looked up at the ceiling to appear frustrated but remained facing the door. "Sir, I think I left the keys to my truck on your couch. Can I please go get them?"

"Dangit, boy!" John exclaimed.

In a flash, Rylan spun his body around, seized the shotgun from the side, and violently slammed his elbow into the old man's face. John's head snapped backward from the blow, and his grip released from the shotgun as he fell to the floor. Stunned, John looked up from the floor at the younger man, now standing over him with his own weapon aimed at him. Anger blazed in John's chest, and he started to get back on his feet, ready to fight.

"Nah nah, bubba. This isn't what you think it is." Rylan stepped forward, put his shoe on John's chest, and forced him back down. "If I gotta splatter your whole head onto the floor behind you, then that's what I'ma do, but either way, you're not getting back up."

Rylan could see in John's face that he registered his defeat as only temporary, and he had no plans to surrender.

"What do you want?" John growled.

"I told you before; I want a little conversation. I tried to be civilized about it too, but then you had to go make it awkward, so here we are."

"You want to talk?"

"I do. Yes, sir, but first, let's get comfy. I need you to roll over onto your chest."

John shot him a skeptical look before reluctantly doing as he was told.

"Good. Now, I want you to take both hands, slide them underneath your belly, and get a nice firm grip on your belt buckle."

Perplexed by what was happening, John figured he should just play along for now and wait for an opportunity to turn the tables.

"Good. You feel that buckle? I want you to describe it to me." Rylan prompted.

"Describe it?"

"Yeah, tell me how it feels on your fingertips." As he spoke, he quietly laid the shotgun on the floor, close, but slightly out of reach.

"It's cold and hard. The edges are...."

Rylan had stealthily straddled John's body while he talked, then, suddenly, he pounced. He flopped down onto the old man's back, forcing all the air from John's lungs and pinning his hands beneath him. With one hand, Rylan snatched John's hair and pulled his head back, then slipped the other arm around his neck, locking in a perfect rear-naked choke. Once John realized what had happened, he tried furiously to buck Rylan off his back until the lack of blood to the brain caused him to pass out.

14

— ・ —

OCTOBER 17, 2003, FRIDAY

ISKANDARIYAH, IRAQ

Nineteen-year-old Rylan sat in the backseat of a Humvee as it drove back toward his unit's operating base. After a twelve-hour guard shift, over-watching a vital stretch of highway, Rylan's platoon returned to FOB Iskandariyah, their wretched home away from home, at around 3:00 am. They quickly followed their familiar routine, downloading the ammo from the Humvees, accounting for all their equipment, and refueling the trucks. By 4:00 am, everyone was on their cots and ready to go to sleep, except for two.

While everyone else was preparing to bed down, Rylan, known as Private Beam to his fellow soldiers, and Specialist Valdez were preparing to set off on yet another guard shift, protecting a new batch of Iraqi Army recruits at a makeshift training compound adjacent to the US Army base.

About to begin their short march to the Iraqi Army training compound, Rylan convinced Sergeant Merlos to loan him his shotgun instead of bringing the cumbersome machine gun he usually carried. Valdez however, attempting the same weapon exchange with his team leader, was denied and stormed out of the tent with his dusty machine gun.

The Iraqi training compound was only a stone's throw away from where the American soldiers' tents were, but the two sites were separated by a ten-foot wall, with additional rows of fencing and concertina wire for good measure. This forced the soldiers to first walk a quarter mile in one direction, pass through the main gate, then walk along the other side of the fence, right back to the general location of where they'd started. The absurdity of the route only fueled their frustration at being picked for the assignment.

Once they arrived at the Iraqi compound, dusty and grumbling, their boots crunching the gravel underfoot, they squinted through the early morning darkness to spot the soldiers from the prior shift. They found them sitting on a low cinder block wall, struggling to stay awake. Upon meeting, the four soldiers quickly discussed the particulars of the guard duty before the outgoing shift happily departed. Valdez perched himself on the low wall where the other team had been, muttering as he settled in for the six-hour guard shift. Rylan sat next to him.

Before long, twenty Iraqi recruits in brand-new uniforms emerged from their barracks. They moved into the nearby administrative building while the two American soldiers sat outside, guarding the entrance, passing the time by sharing stories of their lives back home. Eventually, the cool air, which crept in nightly from the nearby Euphrates River, was chased away by the warmth of the coming sunrise and the sun finally peeked above the horizon; bold yellow, then orange, radiating into pinks and shades of purple in gentle gradation across the sky. Without a word exchanged between them, both men took a minute to appreciate the peacefulness.

Hours later, after the sun had ascended and grown in intensity, the Iraqis reemerged, sat in the shade of the building and began eating. The two Americans, in constant conversation since sunrise, pulled out their MREs to begin eating too.

Without warning, the calm was destroyed by an explosion that sounded like an enormous bang, more than a boom, as if God had clapped his massive hands directly above their heads. The two men instinctively ducked in unison, crouched, and reached for their weapons. They took cover behind the low cinder block wall on which they had been sitting, their weapons over the top, aimed at the Iraqis scrambling in the gravel for safety.

Hyper-alert, confused, and afraid, the two young soldiers were moving by muscle memory alone, struggling to determine where the explosion came from and what to do next. Valdez yelled at the Iraqis to get into the building. Not understanding English, they gaped at him dumbfounded and panicked until he started pointing towards the building, jabbing at the air; some understood and ran for the doorway, and the rest soon followed. The two American soldiers then looked at each other, searching each other's faces for answers.

Rylan began, "What the f...."

Another boom interrupted him, much closer than the first. The two men ducked again, closer to the ground, tighter to the wall, and braced for impact. None came, but it was now clear where the explosion originated. It was behind them, on the other side of the ten-foot wall; it came from the American base.

Over the wall, they could see two gray plumes of smoke rising into the clear blue sky. The first was much taller and further away, and the second plume was wider and much closer.

"Mortars," Valdez murmured to himself.

Rylan, staring at the billowing smoke, tried to process rough calculations of distance, then came to a heart-stopping determination.

"That's our tents." He turned to Valdez, wide-eyed and terror-stricken, pointing at the smoke. "That's our TENTS!"

Recognition washed across Valdez's face, bringing with it the paleness of shock. His mouth hung open and his machine gun nearly fell from his hands. Rylan, in a panic, darted one way, stopped, and then darted another, only to stop again, his body reacting before his mind had decided what to do.

"What do we do?" Valdez shouted at his partner.

Rylan had been momentarily stuck in a mental loop, unable to break free, then another mortar exploded, closer than the two previous. The men ducked again for cover as rocks and other debris rained down into the gravel near the wall, some hitting the fences, sending a dull ringing sound rippling along the barrier. The men got up and saw a third, closer plume rising above the wall. Rylan could see that his earlier calculations were incorrect. The first two mortar strikes were not near the tents, but the third was. The new smoke plume was as wide as the length of a Humvee.

"Get them in the building." Rylan pointed at the few Iraqis still hunkered outside, "I'm going."

He hopped up and rushed toward the main gate while Valdez sprinted in the opposite direction to round up the Iraqi Army recruits.

As Rylan ran, shotgun in hand, along the fence toward the main gate, he tried to shake the images in his mind; the tents in flames, soldiers trapped inside, screaming. He wanted to vomit but somehow held it down. Another mortar exploded in the same area as before. He recoiled but kept running. A few more strides and Rylan could see the gate guards on high alert, weapons aimed outward, ready to repel an attack.

"Friendly!" he howled through a dry mouth, hacked, then shouted again at the gate guards, "Friendly! Friendly! Friendly coming in!"

"We see you! We see you! Come in!" Two guards were yelling back at the same time, waving him in.

As he raced through the gate, a Sergeant yelled, "Go get those motherfuckers!"

Turning the corner, he saw five separate columns of smoke roiling into the sky and though his lungs burned with exertion, he quickened his pace. Despite his best efforts, two more mortars hit inside the base before he finally arrived at the tent city.

The road Rylan was on continued alongside the tent rows, at the top of an almost ten-foot embankment from where the tents had been erected. Rylan stopped where the tents began, accessing the carnage, trying to decide what to do. Directly to his left, five of the nearest tents were ablaze, with the rest obscured by the towering flames and thick black-grey smoke. To his right, a row of tan-painted Humvees was parked along the perimeter wall, and Rylan could see the faces of terrified soldiers peeking from behind the vehicles they used for cover.

Turning back to the widening inferno, he spotted two soldiers scrambling up the sandy embankment toward the road. One of the two, Specialist Munson, was wearing what was once a gray PT shirt and shorts, now covered in blood. The other soldier, unfamiliar to Rylan, was shirtless and blood-smeared, weakly clinging to his savior's shoulder. Rylan sprinted to help as Munson shoved the bloody soldier up to him.

"Help him!" Munson shouted then turned to run back toward the burning tents.

Rylan gawked for an awestruck moment at the young man willfully running toward certain death, before remembering the one bleeding in his arms. He pulled and dragged the barely conscious soldier the last few feet up the embankment and onto the road. Once on the pavement, the soldier nearly collapsed in exhaustion and fell heavily into Rylan's arms. The metallic smell of blood and smoke was suffocating, and Rylan craned his neck to find air.

Rylan threw the soldier's arm over his shoulder and tried to walk him to the line of armored vehicles, but after five steps, the soldier's body had gone almost completely limp, and the greasy combination of blood and sweat on the soldier's bare skin made grip impossible. He carefully lowered the man to the ground.

Rylan roared in the direction of the soldiers peeking from behind the trucks, "Help me!"

Three soldiers immediately sprang from their shelter to assist, just as another explosion pounded the earth, not far beyond the tents. They ducked instinctively as they ran, but never stopped. The four of them struggled to grip the man's body, now slick with a red slime, while carrying him to safety behind the trucks.

The bloody soldier's eyes rolled in their sockets as they laid him, face-up, on the hot pavement. He was barely conscious, his breathing was ragged and wheezy, and while a cacophony of voices cried out for a medic, Rylan finally saw the source of all the blood. The soldier had two separate inch-wide puncture wounds on the right side of his chest, one near the bottom of his ribs and the other high, below the collarbone.

Remembering his first-aid training, Rylan laid his hands flat onto the hole near the collarbone and pressed down, hoping to slow the bleeding. Beneath his weight, two fractured ribs gave way and, through his palms, he felt the jagged ends of the shattered bones grinding hard against each other. He retched and tried to close off the back of his throat.

Another soldier applied pressure to the other wound just as two medics arrived, nearly out of breath. The medics hastily dropped down on their knees, flipped open their aid bags, and shouldered Rylan out of the way to begin work on the wounded soldier. They swiftly assessed the frontal wounds before rolling their patient over to find the exit wounds in his back.

Rylan stared, in horror, at the dark red puddle spreading on the asphalt beneath the soldier. He hadn't even considered the exit wounds. His heart sank into his stomach, and vomit welled up in his throat again. It occurred to him that if the medics hadn't arrived, the man would have bled to death while he cluelessly pressed down on his chest.

First Sergeant Duran's booming voice saved Rylan from the whirlpool of his catastrophizing thoughts. Duran shouted at someone to get a Humvee started as another mortar hit somewhere beyond the tents. Everyone flinched, but no one stopped working. A flatbed Humvee parked next to them started up, blowing exhaust fumes in the face of the medics and their patient.

Rylan recognized that First Sergeant Duran was trying to move the wounded soldier to the CCP, the Casualty Collection Point, which, according to emergency plans, would be at the dining facility. He jumped up into the bed of the truck and started tossing off boxes of MREs, water cans, and empty ammo cans, trying to make space for the soldier. He had only begun before six soldiers, including the medics, lifted the patient onto the flatbed. Rylan helped drag him toward the front of the truck while four other men crowded into the back with the casualty. Rylan vaulted over the roof of the cab to get out of the way, then jumped off the truck's hood. First Sergeant Duran, standing at the rear of the vehicle, slapped the tailgate, yelling at the driver, "Go! Go! GO!"

As the Humvee sped off toward the CCP, Rylan was left standing in the middle of the road and could finally assess the destruction the fires had inflicted. When he had initially arrived, a light wind was blowing the smoke in the direction of the main gate, obscuring the rest of the tents, but he now had a different vantage. Of the roughly twenty-five tents, all gathered tightly together, at least a third were actively on fire. As the wind kept pushing the fire from one tent to the next, and the next, the realization that all the tents might eventually burn down, paralyzed Rylan. He stood alone on the road, stunned and indecisive, asking himself if he should run down to the tents, like Munson, and search for survivors, or seek shelter from the continuing bombardment.

"BEAM! The fuck are you doing?" A voice barked from behind Rylan, and he whipped around to find First Sergeant Duran standing behind the corner of a Humvee, "get your ass over here!"

The young soldier briefly considered defying the order, convinced he could help down by the tents. Another mortar exploded on base, just beyond the tents, and as Rylan ducked, Duran roared again.

"BEAM! Get the fuck over here!"

Rylan gave in and retreated to safety. Once behind the trucks, he saw a few faces he recognized, all scared and clinging to the backside of the vehicles for protection. The explosions had indeed been mortar impacts, and they kept coming, roughly thirty seconds apart, some closer, some further away.

For weeks, insurgents had unsuccessfully attempted to drop mortars inside the base. They would stop a pickup truck somewhere across the river, hastily set up the baseplate and tube, then launch a few mortars hoping to get lucky and leave before we could affect a counterattack. Although close a few times, until that day, the insurgents had never successfully hit inside the compound, but after stumbling upon the correct distance and angle for their mortar tube, they seized the opportunity to continue sending round after round, pulverizing the base.

At one point, a mass of gunfire and smaller explosions erupted. The initial thought was that the enemy had infiltrated the base, and a gunfight had broken out, but since it was over so quickly, the First Sergeant said it was probably an ammo storage shed cooking off. He decided it was time to move to the CCP and yelled down the line for everyone to come to his location.

As soldiers arrived, the First Sergeant took stock of the personnel present. There were seventeen soldiers in total; only three were wearing their full-battle-rattle, some only had a helmet or body armor, some wore just their PT uniforms, one didn't even have shoes, and some wore camouflage pants and a tan t-shirt. Only half of the group had weapons, the rest had abandoned them in their tents in their rush to safety.

Rylan noticed Sergeant Addis sitting on the ground, holding his head, looking disoriented. Rylan squatted down and put a hand on the young leader's shoulder.

"Sergeant, you okay?"

Addis slowly, carefully, let go of his head, as if he thought it might tip over. He raised his head only a few inches, and appeared confused, as though he'd heard a distant voice, but was unsure if he had heard anything at all. His face was pale, slack, and fatigued like he hadn't slept in days. Rylan repeated the question, and Addis, reacting to the sound, blinked with heavy eyelids. Hunching down a little lower to see Addis' eyes, Rylan found his pupils dilated.

"Sergeant, did you hit your head?"

"Hmmm?" He moaned.

"Did you hit your head, Sergeant? Are you okay?"

"I-uhno." He mumbled.

Rylan scanned for a medic among the soldiers along the wall, then remembered they all had gotten into the back of a Humvee earlier.

"Shit." He grumbled. Looking back at Addis, "Sergeant, we have to move you to the CCP. You need to see the medics. Can you walk?"

"Yuh," Addis whispered.

"You sure? We can get a couple guys to carry you."

"Nuh," he shook his head weakly.

Rylan hunched over again to get right in front of Addis' face.

"Sergeant, look at me. Look me in my eyes."

Addis' wandering gaze eventually found Rylan's eyes in a roundabout way, but even when he was able to make eye contact, he couldn't quite lock on. Rylan decided the best he could do at that moment was reassure and encourage the young leader.

"You're going to be okay. Okay? We're gonna get you to the medics. You're going to be okay. Here, lemme help you up."

Just then, the First Sergeant started barking in his graveled baritone, "Look here, people, we're going to follow the wall and make our way around to the CCP. Stay with the group. No detours. Jackson! Beam! You two take point. Sprague, get over here and help Sergeant Addis. Sergeant Harrison, you and McGill take trail; make sure no one falls behind. Everybody got it? Good. Let's move out."

The last of the mortars fell as the group worked their way toward the dining facility, and though the distance was not far, the time it took to travel seemed long. Everyone was in a state of shock and moved as if floating through a dream. When they finally arrived at the dining facility, the group carried Sergeant Addis, who had lost consciousness, to the medics, and some of the others, with minor injuries, stayed to get checked out. Everyone else dispersed to locate their people among the huddled masses.

The air in the building was hot and thick with the smell of dust, body odor, and smoke. There were hundreds of dazed soldiers dressed in the same hodge-podge way as the group from behind the Humvees. The soldiers had coalesced into large groups centered around their company guidons, and individual leaders were searching the crowds for missing members of their teams, stragglers, and other disoriented soldiers who had just wandered in.

With their adrenaline surge starting to wane, uncertainty began to spread like a virus. Many soldiers had trouble accepting the reality of their situation, that some of their fellow soldiers had died, others were badly wounded, and they were now homeless with nothing but the clothes on their backs and the items carried in their hands. Everything else was now gone. The photographs and hand-written letters from loved ones, mementos from their lives before they had come to this god-forsaken country; it was all ashes now. Many soldiers were downtrodden, others paralyzed with fear and self-doubt, some merely angry while others were nearly rabid with rage.

Rylan found his platoon and was relieved to discover that everyone had miraculously survived, including Specialist Munson, whose shirt was smeared with blood and ash, and Valdez, who had found his way back from the Iraqi compound. Everyone stood around sharing their experience of the attack, then vehemently expressed their hunger for revenge.

Minutes later, two Blackhawk helicopters arrived to evacuate the wounded. They briefly landed in an open area near the hangar, kicking up a massive cloud of dust, then ascended back into the sky as soon as the casualties were aboard. Many soldiers watched the choppers disappear into the horizon, sending prayers in their wake.

After a while, leaders sent small groups to fetch water and MREs, and although the soldiers had no appetite, they forced themselves to eat, if only to have enough energy to fight. They planned defensive tactics in case the insurgents decided to mount a ground attack, though, thankfully, no such attack came. Confined to the hangar area and barred from exploring the smoldering ashes of their tents, the displaced soldiers, all still clamoring for vengeance, sat around restlessly for hours with nothing to do.

News of the mortar attack on FOB Iskandariyah had spread quickly, and in response, the commanders in charge of the two closest Army bases ordered all their troops to donate one full uniform each, including boots, to help refit the survivors. Eventually, four Humvees arrived. They parked outside the hangar while soldiers with unfamiliar faces got out, toting trash bags full of uniform items into the building. The newly destitute soldiers eagerly picked through the bags to find their sizes, and in the end, each soldier received at least one combat uniform that fit, or was close enough.

Sometime after lunch, Rylan fell asleep on the sandy concrete and woke up in the late evening to find almost everyone else asleep. The sun was down, and the air was cooler, but the smell of body odor and bad breath had lingered in the enclosed space, and at least ten different snoring soldiers had combined to form the world's most obnoxious chorus. Surveying the dimly lit hangar, Rylan found First Sergeant Duran standing outside, just beyond an open doorway, smoking a cigarette with the moonlight shining on him like a spotlight. Rylan stood up, and wending his way around the sleeping troops, approached Duran, who motioned for the young soldier to come closer.

"Beam, how you holding up?"

Rylan blew out air and simply shook his head.

"Yeah. Me too." Duran took a hard pull from his cigarette, then continued, "You did great work out here today."

"Just doing my job, First Sergeant."

Duran turned his gaze up to the moon to ponder the young man's words. "You know, Beam, it looks like Specialist Gilmore is going to make it."

"Specialist Gilmore?"

"The guy you were dragging across the road this morning."

"Oh! Yeah? That's great!" Rylan was surprised and delighted by the news. "How did, or how is Sergeant Addis doing?"

Duran's face bent in anguish, and Rylan knew the answer before the words came.

"Didn't make it. Died on the chopper. Brain bleed." The First Sergeant angrily crushed the cigarette in his hand.

Rylan felt dazed and woozy. Everything suddenly seemed surreal. He tried desperately to anchor himself, grabbing the door frame for support. Rylan had never said more than two words to Sergeant Addis, who was from a different platoon, but that morning, he'd been standing right in front of the man while he was dying, telling him that he would be okay. Rylan wanted to vomit. He replayed the scene in his mind, questioning everything. What did he miss? Should he have known? How could he have known?

"You alright?" Duran asked, noticing Rylan's unsteadiness.

"Yeah. I'm good." He reassured Duran, although the ground hadn't stopped moving yet.

"You're doing a lot better than I am, then. Truth be told, I'd cut off this pinky finger for a glass of whiskey right now."

Rylan didn't drink alcohol, but at that moment, he agreed. He would've tried anything to help cut through the grief and guilt.

Duran spit on the ground and then took another drag of smoke.

"Those bastards really hit us hard. We lost four men today, including Addis. Another ten casualties had to be airlifted, and of those, three are still in critical condition."

"Who were the other three?"

"Sergeant Ragan and Private Pinkston from first platoon, and Specialist Cooper from second."

Rylan didn't recognize the soldiers' names. He searched through his memory but came up empty, then felt ashamed for not knowing them. The two men stood in silence for a while. Duran pulled the pack of cigarettes from his cargo pocket, looked longingly at the four remaining, then decided to save them for later.

Rylan tried to shift the conversation. "First Sergeant, a lot of the guys wanna know when we're going back across the river."

"To find the motherfuckers that did this? Well, you can bet your ass we're going over that bridge as soon as we get refit. Battalion already informed the commander that we'll have Chinooks inbound in the next two hours to drop pallets of body armor, weapons, and ammunition. We should be combat effective again by sunrise."

"Damn. That's crazy." Rylan was amazed at how quickly they could get resupplied.

"It's like I keep telling you guys; no matter what happens, 'the Army goes rolling along'."

First Sergeant Duran frequently quoted the Army song to emphasize the resiliency of the force, a habit which often elicited eye rolls from the troops, but at that moment, Rylan understood his meaning. It made him feel proud to be part of something enduring, but at the same time, it also made him feel insignificant. Sergeant Addis had died, three others too, and everything had burned down, but none of it mattered; the military could just drop a pallet of gear and get the rest of the boys back in the fight.

Duran checked his watch. "I've gotta go send up another report to Battalion. You gonna come help download the pallets when they arrive?"

"Of course, First Sergeant." He responded as if he had a choice.

Duran patted Rylan on the shoulder as he walked past him, then disappeared back into the hangar.

Rylan stayed outside for a while longer. The cool breeze from the river was heaven compared to the humid musk within the hangar, but more importantly, he needed some time alone. He was racked with guilt and regret, and struggled to wrap his head around the fact that Sergeant Addis was dead.

It had been a little over two months since his unit deployed to Iraq, and only one other soldier had died in that time despite numerous roadside bomb attempts by the insurgency. The repetitive nature of the daily patrols and the infrequency of enemy encounters had begun to wear down the soldiers' vigilance. When attacks did come, the enemy's low success rate gave the soldiers a sense of superiority over their faceless foes, and most were left with little respect for the enemy threat, but the mortar attack on FOB Iskandariyah had changed everything.

From where Rylan stood, his back to the hangar with his fellow soldiers-turned-refugees sleeping inside, he gazed across the Euphrates River at the palm groves on the far bank. He remembered a conversation with his mom the week before he boarded a C-17 transport headed to the Middle East. He told her he was conflicted about one of the Bible's commandments, specifically the verse stating, "Thou shall not kill". He had struggled to reconcile the fact that he might have to take someone's life to preserve his own but would also be judged and punished for it in the afterlife. She told him that the Bible's translation from the original Hebrew scripture into various languages and countless versions over the millennia had changed the interpretation of the message, and that the earliest translations were closer to "Thou shalt not commit murder". She asked if he intended to murder Iraqi people, which he wholeheartedly denied. He stated the American mission was to capture Saddam Hussein and to help stand up the new Iraqi government, and technically, they didn't really have to kill anyone unless attacked first.

Recalling that conversation with his mom had stoked an ember of anger in Rylan as he glared intensely across the river, searching for any sign of movement. The nearly full moon had cast a soft grey light on the forest of palm trees lining the far riverbank, the same trees the enemy had used for concealment that morning while they launched mortars into his base. He could feel fresh rage begin to burn in his chest, and he wanted to use it to set fire to the forest and everyone in it. He had spent two months in an actual war zone and hadn't killed anyone yet, but for the first time in his life, he wanted to.

15

— · —

APRIL 3, 2017, MONDAY

CALDWELL, IDAHO

Rylan quickly pulled the last zip-tie tight then plopped himself down a few feet away, his soaked clothes slapping against the linoleum as he landed. He had rushed to set John's restraints before the old man woke up, having correctly assumed that unconsciousness from a blood choke around the neck, wouldn't last as long as blunt force trauma to the base of the skull. So, as soon as John was out, Rylan stripped his victim down to his underwear, ran out into the rain to grab the PVC poles and zip-ties from the trunk, then barely managed to get the old man tied down before he regained consciousness.

He sat with his back against a storage rack, chest heaving, breathing heavily through his mouth while rainwater and sweat dripped down his face. He used his hand to squeegee the water off, then realized that, in his mad dash to retrieve the supplies from the truck, he had forgotten to grab the brown overnight bag with the hammer and duct tape inside. Now, without a way to silence his captive, he braced himself for a verbal onslaught.

John slowly opened his eyes and went through the same progression as Edward and Toni; confusion, then realization, followed
by panic and anger. The overhead fluorescent lights provided a
much clearer view of his victim compared to the little camping
lantern, and Rylan could see all the subtle expressions in detail.
John had jerked at the restraints in the same way as the other two,
but surprisingly, he never became visibly frightened, and when he
scanned the room and found Rylan sitting on the floor, he just
stopped.

The two men stared at each other for a while, a prisoner facing
his captor for the first time; John's glare trying to silently communicate his defiance while Rylan's conveyed his confident indifference. Once John realized that intimidation tactics wouldn't help
his situation, he decided to talk and wait for an opportunity.

"What're we doing here, Paul? What is this?" He calmly asked,
tugging at his wrist-ties for emphasis.

"I don't want to lie to you anymore, John. So, first off, my name
is not Paul, but we can stick with it for now, and as far as 'all this
'...'" he gestured his hand in John's direction, "If you'll just give me
one minute, I'll explain. I've got to run back out to the truck first,
okay?"

"Yeah, sure, I'll just wait here," John answered sarcastically.

Rylan smiled as he rose to his feet, "That's funny. I'll be right
back."

Rylan exited through the garage out into the raging storm, retrieved what he considered his 'hammer bag', then sprinted back
into the house. Stepping back into the utility room, it was obvious
that someone else had also been busy. The PVC frame upon which
John was fastened had shifted noticeably, and although the old

man was now lying motionless, he was panting, and beads of sweat had bubbled up on his forehead.

"Looks like we both need a minute to catch our breath, huh?" Rylan joked, then slogged back over to the spot he had been sitting previously and plopped back down again, setting the leather bag beside him.

"This is a sturdy thing you got here," John remarked about the frame.

"Yeah, so far, it seems to get the job done."

"What's that mean?"

"What?"

"What'd you mean, 'so far'? You done this before?"

Rylan shook his head in amazement, "Damn, you're sharp."

"Is that a yes?"

"We can talk about that later, John. I want to talk about you first, if you don't mind."

"You haven't answered my question, though."

"Which one?"

"What is all of this?" He tugged again at his wrist restraints.

"Ahhh, right." Rylan sucked in air through his teeth and grimaced, finding himself surprisingly reluctant to voice the true nature of his business. He contemplated how to break the news, then another thunderclap shook the house, and he drew inspiration from the suddenness.

"I've come here to kill you, John."

The older man didn't respond. He didn't move, not even a twitch. He studied Rylan's face carefully as though he was trying to understand what he was seeing. After a while, Rylan spoke again.

"You, uh, you got anything you want to say?"

"I've been waitin' for you nearly my whole life. It's been a long time, but I just knew, someday, you'd come for me."

Bewildered and speechless, Rylan could only stare back, fascinated by the old man.

John continued, "I always wondered what you'd look like when you finally came. I wondered if I'd be able to recognize you, and I had myself convinced that I could too. I thought that maybe if I could see you comin', then maybe I'd be able to put up a fight. Looks like I was wrong, and now, I'm here... all splayed out."

Rylan sensed John wasn't actually addressing him, but rather some spiritual entity, Death perhaps, or maybe God, and he was unsure of how to reply. His mind rapidly shuffled through many responses before he decided to lean into John's religion.

"John, the end is near, but we have a long way to go before we get there. This would be the right time to confess your sins. Tell me about Redemption Baptist Church."

John let out a long sigh, "What do you want to know?"

"I want to know why."

"Why?" John turned his head to look at the ceiling. "It's been almost fifty years now, Paul. I've asked myself that same question every single day, and I'm ashamed to say it, but...." Tears started to flow down the deep wrinkles at the corners of his eyes. "I think I did it because... I hoped it would make people care that I was alive."

"Help me understand that, John."

"Up until that day, I was worthless."

John stopped cold, those three words had exposed something he had long ago shoved into a distant corner of his mind and tried hard to forget, but like startled moths suddenly taking flight, the uncovered memories now fluttered aimlessly through his brain.

He was momentarily spellbound and paralyzed by the overwhelming discord in his mind until everything slowly settled, and he could think clearly again.

"No one ever cared about me. The day I was born, the doc had to cut me out Mama's belly, and my old man blamed me for it; hated me for scarring his wife. To him, she was damaged, and he wouldn't look at her no more. Instead, he had girlfriends. Mama knew. He lied to her about it, but she always knew. 'Cuz of that, she drank a lot, slept a lot, and when she was awake, she yelled a lot, and she beat me, but I don't rightly blame her, 'cuz my old man was doin' the same to her. I spent most of my childhood up in my room, hidin' from the both of them. When I wasn't, I was somehow always in their way, and they never missed a chance to let me know. See, I had some immune system disorder as a young child, so I was always sick and weak, and had to go to the doc regularly, which of course, only made my folks hate me even more. Then at school, I was that sickly and uncoordinated kid who got beat on every day. I was tall and skinny, so the kids called me Daddy Long Legs, and they would sneak up on me from behind and punch me, or kick me, and yell, 'smash the bug!'"

John's neck twitched, and his head moved with it, dodging a phantom blow from his past. He shut his eyes for a moment, trying to hold his emotions in check, then he began again.

"I remember once when I was in third grade, I think, I went and told the teacher what they were doing to me, the teacher called Mama, and she came down and talked to the principal, but when I got home, she whupped me for embarrassing her. After that, I never said another word about it. I just took my lumps from the other kids instead. I had no friends. I was like a magnet for taking beatings, so no one wanted to be around me. The only time I really got to play with other kids was at the weekly Klan meetings. While our fathers were inside ranting and raving about how they were getting cheated by the coloreds, we were outside playing cowboys and Indians, and then, of course, when we got older, we turned to playin' cards or throwin' dice."

A hint of a smile curled the corner of John's lips as he recalled a few fond memories from his youth, but then the smile quickly disappeared as John remembered something else.

"One night, at one of the meetings, I was sixteen by then, my old man pulled me into a room with two other boys and their fathers. Randy's dad, one of the high-ranking members, was there, and he talked to us; said they'd pulled us boys together for an important mission. He told us the whole town was counting on us to right a wrong, and asked if we could do a hard thing to keep our mothers and sisters safe from villains. Before even knowing what they were asking, we all swore we would; then Randy's dad told us a story about two black men who had attacked a white woman a week ago, out near Roanoke. The men had run off and were hiding in a black church on the outskirts of town. We were told that because of the laws, the cops couldn't go inside a church to arrest them, so they needed us to help flush 'em out. Of course, the three of us boys were outraged and willing to do damn-near anything. The plan was, the next morning, during Sunday service, Josiah and Randy would use gasoline to set fire to the front and back doors, and I would stand on one side of the building with a shotgun in case anyone tried to come out through the windows on my side, then, on the other side, the cops would be in the woods, waiting to spring the trap when everyone came out those side doors.

"Hold up, John; I don't mean to interrupt, but... during Sunday service with all those people trapped inside? That didn't raise any red flags?"

"No. You've gotta understand, to three teenage boys, this was exciting; helping the cops to set a trap to catch bad guys? And I got to hold the shotgun, too? I could hardly see past that to even begin questioning the legitimacy of the thing. Besides, our parents already coordinated with the cops and had everything planned out. What was there to question?"

"Everything. The plan doesn't even make sense."

"That's because you're looking at it with the benefit of hindsight and life experience. We were nothing but children at the time. The adults, our parents, told us they trusted us to do this one thing. You're crazy if you think we'd have voiced reservations, even if we had second thoughts. My father; for the first time in my life, actually looked at me with something less than anger, and to me, it was like I might finally be able to do something right in his eyes."

"That still doesn't explain how you didn't know people would get hurt, John."

"Look, the plan was to force everyone from inside the church out through the side exit doors where the cops would round everyone up. In our minds, no one should've gotten hurt, but truth be told, there wasn't a whole lot of time for deep thought on the matter. We left that meeting around eleven at night and were supposed to be at the church at eight-thirty the next morning. That might seem like a lot of time, but I promise you it ain't."

"You make it sound like you were just following orders, but I'm not buying it. You guys set fire to a building full of people. You had to know."

"Know what?"

"That what you were doing was wrong."

"See that-there's the point. It wasn't wrong. Not to us. The way it was explained to us, we were doing the right thing."

Rylan's hands shot up to the top of his head in sudden revelation, "Wow." He dragged his hands down his still-damp face, then let them drop to his lap. "I'm just... dumbfounded, I guess. How could a parent, let alone three of them, trick their own kids into doing something like that?"

"That's a tougher question than you think. Morally, there's no way to defend what they did, it's reprehensible, but looking at it in a tactical, practical way, then it makes perfect sense."

Rylan scowled, but John cut him off before he could say anything.

"Think about it. There ain't no court that would've convicted three kids, especially three white kids, and sent them to prison. Hell, you see how easily I got off, and three people died by my hand!"

"Right! Tell me about that... wait, no, before we get there, tell me what happened at the church first."

John shifted his body again, indicating his discomfort with exploring the memory of the actual event. "How much do you already know?"

"Just what I found online but pretend like I don't know anything."

John let out a heavy breath before beginning. "Me and the other boys got dropped off at my Uncle Joe's bakery a little after eight o'clock. The bakery was right around the corner from the church, and to this day, I can't eat sourdough on account of the smell in there that morning. My old man put his shotgun in my hands, stared at me, and said, 'We're counting on you, boy. Don't muck this up.' Then he and the other boys' fathers, got back in the truck and drove off, leaving us to do the work. We were so hopped up and ready to go, we ran straight to the church and got straight to it. I remember coming around that corner, we could hear the voices of the folks inside singing, 'Wade in the Water'. You know that hymn? It's usually a somber song, but the way they sang it that day, I swear they must've been dancing in the aisles."

John retreated into his memories for a moment, and Rylan watched the old man's face twitching. John eventually caught himself and returned to his story.

"So we got there, and Randy ran to the rear while Josiah started dousing the front entrance with gasoline. I stood guard on the north side of the building, watching the windows. I couldn't see inside the windows due to the angle, with the church being raised up 'cause of the floods and all. Josiah struck his match first, and straight away, I could see the orange flickers peeking around the corner and that oily smoke coming up on the wind. He came stumbling backward into my view, landed on his rump, then turned tail and ran back toward the bakery; then, not five seconds later, Randy lit up the backside and hightailed it down the street. There were a few seconds I stood there completely alone, two opposite ends of that church on fire, the folk inside still singing that chorus like a chant, clapping and stomping, the burning wood outside crackling and snapping... I tell you now; I've had whole nightmares where I'm stuck in those three seconds for what seems like all time. You know, if I feared anything in my lifetime, it's been the thought of Saint Peter turning me away at the gates and sending me back to that moment for all eternity."

The old man stopped, swallowed hard, and glanced sideways at Rylan. It was only for an instant, but for the first time, Rylan had seen real fear in the old man's face. John cleared his throat.

"Could I have some water, Paul? I can't remember the last time I've talked this much."

"Yes! Gosh, yes."

Rylan, who had been mesmerized by the old man's tale, popped up to his feet, freed a bottle of water from the stacked cases against the wall, and brought it back to John. He knelt down and carefully tipped the bottle's rim to the man's lips so he could drink.

"John, I want you to know I appreciate you being so candid about all this. I can tell it's not easy for you."

"No, it's not. These things happened over fifty years ago, but I've never spoken of it to anyone. I've tried to pretend it never happened, but my dreams always remind me. Those nightmares where I'm back in Nam are scary, gory, violent things, but these ones... they're a different kind of scary. I don't know how to explain it." John paused for a second, took another drink of water as Rylan tipped the bottle, then asked, "You know how to swim?

"Me? Yeah, I can swim." Rylan answered as he returned to sit in the shallow puddle he had created on the floor.

"Can you tread water?"

"Of course."

"Alright, imagine you're in a pool alone, and you're treading water. There comes a point when you start getting tired, and you can feel the lactic acid start burning in your arms and legs. Your mind sets off a little alarm, and you start looking for the edge of the pool because, you know, if you don't reach the edge before your muscles give out, you're going under. Drowning is terrifying to think about, but it's that threat of drowning that ultimately motivates you to move, get to the edge, and save yourself. But in my dreams where I'm standing outside the church, it feels like I'm in the pool, stuck in that moment when my muscles start burning, and I start looking for the edge, but there's nothing there. The edge is gone. There's nowhere I can go for salvation. I can only keep treading water in the same spot while my muscles burn."

Rylan shuddered. "That sounds awful."

"It is."

Rylan took a sip from the same water bottle and then set it down.

"You know, John, since Iraq, I never remember my dreams."

John's face showed confusion, "You don't remember them when you wake up?"

"Nope."

"Never?"

"Not since." Rylan shrugged. "I know I do have dreams, though. My wife used to say I talked in my sleep when I came back from Iraq. She said I hit her a few times while asleep, too, fighting with someone in my nightmares. Fortunately, I didn't seriously hurt her, but still... it's crazy. I dunno how to explain it; I just never remember my dreams."

"Is that some kind of a mental block?"

"That's what my old therapist said."

"It must be nice."

"After listening to your stories, I'm starting to see it as a blessing. Maybe that's what has kept me sane all these years."

John looked at Rylan in all seriousness and pulled hard at the zip ties around his wrists.

"This doesn't bode well for your claim to sanity, Paul."

Rylan laughed and smiled in embarrassment, "You make a good point. Alright, alright, that's enough about me. Let's get back to your story."

"My story... where was I?"

"Um, we were talking about dreams, and uh, before that, you were... you were stuck...."

"At the church," John said solemnly.

"Right! The church."

John laid his head back down again and stared at the ceiling as he spoke.

"I was standing beside that church, the front and the back were on fire, and the congregation was still inside singing. Someone, a woman, screamed, and the singing stopped. I heard the commotion start; more women screaming, men yelling, shuffling, and stomping, pews making a scraping sound on the hardwood as they were shoved aside. I heard someone yell, 'The side doors! Get out the side doors!' I was standing there, thinking everything was going perfectly, then a bible crashed through the window and landed not a foot away from my feet. It startled me, and when I looked back up to the window, there was two black men trying to clear the glass shards from the frame, getting ready to climb out. Now, the plan was, if someone was trying to come out through the windows on my side, I was to shoot over their heads to scare them back the other way. The problem was, I had only ever shot a rifle before that day. So, I pulled that shotgun up to my shoulder the same way I would've Grandpa's old bolt action, drew a bead on the window frame right above their heads, and right as I was squeezing the trigger, another boy popped his head into the frame."

John's voice trembled at the end. He reflexively held his breath, attempting to contain the coming surge of emotion for as long as he could, but as tears trickled down his temples, a desperate gasp for air was his undoing. He crumbled like a dam buckling under the weight of a mighty river. Crying quickly turned to sobbing as his body convulsed with each successive gasp.

For Rylan, witnessing the tough old man break down so completely was heart-wrenching. He turned his eyes to the floor out of decency and respect, and soon, overcome with pathos, his own tears started to fall. He sat quietly, unmoving, as John cried himself out.

Eventually, John glanced sideways at Rylan, ashamed of himself. "I'm sorry. I don't...."

"You don't need to apologize to me, John. I understand."

"Thank you. Just give me a minute; I'll finish the story."

"No, it's fine. Take your time."

John closed his eyes and took a series of deep breaths, which started shakily but progressively got smoother as he regained his composure.

"I pulled the trigger." The words caused his lower lip to shiver, but John fought to keep going. "I pulled the trigger, and the recoil knocked me onto my backside. I was surprised by it, but I quickly recovered and looked back up to the window, expecting to see the men still there, but it was empty. More screaming started inside the church, and a man's voice shouted, 'GET AWAY FROM THE WINDOWS!' There was splintered wood all around the window frame, and blood dripped down the bottom-right side, where one of the men stood a moment before. It took a second before I understood what I was seeing, but then it dawned on me that the shotgun had been loaded with buckshot. Right then, another voice yelled out, 'They shot Ray-Ray, Roose, and Willy.' Now, I can't tell you if my body went cold, or hot, or both at the same time, but I do know that my hands gave out, and I dropped the shotgun right there at my feet. All the sound in the world felt like it got turned off, and I dropped to my knees, and my bladder let go. I don't know how long I was like that while the church was eaten up by the fire, but the first sound I heard was someone hollerin', 'Hey you!' That snapped me out of it, and I snatched up my Papa's shotgun and ran like the devil was chasing me."

John stopped, but Rylan could tell he wasn't done. He waited patiently, and soon, John continued.

"It wasn't until later that night that I found out one of the men, Raymond Calhoun, and the teenage boy, William Bradford, had been killed instantly, shot in the head. The other man, Roosevelt Bradford, the boy's father and a deacon at the church, had taken buckshot through his eye and into his brain. He ended up in a coma for two weeks before the Lord took him."

John's lip quivered again, and he pinched them both tightly shut. Rylan sat quietly, wanting to say something comforting, but in his head, everything sounded patronizing. John sighed, letting out an almost imperceptible whimper, then spoke again.

"According to the plan, we were supposed to meet up at the bowling alley on Lee Street, four blocks over. When I got there, the building was empty except for Josiah and Randy. Since it was Sunday, everyone else was at church on the other side of town, making sure they had a rock-solid alibi. Mr. O'Leary, who ran the bowling alley, had left the front door unlocked and had set six cold bottles of Coca-Cola out on the counter for us. Randy and Josiah were in there jumpin' around and slappin' each other on the back, and they wanted me to join in, but I couldn't bring myself to tell them what I'd done, so I said I needed to run home to grab something. I mostly needed to change my britches before my old man found out about my little accident. When I got home, I sat in the bathtub and cried. I hadn't ever shot anyone before, and it wasn't as though I'd been trying in the first place. I was so scared; scared of going to prison, sure, but I was even more scared of my old man. I thought he was gonna kill me."

"What about your mom?"

"I could've been dead, and my Mama would've rather not be bothered about it."

"Damn."

"Yeah, well, that's just who she was back then. My old man wasn't much better, but a young boy needs validation from his father, so I never stopped trying with him. I went back to the bowling alley before church let out, and waited with the other boys until everyone arrived, and when they did, it was like we had won a race. They threw a party right there, clapping, toasting us, and congratulating each other. My old man actually hugged me and told me he was proud of me. I couldn't say anything. It didn't feel real. None of it."

"Did they know you had killed two people?"

"They sure did. They had heard all about it by the time church let out, but they weren't angry; they were downright jubilant about it. They acted like we were heroes. I couldn't understand it."

"When did they arrest you?"

"Arrest me? That never happened."

"What?"

"Two constables eventually did come to the bowling alley. They cracked a few beers, laughed with the rest of the crowd, then left. They were Klan too. Everybody was. Heck, you know who else was at that party? The judge that ended up presiding over my case. I'm telling you, everyone in the whole dang town was either Klan or related."

"That's crazy."

"That was common in the South in the late sixties."

"So if they didn't arrest you, how did you get caught?"

"Someone spotted me at that church with a shotgun in my hands. You probably know about the protests that came afterward. Hundreds of blacks showed up from all over the state. The police tried beating them with batons to quell the uprising, but that only made it worse. More came, then the media took interest, and the mayor ultimately had to make a public statement that I had been arrested, but I only spent two hours at the station before they sent me back home. The trial was a joke. At night, my attorney, the sheriff, and my old man would have strategy sessions with the judge in his office. The entire defense was the judge's idea!"

"Are you serious?"

"Dead serious. We were in his office the night before the trial, and he told me to tell the jury, an all-white jury by the way, that I was bringing the shotgun home from my Uncle Joe's bakery, but on the way, I smelled smoke and went to see where it was coming from, then saw the church on fire, people screaming, and some guys who appeared to be fleeing the scene. I brought the shotgun up to scare them, but it went off in my hands."

"They bought that shit?"

"All-white jury, a white child on the stand, crying? You already know how it went."

"That makes me nauseous."

John nodded, "It should."

Silence fell over the two men as Rylan thought deeply about John's story. Seconds turned to minutes, and John finally broke the silence.

"Sounds like the storm blew over."

Rylan grunted his acknowledgment, noting that he hadn't heard the thunder in a while, "Sounds like it."

"I reckon you'll be heading out soon then, huh?"

Rylan looked at John. "Soon, but not quite yet."

"Still got business to attend to?"

"Yes, I do."

"Right. Well, first, can you answer my question from earlier?"

"I thought I already did."

"No, if you recall, I remarked about the sturdiness of this pipe frame you got me tied down to, and you said something about how it had been working 'so far'. What did you mean by that? Have you done this kind of thing before?"

Rylan scrunched his face in hesitation before admitting, "Yes, I have."

"You have?" John was shocked by the blunt confession.

"Yes."

"Well, how many?"

"Before you? Two."

"Two?" John exclaimed, "What, what are you?"

Rylan frowned modestly, "I'm nobody."

"You some kind of serial killer?"

Rylan considered the thought for a moment, "Probably. Technically." He shrugged.

"Why me then?"

"Because of what you represent."

"What do I represent?"

"Racism. The systematic suppression and persecution of a large group of people over something as trivial as the color of their skin."

John opened his mouth to protest, then caught himself and shifted course. "I am not a racist." He said sheepishly.

"You know what, when I drove here, I had a completely different opinion of you than what I have now. You might not be a racist. I mean, you might very well be, but I don't believe you are. All that's irrelevant, though; I'm not here to judge you. Like I said before, I chose you for what you represent."

"You're saying," He paused to choose his words, "It doesn't matter if you think I'm culpable, or even penitent; I'm to be made an example?"

"Yes."

John huffed, "I don't understand you at all." He was visibly agitated, squirming frequently, and his voice was getting sharper. "Why did you kill the other two?" He demanded.

Rylan noticed the fresh boldness in John's voice. He stopped and appraised John through narrowed eyes, measuring just how long a leash he should allow. He chose to ignore it for the moment.

"The first one was a child molester. Four children, well, at least that's what he was charged with. Apparently, there were more, but their parents refused to participate in the investigation. The second was a woman who killed her daughter, then lied, trying to cover it up."

"So, what is, what are you doing? Killing bad people?"

"I'm trying to, but...." Rylan struggled to articulate his thoughts, "It's not just the killing, though; there's more to it than that. It's more about sending a message."

"What message? Don't do bad things, or some lunatic is gonna come kill you?"

Rylan smirked, "In a way."

"Kid, you've completely slipped out of gear."

"What does that mean?"

"You're crazy! Certifiable. You really think anyone will even notice you? Killing me might make page four; page three of the newspaper, at best. No one will get your message because no one cares."

"Oh, I agree with you one hundred percent. The message has to be loud enough for people to hear." Rylan opened his bag and pulled out the hammer. "That's why I have this."

For only the second time, Rylan saw real fear on John's face.

"W-What is, what's that for?" John stuttered.

"This is how I'm going to get peoples' attention. I'm going to take this hammer, and I'm going to break two bones in each of your legs, two in each arm, your collar bone, and your pelvis.

John lay motionless, except for his eyelids which blinked irregularly.

Rylan watched John's peculiar twitch with fascination and mild concern. "You rebooting your system over there, John?"

"What kind of sick fuck are you?" John muttered.

"Whoa! That's the first time I've heard you cuss."

"You get off on hurting people like that?" John demanded.

"No! No, no, no. I don't enjoy this at all. I'm not doing this because it gets me off. I'm doing it because it's the right thing to do." Rylan defiantly retorted.

"You believe that?" John's words were heavy with disgust.

"Of course, I do."

"Of course, you do," John commented sarcastically.

"What's that supposed to mean?"

"You think you're on some righteous crusade, but you're not. You take pleasure in killing just like any other serial killer. You're not special. You're the exact same shit, from the exact same butt-hole as Dennis Rader, Dahmer, Gacy, and Berkowitz."

Rylan recoiled like a child being reprimanded by an imposing adult. "I'm not."

"You are, and I think you know it, too."

"No. No, I don't think..."

"Spare me. Spare me, Paul, whatever your name is. It doesn't matter to me. You're obviously going to do whatever you're going to do, but don't sit there lying to yourself about it. You're a serial killer. That's who you are."

Rylan's stared down at the linoleum near his feet. "I don't enjoy doing this, John."

"Keep telling yourself that. Say it over and over like a mantra or something, but don't waste your breath on me. I'm not buying it."

Rylan fell silent, lost in self-reflection, wondering if John was right. After a few minutes, Rylan was startled when the old man spoke.

"Paul, listen, I have five thousand dollars, cash, stashed in that coffee can on the shelf behind you. If you cut me loose, take the cash, and walk away; my hand on the Bible, I swear I'll never say a word to anyone."

Rylan shook his head slowly, "I wish I could, John. I really do, but I can't. I won't."

"I know," He replied with disappointment weighing heavy on his voice. "I had to try, though."

"Yeah."

"Can you at least do me a favor?"

"What's that?"

"Can I get a wooden spoon or something to bite down on?"

"Absolutely. In the kitchen?"

"Drawer beside the oven, on the left side."

"Got it. I'll be right back."

Rylan placed the hammer on the floor, stood, and walked down the hall toward the kitchen. As soon as he was out of sight, he could hear rustling sounds coming from the utility room behind him. He knew John was making a last-ditch attempt to escape, but Rylan was confident his bonds would hold. Once in the kitchen, he found a wooden spoon in the drawer and began walking back, but his eyes caught the vacation photos of John and Charlene hanging on the wall. He stopped to browse and could hear the continued struggle in the room at the end of the hall.

"Don't tire yourself out, John. It's not worth the effort."

All at once, the sounds of struggle stopped, and everything was quiet; then John called out, "That's easy for you to say."

Rylan nodded to himself, "That's fair." He looked over the photos of John in happier times, and was struck by a feeling of deep sadness, knowing that the man grinning and smiling in the photos would soon be dead. Rylan tried to push the feeling away.

"Hey, this photo of you and Charlene on a beach. You're wearing a snorkel. Where is that?"

"Puerto Rico," John replied, his voice low and regretful.

The words caused a painful sting from the past to pierce Rylan's heart. He turned away and returned to the utility room. "Looks beautiful."

"It was."

"John, I'm honestly gonna miss you." Rylan was surprised by his own candor.

"I, I don't know what I'm supposed to say to that."

"I'm not sure why I said that out loud." He said bashfully, then decided to change the subject. "Look, before we begin, you said something earlier that I wanted to touch on."

"What?" John asked.

"When I asked why you killed those people, you said something like; so people would care that I was alive."

"What about it?" John asked cautiously.

"By 'other people', you meant your parents?"

"Not just them... back then, I felt like I needed to do something that would make everyone, anyone, care about me for just a moment."

"That's... so sad."

"That's life sometimes."

Rylan nodded sympathetically. "John, I recognize that the adults in your life manipulated you when you were a kid, and what you did was an accident, but that doesn't absolve you of your crimes. You killed three people. Accidents have consequences, too. I know it's cold comfort, but for what it's worth, I'm going to do my best to make this go as fast as I can; then, in the end, I promise to shoot you in the head instead of letting you suffocate."

"Holy shit. This is really happening, isn't it?" John began hyperventilating.

Rylan worried the old man might have a heart attack. "Slow down, John. Slow your breathing. Try to calm down."

It took a few minutes, but John finally got himself under control.

After a while, Rylan reluctantly continued, "This is happening, John, and I'm not going to drag it out any longer. Here, put this between your teeth."

John's entire body started to tremble, but he opened his mouth, bit down on the wooden spoon, and shut his eyes tightly.

"Try not to move, okay? Neither of us wants me to miss."

Rylan knelt beside John's abdomen and looked down at the old man's outstretched right arm. The skin around his wrist was raw from the zip ties, but besides that, his skin was remarkably taught for his age, muscled, and veiny. He had obviously taken great care of his body throughout his life, and now Rylan was about to destroy it. He took a deep breath, clenched his teeth, and seized John's elbow to pin it down. He could feel the arm jerk reflexively beneath his hand while he drew the hammer above his head. In his peripheral, he could see John's eyelids pop open, unable to stop himself from watching the hammer come down.

The hammer's head crashed into the meat of his upper arm, instantly snapping his humerus in two. Rylan heard the wood compress between John's teeth as he bit into the spoon handle; a split second later, the old man howled louder than ever in his life.

Rylan tried to block it all out and quickly slid over, grabbed John's wrist, and bashed the hammer into his forearm. The force of the blow caused John's limp hand to flop up, and his fingers came to rest against Rylan's wrist. The younger man yanked his hand away and tried to stifle his gag reflex. Suddenly, Rylan was struggling to keep it together. Everything, the swirling thoughts and emotions in his head, the vomit bubbling up in his throat, the sound of John's muffled cries with spit spraying forcefully from around the edges of the spoon handle, his nearly naked body twisting and flailing in agony; all of it at once became overwhelming.

Determined to keep his promise to John, Rylan needed to get to the left side of the man's body to work on the other arm, but he knew he couldn't stand, or he'd pass out, so instead, he clumsily crawled over John's abdomen. As Rylan made his way, John's muffled howling changed, replaced by the sounds of pleading.

Rylan got into position and squeezed his eyes shut, reset his clenched jaw, and tried to ignore everything. He positioned himself high on his knees and clenched the arm near the shoulder joint while John fought against his captor's grip. Rylan used his body weight to immobilize the limb, then swung the hammer down into the space between John's bicep and tricep muscles.

John's whole body convulsed upward with the force of the blow as though someone had violently stomped down onto his stomach. The old man screamed behind the spoon handle. Rylan stayed in place, using his body weight to pin him down by the shoulder. With John writhing in agony beside him, Rylan fought to maintain focus. The tortured cries of a man he had come to respect, a Vietnam veteran no less, were clawing at his psyche like a wild animal.

As he stared at the mangled arm, Rylan watched a single drop of water splash onto the bruised purple skin, then run along the curvature to disappear beneath, leaving a thin wet trail behind. The unexpected sight was initially puzzling, but then another fell, and he realized the drops had fallen from his eyes.

Rylan felt panic begin to swell up inside his chest, and all at once, everything seemed to be moving fast. Afraid he was on the verge of a breakdown; he was determined to finish quickly before he lost it. He slid over to John's forearm, pinned down the elbow, raised the hammer again, and then stopped.

John had spit out the wooden spoon, and it landed beside Rylan's left knee. He glanced down at it; the teeth marks were deep and defined, as unmistakable as the blood soaking into the surrounding wood fibers. Rylan forced himself to turn away and attempted to refocus his aim, but his vision was vibrating.

With the spoon handle out of his mouth, John choked and coughed, spraying bloody saliva from his mouth as he tried desperately to speak. Rylan could somehow understand the word 'stop' amidst the guttural sounds being repeated as John gasped for air. Rylan, intent on continuing, squinted to narrow his shaky vision, searching for steady aim while holding the hammer above his head, but it was taking too long, and he quickly became desperate. Fearing he might pass out, he forced himself to make a hasty swing, hoping for the best.

The head of the hammer came down dead-center of John's forearm, simultaneously snapping both bones beneath the skin. John's left hand flopped upward, like a floundering fish suffocating on air, then fell to the floor.

Rylan, relieved that his rushed strike had been successful, almost smiled, but suddenly, a cold rush came to his head, his peripheral vision darkened, and his skin tingled. As his body tipped sideways and everything faded to black, he could hear John's screams getting further away.

When he opened his eyes again, Rylan found himself lying on the floor, facing the lifeless left hand of his latest victim. He could hear John yelling for help, and although he was within arm's reach, he still sounded far away. Rylan sat himself up, ashamed of what had just happened. When John saw his tormentor had awoken, he immediately tried to squirm away and plead.

"Nonnnoonnonono, stop, stop, stop, please. You don't have to do this. Any-Anything, anything, ANYTHING you want. I'll get it. I'll DO it. Anything. Just please, please s-s-stop." He began to sob.

Rylan studied the old man. His white hair was drenched in sweat and stuck to his face in clumps. His eyes were wild, red, and swollen. Blood had dripped from the corner of his mouth down the side of his cheek. His arms had bloated to double their original size and were discolored in colorful blotches and streaks, both beautiful and revolting. Rylan knew this was the same man who, not more than thirty minutes ago, had served him a slice of his homemade banana bread, but it also wasn't that man, not anymore. Rylan had transformed him into something less. He had reduced him to a sniveling, broken animal caught in a snare, willing to do anything to free itself.

Rylan sat on the floor beside John, overwhelmed with sadness. He brought his knees up to hide his face behind and cried. He truly wanted to stop, to be merciful, and end John's suffering, but he knew he had to continue. He pulled himself together, wiped his tears, then looked at John. The naked terror in the old man's face was enough to bring tears to Rylan's eyes again, but his mind was made up and would not be deterred. He moved to a kneeling stance and picked up the wooden spoon.

"John," Rylan began, "I am sorry, but I'm not going to stop. I can't, and I won't."

John began to blubber and sob. Rylan's tears began to trickle down his cheek again, but he blocked them out.

"I'm going to put this spoon back in your mouth. It might help."

John kept his lips tightly closed, his face twisted in anguish and fear.

"Please, take the spoon. I swear, I will try to go through this as fast as possible."

John reluctantly opened his mouth, and Rylan gave him a different length of handle to bite down on.

"I know you're a religious man, John, and I respect that. This would be the time to pray for swift deliverance."

John snapped his eyes shut, and his lips began to move. Rylan slowly made his way down to John's left ankle, giving him a few extra seconds to pray. When he was set and ready, he glanced back at John's face. The old man's eyes were still shut while his lips continued to ripple around the wooden spoon handle. Rylan brought his attention to the lower leg lying in front of him. He noticed a wide scar that ran diagonally across the front of the leg, no doubt a painful souvenir from some long-past exploit, but beneath the skin, the shin bone was easily discernable. He closed his eyes, filled his lungs, then let out a long exhale before reopening his eyes.

Ready, though still unsteady, he raised the hammer, grabbed the ankle, then sharply brought the hammer down again.

16

— · —

SEPTEMBER 23, 2004, THURSDAY

FORT DRUM, NEW YORK

Rylan stood nervously, shifting his weight back and forth between his feet. He looked around to see many of his fellow infantrymen also struggling to contain their excitement. The members of Alpha, Bravo, and Charlie Companies had completed a
twelve-month deployment to Iraq and finally returned to their
home base in upstate New York.

They stood outside a building that housed a large gymnasium,
and their family members were inside, waiting for the welcome
home ceremony. Arranged into three long columns outside the
building, the soldiers were facing a closed set of double-doors
leading into the gymnasium. The plan was that, once the doors
opened, they were to march into the gym and stand in formation
while the battalion commander said a few words, then they would
be dismissed and free to go home with their families for a four-day
weekend.

Rylan heard the muffled words of a faceless announcer from
the other side of the doors, asking the gathered friends and family
members in the audience if they were "ready to meet their heroes."

Rylan cringed at the word. In his mind, he had done nothing during his deployment that rose to the level of heroism, and he loathed any suggestion otherwise. As he stood, lamenting the announcer's word choice, the double-doors suddenly flew open, and the speakers blasted Toby Keith's patriotic anthem, "Courtesy of the Red, White, and Blue."

The infantrymen marched into the gymnasium amid loud cheering that nearly drowned out the music, and Rylan thought if his heart beat any harder, it would explode. He reminded himself to breathe and be patient, fighting the urge to turn his head and search the bleachers for his mother and sister, who had made the drive up from South Carolina.

Abruptly, the column of soldiers came to a halt and faced the bleachers. Rylan's column became the back row, which limited his view, but he still tried, without moving his head, to scan the crowd for his family.

Of the few hundred people in attendance, some were soldiers' parents, but the crowd was mostly comprised of wives with their children in tow. Many held up homemade signs with their soldier's name painted in big letters and decorated with colorful stickers, drawings, and photographs arranged in collage. Rylan searched the portion of the crowd within his view, and although unable to find the faces he longed to see, he reassured himself they were in attendance.

Shortly after the formation was in place, the battalion commander was handed the microphone and delivered some laudatory statements, but Rylan, like many of his peers, never heard any of it. The anticipation had grown enough that his pulse, thumping in his ears, had muted the sound of everything else. To his credit, the commander kept his speech brief, and less than a minute later, he turned to face the formation and yelled the single-word command they had all been impatiently awaiting: DISMISSED. The crowd in the bleachers howled in celebration and surged forward, rushing across the polished wood basketball court to find their returned loved ones.

Rylan wandered, alone in a room full of people, for what seemed like an eternity. He searched through the crowd, unable to find his family, and with each passing moment, his heart sank further. He witnessed joyous gatherings happening all around him and was grateful for his brothers' reunions, but the dawning realization that his family had not arrived became like a weight in the water, and he rapidly sunk into despair. His heart was gradually, mercilessly, being crushed in an invisible fist. He tried to console himself, envisioning excuses for their absence; wrong directions, traffic, sickness, even death. His mind seized on the possibility of their demise, and he spiraled down into a dark place in his imagination where his loved ones had perished on their way to visit him. He became nauseous as terror set in.

"Rye!"

He spun around to see a woman halfway across the room, her face full of elation. Though her hair was different, he easily recognized the woman, but his mind couldn't reconcile her presence in that space. He asked the question out loud to himself, "Is that Abigail?"

The woman turned her head to the side and briefly called to someone, then turned back to Rylan and sprinted in his direction. She closed the distance in no time and threw her arms around him, her momentum nearly sending both of them to the floor. Rylan held onto her for stability, though still in disbelief, until he caught the scent of her skin. He coiled his arms around her like a python, and if he could've squeezed her hard enough to merge, like two spheres of clay becoming one, he would have.

Emily and Jean came trotting up but stopped short, not wanting to interrupt the moment. Rylan saw and wanted to go to them but couldn't bring himself to let go of Abigail. Over his shoulder, he heard his ex-girlfriend's breath hitch twice in rapid succession and realized she was crying. He buried his face in her shoulder and whispered under his breath, "I've missed you," unaware the words had slipped through his lips until she softly said she had missed him too.

"Hey, we're here too!" Jean interrupted, and her mother lightly swatted her arm.

The former couple giggled nervously and slowly released each other. Abigail wore an embarrassed look on her face. Rylan, still in shock, wanted to ask her so many questions, but he restrained himself and turned his attention to his mother and sister. Rylan held his arms out wide as they both ran in to embrace him, and once again, he had to reset his feet to not fall to the floor. Abigail stood to the side and laughed, more from overflowing happiness than humor.

After an emotional hug, the four stayed in place to talk. The women gushed about how proud they were of him, how he appeared more 'muscled up', and how relieved they were that he wasn't 'over there' anymore. Rylan, who had always been uncomfortable being the center of attention, downplayed everything, then purposefully mentioned he was hungry, to which his mother immediately insisted they leave to find a place to eat.

They walked outside to find the baggage cache and retrieved Rylan's duffle bag from his company's rapidly dwindling pile. Jean asked her big brother if she could carry his duffle to the car. He hesitated, considering the clunky contents of his bag, but he reluctantly agreed and helped her heave it onto her back. Even though it was heavy and incredibly imbalanced, she was determined to demonstrate her grit.

Arriving at Emily's car, Rylan helped Jean deposit the bag into the trunk, then walked to the front passenger door. He reached for the handle, but Jean grabbed his arm and told him to sit in the backseat instead. Before he could protest, she swiftly darted her eyes to the left in Abigail's direction. He immediately understood and complied without objection.

As they drove away, discussing various fast-food options, Rylan compulsively scanned his surroundings through the windows, leaning toward the center of the car to have a better view through the windshield, paying especially close attention to the road ahead. They decided to leave the military base and explore the more varied food options near their hotel in Watertown, so, Emily drove through the main gate and began the twenty-minute journey down the highway.

While the car was filled with lively conversation, Rylan was surprised to feel a bead of sweat run down his back, which drew his attention to the perspiration accumulating on his forehead. It suddenly occurred to him that, despite being back in the relative safety of the United States, a yearlong fear of roadside bombs had left him anxious when traveling by car. Recognizing the absurdity of his fear, he tried to calm himself and relax but found he couldn't stop himself from scanning the surroundings for possible threats.

Over the course of his deployment, Rylan had become wary of objects lying along the edges of the roadway, and he spotted the animal carcass lying on the road shoulder from nearly three hundred meters away. He squinted to focus his vision as they drew closer and could tell it was roadkill, likely a deer.

"Mom, roadkill up ahead-right." He reported, then instinctively shifted his attention to the woods directly behind it, searching for signs of someone using the forest as concealment.

"What, hon'? Oh. Probably a dear. Poor thing." Emily replied.

"Make sure you go around it." He offered as a reminder, then shifted his attention back to the dead animal, now only a hundred-fifty meters away and closing fast. He narrowed his vision to search the tall grass between the trees and the carcass for wires.

"What're you... what?" She stumbled, befuddled by her son's request.

Jean scoffed, "It's on the side of the road, Rye."

"No, Mom! Switch lanes! Go around wide! Go..." He shouted in panic, grasping the seat in front of him to brace for impact, but they passed by the dead deer harmlessly.

The car fell silent. All at once, Rylan felt dazed and embarrassed. He hung his head, unable to look at anyone. After a few uncomfortable minutes, Rylan decided he should be the one to break the awkwardness.

"I'm sorry, everyone."

All three women responded simultaneously, generously downplaying his outburst, and entreating him not to feel the need to apologize. Abigail grabbed his hand and gently squeezed it to remind him she was there for him. He squeezed hers in return, then reluctantly met her eyes. Seeing the compassion on her face was both comforting and painful. He wanted to get out of the car, to find some space alone to breathe, but couldn't, and was disinclined to draw further attention to his anxiety by asking his mom to pull over.

Since the conversation inside the vehicle had unexpectedly fizzled, Emily clicked on the radio. Tuned to a local golden oldies station, a doo-wop song from the fifties played softly in the background while everyone retreated into their own thoughts for a while.

As they approached the central part of Watertown, Emily asked the returning service member to decide where to eat. He chose the bar and grill a few blocks up, and as Emily pulled into the parking lot, other veterans were strolling into the restaurant with their families. She parked the car, everyone got out, and she walked directly over to her son and hugged him tightly. Though caught off guard, he was grateful for the comforting embrace, and once it was clear she wasn't going to let go, he hugged her with equal intensity in return.

Jean and Abigail stood nearby and acted as though they were distracted by their cellphones. Eventually, the mother and son released each other, and Rylan, feeling a little less like a pariah, invited them to follow him inside.

The aroma of hickory and oak, grilled meats, ground pepper, and beer hit them even before they had walked through the front doors, and Rylan began to salivate immediately. The restaurant interior, decorated like the typical American sports bar, consisted mainly of sports memorabilia, pennants, flags, jerseys, and photographs. The wall behind the bar was completely covered with televisions, most of which provided live broadcasts from various sporting events, though a few were tuned to a news channel.

A cheerful hostess greeted, then seated them at an open table, but as soon as everyone had gotten situated and begun perusing the menu, Rylan started feeling anxious again. With his seat facing away from the center of the room, the commotion behind him rapidly became unnerving. He could hear the conversations of various groups of customers scattered throughout the restaurant, and as much as he tried to suppress it, he couldn't stop flinching at their sudden outbursts of laughter, jeering, or cheering for their favorite sports teams. He did his best to calm his frazzled nerves, but when a waitress strode briskly behind him on her way to the kitchen, Rylan felt the swirling wind in her wake sweep across the back of his neck. He jumped out of his seat, drawing the concerned attention of the three women at his table. Rylan stood awkwardly in place for a few seconds, unsure of what to say, then he cleared his throat and sheepishly asked to switch chairs with Abigail, a request she didn't quite understand but, nonetheless, eagerly granted.

Not long after, a heavyset waiter named Billy appeared, took their drink order, and then hurried off to another nearby group. The four, left alone at the table again, tried to lighten the mood with idle chit-chat, commenting on various items displayed around the room or discussing the fashion choices of other customers. While they talked, Billy quietly returned with their drinks, then hustled off again to service yet another table.

Rylan raised his beer bottle in a toast, "Not to get all serious or anything, but I just want to say how truly grateful I am to have you all here. Thank you. It means the world to me. You are the most important people in my life, and I love you."

All three women aww'ed at the same time, then they all clinked their glasses together and took a sip.

"So, what's up with the beer, Rye? I thought you didn't drink." Jean asked.

"Yeah, well, since I'm a full-fledged veteran now, I figured I'd pick it up as a hobby." He joked.

Emily scoffed at Rylan's comment and took a sip of her ice water.

"But seriously, this beer tastes like shit. I might have the waiter bring me a Jack and Coke or something." He scanned the room for Billy, but their server was nowhere to be found.

"Geez. Your first sip of beer, and you're already graduating to hard liquor? This won't end well." Abigail derided.

"How did they not card you?" Jean demanded, "You're not old enough to drink yet."

Rylan shrugged. "Packed house, lots of other soldiers here with their families; he doesn't care if I'm twenty-one or not. He's busy running his ass off around here."

"He sure is." Abigail said, "Poor guy. You better leave him a big tip."

"Just the tip?" He smirked.

"Dirty boy!" His mom exclaimed and swatted his arm while the other two women giggled.

"Yeah, Rye. Grow up." Jean piled on as she restrained her laughter.

Rylan glanced around the table and saw smiles, even from his mother, who was trying to hide hers to avoid encouraging her son's crude behavior. He felt like the mood at the table had finally normalized. He began to relax, even though his mind kept attempting to drag his thoughts back into the deserts of Iraq. It became a chore to push his miserable memories away, stay focused on the present, and savor the precious moments with his family.

Rylan spotted his waiter marching past his table and waved him down. "Excuse me, could I get a Jack and Coke?"

"Jackcoke? Sure. Single or double?"

"Huh? Oh, uh, just one, thanks."

The waiter flashed a dubious expression on his face, but only for an instant, "You got it; one Jackcoke." Then he briskly stepped off to continue his rounds.

Abigail shook her head.

"What?" Rylan asked.

"He wasn't asking if you want one or two whole drinks." She corrected, "He asked if you want one or two shots of liquor in the glass before they top it off with coke."

"Oh." Rylan blushed, and everyone laughed again.

"How embarrassing for you, big brother." Jean jeered, and Rylan glared back at her.

"Ah, I guess everyone's just gonna pick on me today, huh?"

"C'mon, don't get all emotional about it. We're just messing with you." Jean replied.

"It's good to have you back," Abigail said as she patted his shoulder.

"It's good to be back."

"I'll bet," Abigail replied.

"So, Rye, how was it over there, really?" Jean lowered her voice to ask, anticipating the topic might be sensitive.

Emily forcefully cleared her throat in her daughter's direction as a signal of disapproval, but Jean acted as though she hadn't noticed.

"Well," Rylan began but stopped to take a sip of his beer, stalling for time to think, "I'm not gonna lie, it was pretty bad, but not all the time. Mostly nothing happens, but then something does happen, and we handle it, then it's back to nothing happening again."

"Did you get shot at?" Abigail asked cautiously.

He shrugged nonchalantly, trying to downplay the reality behind his answer, "Yeah, a few times."

"Did you have to kill anyone?" Jean asked bluntly.

Rylan hesitated. Glancing around the table, it was obvious everyone else was eager to know the same thing, and right away, he saw the question posed a dilemma. He could lie to give them solace or tell the truth, forever altering their perception of him.

"That's kind of a tough question." He waded carefully into the quagmire, unsure of his course, "For the most part, the hajis didn't like to stick around to get into firefights with us. It was a lot of ambush, guerilla-type tactics where they tried to blow us up, then they'd shoot at us, then they'd run away. Of course, I shot back, but so did everyone else so..." He shrugged again, attempting to communicate uncertainty and indifference.

Everyone at the table knew he hadn't answered the question but was reluctant to probe any further. Rylan took another drink of his beer while Abigail and Emily exchanged uneasy glances, silently agreeing to drop the query before looking to Jean, the most likely to continue pushing the issue. Her face showed concern but not intent.

Rylan put down his beer bottle and tried to change the direction of the conversation.

"You know, I'll say this: I understand now why all those old veterans that fought in places like Vietnam, Korea, and Grenada are so patriotic. Seeing the poverty in some of these countries, and the total lack of opportunities for the people to rise up from the muck really gives you an appreciation for the country we have."

"Is it that bad?" Jean asked.

"I once saw raw sewage running through the street like a creek flows through the woods." He declared.

"No!" His mom exclaimed in horrified disbelief.

"I swear it, Mom. That was in Baghdad, their capital city, and some of the smaller cities were even worse, but what's frustrating to me is that country generates tons of money in oil, but Saddam kept most of it for himself and his shit-stain sons. Seriously, you should see some of his presidential palaces. Like the one at Babylon, for example, the land in that area is flat, okay, but this guy had an entire humongous hill created just so he could build a massive palace on top, all marble, granite, and gold, overlooking the birthplace of civilization."

"You mean, like, the actual city of Babylon? That's in Iraq?" Jean asked in astonishment.

"Well, it was... but here's another fun fact; Saddam pledged to have the ruins of Babylon fully restored, but because the restoration was taking too long, he became impatient and had the whole thing bulldozed, historical ruins and all, to build a cheap replica in its place."

The women stared back at Rylan in slack-jawed bewilderment.

"That can't be real," Abigail said.

"Oh, it's real. Look it up. I took lots of photos while we were there, too. I'll show you what I'm talking about once I get them developed."

Billy, the waiter made a brief appearance to deliver Rylan's cocktail and assure everyone their food would be along shortly; then he sped off again to service another table. Rylan took one sip from his glass and felt like he had discovered a new friend.

"How could he do something like that?" Emily cried.

"Easily," Rylan answered. "He was the undisputed ruler of the country. He did whatever he wanted. Look, bulldozing Babylon was stomach-churning, but it pales in comparison to the shit that man and his sons did to the people across the nation. There are thousands, *thousands*, of reported cases of torture, rape, kidnappings, mutilation, and murders by their order. Those dudes were legitimately evil."

"Good lord," Emily murmured to herself.

"So, you agree we should be at war with Iraq then?" Abigail asked.

"Hell no." Rylan exclaimed, "To Afghanistan? Sure. Those Taliban assholes helped Bin Laden blow up The Towers. But Iraq? Look, everyone knows Saddam is a piece of shit that deserves to have someone bash his head in with a brick, but really, that's none of our business. In my opinion, we shouldn't even be over there, but I don't make those decisions. I'm an infantryman; I fight where I'm told."

"That's kind of surprising to hear. I expected the soldiers to be more supportive of the war." Emily said.

"Well, keep in mind, two different wars are happening at the same time. Most of the troops support the idea, or at least the purpose of the war in Afghanistan, but it's not the same for Iraq. I know the president keeps saying Saddam had weapons of mass destruction, but..." he cocked his head to the side with a quizzical expression on his face, "Saddam knew we were coming, the whole world knew it, so if he had the WMD's, wouldn't he have used them against us as we were invading? The whole thing is suspect."

"Can't you guys just refuse to deploy?"

"Not really. We're kinda stuck in a tough spot. We're under contract with the government. Refusing a lawful order counts as insubordination, and if you run, that counts as desertion. So yeah, it's basically go to war or go to jail."

"That's so sad," Jean commented.

"Infuriating," Emily added.

"But honestly, even if I could, I wouldn't try to get out of a deployment. It's not like we're over there slaughtering people mercilessly. We got the Corps of Engineers out there rebuilding roads, hospitals, and schools, we're training their police and military, spending ridiculous amounts of money to equip their national defenses; we're doing good things for those people."

"And they still don't want us there," Abigail muttered.

"Of course, they don't want us there!" Jean exclaimed, "Have you seen the number of civilian casualties? There's thousands."

"But isn't that more the fault of the insurgency?" Emily responded to her daughter, "I might be wrong, but aren't the vast majority of attacks started by them? If they would stop trying to kill our troops, and instead use that energy to help rebuild their infrastructure and stand up their new government, we'd gladly leave that dreadful country behind."

Abigail thought about it. "I agree with you, but it's got to be hard to shake off the desire to defend your home, right? Remember, we invaded their land. Imagine if something like that happened here in America, and another nation tried to take over. Everyone and their ten-year-old daughter would be out, gun in hand, fighting off the 'bad guys', right?" Abigail asserted.

" Damn right," Rylan nodded, "but... I'm sorry, can we please change the subject? I know y'all have a bunch of questions and strong opinions about Iraq, but I'd rather talk about something else. Anything. Like Jean... you're graduating this year; you know what you want to do?

"What do you mean? Like for a job or college?"

Rylan shrugged, "Both."

"She's been talking about going into teaching." Emily chimed in proudly.

"Teaching? Really?"

"Thinking about it." Jean modestly admitted.

"That's great! What level? Grade school, middle, or high school?"

"Oh, it would be grade school, for sure. Can you imagine me having to deal with teenagers and all their attitudes? I might have to slap someone's smart-mouth son or daughter, and then I'd end up arrested." Jean declared.

Everyone laughed and nodded their agreement.

"Yeah, teenagers are the worst, right?" Rylan joked, trying to highlight the irony in her statement.

"They really are," Jean agreed, ignoring his implication, "but I'm not sure that's the direction I want to go, though. Abigail and I were talking about her Psychology classes on the drive up, and it's such a fascinating subject to me. The human mind is so wild, isn't it?"

"It really is," Rylan admitted. "So, you thinking about going that route then? Psychology?"

"Maybe. Human behavior interests me, but I don't want to be a counselor, and I don't want to be a researcher either. I don't know." She blew out air in apparent exasperation.

"Okay, you don't need to stress about that right now. You've got time." He tried to calm her by changing course, "Do you know which colleges you want to apply to?"

"Well, you know, the good 'ol University of South Carolina is always a fine option, Clemson too, and Abigail has been trying to sell me on Penn State, but I really miss being out West. Mom doesn't like the idea of me being so far away, but I might look into a few schools out that way, like UNLV, Colorado, Arizona, or Utah. I don't know. We'll see."

"I'm sure you'll have a lot of options but don't stress on it too much. You've got plenty time to think it through." Rylan turned to Abigail, seated beside him, "Speaking of higher education, how's the college experience?"

"It's good." Abigail admitted, "Challenging, for sure, but good. I have some amazing professors, I love the campus, love football season, and my dorm-mate is quiet and minds her own business. I can't complain."

"That's great. Really great. It's great to see you, by the way. And you look great too."

"Is it great, Rye? How 'bout her shoes? Are they great too?" Jean teased, and Emily snickered.

He sneered at his sister, then turned back to Abigail. "So, what do you do in your free time? You on a sports team, got a job, boyfriend?" He swallowed nervously.

"I thought about trying out for the volleyball team, but," she shook her head, "maybe next year. Right now, I work at a pizza parlor a few blocks from campus during the week, and then, I volunteer at a homeless shelter on the weekends."

Rylan, his interest piqued, shifted in his seat, "A homeless shelter? Interesting. How is that?"

"Well, it is interesting. Seeing the different personality types out there has been a real eye-opener for me. We have some of the sweetest, kindest folks who come through the shelter, and then we also get some of the grumpiest, meanest, and rude clients too. Some are so smart they're dumb, and then others are so ignorant they actually think they're smart. They're all so fascinating to talk to, and I learn so much from them every day."

"Sounds like a zoo," Rylan commented.

Abigail's face became deadly serious. "No. Don't do that. That's very disrespectful."

"No, I didn't mean it like that. I was saying 'zoo' like where you can see all kinds of different animals... I mean, not animals, well yeah, animals at a zoo, but at the shelter, its different types of people you're seeing."

"I understand what you're trying to say, but you're still implying that these people, whom life has kicked around, exist in this space to be gawked at," Abigail stated firmly.

"The term 'zoo' has a negative connotation when it applies to humans." Emily offered.

"Maybe that's it.' Rylan accepted, "Look, I'm sorry. I didn't mean any disrespect to your friends, clients, or whatever; I was trying to liken it to something to which I could relate. I mean, the last time we stayed at a homeless shelter, I was, what..." he looked to his mother for help, "six or seven years old, maybe?"

"In Vegas?" Emily furrowed her brow.

"No, Mom, that was the domestic violence shelter. I mean the homeless shelter in LA. Remember, we got kicked out because Dad tried to fight the manager?"

"Oh. Yeah, probably around six, I think, because Jean couldn't have been more than four. She hadn't started kindergarten yet." Emily recalled.

"Right, so yeah, I was six, and I only have broken memories of those days. Just glimpses, really, so I'm trying to imagine what you're describing at your shelter. I guess I'm not doing a very good job. Again, I'm sorry if I offended," Rylan apologized.

The conversation paused momentarily as Billy arrived with their entrees, and once everyone was served, they all thanked him, and he disappeared once more.

"We good?" Rylan asked his ex-girlfriend.

"Of course, we are! I know you weren't trying to ruffle any feathers; I just get passionate about it sometimes, that's all."

"You know," Emily interjected, "I was having lunch with one of the new doctors we have at the hospital, his family is from Ghana, and he was trying to explain how rich America is compared to the rest of the world, and he used the homeless population in America to highlight his point. He said that with the abundance of charities and government assistance programs providing free shelter, food, clothing, and medical services, our homeless would qualify as middle class in most countries of the world."

"What? That's crazy." Jean cried.

"Even crazier, he said that even if our government suddenly canceled all those programs, and the charities went away, the simple fact that our homeless have access to clean drinking water puts them at a huge advantage over many nations in Africa, South America, and Asia."

Abigail added, "My international affairs professor said something similar. You know, the sad part is that the homeless population in America is so huge that all of those government programs and charities are constantly overwhelmed, and a huge percentage of impoverished Americans are left without basic needs."

Rylan had been engrossed in devouring his twelve-ounce steak while the women carried on the conversation, but he suddenly groaned loudly. He hadn't realized he had made a sound until the discussion unexpectedly halted, and he glanced up to see them looking at him with concern.

"Sorry," He started to speak but stopped to finish the bite of steak in his mouth before continuing, "I might be in the minority here, and I swear I'm not trying to stir up an argument, but I don't believe that all those people should be eligible for aid."

"How can you say that?" Emily questioned her son, demanding an explanation for such an insensitive comment.

Rylan saw everyone's attitude had turned hostile towards him.

"Don't shoot." He joked and raised his hands in a mock-surrender gesture, "I just think some of those people are on the streets by choice. It's not so much that they've fallen on hard times. It's their choice. Some of them. Not all, but there are definitely some who are just lazy and don't want to work. They don't want to contribute positively to society. They would rather leach off of the rest of us because they are enabled to do so."

Both Emily and Jean's heads simultaneously snapped to Abigail, anticipating a fiery volley in return.

Abigail gawked at Rylan, stupefied by his statement. "Tell me that's not how you actually feel."

"Of course, it is. A lot of those assholes could easily help their situation, but they don't want to. They're happy to hold out their hand and beg for the rest of us to support them instead."

"No, that's wrong," Abigail raised her voice. "Many of the people in the shelter are survivors of all kinds of trauma, barely hanging on, carrying with them crippling mental disorders, severe injuries, and extensive histories of abuse, with no money to get the medication, therapy, or counseling to recover. Many turn to substance abuse because they can't cope."

"I believe you, but you're not going to convince me that some of them aren't just lazy bloodsuckers." Rylan defiantly proclaimed, then resumed eating his dinner.

"Oh, my god," Abigail muttered in utter disgust.

"Wait. Are you saying that," Jean started, "you're saying 'some' of them, right?"

"Yeah, some, not all." He conceded.

Jean saw an opportunity to mediate. "Like how much then? Give me a percentage."

"I dunno, maybe ten or twenty percent. It's probably a small percentage, but they're content with taking advantage of the system, and I don't think they should be eligible for assistance. She said the system is overwhelmed, right? Well, if you scrubbed out those degenerates, it'd free up resources for those that truly need it."

"Okay. Okay. I see what you're saying," Abigail conceded, "and I suppose I don't completely disagree, but how can you distinguish between those that need it and those that are taking advantage?"

"That's a great question." He thought about it for a second, "I don't have an answer."

"In the end, there might not be a good answer." Emily hoped to bring an end to what had become a heated discussion. "It's an altogether broken system."

"It's not fair," Jean added, then caught herself. "Sorry, Mom."

Emily patted her daughter's hand to acknowledge her apology.

Rylan looked back and forth between the two, "What're you apologizing for?"

"Oh, Mom's been on me about saying 'it's not fair'."

Rylan, still confused, shook his head. "I don't get it."

Emily explained, "I told her that only children say things are not fair. Adults already know there is no such thing as 'fair'."

"I've never heard that before." Abigail said, "It's kind of a pessimistic view, don't you think?"

"Maybe," Emily admitted, "but it's also the truth."

"Maybe," Abigail deferred, sensing the idea required a little more thought.

The conversation paused, everyone could feel the temperature had risen at the table, and they were happy to take a few minutes to eat in silence. Rylan, who had mercilessly attacked the steak and baked potato on his plate, finished first, then sat back, stuffed and satisfied. He sipped his drink slowly and patiently waited for the rest of his party to finish.

"You okay, baby?"

Rylan blinked, unaware his consciousness had retreated into his memories until the sound of his mother's voice brought him back to the present.

"Yeah." He assured her, then bashfully smiled, "Thanks."

Emily rubbed his back. "You're safe now, Rylan."

"I know. It's like I'm physically here, but my mind is still somewhere between."

"That's how it was with your dad. It's going to take a while. Try to be patient with it, okay?"

Jean, who had been watching the TVs, pointed at the news broadcast. "Hey Rye, did you guys hand out soccer balls like that?"

Rylan looked up and saw a squad of soldiers in full body armor, rifles at the low-ready, completely swarmed by smiling Iraqi children, while their lieutenant tried in vain to hand out soccer balls in an orderly manner.

"Man, fuck those kids!" Rylan exclaimed in anger.

Everyone at his table, and the couple at the neighboring table, turned to stare at him in stunned outrage. Rylan didn't notice.

"I thought you liked kids." Abigail quietly muttered.

"What?" Rylan asked, then saw all the gawking faces and realized what he had said.

"No. I mean, yes. I do like kids, but not those kids." He explained, gesturing sharply at the television, which had already switched to another video clip. To his surprise, his simple explanation did not appear to appease the group.

"What's wrong with those kids?" His mom questioned.

"I don't trust those little bastards." He let slip the words, immediately regretted it, and shifted to damage control, "You don't understand. When we're out on patrol, we have to keep moving. If we stay in one spot for too long, the enemy uses that as an opportunity to attack us, but when we're in a situation like that," he again gestured to the TV even though it no longer displayed an example, "some of those assholes will give a hand grenade to one of the younger kids, pull the pin, and tell them, 'go trade this with the Americans, and they'll give you a soccer ball, or a bottle of water, or an MRE'. The kids don't know any better. They'll just trot over, all smiley-faced, and blow up a soldier along with some of the other kids in the area. Which is horrific enough, but now we're stuck there treating injuries and evacuating the dead while the insurgent shitheads are calling their buddies to bring their AKs and mass on our location. So yeah, I guess it's not the kids I don't like; it's what they represent." He tipped his glass back to swallow the remainder of his drink, then immediately started looking for the waiter to order another.

"Holy crap," Jean said under her breath.

"Yeah." Rylan agreed.

No one else spoke for a while. Rylan eventually got Billy's attention while he was serving a nearby table, then gestured to his empty glass. The waiter nodded his understanding, and Rylan mouthed the words 'thank you' in return. He brought his attention back to the table, lamenting the somber tone that had settled, and hoped to improve it.

He turned to Abigail. "You hear from Joey lately? I know his unit came back a few months ago, but he hasn't written to me since June. We were talking about taking a trip to Puerto Rico together."

Abigail pulled her hands from the table and laid them in her lap, then shot an alarmed look across the table to Emily. Rylan followed her gaze and saw his mother staring back at her with an equally uneasy look.

"What? What's up?" Rylan suddenly felt nervous.

His mother laid a hand on top of his and looked at him with deep compassion.

"Rylan," her voice hitched, and she tried to swallow it down and continue, "I'm so sorry, honey, we were hoping to wait to tell you, but Joey's Humvee hit a roadside bomb in July. He's alive, but they sent him to a military hospital in Germany. They said..." She took a moment to breathe, "they said if he ever wakes up, he's going to be in a vegetative state."

Rylan's mouth hung open and his gaze fell to the table. While he stared vacantly into the lacquered wood, his mind retreated into the depths of his psyche. He could hear the voices of his family, the sound, but not their words, blending into a quavering ambiance distorting everything around him. He became lost and disoriented, vaguely aware that his mother said something important, but hadn't made any sense. What had she said? He tried to think, but only found fragments of memories, all slipping through his fingers like liquid turning to smoke before disappearing into the ether. Each failed attempt to hold a coherent thought increased his sense of dread until he was near panic and couldn't breathe. Suddenly, a whiskey glass appeared, cutting through the nebulous atmosphere, focusing his attention.

"Your drink, Sir. Can I get you anything else?"

Rylan blinked, and he was suddenly back, seated at the sports bar with his family, and the realization that Joey was lying comatose in a hospital in Germany hit him like a freight train. He looked up and saw his waiter standing beside him, sweaty and smiling.

"What the fuck are you smiling about?"

"I'm sorry, Sir?"

"What the FUCK are you smiling about?" Rylan stood up fast enough to tip his chair over behind him. The sound drew the attention of most of the restaurant patrons, many of them returning veterans, who turned around to identify the source. Rylan stood mere inches from his confused waiter, who stepped backward in defense, bumping into Emily.

"Sir, sir..." Billy stammered and glanced around for help.

"Rye!" Abigail cried as she stood.

Rylan grabbed fistfuls of Billy's shirt near the collar, pulled him closer, and yelled in his face, "Tell me! What's so goddam funny?"

Abigail put her hand on Rylan's shoulder to try to pull him away, but he shrugged her off. Out of nowhere, a large soldier stepped in between her and Rylan, threw his arm around her ex-boyfriend's neck, and used a choke hold to drag him backward.

"At ease, soldier," the large man firmly commanded in Rylan's ear.

At first, Rylan's rage spiked, but then as Abigail watched, his anger inexplicably drained from his face as if the phrase had broken a spell, and his body relaxed within his captor's clutch.

"You good, bro?" The large soldier asked Rylan.

"I'm good." He replied as he tapped his open hand on the bigger man's forearm.

The big man released Rylan. They faced each other, shook hands, and Rylan thanked him before the stranger walked back to

his table. Rylan turned back to his party, red-faced with embarrassment, then faced Billy, who was breathing heavily with fear.

"I am so sorry. I... I don't even know how to... I'm sorry. I'm...
I'm just going to leave." Rylan stumbled through his apology, and
as Billy scampered away, he looked at the horrified faces of those
standing around his table. "I'm sorry." He pulled out his wallet and
placed his bank card on the table. "I think I'd better stand outside.
Mom, can you please pay the bill for me and add a hundred for the
tip?"

Emily, frozen in shock, didn't respond. She just watched her
son with deep concern. Rylan began to turn away but noticed the
freshly prepared whiskey and cola on the table. He swallowed it in
three gulps, then calmly put the glass down and left the restaurant
alone.

17

— · —

APRIL 3, 2017, MONDAY

CALDWELL, IDAHO

<u>Notes: John Burbules in Caldwell, Idaho</u>

John didn't deserve to die like that. They set him up: his father, the judge, the police, all of them. They set him up, back then, for what I did to him today. He didn't deserve it. He didn't.

But I did it anyway.

What was I supposed to do? Let him go so he could give the cops my ~~discription~~ description? He swore he wouldn't, but I couldn't take that risk. So, then what? Forget the hammer and just shoot him? He said it himself; no one would notice his death. No one would care.

I liked John.

His death needed to mean something.

Back when I was reading up on him, the news clips only talked about a 16 year old white kid who murdered 3 blacks after setting fire to their church. That sounds like some kind of demon, but that's not the man I met. The story he told broke my heart. He didn't deserve what I did to him, and I don't know how to deal with it. Toni deserved it. Edward definitely deserved it, but not John. He probably should have spent a couple decades in prison for what he did. His father should've been the one that got the hammer, and truth be told, if he wasn't already long dead, I'd make a special visit.

I feel like I killed the wrong man. I want to puke. ~~It feels like my mind is going to snap.~~ I don't want to do this anymore, but I can't stop. I can't.

But can I even keep going? And for how long? Or does it even matter? This was always a one-way trip, but it's all getting so heavy. I think I'm losing it. I keep seeing people who look like Edward and Toni everywhere I go. The woman pumping gas in the middle of nowhere, the man reading a book in the hotel lobby, another one coming out of the restroom at an Applebees, a girl crossing the street while I was stopped at a red light, they're everywhere! Is this what a haunting looks like? Am I going to start seeing John everywhere, too?

I promised myself I'd keep going until I couldn't or until someone stopped me. If this next one breaks me, then so be it. Maybe that'd be for the best.

-I want to make this clear to anyone who may end up reading this: I shot John Burbules in the head as a sign of respect. I didn't want him to suffer further by suffocating to death. To me, that was mercy. ~~I didn't know what I was doing.~~ I fucked up by going into his house before I was ready. I was on my heels the whole time.

-Having the PVC poles pre-drilled saved my ass. I barely had enough time to get him tied down. If I was still trying to set everything up with the old 2x4s, he would have woken up, and everything would have gone sideways real fast.

-He sniffed me out as fake while I was in his house. Pulled the shotgun on me. I'm lucky he didn't shoot me for trespassing or call the

cops on me right then. He wanted me to leave, and I almost walked out. That would have been a ~~catastistrophic~~ *catastrophic mistake for me. Just another example, in a parade of mistakes I made, or almost made.*

-I took his cash from the coffee can. Need to find a charity to donate it to. Something racial-equality-based, I think would be fitting.

-As far as how long everything took, I was in his house for over four hours. There's no point in keeping time anymore. I can't measure efficiency this way.

-I worry about the neighbors being able to identify my truck to the police. It might be time to burn it and get something else.

I'm beginning to wonder about all the fingerprints and DNA I'm leaving everywhere. I wonder if it's a tactical mistake. I shouldn't pop up in any databases. My fingerprints have never been taken, except for when I joined the Army, but as far as I could find on the internet, those don't get shared with law enforcement. So, I should be invisible, but still, I wonder about my fingerprints ~~at the crime scenes at the place of their death~~ *at the crime scenes. I guess I'll find out soon enough.*

I'm surprised that they haven't found Toni yet. I know the house I chose was kind of out there in the sticks, but it's been 5 days now. It can't be much longer, right? I'm getting anxious. I want to hear what the news says about it. With Edward, there wasn't much. They talked about the gruesome scene, how the murderer had used a blunt object, and then the news rehashed his trial and ~~speckulated~~ *speculated that the killer may have been a relative of one of his young victims. They did say there were no suspects yet, which is good. In time, the killings will link together, but at first, it would be ideal if they look like isolated incidents left to the local cops.*

John called me a serial killer. ~~I don't feel like that's right.~~ I know that, technically he's right, but I'm having a tough time accepting the label. Sure, I've studied some of the notorious serial killers before, but when I think about them now, all I can think about is how hard it must have been to dispose of the bodies. Moving dead weight, a completely limp body, is hard to do. Dragging and carrying it is hard work. Burying it, burning it, hacking it into smaller pieces, dissolving it in acid, submerging it in a lake; I imagine all that is even harder work, but I don't have to worry about any of it. I want the bodies to be found. That's the point. In an odd way, and I'm sickened to admit it, I pity the serial killers who had to endure the disposal process.

Afraid of the direction his journal entry was heading, Rylan slammed his notebook closed and shoved it back onto the black backpack. He stared at the canvas bag beside him as if his journal might find a way to crawl back out. The tenor of his written words had left his skin feeling slimy and his mouth tasting acidic. He spit on the grass in front of the park bench, then looked around for a distraction.

A few more people had entered the park since he had first sat down an hour ago. There was now a group of about eight parents standing in a rough circle, chatting and laughing while their children tossed frisbees, voiced imaginary conversations between their dolls, or chased the cocker spaniel who refused to relinquish a fetched tennis ball. Further, in the distance, Rylan could see a young couple seated on a plaid blanket, taking advantage of the beautiful, sunny spring day for a picnic. They gazed lovingly into each other's eyes while the light-haired lover fed her brunette girl-friend a strawberry. The blonde's face lit up with glee watching her sweetheart savor the sweet tartness of the fruit, and she followed it with a quick but tender kiss.

Rylan watched the couple for a while. Although they were too far away for Rylan to hear their discussion, the love communicated to each other non-verbally was palpable. They sat in the warm afternoon air, blissfully lost in each other's presence, unconcerned with the world around them.

To Rylan's relief, the young couple never noticed the members of the parents' group casting disgusted, judgmental glances in their direction, but he did notice their behavior, and it reminded him of his sister, Jean.

Near the end of her junior year in high school, Jean fell in love with a girl on her soccer team, and they carried on a semi-secret relationship for almost a year. During that time, Rylan was on his first deployment to Iraq, and the two siblings had kept in touch, mailing weekly letters back and forth. In a few of her letters, she described some of the disgusted, disapproving looks she would re-ceive from classmates, teachers, convenience store attendants, and fast-food workers whenever she was out with her girlfriend. She described how people she had known for years, who had always treated her kindly, had suddenly begun treating her like a vagrant begging for money to support a drug habit.

Though Rylan never told her so, reading that sort of news from his younger sister infuriated him to his core. In his correspondence, he tried his best to seem optimistic and supportive, but secretly, he just wanted to hurt those people who hurt her. He was angry, but his remote location in the world left him feeling helpless and isolated.

She had written to him once about how she was terrified their mom would find out about Sandy, her girlfriend, knowing her mother's devout Christian views would have prevented her from accepting her daughter's lesbian relationship. Rylan, having grown up in the same religious system as his mother, also disapproved of, what he saw as Jean experimenting with homosexuality, but because he was so far away, and forced to read her letters without the ability to quickly respond, he was able to listen to her words and fully digest them before committing his opinion to paper.

In one of her letters, Rylan recalled a paragraph that proved to be particularly impactful to him: "So many people plod through their lives, day after day, lonely and depressed, while their friends, one by one, find companionship around them. Alone, those lonely people wonder, 'Why not me', then many eventually arrive at the false realization that they must be unworthy of love. I don't want to be one of those people. If I find love in a woman, and she loves me too, how is that wrong? If she makes me smile from my soul, how can that be wrong? Is God really going to deny me at the gates of eternity because someone loved me, and I loved them in return? Why? Because it's unnatural? Is it, though? Homosexuality has existed since at least Jesus's time, before Moses too, so who decided it was wrong? Really, and truly, it doesn't matter. If my body and mind tell me I am attracted to someone, and I feel safe and confident enough to pursue the possibility of love, in any form, then I'm going to do it. It doesn't matter what anyone thinks. I don't intend to offend anyone who may have a problem accepting my relationship, but at the same time, I have a right to pursue my happiness."

Her words had not changed his views, but they had fractured his opinions just enough. Although Jean was two years his junior, Rylan always respected her mind. She possessed an uncanny wisdom for her age, and regardless of whether he agreed or not, her insights had always been, at least, worthy of consideration.

In her letter, she asked hard questions, and Rylan saw that any response he could come up with would have been weak. He wanted to pull quotes from scripture, but he knew that simply quoting the Bible wouldn't work on her. In previous conversations, she had declared her doubts about the purity of the divine text, stating, "Man wrote the Bible. Men. Not God, and men make mistakes. They have agendas. They have opinions. To be reading the Bible literally, hanging on every single word of men from an ancient time, is plain ridiculous."

In the end, after a few days to ruminate, he realized he was ill-equipped to mount a strong enough defense. He simply acknowledged her feelings and reminded her that he and their mom were only concerned for her safety. He reassured her that they would always love her and want her to find happiness, but in their beliefs, she was making a mistake that would have devastating consequences in the afterlife. He reminded her that, ultimately, she would be held accountable for her decisions, but those decisions were hers, and hers alone to make, and he would always defend her right to determine her fate, even if he disagreed with her. Before closing his letter, he asked her to keep hiding the relationship from their mom as long as possible. He was worried about his mother's emotional state with her son deployed to Iraq and her daughter about to graduate and move out of the house soon.

A week later, she wrote back. She thanked him and agreed with his request.

Rylan sat on his park bench, observing the parent group's conduct toward the young lesbian couple, and felt that old itch from long ago resurface. He remembered wanting to hurt those who treated his sister with disdain, and seeing the parents' sneering faces, triggered something in the back of his mind.

Without thinking, he jumped up and marched straight toward them, aiming to attack the largest male first. No one noticed his approach, and as he drew closer, their smiles and the sound of their laughter only increased his blood pressure. He balled up his fists and measured his steps in stride to ready the onslaught.

Suddenly, a yellow frisbee flew past, inches away from his face, and a little girl came chasing after it. He had been completely locked in tunnel vision and hadn't seen either of them coming. The frisbee gave him a fraction of a second to react and slow his momentum before he collided with the child, catching and holding onto her to keep her from tumbling to the ground. She yelped in surprise.

The sound caught the attention of the entire parents' group, and they turned in unison. Rylan apologized to the little girl and asked if she was okay, she said yes, and he released her. One of the male parents' voices called out.

"Hey! Let her go."

"I did." Rylan raised his empty hands to show proof. "We just ran into each other."

The parents stepped out of their huddle but stayed in place, all scowling at him. The little girl, unbothered, trotted over to the frisbee, plucked it from the grass, and ran back toward her friends.

"Cindy, you okay, honey?" One of the women asked.

"Uh-huh. I'm fine, Mom," Cindy called over her shoulder as she scampered away.

"You from around here, buddy?" Another man in the group asked Rylan.

"No, I'm not. Just passing through."

"It's time to be on your way then, huh?"

Rylan held his tongue. The fire in his belly had extinguished when the little girl unexpectedly stepped into his path. He felt embarrassed and deflated but still felt like he should say something to the parents before leaving.

"I was just coming over to say; those girls over there..." he pointed toward the couple on the picnic blanket, still blissfully oblivious. "They seem to be happy and minding their own business. Maybe all of you should do the same and leave them alone."

"How about you? Maybe you should mind YOUR own business." One of the women spoke up.

"Maybe," Rylan responded.

"Alright, now, it's definitely time for you to leave." One of the men added, taking an aggressive step forward.

"Yeah, I'm going. Just set a better example for your kids next time, huh?"

Walking back to the bench to collect his backpack, he could hear the parents' hushed voices behind him, and a few curse words amongst the murmuring. Rylan didn't feel good about the interaction, and as he walked out of the park, he reflected on the incident.

He recognized he had let his emotions get the best of him and had acted impulsively, which was uncharacteristic and worrisome. He had always been deliberate, even methodical, in his actions, but ever since yesterday morning, when he first met John, he had taken chances that he otherwise wouldn't. He speculated that he needed to vent some pent-up energy to help clear his mind and decided to find a gym.

In his life before embarking on his journey along the Garbage Route, he had been an avid gym-goer, considering his time spent lifting weights to be just as much mental therapy as physical, but he hadn't been in a gym in weeks, and he figured he should find one offering a free trial membership at his next stop.

Rylan opened the driver-side door to the Trailblazer, slid in behind the steering wheel, and tossed his backpack into the passenger seat. His mind returned to the lesbian couple and the passive-aggressive parents' group, then to his sister again. He missed her dearly. They hadn't spoken since the funeral, when she said she never wanted to talk to him again, but it had been almost three years since, and Rylan wondered if her frigid stance had thawed any.

Pulling out his cell phone, he stared into the blank screen for a few minutes, trying to make up his mind. Finally, he woke the phone, found Jean's phone number, and typed a single sentence, "I miss you," then quickly hit send before he could talk himself out of it. The deed now done, he stared at the screen with the widened eyes of nervous hope. After about thirty seconds without a response, he forced himself to put the phone down in the passenger seat. Turning the ignition, he shifted the truck into reverse, but before backing out of the parking spot to resume his transcontinental journey, the phone vibrated.

18

—◦—

April 8, 2017, Saturday

Washington, DC

Helio had lived in DC for more than a year and had long ago made "The Lincoln" the turn-around-point of his morning run route. He had visited the Lincoln Memorial countless times and was always struck by the restrained elegance of the place. The design was simple but also magnificent, a vision of grand modestly befitting the man it was designed to honor. The statue, much like the building that housed it, was huge, but not excessively so, depicting the former president seated, gazing past the fluted columns and across the National Mall, with his eyes forever fixed on the Capitol building in the distance. Helio felt there was something compelling in the way the statue was posed. He saw a stoic readiness in the way the stone president was seated, as though he was prepared to stand and go back to work if called upon.

Every time Helio visited the monument, from the bottom of the stairs, he could feel an inexplicable compulsion to ascend the steps and lay eyes on the statue of the former president; in the same way a loyal subject might pay tribute to a revered ruler. Then, once at the top, Helio would often stare up at the statue, feeling as though the carved marble was trying to tell him something, but invariably, the message would prove as elusive as a whisper in the breeze.

Helio doubted his ex-fiancé, Lee, had decided to scale the steps while carrying their one-year-old son, but couldn't entirely rule out the possibility, so his legs began stepping before his mind had even made the conscious decision.

During daylight hours, the central hall of the memorial is regularly full of people posing for photos or just admiring the view, and that day was no exception. Helio weaved his way through the crowd, scanning faces to no avail, then emerged from the building as his frustration intensified. He stood at the top of the steps and checked his watch; one minute to noon. He thought about calling her cell phone, but he used the high vantage to survey the area below one last time. Finally, he spotted Lee pushing a light blue stroller, and he hurried down to meet her.

"You should have let me pick you up. I told you parking downtown during the festival would be a nightmare," he said as he walked up behind her.

Lee let out an exasperated sigh before responding sarcastically. "It's good to see you too, Helio. I'm doing well, thanks for asking."

Helio ignored her and walked around to the front of the stroller to peer at his sleeping son under the sunshade, his tiny body covered by a thin, blue blanket with cartoon puppies printed all over.

"Can I wake him?" He whispered to Lee.

"No, you can't wake him. Let him sleep." She cried incredulously and pushed him away.

"Okay, okay," He backed away, then stared at Lee as though he had only recognized her at that moment. The look on his face made her feel uncomfortable and self-conscious.

"What's wrong? Why are you looking at me like that?" She demanded.

"Nothing. Nothing's wrong. How are you doing?"

"Oh," She exhaled in relief, "I'm okay, I guess. We're okay. You know, just making it work. How are you doing? How's the shoulder?"

"It's good, healing fast. Listen, I want you to know I appreciate you making the drive up from Richmond. Once I return to work, I'm uncertain when I'll have some free time like this again."

"Yeah, well, I felt bad since you were in the hospital the last time we visited."

"Right." Helio pushed the stroller slowly alongside the reflecting pool, away from the Lincoln Memorial, and Lee followed at his side. "Well, I am grateful, Lee. Also, I wanted to discuss something with you."

"Oh no." She grumbled.

"What?"

"Nothing. Just bracing for bad news."

"No, it's not bad news. It's that... well, to say this past month-and-a-half has been an eye-opening experience for me, would be an understatement."

"Yeah? I imagine a bullet through the shoulder can do that." She interjected sarcastically.

He shot her an unamused sideways glance.

"Alright," she said, "I'm sorry. Please continue."

"I've been evaluating the value of things in my life, and I've had a few moments of revelation. In one such moment, I realized I took you for granted while you both still lived here. Jack deserved better, and truthfully, I should have paid more attention to you as well."

She nodded, "Well, I can't argue with that."

"Furthermore, if I can, I'd like to make amends."

"What does that mean?" She asked cautiously.

"To be completely transparent, it means I want you back."

Lee winced and stopped walking. "Helio, it's been six months. I've moved on."

Helio stopped and turned to face her. "Moved on? Meaning you're in a relationship?"

"I have a boyfriend."

"Oh." His tone betrayed his disappointment. "Is it serious?"

"It might be. I'm not sure, but we've been dating for a few weeks now."

"Well, congratulations!" He forced himself to smile, though the result appeared more menacing than joyous, "You should have brought him with you."

"Right." She rolled her eyes.

"What was that for?"

"Why would you want me to bring him, Helio? So you could try to intimidate him?"

"No, of course not, but I have the right to know who you're going to be bringing around my son."

"No. You're wrong. It doesn't work that way. I don't need to check with you, I don't need your permission, and I sure as hell don't need your approval about who I date."

"I disagree, but I don't want to argue with you. Just, at least let me run his name through the database at work and confirm he doesn't have any red flags on his record."

She started to protest, but stopped herself and took a moment to appraise the offer. Her face showed skepticism, but she ultimately said, "Maybe," and they resumed their stroll.

They walked together for a while, silently contemplating possibilities as they wandered into the World War II Memorial. While they meandered around within the expansive memorial plaza, near the gentle roar of the water jets in the central fountain, Jack began to whimper, and Helio walked around to the front of the carriage. Lee watched him closely as he covered the shoulder of his sports coat with their baby's blanket, then carefully lifted the child from beneath the shade and delicately held him to his chest. Lee thought she detected something different in how Helio moved; a patience that seemed unfamiliar.

"What else did you learn after getting shot?" She asked.

"Hmm?"

"I said, did you learn anything else after getting shot?"

"Maybe." His answer was uncharacteristically coy.

"Maybe?" Lee responded quizzically.

Helio frowned. "It forced me to examine many things in my life more closely. Most notably, the people and relationships I have, as well as those I have lost over the years." He took a deep breath, "Then, a few days ago, I was attending Frank's retirement,

"Oh? Frank finally retired?"

"Yes, he did, but that's not the point of my story."

"Sorry, sorry, please continue."

"At his retirement, I had a conversation with someone that made me think... it's possible I might be treating people a bit harshly."

Lee took a step backward in abject astonishment.

"It's just that, my entire life, I've continually held myself to an extremely high standard of excellence without compromise, and in those very rare instances where I've fallen short, I've been hard on myself, often excessively so. I've stomped my way through life up to this point, using ruthless self-accountability to push myself to go harder, but along the way, I suppose I've also expected the same high standards of others, and as a result, I have been frequently, almost constantly disappointed in people. You know how I am, Lee, it's hard for me to hide my emotions or biases, and if I'm disgusted with someone, they will certainly know it. These last few weeks, I have been reflecting on some past interactions, and it appears likely I've been a veritable asshole to people that don't deserve it." He paused and gazed pensively into the fountain before continuing, "I'm beginning to think I might be a bad person."

Lee stepped forward and put her hand on his shoulder. "You're not a bad person, Helio."

He turned to see the warmth in his former lover's eyes and said, "Thank you."

"But..." She teased, "You're definitely bad at being a person."

He chuckled. "Thanks."

Lee smiled, then turned serious. "You know, all kidding aside, this is the most open and honest I've ever heard you. I am genuinely surprised, and impressed."

Helio glanced down at his son, who had already fallen back to sleep listening to the vibrations of his father's voice.

"I don't want people to hate me, Lee. I want to do better, but I just don't know how to change."

"I think, for starters, you should try to cut people some slack."

Helio turned his body away slightly and narrowed his eyes.

"Listen, not everyone... actually, very few people are as ambitious as you are. Those high standards you talk about are not important for most of us. Most people you meet, or pass on the street, are content just getting by. As long as their bills are paid, and they have a little money left over to have fun with, that's a good enough living."

Helio shook his head, "That runs completely counter to what I believe in."

"Oh, you don't have to tell me. I know exactly how you are. You expected me to have the same drive as you, then treated me like shit when I didn't."

"Because you had, HAVE, so much potential," Helio asserted.

She shot him a look of contempt.

"Alright. I get it." He bent down to place the sleeping baby back under the shade of the carriage, kissing his forehead and gently squeezing his son's impossibly soft hand before standing back up to face his baby's mother. "I am sorry. You deserve to be treated with respect, and that's not what you've received from me in the past."

Lee couldn't remember the last time Helio had apologized to her or the last time she had witnessed him apologize to anyone. She skeptically searched his face for signs of mockery but only found earnestness.

"I appreciate you saying that."

The two stared into each other's eyes, feeling an old familiar pull of attraction. Helio stood hoping for a future with a woman who had every reason to reject him, while Lee stood in disbelief of her warming feelings towards a man whom she had believed was beyond redemption. She couldn't help but wonder if the version of

Helio standing before her was nothing more than a clever facade, or perhaps a short-lived reaction to having a bullet tear through a part of his body. Either way, she was intrigued by the idea of Helio as a reclamation project.

As a prospect, she recognized that she could do a lot worse. Helio was intelligent, confident, and determined. He was a well-dressed, handsome young man with a very well-paying job that came with eyebrow-raising status when mentioned to new friends. She knew that with those characteristics, Helio Sangria would be seen as a bonafide catch to most women, but she had also witnessed the unseen; she knew of his demons. With their shared past as a painfully lamentable reference, she began to warily assess if this new Helio was worth the effort.

While they stood staring into each other's eyes, something suddenly stole Helio's attention. He quickly zeroed in on something over her shoulder, and then, without warning, yelled, "HEY! Pick that up!"

Lee spun around to see a loose crowd of people who were, at the same time, turning to look back in her direction, trying to discover the source of the yelling.

She quickly glanced back at Helio, then followed his icy glare to find two teenage boys looking guilty and embarrassed; a discarded red and white candy wrapper lay on the grey stone floor at their feet. While one of the young men stooped to retrieve his trash, the other scowled at Helio. Lee could tell the teen wanted to say something peevish but held his tongue. Lee brought her attention back to Helio, who was now smiling condescendingly and waving.

"Thank you for not littering." He said with a patronizing grin.

Lee rolled her eyes. There was the old Helio. His outburst made her question how deeply committed he was to changing. She hunched to peek under the carriage shade and ensure Jack had not been awakened by his father's loud reprimand, then without a word, she began walking away, pushing the carriage ahead of her.

"Let's go, Officer Sangria." She called over her shoulder.

Helio followed and caught up to her. "It's Agent Sangria, and those punks need to show some respect for the memorial. It represents all the..."

Lee cut him off, "I don't need a speech. I agree with you, but you didn't need to be an asshole about it. You could have calmly walked up to them and asked them to help us keep the area clean, because respect and blah blah blah, but instead, you chose to embarrass them in public."

Helio knew she had a point. He wanted badly to retort but also knew anything he would say would just be bullshit, so he kept his mouth shut. Lee kept walking, fully expecting a snappy response from her ex-lover, which in the past would have led to a heated argument, but when none came, she found herself in an oddly disorienting silence.

The pair walked quietly together, leaving the World War II Memorial behind, and eventually joined the large crowds of visitors converging on the banks of the Tidal Basin. Just like every year at the start of spring, thousands of people from all over the world traveled to the nation's capital to attend the Cherry Blossom Festival and take photos in front of the man-made pond ringed with Japanese cherry trees. As Lee and Helio continued their stroll toward the basin, the trees' vanilla-colored blossoms had only begun to turn pink, and the spring breeze had freed many of the petals to flutter along the sidewalks and streets, gathering at the edges of the grass like drifted snow.

Lee smiled, remembering a trip her family had made to Washington DC, seemingly a lifetime ago, when the blossoms had fully transitioned to their final pink hue, and she had remarked that the trees looked like cotton candy. Her mother and brother laughed, but her father, missing the point, stated that spun sugar didn't actually grow on trees, then didactically described the process of how cotton candy was truly made. She remembered how, as a young girl, she used to hate it when he would do that.

She had always been a dreamer who enjoyed grand romance and mystery, and her father had a habit of, while intending to be illuminating, destroying the magic of a wonderous thing by exposing its inner machinery. Recognizing an ironic parallel, she glanced sideways at Helio, who was still lost in contemplation as they reached their destination. They stood together, quietly appreciating the view until Helio finally spoke.

"Would you say that I do that often?"

"Do what?"

"You mentioned how I embarrassed those kids in public. Do I do that often?"

"That's an excellent question, actually. I would say yes, but also no."

Helio scowled in confusion, "Explain, please."

"You're asking me if I think you're actively trying to embarrass people, right?"

"Yes."

"Then, no. I don't think you're trying to embarrass people, Helio, but that's what ultimately happens. It's the way you choose to go about 'correcting' people that frequently ends with them feeling embarrassed, or more often than not, demeaned."

He nodded slowly, processing the information. "Okay."

Lee noticed the muscles at the back of his jaws flexing. He had always had a nervous habit of chewing at the inside of his lips while deep in thought.

"You are trying to change, aren't you?" She asked.

His face flashed with indignation, "Why do you seem so surprised?"

"Well, I guess you've always seemed so self-assured. I've never seen you so... introspective."

"I'm constantly analyzing and assessing myself, Lee." Helio defended himself.

"I'm not disagreeing with that at all. Lord knows how much you love to look at yourself, but you seem different now. Like you're seeing yourself from a different angle."

"Hmm, perhaps." His eyes dropped to the concrete sidewalk, and he took a moment to ponder her point. When he looked up again, a sly smile had crept across his face. "You know me so well, Lee. That's why I need you. I need you with me, to help straighten me out."

The tips of Lee's ears warmed, and the tiny hairs along the back of her neck prickled. That particular smug smile on Helio's face, the mischievous one that says he knows something he shouldn't, had always been her undoing. Maybe it was the hint of a dimple in his left cheek, or the way his eyes glistened like whiskey over ice, or the half-hearted way he tried to keep the corners of his lips from curling up like the Grinch who stole Christmas; whatever it was, it was damn-near irresistible to her, and he knew it.

She groaned and dramatically turned away from him, but he stepped closer and ensnared her with his arms from behind. He held her body firmly against his while he whispered in her ear.

"I can't do this without you, Lee."

"You and I both know that's a lie." She shot back.

"Okay. I don't want to do it without you. I want you and Jack to move back in."

"Helio..." She pleaded.

"I don't need an answer right away." He cut her off, "I'm only asking you to think about it. Will you do that for me, please?"

She groaned again, partially because his embrace had tightened, but also because she knew she was about to do something she would likely regret.

"I'll think about it. That's all I can promise."

"I'll take it!" He exclaimed, then released her. "Thank you."

"Yeah, well, don't get your hopes up. We're a long way away from renting a moving truck. I need to see you make sustained progress toward becoming a more compassionate human being."

Helio raised an eyebrow. "Compassionate?"

Lee raised one of her eyebrows, partly to mock her former lover but also an honest reaction to his dubious response. "What's wrong with that?"

"Nothing." He shook his head. "Nothing."

"Helio, if this is all bullshit, please, please, let me know now. Don't waste my time."

"I'm not." His voice began to show signs of annoyance, "Why can't you trust me?"

"Why? Because you hurt me, Helio, so forgive me for not rushing in to let you hurt me again."

"This again?" Helio threw his hands up in exasperation, "I didn't mean to push you that hard, Lee. I told you before…"

"I'm not even talking about that, which is a whole other topic that we will absolutely revisit… but right now, I'm talking about your words. You don't even realize how cruel you are sometimes. You say vicious, vile things when you get upset, and then later, once you cool off, you act like it's all behind us, and you expect us to move on. You can't expect me to be cool after you bold-faced accused me of infidelity, and for no reason other than because I smiled when the maintenance man complimented my dress."

"C'mon, it was obvious he was hitting on you right in front of me." His reply crackled with resentment.

"No! It was NOT obvious," Lee fired back, "sometimes a compliment is just a compliment, but hold up," she stepped closer to Helio. From only a few inches away, she stared angrily into his face, "Even if he was hitting on me, how the fuck is it my fault? How did you come to the notion that I was fucking him?"

Helio stepped back in sudden embarrassment and glanced around at the people passing by, noticing they had drawn the attention of a few.

"I never said that."

Scowling angrily, she growled," You called me a whore."

"That's, no, that's not at all what I meant."

"Well, that's what you said. Words have meanings, right? Isn't that a phrase you're fond of saying?"

Helio opened his mouth to retort, but nothing came out. He had nothing to say. Reflexively, his mind searched for an insult to throw, but he snapped his mouth shut before one could escape.

Fuming, he stepped to the edge of the walkway, rested his forearms on the top of the railing, and gazed across the Tidal Basin.

On the far bank, the Jefferson Memorial sat neatly nestled among the Japanese cherry trees extending out along the water's edge. Even from that distance, the silhouette of the bronze statue inside was visible, though cast in shadow by the overhead dome, and framed perfectly by the bright white marble columns outside beaming under the heat of the mid-day sunlight. The entire scene was exquisite in its vibrancy, but all Helio could focus on was the darkened statue of the Founding Father subdued within the memorial. To Helio, the figure appeared resolute but simultaneously sorrowful; a juxtaposition of emotion with which he could relate.

For so long, he had been sure of his direction in life. At every turn, the path had always been clear, and he had progressed unencumbered, until one night, when a scorching-hot slug of copper-jacketed lead ripped through his shoulder, miraculously missing his bones, but shattering his once impenetrable sense of certainty. For the first time, he seemed lost in a world he had felt destined to dominate, and the very ground he stood upon now seemed infirm and the air foreign.

The words of Frank's wife had been ringing in Helio's ears for the past week: "If you feel the world is full of enemies and you're at war, you're tremendously outnumbered. Build a deep network of allies, or you will lose by attrition." He glanced over his shoulder at Lee, who had turned her attention to their sleeping son.

He remembered, six months ago, when she stood in the kitchen of his apartment and declared that she was taking Jack and moving out. He didn't protest or beg for her to reconsider; instead, he chose to show no emotion.

He loved her more than anyone he had ever known, but in a practical sense, it was easier to just let her go. The way he saw it, on his own, he could focus on his career and provide financial support for their child and wouldn't have to endure her repeated claims that he wasn't affectionate enough, or never spent enough time with them. He convinced himself that it was the best outcome for everyone involved, and even as the tears streamed down Lee's face, tormented by her fiancé's lack of concern, Helio calmly helped her pack Jack's things and remained silent. A decision he could not have imagined he'd regret so deeply.

As he stood by, observing Lee attending to their son under the shade of the cherry trees, an older woman humbly approached her and asked if she would take a photo of the woman's family with the blossoms as a backdrop. Lee graciously agreed with a warm smile and obliged cheerfully while exchanging light banter with the family of strangers, before finally bidding them safe travels back home from their vacation. Helio felt like he was seeing her with new eyes. He knew he had often treated her as less than an equal and had committed a grave mistake in letting her go, then made it even worse by doing it so coldly. He was unsure if he could get her back but knew he had to try.

"Let me ask you something." He entreated.

Lee turned to him. 'What's that?"

"Who am I?" He asked.

"What?" She replied, puzzled by the question.

"Who am I?" He asked again before providing context, "As in, if I died today, how would you describe me in my eulogy?"

"What makes you think I'd agree to speak at your funeral?"

"Lee."

"Okayokayokay, hold up." She folded her hands in front of her mouth and considered her words. "I'd say, here lies a man who would have been successful at anything he had chosen, but chose to become an FBI agent to prove that he could. Then once he did, he set about to prove he was better than all the other agents by trying to prove that no criminal could outsmart him. That was Helio. That's how he lived his life; he never stopped trying to prove himself to someone. He was also impossibly demanding, emotionally closed-off, inconsiderate of other's feelings, and arrogant, but besides that, he was nice to look at, had great fashion sense, was meticulously organized, was great at solving puzzles, and could cook the most amazing chilaquiles." She closed her speech, then asked, "How's that?"

"I think... I think I don't want you speaking at my funeral."

Lee laughed. "Aww, c'mon! It was good."

Helio scoffed and looked away.

"Seriously? Come on, do you really disagree with what I said?"

"I suppose it's not that I disagree, there's probably some truth there, but it's more that I don't like hearing it."

"That's fair. I hope you know I wasn't trying to be mean."

"No. I know. I trust your opinion. I trust you." He shrugged, "It's just that... truth has teeth. A big part of my job as an investigator is to analyze other people and search for patterns and weaknesses to help predict their behaviors, but turning that same level of scrutiny inward is a new concept for me. It's a bit jarring, if I'm being honest."

"For whatever it's worth, I am glad you are, but it's unfortunate that it took a near-death experience to get you there, though."

"I wouldn't classify it as near-death." He tried to downplay the situation.

"Three inches away from your neck? I'd say it was pretty close."

"Perhaps." His words trailed off, along with his thoughts.

Lee decided to change the subject, "Hey, I wanted to ask: how are your parents doing?"

"They're fine. Adjusting. The assisted living staff have been very accommodating. They joined the gardening club and attend yoga classes every other day."

"Yoga? Your dad too?"

"Surprisingly, he seems really into it, but you know how he is; I suspect it's because he's eyeballing a few of the other ladies."

Lee laughed, "I'm sure he is! That old dirty dog."

Helio chortled knowingly, but his smile faded quickly, "Mom's memory is failing faster than expected, though. My father is doing the best he can with it, but I'm just glad that they agreed to move into that facility. I can't imagine him doing it all on his own. He's not exactly a patient man."

"Pfft. You don't need to tell me. I know where your bedside manner comes from." She scoffed. "I'm sorry to hear your mom is getting worse, though. The next time you visit, tell them I send my love, okay?"

"I will, but you should bring Jack by to visit his grandparents one of these days. The last time they saw him was Thanksgiving."

"I should." She agreed, then checked her watch, "We could stop by after lunch if you have time."

"Yeah? That'd be terrific."

"Speaking of lunch, where are we going?"

"Oh man, I want you to try this place called Farmers and Distillers. It's a few blocks down from my apartment. They have this dish; it's fried chicken served with a house-made glazed donut and a tangy barbecue sauce. It sounds bizarre, but is undoubtedly one of my favorite dishes right now."

She raised an eyebrow. "With a donut? Like you're supposed to eat them together?"

Helio nodded with a provocative expression on his face.

Lee shrugged, "Okay, so it's like chicken and waffles, then?"

Helio pointed his finger at her in acknowledgment, "That's a good reference point, but it's different. You just got to try it."

He started pushing the baby carriage, and Lee went along with him. They strolled along together for a while, feeling like a family until Helio suddenly stopped and turned to her; the expression on his face was of grave concern.

"Lee, before we go any further, I want to be clear and ensure we're on the same page about something."

Lee scowled quizzically while Helio firmly gripped her upper arm.

"You are not, under any circumstances, allowed to deliver my eulogy."

Lee rolled her eyes and shrugged her arm away from his grip, "Honey, you'll be dead. You won't have any say in the matter."

She immediately started walking away, pushing the stroller ahead of her, while Helio stood his ground, smirking.

"Lee!" He called after her as she drew further away.

"Can't stop me!" She hollered over her shoulder.

Helio smiled and jogged to catch up with her.

19

— · —

NOVEMBER 18, 2004, SUNDAY

FORT DRUM, NEW YORK

As soon as Abigail got into the young soldier's car, she regretted her decision. The sleazy way he stared at her, then licked his lips before mashing the accelerator, was proof enough of her mistake, but as the car fishtailed on the recently plowed street, still slick with residual snow, she braced her hands against the dashboard and prayed her error wasn't a fatal one.

Minutes earlier, she had called Specialist Turbeville, who went by the nickname "Turbo", from the main gate and asked him to sponsor her entry onto the Army base. She had driven all the way from her college dormitory in Pennsylvania with hopes of surprising Rylan, but after a heated discussion with the gate guards over an expired inspection sticker on her car, she was forced to park her vehicle and catch a ride with Turbo.

As she sat in the passenger seat while Turbo regained control of his car, she hoped the rest of the ride to the barracks would be quieter, but unfortunately, Turbo started talking. Over the short five-minute drive to the barracks, he had twice remarked about how beautiful she looked and how she must spend hours in the gym to maintain such a 'tight body'. Abigail repeatedly tried to diffuse the increasingly uncomfortable situation by quickly thanking him for the compliment and trying to move on, hoping he would get the hint, but he proved relentless. No matter how she tried to redirect the conversation, Turbo kept trying to splice in flirtatious comments or innuendo.

She couldn't help but wonder what Rylan, who had introduced them at his unit's Halloween party, would say, or do if he became aware of how his squad mate was talking to her. Imagining a tense confrontation leading to a fistfight, she had no plans to inform her boyfriend of Turbo's behavior.

As soon as the car was parked, Abigail stepped out into the sub-zero temperature. Noticing the parking lot was only sparsely lit by streetlamps, with large portions cast in darkness, she folded her arms tightly across her chest, thanked Turbo for the ride, and marched toward the barracks. Turbo quickly popped out of the car and called after her, asking if she needed any help finding Rylan's room. She assured him she remembered the way, but he trotted to catch up anyway.

At the edge of the parking lot, she found the plowed sidewalk, a singular path carved through the otherwise undisturbed two feet of snow covering the ground, then followed it toward the barracks as the salt crystals scattered on the concrete made a crunching sound underfoot. She popped up the collar of her coat to block the icy breeze from tormenting her neck and wondered which was more chilling, the frigid temperature outside or the creepy way Rylan's coworker was hounding her.

"Hey, if you need anything else, remember I'm only a phone call away." Turbo offered as he followed closely behind her.

"I'm pretty sure I will be okay from here. Thank you again, though." She intended to sound sugary, but instead sounded snide.

He didn't respond.

Outside the entrance of the building, two male soldiers were braving the cold to appease their nicotine addiction, their warm breath, in between puffs of smoke, rising like steam into the cold night air. They spotted her walking down the sidewalk and immediately halted their conversation. She could see them looking her up and down as she approached. They made no effort to greet or otherwise acknowledge her; instead, they stared like hungry wolves watching a young doe foraging for food along the forest floor. She refolded her arms across her chest and flexed her shoulders a little higher, hoping to project confidence in the face of the male soldiers, but with Turbo walking so close behind her, she felt especially vulnerable. She tried to reassure herself that they wouldn't do anything to hurt her, but everything, when viewed together, felt ominous.

The two soldiers made just enough space for her to pass between them without stepping into the snowy embankment edging the sidewalk. She lowered her eyes, quietly passed by, and then hustled through the barracks doors into the safety of the fluorescent overhead lights. Once inside, she hurried to the front desk to check in with the uniformed soldiers on duty.

Turbo passed behind her and continued walking. He headed toward his room, but not before commenting over his shoulder to the guards. "Make sure you check her ID, guys."

The sergeant on duty called back, "Hey, we got it from here, Turbo. G'head, scoot on back to your cave now."

While the sergeant checked her identification and added her name to the visitors' log, the other guard, Specialist Merriweather, watched Turbo walk away, and Abigail could hear him mutter, "turd," under his breath.

The Specialist studied Abigail's face for a moment, then mentioned that he remembered her from the Halloween party. Even though she didn't recognize him in the slightest, she feigned a vague recollection to spare his feelings. She explained that she had come to visit Rylan and had hoped to surprise him. After the sergeant finished logging her information, Specialist Merriweather offered to escort her to Rylan's room on the second floor.

After climbing the stairs, Merriweather and Abigail stood in front of Rylan's barracks room while the uniformed soldier pounded on the door. Before long, the deadbolt unlocked, and the door cracked open. The expression on Rylan's face was initially one of annoyance, which then turned to confusion when he noticed Abigail standing beside the guard.

"Your girlfriend is here, Beam." The guard announced, then turned and flashed a warm smile at the young woman before walking away.

Rylan and Abigail stood on opposite sides of the doorway, peering at each other as the door slowly drifted open. Rylan squinted at her as though he was unsure of what his eyes were seeing.

"How? What are you doing here?" He asked.

"I came to surprise you. SURPRISE!" She exclaimed, hoping her enthusiasm would ignite Rylan's excitement, but his confused expression persisted.

He opened the door a few more feet, holding out his arms, into which she eagerly rushed. Throwing her arms around him, Abigail could smell the alcohol on his breath.

"You happy to see me?" She asked, giving him another opportunity to show his appreciation for her journey.

"Of course, I just wasn't expecting you." Rylan said flatly, "You should have called me."

"Then it wouldn't have been a surprise."

Rylan was the first to let go, kissing her cheek as he took a step back.

"Well, either way, it is good to see you. C'mon in." He invited, then turned to walk deeper into the room.

Abigail couldn't help feeling underappreciated and slightly unwelcome as she closed the door behind her. Standing in the darkened kitchenette, she noted the only illumination in the room was coming from the big screen television in the adjacent bedroom and asked, "You want me to turn on a light in here?"

"Not really." He called from inside the bedroom, "You can come in here, though. Help yourself to some pizza if you're hungry. It's there on the counter."

Abigail had twice before visited Rylan's barracks and was easily able to navigate the simple two-room layout in the semi-darkness. As she approached the bedroom doorway, dramatic theme music was heard from within, accompanied by sporadic gunfire and explosions. Rylan was sitting on his bed wearing a pair of basketball shorts and a hoodie. He was holding a video game controller in his hands while his thumbs feverishly worked the buttons.

Abigail removed her coat and carefully sat down at the foot of the bed, trying not to disturb him. Rylan was focused on the action on-screen and hardly acknowledged her presence in the room. She sat silently watching Rylan's video game avatar run, crawl, and shoot its way through a virtual war zone for fifteen minutes. The entire time, Rylan grunted and cursed at the screen while stealing quick sips from a tall plastic cup on the nightstand beside a half-empty bottle of whiskey and a can of Coca-Cola Classic.

Abigail had no interest in video games and was unfamiliar with the game her boyfriend was playing, but he appeared to be fairly good at it, and although she found the game mildly entertaining, all she could think about was how disinterested Rylan seemed to be in her.

She began replaying their phone conversation from last night in her head, searching for any indication of why he might be upset with her. Unable to find any viable reason, she began thinking of how best to broach the subject with her boyfriend. Thankfully, it wasn't long before he completed a portion of the game and decided to save his progress. He finally put the controller down, switched on the lamp beside his bed, and turned to Abigail.

"You want a drink? I got some Jack Daniels over here and more Coke in the fridge."

"No, I'm fine, thanks," Abigail replied.

He took a sip from his cup, then cheerfully asked, "So, wassup?"

She rotated her body to face him and saw his attitude had completely changed.

"I dunno, what's up with you?"

"Nothin'," he shrugged, "Just chillin'. It's good to see you, though."

"Good to see you too."

The conversation unexpectedly stalled and they shared an uncomfortable silence until Abigail spoke again.

"I didn't mean to bother you, Rye. I'd hoped to surprise you, and I guess I thought you'd be happy."

"Of course I'm happy. You don't think I'm happy to see you?"

"I don't know. You didn't look too happy."

"It's just this game. It's been kicking my ass all night. I was frustrated."

"Oh," Abigail responded skeptically, "Well, I thought you were mad at me."

"For what?"

"I don't know. That's what I was wondering."

"No, babe, I'm not mad at you. It's good to see you, and I'm glad you surprised me. Thank you."

Rylan put his cup down, scooted closer to Abigail, and hugged her. The smell of alcohol on his skin was strong enough for her to wrinkle her nose, and she questioned the timing of her visit. She reminded herself that since Thanksgiving was next week, and they would be spending it together at her parents' house, what she needed to discuss with him could not wait.

While they held each other, Rylan began softly kissing her shoulder, then started making his way toward the base of her neck. She knew what he was trying to do, and even though she wanted to talk to him, being touched, being desired, felt wonderful, and she didn't want him to stop. His lips, warm and soft on her neck, made her blush, and gooseflesh tingled on the back of her arms. She moaned as she exhaled and tried to summon enough willpower to try slowing him down.

"Rye."

"Hmm?" He hummed, and her body shivered.

"Rye." She tried again. "I, uh, I need to talk to you."

He briefly paused to whisper, "I'm listening," then continued.

"Could you um, uh...stop? For a minute."

"You sure?" Rylan asked as he kissed below her ear.

"No... but yes." She fought against her desire.

Rylan persisted.

She begged, "Babe, please."

Rylan groaned and slowly pulled away. He reached again for his cup feeling dejected.

"Alright, what do you wanna talk about?"

"Babe, don't be mad. I need to talk to you first."

"I'm not mad at all." His pretense was thin enough to betray his annoyance as he sat back against the wall and petulantly sipped from his cocktail.

Though she wanted to address his attitude further, Abigail saw no outcome that didn't involve an argument, so she chose to ignore it, remembering she had more important business to discuss.

"Well, okay, this is not how I had envisioned this happening, but I guess, here we are." She started, then stopped to gather herself.

The realization that such a pivotal moment had suddenly arrived sent the beating in her chest into overdrive, and her thoughts started to spin wildly. She tried to take a deep breath, but her throat felt as though it was nearly swollen shut. Afraid but undeterred, she bravely took what air she could and hoped for the best.

"I'm pregnant, Rye."

Rylan froze; his eyes widened in shock. It was a full ten seconds before he even blinked. He mechanically brought the cup to his lips and gulped down the remaining liquid before speaking.

"Are you sure?"

"I took three pregnancy tests this morning. All positive." She confidently stated, then waited for a reply, but none came.

Rylan only stared down at his bedspread, dumbfounded by the news.

She continued, "Not going to lie; I started to freak out. I sat crying on the floor in my dorm room for a while. I was this close to calling you, but I wanted to tell you in person, so I got in the car and drove the five and a half hours from State College to come see you."

Rylan continued to stare absentmindedly down at his bed with his jaw hanging open, struggling to grasp the enormity of the situation.

"How did this happen?"

"Well, usually, when a man and woman are attracted to each other, they eventually get together, and he puts his penis into her..." she joked, hoping to lower the temperature in the room.

"Funny," he said flatly, "I meant... it had to be right after the Halloween party, right?"

"Yeah. Had to be."

She searched his face for any emotional response but found none. He just sat there, motionless, except for his eyes which moved back and forth as though reading an invisible book. She wanted to give him time to process the information, but the electricity in her skin wouldn't let her wait any longer.

"Can you tell me what you're feeling right now?" She asked.

"I'm just shocked, I guess."

Abigail bristled at his answer and its lack of fidelity. She desperately needed to know how he felt, and her anxiety began to boil over into anger.

Rylan closed his eyes again and rubbed his head firmly with both palms, "Don't get me wrong; I'm happy." He opened his eyes and squinted down at the bedspread. "I'm happy." He repeated, though it vaguely sounded like a question. When he finally looked at Abigail and saw the worry on her face. He hugged his pregnant girlfriend. "I'm happy." He reassured her, then exhaled, and reassured himself, "I am happy."

They held each other tightly for a long while, neither saying a word.

"So, what are we going to do?" Rylan eventually asked.

"What do you mean?" Abigail questioned.

Rylan released his embrace so he could look deep into Abigail's eyes. "I know we've never talked about it, but would you want to get married?"

"Oh god." A swarm of butterflies instantly took flight inside her abdomen. Startled, she reflexively clutched at them. "Are you, are you asking me?"

"I mean... I don't...." He quickly glanced around his room, then stopped at his nightstand. "Hold on."

He got up and quickly rummaged through the drawer before pulling out a small wad of green paracord and a knife. He cut off a short length, then tossed the rest back into the drawer. He knelt on the floor beside Abigail and gently pulled her left hand to him.

Abigail watched him with rapidly swelling panic. She felt like she was both hyperventilating and suffocating at the same time, her arms and legs had gone numb, and the room seemed to be either slowly rotating or melting; she couldn't tell which. As Rylan looked up at her like a timid child begging permission to have a treat, she feared she would pass out.

"I am sorry this is all so hasty, and I swear I will get you a proper engagement ring tomorrow morning, but...." He carefully tied the paracord around her ring finger. "Abigail Jameson, will you marry me?"

Warm tears trickled down her face. Each drop, a bittersweet out-pouring of conflicting emotions. While excited by the prospect of becoming a mother and a wife, all at once, she realized her life had changed forever, and she was terrified. She feared her youth had abruptly vanished, and her plans for the future had been stolen, leaving her with nothing but the idle fantasies of a lovesick young woman. Now, as this young man, whom she loved deeply, but may have returned from war irreparably damaged, proposed to her, it didn't feel like there was anything else she could do. She felt hopelessly trapped, and to make it worse, she worried he might also feel trapped by her.

She closed her eyes and lowered her head. "Don't," she softly pleaded.

"Don't what?"

"Don't do this."

"Wha-why not?"

"Because... I don't want the reason you propose to be that I got pregnant." She glanced at the whiskey bottle on the nightstand, "You're also drunk."

Rylan stood up and took a step rearward, clearly agitated. "I'm not drunk! I've barely caught a buzz." He paced back and forth in the small bedroom, formulating a response, then he stopped and knelt again.

"Don't you want to marry me?"

"Rye, that's not what I'm saying."

"Then what are you saying?"

"I'm saying it's not as simple as you're making it out to be. My fear is that you view this pregnancy as a problem and think that marriage is the practical solution, as if you're somehow doing me a favor by putting a ring on my finger."

"I don't...." He started, but Abigail waved her hand to signal she wasn't done.

"Listen, you must understand; I don't need you, Rylan. I never have, and I never will. I can absolutely raise this child without you." She paused for emphasis. "With that being said, I love you, and would love for you to be in my life, our lives," she placed her hand on her abdomen, "but I don't want you to feel obligated to meet me at the altar."

Rylan stayed silent for a while. Before long, his eyes left hers and began traversing the surface of her face as if he was trying to commit every contour to memory. When he finally found her gaze again, he had a twinkle in his eye as though he had fallen in love with her all over again. He gently pulled her left hand back toward him.

"I understand." He stopped, allowing the statement to stand alone before continuing. "And thank you."

He carefully untied the knot in the improvised engagement ring. When he was done, he looked into Abigail's eyes for a moment before returning to the paracord to tie a much more secure knot around her finger than the original. He moved slowly and solemnly as if each loop and twist held deep meaning. Once it was finished, he brought his eyes back up to hers.

"Abigail Jameson, I need you, and I love you. Would you grant me the honor of being your husband?"

With tears full of joy streaming down her cheeks, Abigail leaned forward and threw her arms around Rylan's shoulders. She kissed his lips tenderly before whispering in his ear, "Yes."

20

— · —

April 9, 2017, Sunday

Washington, D.C.

Rylan sat on his plastic crate only a few inches from the uncon-scious man's feet. The man was wearing only a pair of boxer shorts, and his short heavyset body was smeared with dirt that had been accumulating on the floor of the dilapidated classroom for years. Rylan thought the grey-brown smudges on the man's skin looked like someone's half-assed attempt at body paint, and given their current surroundings, he fit right in with the distressed motif.

Listening to the sound of the man's gurgling snoring was as unsettling as it was grating. Rylan sat watching with morbid fas-cination as his captive's grime-streaked belly vibrated with each stymied breath until something out the corner of his eye caught his attention. He snapped his head to the left, convinced another rat had scurried along the edge of the room but found nothing moving around in the shadows. Once more, he nervously scanned the room and wondered if his mind was playing tricks on him.

He hated being in the abandoned elementary school. The air felt chalky in his nostrils and smelled strongly of dead rats and urine. The dusty linoleum floors were littered with cigarette butts, smashed beer bottles, broken syringes, discarded condoms, and fast-food wrappers. Spider webs occupied almost every corner of the building, rats boldly scavenged throughout the classrooms, and Rylan was sure the scratching coming from above the ceiling tiles was from bats. Seated in this miserable environment, he admitted to himself that he had made an egregious mistake in selecting the school. He lamented his impatient decision and wished he had continued searching instead.

Abraham Poindexter's apartment was in a poverty-stricken neighborhood in the southeast of the city, and even though there were many homes for sale in the area, none offered the seclusion and privacy Rylan required. Then, two days ago, while driving through a slowly deteriorating neighborhood, he stopped at an intersection and noticed the elementary school across the street, fenced off, boarded up, and long overgrown with weeds. Although there were multiple apartments and small homes surrounding the campus, and against his better judgment, he convinced himself it could work, a decision he would come to regret.

The unconscious man's breathing abruptly stopped, drawing his captor's attention. Abraham remained breathless just long enough for Rylan to become worried, then, all at once, the man gagged and coughed, eyelids fluttering as he gradually regained consciousness. Rylan remained still as Abraham opened his eyes, then allowed the natural progression of emotions to proceed as the captive discovered his dire situation.

Abraham surveyed his musty surroundings and found Rylan, pistol in hand, calmly seated beyond his feet, and immediately locked eyes with the man who had abducted him. From the start, Abraham was ablaze with anger, snatching at his restraints long after he realized the futility and continued firing off muffled expletives through the tape covering his mouth. After a few minutes, Rylan attempted to calm his quarry.

"Hello, Abraham. You mind if I call you Abe?"

Abraham huffed, his eyes burning with rage.

"Well, I'm gonna call you Abe." Rylan shrugged. "Hey, look, before we talk any further, I want to apologize for the surroundings. This place is clearly substandard. If it's any consolation, I don't want to be here any longer than you do."

Abraham stopped tugging at the zip ties.

"I'm sure you have many questions; why you're here, who I am, and what this is all about, right? Well, for now, I'll just say we're going to have a talk. I'm going to ask you some questions, and I expect you to answer them."

Rylan put the pistol into the bag lying between his feet, then pulled out the hammer, holding it up for Abraham to see.

"If you refuse, I'm going to hurt you, and if you lie to me, I'm going to hurt you more." He paused to allow Abraham to digest the seriousness of the situation, then watched as Abraham's face remained still. "So, how quickly this night progresses will be entirely up to you."

Rylan waited for a reaction, but despite his grave situation, the man showed no change of emotion. He only stared menacingly back at his captor, and Rylan wondered how the rest of the night might transpire. He lowered the hammer into the bag, resting it beside his revolver, then pulled out the folding knife.

"Now, I'm going to walk over and cut the tape off your mouth, but before I do, understand that if you yell, I will slit your throat and leave you here for the rats."

Rylan stood, stepped over Abraham's outstretched body, and knelt beside him, snapping open the blade with a practiced flick of the wrist.

"Don't move; I'd hate to cut you unintentionally."

As soon as the tape came off, Abraham launched his defense, "Yo, this is bullshit! Y'all can't prove nothin'!"

Rylan returned to his seat, bewildered by the man's claim. "What are you talking about? Two witnesses clearly saw you."

"The fuck? Ain't no fuckin' way." He paused to think about it for a second, "Yeah, naw, there ain't no way. Wasn't no one else there. She lyin'."

Rylan was dumbfounded. "What the hell are you talking about? Her sister and her coworker were standing right next to her."

Abraham's confusion had turned to disgust. "Someone told you wrong. Hear the words comin' out my mouth; there wasn't no one else in that bedroom but the two of us."

"Bedroom?" Rylan cocked his head like a dog hearing an unfamiliar sound.

"Damn fool, can't you hear?"

"Hold up; I'm lost. The news said that Jannette Tripper was walking out of the restaurant with...."

"Jannette?! This is about Jannette Tripper? Aww, man, that's old shit. I already paid for that. They locked me up for three years over that bullshit."

"Riiiight." Rylan drew out the word while his mind attempted to process what Abraham had said. "So... who were you talking about then?"

Abraham laid his head down so he wouldn't have to look at Rylan. "Nothin'. I ain't got shit to say about that."

"From what it sounds like, you have a lot to say. We will be coming back to that, but for now, let's start with Jannette, okay?"

"Why? Who the fuck you s'posed to be anyway? You obviously ain't cops. You her cousin or somethin'? Uncle?"

"I'm nobody. Just a concerned citizen."

Abraham's head shot back up, "A concerned what? You gotta be fuckin' kiddin' me. Bitch, you better be plannin' to kill me 'cause when I get out of here, my people gonna fuck you up." He jerked his wrists against the zip ties again to punctuate his threat.

Rylan, unfazed, only nodded, "Noted."

The two exchanged intense eye contact before Rylan abruptly ended the staring contest.

"Alright, look, I don't want to be here all night, so let's get back on track, okay? Let's talk Jannette. The story I gathered from the news reports is; you threw a jar full of nitric acid in her face because she wouldn't go out with you. Is that right?"

Abraham remained silent and continued to stare defiantly at his abductor. Rylan hung his head, already fed up with Abraham's attitude.

"Abe, this isn't gonna go down like you think it is, bubba. I'm sincerely asking you to work with me before I do something you'll regret."

"How 'bout this? Go fuck yourself."

Rylan sighed. He put the knife back in the bag, pulled out the roll of tape, tore off two long strips, then connected them to create one double-wide strip. Amidst a steady stream of crude threats, he stepped around Abraham's body, stopped at the head, and immediately pounced. Once the tape strips were in place across his victim's mouth, he returned to the bag to retrieve the hammer.

Abraham continued yelling obscenities through the tape, bucking and twisting his body like a freshly caught fish trying desperately to return to the water. Rylan didn't acknowledge him. He simply positioned himself beside Abraham's right leg and grasped the knee. As he drew the hammer over his head, he heard a short gasp, then stone silence. He brought the hammer down hard onto Abraham's shin, snapping the bone like a pretzel stick.

Proud of his aim, Rylan stood and returned to his crate to wait. Abraham howled and began choking on his spit, causing snot to spray from his nostrils. He gasped for air, gawking in disbelief at his smashed leg until his vision began to blur and darken around the edges.

"Hey! Stay with me." Rylan clapped his hands loudly. "Don't pass out. Just breathe."

Abraham blinked rapidly, trying to regain focus.

"Go ahead and lay your head down on the floor there. Let your neck rest some." Rylan suggested, and Abraham took his advice. "Abe, I promise, this isn't how I wanted us to start off, but at the same time, I don't have the patience to endure your attitude. So, I'm going to say it again: how quickly we finish up here is entirely dependent on your participation in our discussion. If you don't answer me, or if you lie to me, I will hurt you. Now, I'll give you a few minutes to pull yourself together, and then we'll start again."

Abraham lay on the dusty linoleum floor, defeated, flinching frequently as the pain rushed through his body in irregular waves. Rylan recalled his sorrow when witnessing John lying in a similar state. He reflected on how the old man's suffering had affected him, then wondered why Abraham's plight didn't stimulate similar emotions. Why, instead of sadness and pity, he only felt annoyance and impatience? After a minute had passed, Rylan finally stood. Abraham's head shot up, chin-to-chest, to see what his tormentor was doing.

Rylan offered, "Okay, I'll give you one last chance. I'm going to take the tape off again, and we're going to talk. Agreed?

Abraham didn't respond. He just stared wide-eyed at the man holding the hammer.

"Agreed?" Rylan repeated, then tapped his shoe against Abraham's right foot.

The immense pain, shooting through Abraham's broken leg, spurred another outburst of tortured agony and a muffled but clearly understood response, "Yes! Fuck! YES!"

Rylan tread around to Abraham's head again, knelt, and peeled the tape from his mouth. He remained in place for a moment in case his quarry decided to yell for help, but when he didn't, Rylan returned to his perch on the plastic crate.

"Alright, Abe, let's start at the beginning. I want you to tell me how you knew Jannette."

Abraham burned with rage as the surging pain from his leg continued to cause spasms throughout his body, but fearing another swing of the damned hammer, he begrudgingly began to speak again.

"I never knew Jannette, okay? I had seen her on Instagram, and that was it; I wanted her. Then I tried a few times to slide into her DM's, but the bitch kept ignorin' me."

"What did you do then?"

"I found her on Twitter and started following her there; then I seen that she liked to go to this club on the weekends. So, I drove down."

"To Memphis?"

"Yeah, Memphis."

"You live in DC but drove all the way to Memphis to see her at a dance club?"

"If you'd seen her, you'd understand. Anyway, I drive down, walk up in the club, and offer to buy her a drink, but this stuck-up bitch takes the drink right out my hand and straight up turns her back on me. I swear I shudda choked her ass out right there, but I didn't 'cause I got self-control."

"Alright. You left the club then?"

"Hell yeah, if I'd stayed any longer, they'd have to call the bacon brigade to bring me some of them shiny bracelets, nah-mean?"

"Sure. When was the next time you saw Jannette then?"

"The next weekend. Had to be Saturday night."

"And what happened that time?"

"Same shit. I drive down again, buy her a drink, but this time she actually says 'thanks' before strollin' away to find her girlfriends. Check that out; I want you to see that, man, see I tried to do it the right way. I tried, but she wasn't havin' it. It's her fault."

Rylan itched to refute his captive's appalling logic, but chose to stay on track, "What did you do then?"

"I left the club; then I'm sure you know the rest after that."

"Tell me anyway. Act like I don't know." Rylan urged.

"Well, I saw on her Twitter feed; she always did this 'hangover brunch' bullshit on Sundays with her friends, and they always went to the same restaurant spot. So, I pull up outside the place. Through the front window, I could see them laughin' and stuffing their fat fuckin' faces. I didn't make a scene in the restaurant. See, I was patient. I let them have their little quiches with their little mimosas, and I waited for them to leave, then I met them at the front door. I splashed her face, and then I left. End of story."

Rylan shivered at the casual way Abraham relayed such a heinous attack. He could feel the temperature in his chest rising rapidly. He swallowed hard, took a deep breath, and hoped the worst of Abraham's story was behind him.

"The news said you'd gotten the nitric acid from your cousin who worked for a fertilizer manufacturer back here in Virginia. That right?"

"Yeah, that's right."

"If you got it here, you must've brought it to Memphis. Were you already planning to splash acid in her face when you drove there on Saturday, then?"

"I was ready in case she did me dirty like before."

"You were ready to ruin the rest of her life over a twenty-dollar cocktail?"

"Naw, naw, naw, don't try to make that shit about money. It ain't have nothin' to do with the cash. It's the principle of the thing. It's disrespectful."

Rylan's neck muscles twitched. "Disrespectful? You said disrespectful? Explain to me, then, what do you call throwing corrosive acid in someone's face, permanently disfiguring her, and leaving her blind in both eyes?"

"I call it getting even." Abraham's eyes twinkled with thinly subdued glee.

Rylan's anger flared up all at once. He jumped up from his seat but was able to stop himself before going any further. He stood over Abraham, seething, with one hand tightly balled into a fist and the fingers of the other biting hard into the hammer's leather-wrapped handle.

Abraham, startled by the unexpected move, recoiled in defense, then immediately grimaced at the fresh agony his movement caused in his leg. Rylan forced himself to turn and walk a few steps away. Facing a dingy wall, he closed his eyes and tried to calm down. He could hear the familiar scuffling sounds of yet another captive attempting to free themselves while his back was turned, but he was confident in the integrity of the zip ties. After two long minutes, he had gotten his pulse rate under control and turned back around to find Abraham suddenly still, sweaty, and looking guilty. Disinterested, he returned to his seat and spoke in a regulated, monotone voice.

"Abe, when you found out the extent of Jannette's injuries, did you regret it at all?"

"You want me to be honest?"

"Yes, I do," Rylan said flatly.

"You gonna control yourself if you don't like what I'm sayin'?"

Rylan took one more deep, steadying breath. "Yes."

"You asked if I regretted it? Hell no. To me, this was the best-case scenario. She needed to be taught a lesson."

"Taught a lesson? What lesson?"

"To humble herself. As a woman, she needed to learn her place is to be submissive."

Rylan could feel his face getting hot again, "So, she was supposed to submit to you? Even if she wasn't attracted to you?"

"Fuckin' right! These bitches walk around with their faces all painted up, tiddies pushed up, ass cheeks hanging out the bottom of their itty-bitty little skirts, straight up beggin' for attention, then they suddenly act outraged when it draws attention. How's that s'posed to make sense?"

"That's not what...." Rylan started to say but was cut off.

"They got shit all twisted. Think back to caveman times; if a man seen a woman he wanted, he took her, didn't matter if she was already with another man; the stronger caveman kept the woman. What'd they call that in school? Natural selection? Women ain't strong enough to survive on their own, so our job has always been to provide protection from the wild animals and hunt for food; then women was supposed to prepare the food, provide us pleasure, and make babies. That's the deal. That's how God intended it. Ask Adam and Eve! So tell me, how, a million years later, did we get the shit completely flipped upside down? Nowadays, these bitches act like they the gatekeepers to some magical place, and only they get to choose who gets in. Naw bitch, that ain't how it's s'posed to work. I swear, someone long ago done fucked up letting these ungrateful bitches think they have any power." Abraham huffed in resentful frustration, "They crazy, man. Straight-up insane. That's why I just stopped asking and started goin' caveman on them."

Rylan closed his gaping mouth long enough to ask, "What does that mean?"

Abraham let a sly smirk stretch into a wide grin. "Nothin', man. It don't mean nothin'."

Rylan shook his head, attempting to realign his scattered thoughts after Abraham's stunning diatribe. "Abe, what do you mean by 'going caveman on them'?"

"Like I said, I just stopped asking."

The two men remained in silence for a while. Though Rylan wanted desperately to dig deeper, he was afraid. His whole body was vibrating with suppressed rage. He convinced himself to shift the line of questioning for a little while, if only to calm down again, before returning to Abraham's potentially incendiary comments.

"I need you to help me understand something. In the news report, you were identified as being part of the incel community. Now, I tried to read up on the subject a little, but I still don't understand it. How would you describe the belief system there?"

"Oh, you read up on it, huh?"

Abraham was vexed at the thought that Rylan would seek to understand him by scanning through a handful of news articles.

"I tried, but there's not much."

"Of course there's not. No one gives a shit about us!"

"Well, I'm trying. Help me understand it."

Abraham huffed again but acquiesced. "The basic book-type definition of incels, or involuntary celibates, are men who ain't got no hope of finding a sexual partner."

"Right, I got that part, but what I don't understand is, why not just use sex workers?"

"Naw, man, hookers don't count. That's just paying for a service. What I'm talkin' about is a deeper relationship beyond just sex. Like everyone else, we want something lasting, meaningful."

"Okay, what about the caveman analogy you mentioned earlier, then? There doesn't seem to be much room for a lasting, loving relationship in that scenario."

"Yeah, don't worry about that. Once I own her, I'll make her love me." He chuckled softly behind a smug grin.

Rylan shivered in disgust. He gawked at Abraham's smiling face and fantasized about driving the claw end of his hammer into the bridge of his nose. Rylan hung his head in an effort to re-center himself yet again. "Okay, okay, okay," he muttered.

Abraham watched the nameless man, who had broken his leg, straining to comprehend the concepts he was describing. He relished seeing the mental anguish he was causing in his tormentor and was becoming more confident that, once he got one of the zip ties to snap, he would be able to overpower the man and win his freedom. Earlier, while Rylan was turned away, Abraham had noticed the rough edges of the holes drilled through the thick PVC pipe, where the zip ties had been threaded, then fastened around his wrists. If another opportunity arose, he intended to use the rough edges of the PVC pipe to grind enough of the zip tie to snap it, but in the meantime, he needed to be patient and wait for the opportune time to act.

Okay," Rylan uttered finally, then cleared his throat and sat up, "please continue."

"Where was I?"

"I think we only got as far as your definition."

"Right. So, in your vast research, did you read up on the 80/20 rule?"

"No."

"Of course not." Abraham rolled his eyes dramatically, hoping to get further under his captor's skin. "The 80/20 rule says that the top eighty percent of women, the 'Stacys,' only consider men from the top twenty percent, the 'Chads,' to be acceptable breeding stock. Now do the math. What does that leave? That leaves eighty percent of the men in America pickin' through the scraps of the remaining twenty percent of women who don't happen to have sky-high standards. That means millions of men, like me, are completely left out of the breeding pool."

"I still don't understand the...."

"Of course you don't understand!" Abraham angrily exclaimed. "You'd never understand what it's like. You're a fucking Chad! You won the genetic sweepstakes at birth. Look at those broad shoulders, the square jaw, and fuckin' perfect cheekbones; I mean, fuckin' look at you! Your goddamned eyes look like balls of liquid obsidian! You probably drive a damn Mercedes, don't you?"

Rylan was caught off guard and completely ambivalent about how to respond. Abraham had blindsided him with what amounted to a compliment, harshly wrapped in a ferocious indictment. Uncertain of how to respond, he chose to ignore it entirely.

"Abe, you mentioned a breeding pool. So does that mean all this incel stuff boils down to a matter of procreation, then?"

"No, this 'incel stuff' is not all about procreation! That's a big part of the problem, though. They're denying us a chance to ascend, and you know what? A lot of it is 'cause all these bitches been fed lies by them rom-com movies for years; they're out there guarding the pussy, clutching onto dreams that one day, one of the Chads will magically fall into their lap."

Rylan shook his head in amazement. "I have to say, that's a dangerously pessimistic worldview, man. Don't you have hope that there is someone out there for you?"

"Aww, how romantic." Abraham mocked. "No, I don't buy into that bullshit. I've learned the hard way that that kind of hope is nothin' but rope fuel."

"Rope fuel?"

Abraham scoffed, "Don't you know anything? Rope fuel drives you toward the noose."

"Oh. I see. Then have you, uh, tried, or attempted suicide before?"

"When I was younger, but not since. A few of my friends successfully swallowed that black pill, though."

"Black pill? Oh. Okay. Sorry."

Abraham turned his head, breaking eye contact for the first time in a while. "They're better off."

Sensing the soreness of the subject, Rylan gave Abraham a moment in silence, then cleared his throat to begin again.

"Alright, help me out; let me know if I'm understanding this thing right. You're saying that by virtue of being a man, you have some, I don't know... some inherent right to sex, and you're being cheated out of it?"

Abraham returned his gaze to Rylan. "There it is. Now you're catching up."

"And it's the women's fault, right?"

"Exactly." Abraham smiled proudly.

Rylan rubbed his head hard with both palms, "Abe, I'm not sure how else to put this, but... that's just mind-blowingly stupid. It's stupid enough that it'd be laughable if you weren't this serious about it."

Abraham's smile disappeared, and his face immediately flushed crimson. "Fuck you!" He spit.

"No, no, hear me out. The truth is, even the beautiful people you call Chads and Stacys have failed relationships, but that doesn't mean there's some systemic flaw in society. People have preferences. I'm sure there are women out there who you'd find repulsive, and if they hit on you, you'd turn them down. Is that proof of some conspiracy against the, how did you call them... the bottom twenty percent of women? No, it just means those women are not your type. Now, are there attributes that are generally more attractive to most women? Sure, probably, but just because you're deficient in some of those attributes doesn't mean you're going to be pushed out of this imaginary' breeding pool'. Though, with that being said... you know what will definitely keep you out of it?" Rylan leaned in closer to Abraham. "Playing the victim."

Abraham remained silent, red-faced, smoldering.

Swept up in his own momentum, Rylan couldn't help but keep pressing. "Now, let's talk about that 'inherent right to sex' thing. Let me see if I can put this plainly for you... you don't have a right to sex. You don't! Think about it this way; let's say I'm a gay man with this same 'right to sex' you're declaring. One day, out of the blue, I see you and decide I want your flabby ass. Do I have the right to just bend you over and take it?"

Rylan didn't think Abraham could turn any redder, but he was wrong.

"Yeah, I didn't think so." Rylan felt like he should stop, but couldn't, "Oh, yeah, about that bullshit caveman theory of yours, look, a million years ago, primitive men were communicating in howls and grunts like animals, so if you're looking to the cavemen for examples of how to handle intimate relationships, bubba, I gotta tell you, it's a damn good thing you're NOT procreating. We don't need any more people like you on this planet, and I, for one, am glad you're gonna die a virgin."

"I'M NOT A FUCKING VIRGIN, YOU FUCK!" Abraham exploded, spraying spit as he screamed at Rylan.

"Oh, no?"

"Fuck no. You thought I was a virgin? Who's fuckin' stupid now? You think I'd actually let these bitches out here deny me? I told you, I take what I want! I have ascended to a whole 'nother level; you can't even imagine. You're lookin' at the proud papa of three children, all boys too, motherfucker, and it shoulda been more, but some of those worthless hoes ran off and got abortions."

Rylan sat back, mystified. "Three kids? Then what's with all this incel bullshit then?"

"Don't get it twisted; it's not bullshit. You just can't see it. You're blinded by your own reflection in the mirror. The struggle is real, very real, for a lot of us, but for me, my time in prison changed my outlook on things. It made me realize life's way too short to be waitin' for somethin' to happen. You got to get up and make things happen."

"Wait, you said some of the women got abortions. That means you got multiple women pregnant?"

"Hell yeah. Got to spread my seed." He winked at Rylan.

"How is that even possible? You've been out of prison less than two years."

"I work fast." He chuckled.

Rylan shook his head. "I don't buy it, Abe. I think you're lying."

"I'm lying? You don't think I've got the stones to rape them bitches?"

All the thoughts racing through Rylan's mind came to a screeching halt. "Rape?" The word fell from his open mouth.

Seeing the look of horrified astonishment on Rylan's face, Abraham stifled his laughter at first, "What happened? You thought they'd all given it up willingly?" He erupted in hysterical laughter at

Rylan's naivety. "Naw man, every single one of them tried to fight me off at first, well... I take that back, a few just froze up and let me do my thing, but mostly they all put up a good fight. They made it fun." A sinister smile spread across his face as he reminisced. "Shit, you know, one of them almost got away! That's when I got smart and bought a gun, a pretty little bulldog revolver like yours. Isn't it lovely what people will let you do to them when you shove a gun in their face?"

Abraham started laughing again, lowering his head to the ground to comfortably revel in his accomplishments. Rylan, who had been listening to Abraham with growing horror, felt a sudden surge of blood rush his brain, and in a single blink, everything turned red.

Before registering a single thought, he lurched forward and swung the hammer in a wide arc until it smashed into the side of Abraham's jaw. Instantly, blood, spit, and broken teeth exploded from the man's lips like shrapnel from a grenade.

Abraham never saw the strike coming, and as the cracked pieces of his dislodged mandible hung loosely askew, held only in place by the flesh of his cheeks, his eyes rolled wildly in their sockets, desperate to understand what happened. It was as though his nervous system, shocked by the speed of the attack, was delayed in carrying the pain signal to the brain until it suddenly arrived like a tidal wave against the side of a brick building, then all at once, the pain was everything.

Abraham's eyes bulged wide with panic. He tried to scream, but his throat was filled with blood. He choked and coughed, spraying gore from his mutilated mouth. As he desperately tried to clear the airway, he could do nothing but helplessly watch while Rylan raised the bloody hammer high over his head. The fearsome image completely stopped Abraham's heart. Rylan's face was splattered with blood and warped by wrath. Foamy spit hung on his lips as he spewed curses through his barred teeth like a rabid animal. In Abraham's final view of his tormentor, he no longer saw a man, but a demon unleashed.

21

— • —

AUGUST 15, 2005, SUNDAY

FORT DRUM, NEW YORK

Rylan waited only seven seconds for the elevator car to arrive before charging through the door to the adjacent stairwell and sprinting up the stairs. The maternity ward was on the hospital's fifth floor, and Rylan knew he should pace himself, but the overwhelming fear that Abigail would bring their child into the world without him was like spurs to a horse's haunches. He cleared three full stairs in each stride, and by the time he reached the third floor, his lungs felt like he was breathing acid and his legs screamed for mercy, but he refused to slow his pace.

Gasping for air, he reached the landing where a large purple number five was painted on the door. He stepped out into the brightly lit hallway, found the maternity ward straight ahead, and darted through the waiting room.

His combat boots screeched to a halt on the tiled floor in front of the reception desk, and even though he was out of breath and his mouth was sticky-dry, he managed to utter his wife's name to the nurse at the desk. Sensing his urgency, she took a quick glance at her admissions roster, then got up to escort him to delivery room number three.

Rylan could hear Abigail crying out in pain as soon as he passed through the security doors into the maternity ward, but before continuing any further, the nurse insisted he stop to clean his hands at the nearby wash station. As he vigorously scrubbed and rinsed, he could hear Abigail's cries of agony down the hall. He swiftly dried his hands and then hurried toward the sound of his wife's tortured voice.

Two steps into the delivery room, Rylan abruptly froze in his tracks as his excitement gave way to crippling fear. Everything had become far too real, too fast. So real that it somehow felt fake, staged. Dizziness floated into Rylan's head as he stood motionless inside the doorway, watching the doctor and two nurses huddled between the knees of his bride. It occurred to him that while he had seen many versions of a delivery portrayed on a television screen, witnessing it in person was nothing short of overwhelming.

Abigail was propped up in bed, her legs folded like an accordion, with her face tightly distorted into an expression of intense anguish, fear, and determination. Random strands of her curly hair had stuck to the sweat on her face. She looked wild and ferocious, a stark departure from her usually kempt appearance. She briefly opened her eyes, snatched a quick breath, and braced herself to push again, but noticed someone standing in the doorway wearing camouflage fatigues. She gasped.

Having already accepted that she would have to face such an unspeakable trial alone, Abigail had done her best to steel herself for the coming storm, but in that restless moment, her immense joy at seeing Rylan was so powerful that it crossed over a threshold into bitter sadness, and tears immediately started streaming down her cheeks. Although she was genuinely grateful for his presence, she couldn't help but feel strangely disappointed in herself.

She released her crushing grip on the bed sheets and reached her hand out to Rylan. The gesture was enough to free him from his paralysis, and he flew to her side. The doctor and nurses briefly glanced up to acknowledge him, then returned to their tasks. Rylan held Abigail's hand, kissed her lips, and wiped the hair from her face. They spoke no words, but their eyes said everything.

Abigail took a forceful deep breath, squeezed Rylan's hand, and then courageously resumed the arduous business of creating life. Rylan stood bedside, and although he reminded himself that his job was to be supportive, he felt completely useless. He uttered words of encouragement, gently rubbed her back, let her squeeze his hand, and occasionally reminded her to breathe, but all the while, he silently wondered if he was helping or not. Ultimately, he was simply too scared to ask. He had never seen anyone exert that much effort for so long. He watched in awe as she strained and pushed, breathed and pushed, screamed and pushed their infant child into the world.

It all felt like a vivid dream to Rylan, whose mind hadn't yet accepted the situation as reality. Adding to the surreal sensation was that he was in the woods with the rest of his platoon only an hour prior, practicing how to set up defensive fighting positions.

The unit was preparing for another deployment to Iraq when the company commander received a phone call from the on-base hospital informing him that Abigail had prematurely gone into labor. He quickly assigned Rylan's two sergeants to deliver the expectant father to the hospital in one of the tactical Humvees.

Rylan left everything behind with his platoon and quickly hopped into the Hummer for the forty-minute trip to the hospital. Along the way, Rylan had tried to call Abigail's phone multiple times, with no answer, ratcheting up the tension in his chest each time. Finally, the Humvee's knobby tires squealed to a stop in front of the emergency room entrance, and Rylan ran in to find his wife.

As he held her hand, Rylan felt humbled and honored just to be standing beside his wife in the delivery room. His demeanor had been one of subdued reverence, but once the doctor announced that the baby's head was crowning, the news boosted the young couple's confidence, suddenly, Rylan became much more animated, nearly yelling affirmations at his wife like a fiery football coach confined to the sidelines. Abigail, already thoroughly exhausted, roared like a lioness and found a reserve of energy from somewhere deep within herself. She pushed as hard as her muscles could take, her voice growing louder with each passing moment of burning exertion.

Suddenly, a newborn child appeared in the world. Everyone fell silent, holding their breath, waiting for the baby to cry, but when no sound came, the nurses sprung into action, working feverishly to wipe away some of the mucus and blood from the infant's tiny gray-pink body. The doctor quickly cleared the child's airway and carefully turned it over. She only patted the limp body on the back twice before the baby issued a tiny gurgling cough and began to wail. Everyone exhaled in relief, and the doctor cheerfully proclaimed that Rylan and Abigail had a new baby girl.

One of the nurses extended a pair of medical sheers toward Rylan, offering the opportunity for him to cut the umbilical cord. Rylan, who had been completely mesmerized by the delivery, was caught off guard by the offer. At first, he wanted to reject the proposal for fear of making some catastrophic mistake, but he reminded himself that it was a once-in-a-lifetime opportunity. He took the sheers into his shaking hand and, carefully following the nurse's instructions, severed the tether between mother and child.

The nurses made quick work of wiping the fluid off the baby's body, then swaddled it in a thin blanket before bringing the little girl back to her parents. She was placed into her mother's waiting arms while her father stood beside her, astonished by what his wife had accomplished.

Once cradled in her mother's embrace, the little girl stopped wailing and nestled tenderly into her creator's bosom. Abigail began crying tears of immeasurable joy. She glanced at her husband with an expression of blissful disbelief, and he could only shake his head in amazement. He leaned in, kissed the top of Abigail's head, and held his lips there for a while.

"I am so happy to be here with you and our daughter, babe. She's beautiful, you're beautiful, and I am just so damn proud of you."

"I'm glad you made it, Rye. I was worried."

"Me too." He laughed nervously, "I didn't expect she'd be coming two weeks early."

"Right?" Abigail agreed. "Well, she's here now."

The new parents kissed, then both looked to their child. Her skin was pale with delicately blended shades of lavender and peach. Abigail lightly brushed the back of her hand across the baby's cheek; it felt cool to the touch and impossibly soft, and although the baby's eyelids had yet to open, her lips had parted just enough to allow the tip of her tongue to poke out.

"So, Penelope, then?" Abigail asked while gazing lovingly down at her daughter.

"Penelope." Rylan confirmed, recalling the agreed-upon name, "Our little Penny."

Before long, the nurse reappeared and asked if she could take the child to be weighed and have her vitals measured. Abigail gently kissed Penelope's forehead, then reluctantly handed her to the nurse, but as soon as she was out of her mother's arms, the baby girl started crying again. She continued to screech while being whisked away to the scale in the corner of the room.

Unable to bear being away from the child, Rylan followed closely behind them. The nurse laid Penelope on her back in the plastic tray and walked around the far side to collect readings while the new father leaned over to get a closer look at the squirming infant.

The sound of her continued crying was heartbreaking to Rylan, and he was tempted to lift her immediately and soothe her, but he refrained. Instead, he gently placed the tip of his finger into Penelope's tiny palm, and her miniature digits reflexively closed around his finger. Unexpectedly, she stopped crying, and Rylan froze, fearing something was wrong, but as he watched with growing worry, Penelope's eyelids slowly parted, and she took in her very first images of her surroundings. Rylan softly gasped, then held his breath as he prepared to meet his daughter. She turned slightly and looked into her father's eyes with wonder and uncertainty. All of a sudden, Rylan's legs felt weak as it occurred to him that his was the first face she'd ever see in the world. He was so overcome with emotion he wanted to cry.

"Hello, beautiful. I'm your dad."

Penelope examined her father's face with blossoming curiosity. Her little body had stopped fidgeting while her grey-brown eyes tried to make sense of what she was seeing. Rylan could almost perceive her newborn brain wrestling with the strangeness of the image, and he tried to remain still so she could study without distraction, but the tip of her tongue poked out between her lips again, and he couldn't contain his smile.

The nurse suddenly interrupted, apologizing profusely for breaking up the moment as she lifted the baby from the measuring tray. She quickly finished cleaning up Penelope, swaddled her in a clean blanket, and brought the baby back to her mother. Rylan returned to their side, glowing from his first interaction with his daughter and delighted to see the two of them together.

The trio remained huddled together, talking and making cooing sounds to their baby before one of the nurses coached Abigail through her first attempt at breastfeeding. Thankfully, Penelope immediately latched on and drank eagerly while her mother lightly stroked her wispy black hair.

Eventually, the doctor came back into the room. She informed the parents that the delivery went well, and the baby was healthy, but as a precaution, they would like to keep them under observation through the night. The young, exhausted couple had no objections, and moments later, another nurse came to transfer the young family to a recovery room. Once there, the new nurse checked the patients' vitals and encouraged Abigail to get some rest, a suggestion met with very little resistance.

Rylan sat quietly in the chair beside the hospital bed, holding his exhausted wife's hand while she began to doze with Penelope already asleep in a nearby bassinet. While primarily concerned with his wife's convalescence, he found it nearly impossible to stop staring at the chubby baby snuggly wrapped in a swaddling blanket. She was so adorable and so perfect he had to keep reminding himself she was real. He remained in a state of mild disbelief at the past few hour's events, even with living proof resting an arm's reach away.

After a short while, Abigail began snoring softly, like the purring of a housecat, and Rylan turned his attention to his daughter. He leaned closer to her bassinet, craning his neck a little further to get a better look. He thought she looked simultaneously fragile and frighteningly formidable, like something transcendent, like an angel. Her tiny facial features appeared deliberately shaped by a master sculptor rather than the result of a natural occurrence. He wondered how he could be so lucky.

"Hey there, pretty baby," Rylan whispered. "It's your dad again. I don't mean to bother you. I'll let you sleep, but I just wanted to let you know I love you. I am so proud of you, Penny, and I hope I can be the father you deserve."

Rylan leaned forward and lightly touched his lips to the top of her head, then lingered for a moment, breathing in the subtle scent of her skin. The delicate fragrance carried the faint notes of her mother's skin in the morning, an approaching spring rain, and freshly baked bread in the distance. He wondered if he had ever smelled something so wonderful before.

Mindful not to disturb his slumbering child, he reluctantly began to retreat into his seat but paused, whispering to his newborn, "I swear to you this: if anyone ever hurts you, I'll murder him and anyone standing in the way."

22

— . —

APRIL 10, 2017, MONDAY

WASHINGTON, D.C.

At four-thirty in the morning, with very few pedestrians out strolling around the National Mall, besides the occasional jogger or wandering vagabond, Rylan was otherwise alone and unencumbered. He meandered among the monuments and memorials, stopping to linger and find inspiration at every monument; each brightened by dedicated floodlights cleverly positioned to give the appearance of carved stone glowing defiantly against the confining night. Within the darkened spaces between the dispersed statues and fluted columns, he was able to roam and find the serenity he so desperately needed after leaving Abraham's broken corpse in the dusty, abandoned classroom.

Rylan was aware that, over the past two years, his entire philosophy of life had been irreversibly altered, and some things had gained in significance while others had waned, but he was surprised to discover how much the memorials, particularly the war memorials, had grown in relevance since his visit as a child. He now stepped upon the grounds with respect and reverence as though walking through a cathedral.

Softening his steps while treading through the World War II Memorial, he recalled his old platoon sergeant, with a thick Bostonian accent, retelling stories his grand-father had imparted on him of old battle-worn doughboys called back to Europe to fight a second war against a German tyrant.

Strolling past the polished black granite wall of the Vietnam War Memorial, Rylan's mind replayed images of John Burbules pensively gazing at the wall of remembrance in his house. The melancholy notes of the old man's voice echoed in Rylan's ears, "Some good men in some bad bush over there."

Eventually, Rylan's route took him to the Korean War Memorial, one of the sites that had not yet been constructed when he last visited. Standing in front of the collection of steel statues, he was unexpectedly overcome with sorrow and sat down in the middle of the walkway to absorb the magnitude of the moment.

In all, there were nineteen statues of servicemen arranged in a wedge formation, appearing to be in the middle of a long patrol. Their postures were slumped from the heavy rucksacks borne beneath their wind-blown rain ponchos. Their rifles and machine guns hung from their tired hands as they trudged through an imaginary field, the grass at their feet intentionally grown long to underscore the unrelenting battlefield conditions on the Korean Peninsula. Under their helmets, each face perfectly portrayed the misery of the warfighter, long in a combat zone, enduring, suffering, and surviving one step at a time through what seems like an endless odyssey back to their home.

Rylan immediately felt a kinship with the metal soldiers, as though they were modeled after his own squad mates, woefully trudging through the Iraqi desert instead of the rice fields of Korea.

He sat on the concrete walkway, quietly reflecting on his experience as a warfighter, and wondered how different it must have been for those in Korea. He imagined it must have been nearly impossible to maintain morale with incessant rains beating down the troops as they dolefully marched through boot-sucking marshlands, but then he recalled something one of his drill sergeants had once said about shared suffering bringing people closer together, and he suddenly understood.

Before long, he noticed someone had left a can of Budweiser along the edge of the memorial. Irritated at the brazen disrespect, he immediately jumped to his feet, intent on retrieving the trash to toss into the closest receptacle, but as he angrily reached down to snatch the can, its contents unexpectedly sloshed and splashed onto his hand. Surprised by the amount of liquid in the canister, he was puzzled as to why someone would open a fresh can of beer only to leave it behind; then it dawned on him that the beer hadn't been discarded. It had been intentionally placed as a solemn tribute from a surviving veteran to his fallen comrades.

Deeply moved by the gesture, he still intended to deposit the can in the trash, but reconsidered and decided to set it back down again instead. With the matter settled, he felt ready to move on. He took one last sweeping survey of the memorial, then resumed his circuitous route towards the Tidal Basin.

As he walked, he noticed the eastern sky had begun to fade into lighter shades of purple and red, and a few early risers had added to the scenery in the park: walking their dogs, practicing yoga, or embarking on a morning run before starting their work day. Despite the additional activity, the atmosphere remained relatively quiet except for the occasional car horn as others set off on their morning commutes. At one point, a young Hispanic man briskly jogged past wearing a t-shirt with the large yellow initials FBI emblazoned across the front, and Rylan couldn't help but smirk at the irony. He wondered if the jogger would be running past any other killers that morning.

Eventually, Rylan arrived at his destination by way of the MLK Memorial. The newest memorial on the mall had been placed among the cherry trees, a stone's throw away from the water's edge. The towering figure of the civil rights leader, carved into a massive sliver of white granite, had unexpectedly taken on a pink hue, reflecting the sky across the pond, which was transitioning into shades of raspberry and grapefruit. The rosy tint from the dawning sky, cast upon the striking image of a man unwilling to yield, perfectly matched the delicate color of the cherry blossoms adorned upon thousands of the surrounding trees and the millions of petals scattered across the ground. Rylan marveled at the breathtaking sight and how his life had brought him to that place, at that time, to witness such an enchanting scene. Unfortunately, the magic proved short-lived as the sun continued to rise, chasing away the color to reveal the pale stone's surface. Impressive nonetheless, Rylan continued to appreciate the artist's skill and ponder the wisdom within the inscribed quotations.

After a while, he strolled over to the railing that outlined the basin's rim, rested his forearms on the rail, and leaned forward to take in the view. The sun, the all-important celestial body that his fellow infantrymen used to call BOB, the Big Orange Ball, had finally crested the horizon, though still obscured by the various government buildings, corporate headquarters, and luxury condominiums that filled the city. The Jefferson Memorial, on the far bank, shone like a beacon flanked by the soft pink of the cherry trees, while a cool breeze, stirred by the arrival of the sun's warmth, gently urged the blossoms to sway and ripples to form on the water's surface.

The resplendent panorama reminded him of Lake Tahoe and how the majestic scenery had moved him. Those fond memories then brought him right back to the moment, only a few minutes prior, when he stood in absolute awe of the dawn's early light upon the MLK Memorial. He wondered if he was becoming a sentimental fool, and if so, if it was such a bad thing.

He remained at the edge of the basin for longer than expected, leaning on the railing, observing life rousing for another day. He was fascinated with the ducks and geese lightly landing on the water and the stray cats sneaking away into the bushes. He was surprised by the number of people out exercising so early while others, already dressed for their workday, were commuting on bicycles. He was particularly amused by the young professionals, wearing full business suits, gliding along the sidewalks on rented neon-green electric scooters.

As Rylan casually observed the people going about their morning routines, one jogger seized his attention. The woman was still a good distance away but was approaching quickly. Nothing about her was particularly noteworthy except her face. It was a face he could never forget. It was unmistakably Toni Caisse. He stood upright, his neck flushed hot, and his blood ran cold. He knew it couldn't be Toni, but his mind couldn't deny what his eyes were seeing. His pulse raced as she ran toward him, beating harder with every footfall, matching her pace. The woman continued to close the distance, and he became convinced she was glaring at him as she ran. His mind began to question itself. She's dead, right? Right?

Rylan attempted to flee his impending doom but found himself welded to the ground. He could only watch in horror as the woman ran him down. As she galloped closer, her image seemed corrupted, distorted, like some hound of hell was wearing the woman's skin, and the wrath burning in her eyes like balls of flame signified his end had finally arrived. He shut his eyes and tried to bolster himself for the onslaught. In what would be his final moment, he felt equally afraid and content, terrified of what might come next but also ready to find out.

In complete darkness, over the loud thumping of his own heartbeat, he heard the woman's strides landing on the concrete as she came closer, then as she passed, continuing her route.

Rylan's eyes popped open, and he spun around to see the woman departing without a single glance in his direction. He exhaled and let a meager chuckle escape. Embarrassed, he glanced around to be sure no one had noticed, then decided to sit down on the nearby park bench for a little while.

He leaned back hard against the park bench to stretch his spine, then settled into the bench and tried to let the unexpected surge of tension subside. In the distance, the sun had just peeked above the tops of the buildings, and the warmth was a pleasant contrast to the cool morning air. Deciding to take advantage of the daylight, he reached into his backpack and pulled out his journal.

Notes: Abraham Poindexter in Washington, DC

-I'm never using an old abandoned building like that again. Disgusting. Rats everywhere. I hate rats, and I can't shake the thought that those nasty bastards are having a feast right now. I have some mixed feelings about that.

-Didn't use the tarp this time. There was no point. The whole building should be condemned.

-I need to get rid of the Trailblazer. I'm a little worried about all the houses near the school. Once the cops eventually find him, all it takes is one person to remember seeing the truck parked there. I think I'm going to make a quick stop in South Carolina to buy a new (used) truck before heading back out West again.

-How can I get some ~~cloroform~~ chloroform? Abe woke up while I was carrying him from the truck to the classroom. I had to drop him off my shoulders in the middle of a dark hallway and choke him out. I imagine chloroform would buy me some more time with them unconscious. On that note, every time I go to knock someone out with the gun, I'm scared I'm going to miss. Is there a better way? I think Chlorform takes a minute to actually knock someone out, right? I don't think it's fast like in the movies. Also, can I still wake them with the smelling salts if I use chloroform? I have some homework to do.

-I lost my cool back there. I tried hard to keep it together, but my temper flared up big time. I wish I could blame it on Abe, but I know it's my fault. I have to do better at controlling my anger, but I think it's getting harder for me to keep my emotions in check. I don't know what to do about that.

Abe really pissed me off, but also... I'm not going to lie; it needed to happen. After John, I had been questioning everything. Everything.

But then Abraham Poindexter happened, and that slimy piece of shit fully restored my faith in my mission. He helped me to remember why I'm doing this. THOSE are the type of people that I'm out here to see.

The six years the judge gave him for the acid attack on Jannette Tripper was a slap on the wrist for what he did to that woman, (especially since he only did three years), but he came out of prison even worse than when he went in! Apparently, he's been raping women since. I mean MULTIPLE WOMEN.

I couldn't control myself.

I nearly blacked out. I never planned to smash his whole face in. That was 100% reflexive.

Okay... if I'm really being honest, ~~I loved~~ it felt incredible burying my hammer in his eye socket. I can't even describe how disgusting, but also satisfying it was to see the whole left side of his skull shattered beneath the skin. It made me feel good knowing this guy would never hurt anyone else ever again. Then, right after, my next hit fell straight on dead-center of his forehead. THAT shit was wild. Cracked him right open. I swear, his head looked like a dropped watermelon! Seriously. The tiny bits of skull in there looked like those little white baby seeds inside the watermelon.

Sorry. Sorry. I wandered off on a tangent. Let me get back on track.

Look, I may seem giddy about bashing in his brains, but I truly do regret it. I really do, but only because it was too quick. He didn't suffer enough. I feel like I let him off the hook. His victims deserved better. I've got to do better.

A couple other things, not about Abraham, but still relevant:

I checked yesterday for updates on the investigations, and so far, there have been "no significant developments" in Edward's case, which is great news, but the weird thing is there's absolutely nothing about Toni or John. I guess that means the bodies haven't been found yet. That works out in my favor, but that's going to suck for whoever finds Toni. It's been a week and a half now, and there's no ~~ventala-tion~~ ventilation in that house.

Alright, last thing, and I hesitate to say this, but it's not as though I can vent my thoughts anywhere else, so... I had mentioned it before, but I keep seeing ~~dead people~~ ~~ghosts~~ the people I've killed. A few minutes ago, I swear I saw Toni jogging. That's now the fourth time I've seen her. Two days ago, I saw Edward (again) working the grill behind the counter at a McDonald's. I told myself he wasn't real, but I still couldn't eat my cheeseburger and had to give it away to a homeless woman. That was the sixth time I've seen him. So far, I haven't seen John anywhere, but if this keeps up, I'm sure he's coming eventually. Abe, too, I guess. I don't know how to handle this. When it started happening, ~~I thought I'd be,~~ I was able to brush it off, like my mind was playing tricks on me, but it's happening more often now, and I think it's getting worse. I legitimately froze up this last time. Seriously. No bullshit. ~~Scared stiff.~~ I don't know what to do. A psychiatrist could probably help, but they ask too many questions. Maybe a psychic? I don't believe in that kind of thing, but I'm starting to question whether this is all in my head or not.

23

— • —

APRIL 10, 2017, MONDAY

WASHINGTON, D.C.

Helio watched the display count the floors as the elevator ascended to the fifth floor. He was eager to get back to work but nervous like a marginal student awaiting the results of an exam. The last of the elevator riders had gotten off on the fourth floor, and as the doors closed, he was left alone in silence for a brief moment. He was grateful to no longer be held captive to the stench of cigarette smoke on a coworker's suit, the incessant fingernail tapping as someone typed a text message on their phone, or the recounting of a weekend fishing trip. The temporary solitude was blissful, and he closed his eyes to relish it until the car stopped again.

He opened his eyes when the doors opened, and Agent Mathis was waiting to greet him with a smug smile. While Helio resented most of his fellow agents for the pale color of their skin, his feelings toward Agent Mathis were closer to actual disgust. He thought Agent Mathis was a spineless sycophant who reminded him of those bothersome little kids in elementary school who always tagged along behind the older kids, begging to be included.

"Good morning, and welcome back, Agent Sangria!" He exclaimed loudly. Then, in a more normal tone, he added, "I am to inform you that Furiosa wants to see you as soon you arrive."

Helio frowned, then deftly stepped back into the elevator before the doors closed. He could feel his anxiety rising along with the elevator as he rode it up two more floors. He closed his eyes again and tried to slow his heartbeat. Thankfully, when he emerged from the lift a second time, no one was waiting to meet him. He walked down the hallway and entered the outer room, which doubled as the secretary's office, but found it empty.

Mrs. Ketchum was not at her desk, screening visitors and casting a judgemental eye on anyone who claimed to have an appointment with the assistant director. Helio took a seat and waited for a minute, but the secretary hadn't yet returned, and with the door to the assistant director's office open, he decided to announce himself.

He stopped in the doorway and saw his boss sitting quietly at her desk, reading a report. She hadn't noticed him yet, so he tugged sharply at the bottom of his suit jacket to ensure he was presentable, then tapped his knuckles on the door frame.

Assistant Director Lauren Coffey was an intimidating woman in nearly every sense of the word. She stood six-foot-three and, despite being fifty-one years old, still possessed the chiseled body of a fitness model, the proud posture of a drill instructor, and the stoic grace of a Greek goddess.

Among the agents in the criminal investigation department, she had acquired the nickname "Furiosa" for how much she resembled one of the main characters in the film "Mad Max: Fury Road" in both appearance and bearing, and although everyone knew her by that name, no one dared utter it in her presence.

Hearing knocking at her door, Coffey calmly glanced up and saw Helio standing in her doorway.

"Agent Sangria, take a seat." She said flatly.

He approached one of the seats in front of her desk and sat down while she watched him like a cat assessing its prey; then, once he was seated, she coolly returned to the report she had been reading.

Helio sat quietly waiting, observing the unique items displayed around her office, but his eyes kept returning to the spear collection on the wall beside him. They looked to have been collected from different parts of the world. Helio recognized some of the styles and symbols; Spartan, African, Shaolin, Celtic, and Roman, but there were others he couldn't identify. He was engrossed in studying an ornately engraved spear with characters that seemed to be Eskimo when Coffey startled him.

"My apologies." She stated coldly, more as a required formality than an expression of regret.

Helio turned to see her casually sitting back in her seat, her gaze locked onto his eyes. Her face was placid and impossible to read.

"How is your shoulder?" She asked.

"Much better, Ma'am."

"That's good. Any mobility issues?"

"No, Ma'am. Ready to go."

"Good." She fell silent for a moment but never broke eye contact. "Agent Sangria, no one likes you. You are aware of this, correct?"

The bluntness of the message was more jarring to Helio than the content. He blinked a few times.

"Yes, Ma'am."

"What are your thoughts on that?"

Helio cleared his throat, "Ma'am; I don't believe I need them to like me. I just need them to do their jobs."

She fell silent again, then continued, "Do you like your fellow agents?"

Helio swallowed. Sensing a trap question, he paused and weighed his response.

"No, Ma'am, I don't."

"Why?"

"They're too slow."

"Is that all?"

Her tone had shifted slightly, enough for Helio to sense she already knew the answer, but he also knew he couldn't disclose his racial bias, so he lied.

"Yes, Ma'am."

She stopped talking for an uncomfortably long period of time and only stared at him. She never moved and never looked away. He felt sweat beginning to bead at his temples.

"I don't like you, Agent Sangria. I don't like you because you're arrogant, dismissive of others, and unwilling to work as a member of a team; as such, you are disruptive to the cohesive nature of my organization. In this way, you are unintentionally subversive. Your considerable intellect, instincts, and work ethic were sufficient to allow you to rise to the top of your class at Quantico and earn a coveted assignment here, but they are not enough to afford you preferential treatment when your conduct is toxic. It is important that you keep in mind: a transfer to a less desirable location is only a pen stroke away. Either you will get with the program here, or you will find your career significantly stunted. Is anything I have just said to you unclear?"

"No, Ma'am."

"I have spoken to your now-retired partner, Frank, at length, about you. From his perspective, despite your boundless potential as an investigator, he is unsure of your ability to make the required behavioral changes. I have also spoken to his wife, Bao, who is a very close friend and mentor of mine. She believes you may be redeemable, mainly because your youth provides you the time and space to evolve. I remain unconvinced but will give you the opportunity, the support, and the accountability needed for growth. Is any of this unclear?"

"No, Ma'am."

"It is worth stating that I agree with your previous observation: I don't need to like you; I just need you to do your job. That being said, I think your assessment of what constitutes 'your job' is too narrow-minded. Your job is to conduct investigations and solve crimes. The way in which you accomplish your investigations is through the use of the Bureau's extensive resources, one of which happens to be our considerable in-house talent pool of subject matter experts and our external network of otherwise talented individuals. That network has been cultivated and maintained for decades by agents who knew the full value of teamwork. It has always been an implied task, but now, for you, its become a specified task to not only maintain those relationships but to build upon them, so future FBI agents may walk in your footsteps and efficiently solve crimes. Is this in any way unclear to you?"

"No, Ma'am."

"In summary, how all of this works is: I entrust you to lead investigations using OUR resources, and thus, WE work together to solve crimes. In the course of your investigations, do your best to preserve our resources, including human resources, and don't ruin them along the way. In much simpler terms, do your fucking job." She paused, then calmly added, "What are your questions?"

Helio had many questions and felt strongly that he should defend himself, but he remembered his mother's words after he was fired from his first job, "If you're getting chewed out by your boss, just keep your mouth shut. You'll only make it worse by speaking."

"I have no questions, Ma'am."

"Good. I intended to have you on desk duty for your first week back, but Agent Schultz has appendicitis and will be out for a while. I want you to help out Agent Mathis with his open case for now, and you will be assigned the very next case that comes up. Do you have any issues with this?"

Truthfully, the idea of working for Mathis was nauseating, but Helio kept it to himself, "None, Ma'am."

"Good. Remember, I will be watching closely how you conduct yourself. If I am unsatisfied, SAC Grantham at the Minneapolis office will find a young agent in a well-tailored suit standing at his doorway instead of mine. You are dismissed, Agent Sangria."

Helio stood, straightened his suit, and thanked AD Coffey before walking out of her office. Mrs. Ketchum was now at her desk, and he could feel her eyes on him as he exited. It wasn't until he reached the elevator that he let himself relax.

He was frustrated by Coffey's harsh words but not angry. He knew enough of her to see she was trying to motivate him, but her words were still a bitter pill to swallow. He also knew she never bluffed and always followed through, so, if she said she would transfer him to Minnesota, she would.

The elevator dinged, the doors opened, and Helio stepped inside, groaning at the thought of working with Mathis. It was obvious Coffey was trying to test him with the pairing, but he accepted the challenge and started to mentally prepare himself for the task. Once again, the elevator dinged, the doors opened, and he stepped out onto the fifth floor. Mathis was thankfully nowhere to be seen, so Helio quietly walked to his desk. He hadn't been there in a month, and to his relief, everything was exactly as he had left it.

Hearing Mathis' obnoxiously loud laugh on the other side of the room, he sighed and told himself to stop procrastinating. He took out a notebook from the top drawer, grabbed a pen, and began the loathsome walk to Mathis' desk.

"Well, if it isn't One-Armed Willy!" Mathis exclaimed loud enough to be sure anyone in his vicinity could hear his witty one-liner. When Helio glared back at him, Mathis quickly tried to defuse the situation, "Just messing with you, man. How is the arm?"

"It's the shoulder, and it's fine. Clean through-and-through."

"Hell yeah. If you're gonna get shot, that's how you want to do it."

"Hmm," Helio grunted.

"I hear Frank smoked that perp right after he shot you, like some fucking John Wayne, Clint Eastwood, type of shit." Mathis mimicked a gunslinger in a standoff, quick-drawing his finger guns.

"He did a good job."

"Good job? Fucking great job! Two in the gut, bang-bang, that piece of shit bled out in a world of pain!"

"Yeah. Anyway, Coffey sent me down to come see you."

"To see me? What for?"

"I'm to assist you with your case." The words tasted sour in his mouth.

"What's that supposed to mean?

Helio repeated himself slowly. "Assist you. With your case."

"Oh, you mean 'assist me' like bringing me a cup of coffee?"

"You can get your own damn coffee, Mathis." Helio bristled at the implication.

Mathis laughed. "I'm sorry, man. Just messing with you." He slapped Helio's injured shoulder and immediately realized his mistake.

Helio winced and stepped backward, holding his upper arm below the wound. Mathis immediately apologized, his face full of regret, but it didn't matter to Helio. In that instant, he wanted to punch Mathis more than anything he had ever wanted in his life, but the assistant director's warning was still fresh in his mind, and he stormed off down the hall instead, trying to cool down. He walked the entire span of the floor before returning to Mathis's desk. The older agent apologized again, but Helio put his hand up to silence him.

"Stop. Moving on. What can I do to help you with your case?" He asked through a clenched jaw.

"Right. Right. Um..." Mathis fumbled his words, then grabbed the notebook on his desk, "Alright, so I've been working with Christman and Andrews down in organized crime. They've been working the Dos Fileros biker gang's drug trafficking operation along I-95 for a few months now, but last week, the Fileros executed three low-level riders from a rival gang. Hacked them up with machetes as retaliation for a dudded pipe bomb that was found at the home of one of the Fileros captains."

Helio was rapidly scratching notes into his notebook, and Mathis gave him a second to catch up, then continued.

"Local authorities have already interviewed the probable suspects, and big surprise: they're not talking. Christman has an informant in the Fileros, though, and he was able to get me a name. I was planning to pay a visit to...."

Agent Davis, their group supervisor, walked up and interrupted.

"My apologies for cutting in here, gents. Sangria! How you doing, man?"

"Sir, I'm okay. I meant to come see you, but Director Coffey called me to her office...."

"Yeah, I'm tracking. Don't worry about it. How's the shoulder? Getting better?"

"Yes, sir."

"Glad to hear it. Good to have you back. Furiosa said to give you the next case that comes up, so here you are." Davis handed him a piece of paper with a phone number and a name scribbled on it, then explained, "DC police picked up a homicide early Sunday morning out in Ward Seven, Marshall Heights. They reached out to us because the MO matches another homicide, about two weeks back, near Baltimore. You were on leave but might have heard about it on the news: some shithead child molester was abducted and tortured, broken bones in all extremities, then asphyxiated."

"That the Edward Chaplin thing?" Mathis asked.

"Edward Chaffin," Helio corrected.

"That's right, Edward Chaffin. So, with the new victim, there are some stark similarities to Chaffin."

"Copycat?" Mathis suggested.

"It's possible, but given the relative proximity of where the two bodies were found, it could very well be the same guy, and since it's interstate, they want us to take a look and see what we see. Call up that Detective Samson on the note there and check it out."

"I will, sir."

"Dammit, sir," Mathis whined. "If he's on that case, who's gonna get my coffee?"

"Would you like me to get you some coffee, Mathis?" Agent Davis responded.

"Fuck no. You'd probably spit in it."

"Yes, I would, but I'd still be willing to make that cup of coffee for you. Just let me know if you change your mind." He began to walk away but stopped to add, "Sangria, I'm curious about that case. Let me know what you find, okay?"

Helio nodded once, and his supervisor continued down the hall.

"Well, I guess...." Mathis began to speak, but Helio immediately turned and walked away.

It had been a rollercoaster of a morning, and as he walked down the hall towards his desk, Helio wore a smile, delighted to have been saved the indignity of working with Mathis. It was, sadly, the closest he had come to real joy in a long time. He didn't care what the details of his new case were, it felt good to be back to work, and he couldn't wait to get started.

24

—·—

APRIL 12, 2017, WEDNESDAY

RICHMOND, VIRGINIA

Rylan sat alone at a table near the window. The smell of brewed coffee beans and the sound of customers' soft chatter filled the air. The brown brew in Rylan's cup was nearly gone, and the second cup on the table had cooled considerably by then. He noticed his hands had begun to shake slightly and wondered if it was nerves or the double-shot of espresso he had asked the barista to add to his cup of joe.

Every two minutes, for the past fifteen, he had been opening the messaging app on his phone to see if she had responded to his last message, "Got here a little early. Bought you a coffee," only to become more disheartened each time.

He peered out through the cafe's front window, watching the parking lot like a pet dog waiting for its owner to return home from work. Each time a car would pull into the parking lot, his pulse would quicken, then slow again in disappointment once the driver was revealed. After a while, he finally became resigned to the idea that he had been stood up and decided to give her five more minutes before leaving.

Three minutes later, on the far side of the parking lot, the front door of a gray sedan opened, and his sister stepped out. Her car had been parked in the lot when he had arrived, but since he was early, he paid it no mind.

Watching Jean walk through the parking lot felt like a dream. It didn't become real until she stepped through the door, and he stood so she could locate him. She took the seat across the table without making eye contact.

"That coffee is for you, but it might be cold by now. I can order you another." Rylan offered.

"No. I'm sure it's fine," she said as she wrapped both hands around the coffee cup and sat quietly, looking down into it.

An uncomfortable silence passed between them for a while until Rylan tried to soothe the awkwardness.

"Jean..." He started, but his younger sister cut him off.

"Before you say anything, let me talk."

Rylan snapped his mouth shut and prepared for an onslaught.

"For the last thirty minutes, I sat over there in my car and wrestled with whether I wanted to come in or not. I nearly drove away five or six times. Even sitting here now, I still want to get up and walk away."

Jean kept her eyes firmly on the coffee cup as she spoke, not yet ready to look him in the eyes. As she paused to consider what she wanted to say next, Rylan kept his lips closed.

"After they died, I started going to church. Catholic church, if you can believe it. I had completely fallen apart. I needed help. The church found me and put me back together. In reading the scripture, I understand that I need to forgive you, I know that, but I haven't. I don't know if I'll ever be able to. Mom and Abigail should be here right now, but they're not." She finally met Rylan's eyes, her stare burning with condemnation. "You are, and they're not. That will never be right."

Rylan did his best to maintain his composure, though he almost collapsed under the crushing weight of his own guilt and his sister's denouncement. He fought to stay upright, to endure his sister's glare, and accept her vitriol, but he couldn't prevent his eyes from welling with tears as she spoke.

"At their funeral, when I said I hated you, I meant every word. Every word. That day, I buried you right alongside the both of them and walked away. I had no intention of ever seeing you again."

"Then why answer my text?" Rylan blurted out.

Chastened, Jean's gaze fell back down into her coffee cup. "I've been asking myself the same question." She shook her head in disappointment, "I've beat myself up over it for the past week. I don't know why I did it." Her voice trailed off as she, once again, searched her mind for an answer.

Rylan gave her some time before speaking, his voice cracking with suppressed emotion. "I've really missed you."

Jean held her breath, sensing the wave approaching, but was powerless to stand against it. She cried, sobbing uncontrollably, as years of pain suddenly overcame her. Rylan watched his sister crumble right in front of him, knowing he was the source of her anguish, and he succumbed to his own torment. The two sat across the table from each other, the closest they had been in almost three years, weeping over lives lost and time wasted.

Before long, Rylan stepped around the table, knelt beside her, and gently wrapped his arms around his younger sister. Her first instinct was to push him away, but her body refused and gradually melted into his embrace. She rested her head against his and the two continued to grieve together.

Time moved slowly for a while. The world around them, everything, became inconsequential as a simmering squall of sadness filled their universe. They remained commiserating in each other's arms until a barista dropped a metal pot upon the tile floor behind the counter, startling the siblings. Rylan released his sister, stood, and planted a kiss on her forehead before sitting back down in his chair. Suddenly aware of their surroundings, the two self-consciously glanced around the room while pulling napkins from the dispenser to dry their eyes.

"I swore to myself I wouldn't cry." She confessed with a nervous chuckle.

"Me too." He admitted.

"I'm pretty sure that's only the third time in my life I've ever seen you cry."

"Yeah, well, it seems like I've been doing a lot of that lately."

"Have you? Tell me, Rye, what have you been doing for the last three years?"

"Me? I moved back to Columbia. I couldn't stay in Myrtle Beach anymore. Too many painful memories there. I'm still working construction, though."

"You still drinking?" Her tone was sharp, like a police officer questioning a prime suspect.

"No, been sober since the day after the funeral. It'll be three years next month."

"That's great." She sounded pleased, but Rylan could hear the subtle hint of bitterness in her voice.

"Yeah," Rylan sought to pivot away from the subject of his alcoholism, "actually, a couple of weeks ago, I stepped away from work to do some traveling."

"Travelling? You? Where?"

"I was out West for a bit. Lake Tahoe, Idaho, then I was heading to California next and figured I should at least try to reach out to you, thinking you were still in Arizona, but just my luck, you'd moved back East."

"You came all the way here just to meet me in a coffee shop?"

"Well, no, not, not entirely. I had some other stuff I needed to take care of, but even if I didn't, yes. Of course, I'd still have driven all the way here to meet you in a coffee shop."

Jean looked down into her coffee cup, considering his words. "You heading back out to California then?"

"In a few days. Got some business to attend to back home first."

"How long you gonna be gone?"

"A couple weeks, maybe, but there are some other places I need to visit on the way back, though."

"How can you afford all that?"

Rylan looked away, ashamed. "Life insurance money. I'd never touched it. It was just sitting there in the bank, but I figured I should... I feel like she'd have wanted me to do something with it, you know?"

"She would have." Jean reluctantly agreed though it didn't feel right.

"What about you?" Rylan asked.

"What about me?"

"What have you been doing?" He clarified. "You still teaching?"

She took in a long breath, exhaling slowly. Until that moment, she hadn't determined if she wanted to share intimate details of her new life with her estranged brother, but the moment had quickly come, and she needed to decide.

"Yes, I'm still teaching, but at a high school now."

"High school?" He was surprised by her answer, "How are you liking that?"

"It's different. Teenage attitudes are exhausting, as you can imagine. Plus, most of the students don't want to be there, so there's much less hunger for knowledge, but on the other hand, the students are more impressionable, so you really have an opportunity to spark passion in them for subjects that do interest them. I enjoy that aspect."

"Hmm. That makes sense. Do you miss teaching at Arizona State, though?"

"Sometimes, but I've tried to embrace where I'm at right now and just focus on that."

"What brought about that kind of a shift in your career?"

Reluctantly, she confessed. "I fell in love with one of my grad students."

Jean immediately looked to her brother, expecting harsh judgment, but was surprised by his reaction.

"Oh! Wow. Okay." He took a moment to process the information. "I'm sure you're not the first professor to fall in love with one of your students, though, right?"

"Yeah, well, I got pregnant."

Rylan's eyes bulged for a moment. "By your student?"

"Yes."

"Oh," Rylan didn't know how else to respond.

"I didn't necessarily have to leave the school, but he was graduating and would be moving to the East Coast to attend the academy, so for me, it made sense. Besides, teaching at the high school level allowed me better flexibility, and social studies isn't a particularly difficult subject for me to teach."

"You're teaching social studies?" Rylan's face showed his disgust.

"Not many high schools have a psych department, Rye."

Rylan laughed, "I guess not. It's just... I remember hating that class."

"It's temporary. I've submitted a handful of applications to the colleges and universities out here and am hoping to find a position for next fall."

"I'm sure you won't have any issues finding a position. You were always a lot smarter than me."

"That's a very low bar, Rye."

Rylan laughed and shook his head. "Same old Jean."

She smiled and wondered if he was right. "You know what? You're the only one who still calls me Jean."

"What're you going by now, then, your first name? You always hated it."

She shrugged. "I've gotten used to it."

"Okay, I'll try to remember that."

"No, it's fine. Honestly, it's comforting. Like a cherished relic from my younger days."

"That's a nice way to think of it." Rylan paused before circling back to a previous subject, careful about asking such a potentially painful question. "I don't want to pry, but if it's okay to ask: what happened to the baby?"

"Oh, he's fine. He's perfect. Making my life difficult, but he truly is wonderful."

"So, I'm an uncle?" The excitement in his voice was evident.

Jean suddenly sat up in her seat and pulled her hands down into her lap. Rylan could sense her discomfort at the notion and realized he might be moving too fast.

"Sorry. That was presumptive of me. Look, I'm very happy for you. I have no doubt you're a terrific mother."

"I try."

"And the father? You married?" Rylan glanced down at her left hand.

"No. We're not married. We were engaged at one point but, its, its been... complicated."

"So, you living together then?"

"No, he lives in DC." Her face beamed with pride, "He works for the FBI."

The blood instantly drained from Rylan's face.

Jean noticed his reaction. "Yeah. It's kinda crazy, right? I wish I could say he's not the stereotypical FBI agent, but I mean, he's pretty intense. He's super smart, though. Maybe one day you'll get to meet him."

Recovering from his astonishment, Rylan cleared his throat. "Yeah. Maybe."

Jean continued, "As far as our relationship goes: we might be working it out. I'm not sure. We'll see what happens."

"Right," Rylan replied vacantly, distracted by his thoughts.

"How about you?" She asked.

Rylan blinked. "What do you mean?"

"You seeing anyone?"

Rylan shifted uncomfortably in his seat. "No. Not seeing anyone. I don't really have the time."

Feeling conflicted by her brother's answer, Jean left it alone. She stayed quiet for a moment and sipped her lukewarm coffee before deciding to lighten up the conversation.

"Okay, so... tell me, what else have you been up to? Hey, have you seen that new movie, *Logan*?"

Rylan met her eyes, and a wide grin spread across his face.

ACKNOWLEDGMENTS

No one truly succeeds on their own.

I am immensely grateful to my refinement and support team, who have provided me with inspiration, advice, encouragement, and critique. Without you, this book may never have been completed. Thank you:

Audrey Santana, Sonia Cline, Linda Santana, Sonia Coley, Christina Santana, Victoria Luna, Karen Darling, Neil Darling, Joshua Fagan, Lynn Williams, Tom Williams, Katherine Henricks, Denise Newman, Lynda Cobb, Alexandra Newman, Danielle Miller, Mary Lou Lawson, Bill Lawson, Marie Lawson, Chuck Lawson, Louis Cote, Delmira Miceli, Daniel Lopez, Nadia Dajani, Tracy Thomas, Travis Crowder, Tommy Crowder, Theresa Benney, Beth Ann Retallack, Nancy Luna, and Luke James, with special acknowledgement and gratitude for the critical eye of Niki A. Mitchell.

ADDITIONAL CREDITS